A charming and lyrical story of masculine ambit[...]
fruition. 1920s Sydney, in all her raffish grandeur, [...]

—MANDY SAYER, author of *Love in the Years of Lunacy*

The Floating Garden is above all a surprising love story, full of turns, transformations and 'slips of the heart'. A wise, tender and beautifully detailed novel.

—GAIL JONES, author of *Five Bells*

Emma Ashmere has written a compelling and lyrical novel of a rough-and-ready Sydney that is in the throes of rapid change; a town where the spiritual is necessary but corrupted, and where sexual lives remain hidden even from those in the grip of desire.

—SOPHIE CUNNINGHAM, author of *Geography* and *Bird*

The Floating Garden is a beautiful and quietly enthralling work. Unfurling in gardens, the rooms of spiritualists, wealthy suburbs and the growing shadow of the Sydney Harbour Bridge, it skilfully renders the range and complexity of women's lives. Ashmere's deft evocation of 1920s Sydney and her luscious descriptions of the natural world signal a writer who is sure of her craft, and who will undoubtedly continue to flourish.

—JESSICA WHITE, author of *A Curious Intimacy*

Emma Ashmere's subtle, wry storytelling takes the reader inside 1920s Sydney ... [I]t is the story of those women who dared to want more than society offered them.

—SARAH ARMSTRONG, author of *Salt Rain*

The Floating Garden follows the fortunes of the unforgettable Ellis Gilbey, the highly strung artist Rennie Howarth, the charismatic theosophist Miss Minerva Stranks, and the delicate Kitty Tate. A beautifully written debut novel.

—JESSE BLACKADDER, author of *The Raven's Heart*

Photo by Delma Corazon

Emma Ashmere's short stories have appeared in various publications including *The Age, Griffith Review, Sleepers Almanac, Etchings* and *Australian Women's Book Review*. She has a Masters in Creative Writing from the University of Adelaide, and a PhD from La Trobe University in Melbourne on the use of marginalised histories in fiction. She has worked as a researcher on several books on Australian gardening history, and women and empire. She lives in northern New South Wales.

Emma Ashmere's short stories have appeared in various publications including *The Age*, *Griffith Review*, *Sleepers Almanac*, *Etchings*, and *Australian Women's Book Review*. She has a Master's in Creative Writing from the University of Adelaide, and a PhD from La Trobe University in Melbourne on the use of marginalised histories in fiction. She has worked as a researcher on several books on Australian gardening history, and women and empire. She lives in northern New South Wales.

THE
FLOATING
GARDEN

EMMA ASHMERE

First published by Spinifex Press, 2015
Reprinted 2015

Spinifex Press Pty Ltd
504 Queensberry St
North Melbourne, Victoria 3051
Australia
women@spinifexpress.com.au
www.spinifexpress.com.au

Editors: Renate Klein and Pauline Hopkins
Copy preparation: Maree Hawken
Cover design: Deb Snibson
Typesetting: Palmer Higgs
Typeset in Century Old Style and DK Kaikoura
Printed by McPherson's Printing Group
Cover painting:
    Dorrit BLACK
    Australia, 1891–1951
    The Bridge
    1930, Sydney
    oil on canvas on board
    60.0 x 81.0 cm
    Bequest of the artist 1951
    Art Gallery of South Australia, Adelaide.
    Reproduced with permission.

National Library of Australia Cataloguing-in-Publication data:
Ashmere, Emma, 1964– author.
The floating garden / Emma Ashmere.
9781742199368 (paperback)
9781742199337 (ebook: epub)
9781742199313 (ebook: pdf)
Australian fiction
A823.4

for Delma

PART ONE

PART ONE

CHAPTER
ONE

So now their standoff had come to this. The last of her lodgers had tossed their belongings onto the back of a cart and clattered off to take up an overpriced fleapit in Woolloomooloo, leaving Ellis Gilbey here, alone, peering from windows, rattling about an empty house.

She wiped her finger across the windowpane and looked along the street. It wasn't clear how much longer she could hold out against the latest barrage of Notices to Quit. The staunch ones claimed they'd hang on until they were prised out like oysters from the harbour seawalls, or at least until they'd seen the colour of the government's promises of compensation. Despite months of garrulous street meetings and the rousing talk of 'power in the union', Ellis had always known no one would pay. Just because the authorities had found enough funds to see off the big stevedoring companies which owned entire streets, it didn't mean they'd do the same for inconsequential tenants like themselves. When she'd tried to warn her neighbours of this, she'd been shouted down. Nobody wanted to hear talk like that.

She glanced around the bedroom. Everything was coated in a chalky sheen: the brass bedstead, the amber-coloured wardrobe with its broken leg, the red and gold satin coverlet inherited from a cherub-faced dancing girl who'd done a midnight flit, the faded sign saying *Private!* nailed to the door, the avalanche of papers engulfing her typewriter, and the prize of her belongings—the picture of a landscape hanging over the desk with its quiet dark valleys and sun-stroked hills. Ellis had inherited it when she took over running the lodging house. *To remind you of home,* the previous landlady had said. But for twenty-seven years this had been her home. Despite the creeping winter damp and the winds whistling Aeolian melodies through the cracks, this dingy room had been her place. Now the resuming men were coming to tear it all down as if the act of demolition was the beginning and not the end. It was a death of a suburb, house by house. Even the milkman no longer bothered clattering his cans over the cobblestones.

Ellis stepped back from the window too late. Girl had spotted her from her balcony and waved a bottle in the air.

'Fancy elevenses, Els?'

Ellis shook her head.

'Later then,' said Girl.

Hell, Ellis thought, but she gave a wave and went back to her desk.

This latest disruption had stopped her from producing anything useful the night before for her monthly column 'The Green-eyed Gardener'. For the past ten years or so, she'd never had any trouble dashing off monthly missives for the *Australian Gardeners' Almanac*. It kept her mind on easier, earthier things while bringing in a small and much-needed regular fee. What had started as an anecdote had turned into a column which now boasted a fervent following.

The *Almanac's* editors attributed the success of 'The Green-eyed Gardener' to two things: the fact it was written under the *nom de plume* of Scribbly Gum; and Ellis' depiction of a man she'd encountered long ago, a mean-spirited green-thumb, Mr Moses. Everybody knew someone like him. 'Putting on a Mr Moses' had even entered the local vocabulary. It was what people said if you crowed about the superior scent of your roses, or rued the progress of other people's runner beans, or were seen ringbarking somebody's almond tree because it blocked your sun, or caught dumping your weeds, snails and prunings over a fence.

Nobody except the *Almanac's* editors knew the true identity of Scribbly Gum. Together with the lodgings' takings and typing out invoices for Clements Brothers' Emporium, moonlighting as a columnist had provided Ellis just enough to scrape by, but now she was left to field the whole of the rent until she found another room for herself. In the meantime she'd finish her book: a compilation of her most popular columns with a smattering of gardening hints and a pinch of arcane gardening lore.

If she worked all night, she'd finish it before Dr Bradfield's men came to breathe down her door. Once it was published, funds would roll in and—and what?

Sitting here at the desk, Ellis was no longer sure. Everyone assumed Scribbly Gum was the well-heeled owner of a rambling productive garden estate. Comments such as *Reveal yourself, Sir!* regularly found their way to the Letters to the Editor, much to the editors' amusement. Apparently maintaining Scribbly Gum's mysterious identity had been a boon for sales. Ellis supposed once her book had come out, it would be easy enough to keep hiding the truth, that 'he' was a middle-aged 'she', soon to be evicted from a sunless and now eerily silent terrace house marked for demolition at Milsons Point.

That was the strange thing. While the digging machines screeched and hammered from dawn 'til dusk, and the force of the blasting could toss the tea cups from your shelves and cleave zigzag gaps in your walls, an unnerving stillness had begun to invade these waiting streets. Sitting here now the stillness was almost visible, lapping across the floors, cascading down the stairs, rising to nibble the hem of her dress.

Ellis left the desk. Her footsteps echoed down the hallway. She unbolted the back door and stood against the doorframe, tapping out the dregs from her pipe, staring out at the nettles and the tumble of nasturtium leaves floured by dust as the city raged on and the silence of the house breathed at her back.

She took out a few strands of tobacco and rolled them between her fingers. Privately, she referred to her tobacco as 'maidenhair' but there was no time now for private jokes. She shoved the pipe back into her pocket and ran upstairs, paused on the landing, opened the cupboard and counted the blankets and pillows. All were there.

In the smaller room overlooking the yard and the old night-cart lane, she could almost see Bradfield's miraculous bridge curve over the harbour beyond the ragtag rooves heaped with broken wheels and lumps of rock. The witch's hat steeple on the church was leaning back even further since the last southerly buster. Over towards Kirribilli, the occasional Norfolk Island pine and jacaranda tree afforded shade over wider, wealthier streets. By some quirk of geography those streets would stay intact while these houses and shops, these little worlds, dissolved into air.

The larger room looked across to Girl's stocking-festooned balcony. Ellis squinted up at the ceiling where tongues of paint were curling off and circles of damp rippled out. There were gaps in the floorboards where they'd buckled to form tiny hills. She swiped at a cobweb hanging down and swept a pile of dust sideways with her shoe. On hearing a voice, she stopped. The voice seemed to multiply as it rolled around the walls. Her lodgers may have gone but something of them remained, their *aural vibrations, their astral transferences*, as Miss Minerva Stranks would have said and Kitty Tate would have tossed her dark shine of hair and smirked behind Miss Stranks' back, mouthing to Ellis, *and what does our apprentice Secretaire Spirituelle make of that?*

Ellis put a hand to her throat. She'd let herself think of Kitty Tate and Miss Stranks and those wretched days back at the Hall. All that was in the past where it belonged. But the past wasn't over. It was here, crowding around her in this cheerless room. She sat down hard on a bed. A quarter of a century may have passed but it was still too difficult to think about Kitty Tate. Time had done nothing to ease her guilt. She'd tried to bury her regret since it had taken root inside of her all those years ago, but now with all the uncertainty of the bridge, it had begun to sprout new shoots.

It was best to keep moving when she felt like this. She set about wrestling the mattresses off the beds, took apart the bedsteads, and managed to manoeuvre them downstairs ready to flog off to the scrap iron man. In the kitchen, she found a knife, ran back upstairs and removed the brass door handles on the upstairs doors followed by the plates surrounding the light switches. If the landlord asked for them before she left, she'd surrender them all. If not, she'd pocket the modest spoils for herself.

She stood back and sighed. So, the house was all hers, but not hers at all.

She cradled a hot strong cup of tea and stared up at the picture shining over the desk. At this time of day the glass reflected oblongs of light, whiting out the sunny foreground, making it a pale lapping sea. Sometimes the lines of the mountain resembled the face of a woman turned upwards towards the sky. She moved her head so she could catch this effect, the profile of a woman reclining, her chin, her nose, her breasts caressed by the soft morning light, the slight smile on her lips as she raised her eyes, just like Kitty had across the bed, on that last beautiful, terrible morning ...

Ellis stood up so quickly she spilt her tea. That was the second time she'd let herself think of Kitty. It was time to get out of here, to begin somewhere else. The end of the week, that's all she'd give herself. If the government hadn't paid up by then, she'd go out and find another room far from the thundering path of the bridge, away from the memory of what had brought her here all those years before. She'd say to her neighbours, Girl, old Mrs Liddy and Clarrie, *I've found somewhere else.* And Mrs Liddy would cry out 'What, dear?' and she'd sit down on her milking stool and weep into her long black skirts, and Clarrie would cough and frown at his beloved poetry book, and Girl would call her a 'scab' or a 'dog' or something just as bitter.

Ellis jumped at the sound of a thump on the front door. It was only Girl, a bottle tucked beneath one arm, her pink feather boa dragging behind her in the dust.

CHAPTER TWO

They sat together on the back step. Ellis tapped her pipe against her shoe and stared at the shadows swimming through the mess of her backyard as Girl talked on about who was doing what nefarious thing to whom.

'This is a change, ain't it, Els?' said Girl. 'Having the place all to yourself.' Girl glugged another shot of port wine into their cups and raised it. 'To the two of us then, the lasts of the lasts.'

Ellis downed it. Girl poured another. 'Your turn, Els.'

'What? Sorry, Girl, I was miles away.'

'It's your turn to christen the next thirsty cup.'

'Oh. To us. The lasts of the lasts. To the dying days of Burton Street.' The wine was beginning to slur her words.

'The dying days?' Girl gave her nudge. 'Cheer up, Els. Alf Ostler reckons the government's going to cough up any day.'

'Does he now?' Ellis packed a good pinch of tobacco into her pipe. 'Then I'll celebrate with a double helping of maidenhair.'

'Of what?'

Ellis felt herself flush. She'd always been careful not to let slip her private jokes, especially not to Girl. In a house full of strangers and a street with flimsy walls and open windows, privacy was hard to win and even harder to keep. Now she'd never hear the end of it.

'What did you call your tabaccy, Els?'

Ellis struck the match on her shoe and watched it flare and stutter out. What did it matter now what she said? 'Tobacco reminds me of the dried stems of the maidenhair fern.' She eyed Girl, careful to keep her own face a blank. 'You know the ones?'

'Yeah,' said Girl, slowly.

'The Ancient Greeks called them ... Oh, don't worry.'

Girl splashed more wine into her cup. 'Go on Els. Loosen up. Nothing better than a good story to cheer us all up.'

'Well, they used to think the stems didn't get wet when they were put into water. And ...' She gulped her wine. 'They thought they looked like women's hair.'

'Eh?'

'You know. Hair. *Down there.*'

Girl threw her head back and roared with laughter. Ellis listened to Girl laughing on, but it only made her feel more alone. She wished she was lying safely in bed staring up at the lodgerless rooms above, her curtains drawn against the world.

'Come on, Els. Treat yourself to a snifter or two. That'll perk you up.'

Girl unfolded a twist of paper and sprinkled a line of Sweet Tooth pain-relieving powder, as she called it, over the dimples on the back of her hand. The crystals sparkled in the darkening air. Girl raised her hand and took a sniff.

'See? Easy as you like. It'll bring them roses back to your cheeks.'

Roses, Ellis thought, with a sigh. According to last month's 'Green-eyed Gardener', Mr Moses' roses won every prize in New South Wales because they were fed a carefully balanced diet of banana skins and chicken manure, a recipe he'd copied by watching his neighbour through a much-used spyhole in the fence. For years he had been incensed by his neighbour's blooms which were larger and brighter than his own. But now, officially, his roses were a riot of colour. At the first sign of a withering bud, Mr Moses sharpened the blade of his bayonet and removed them with military precision. *Do not blight your garden with specimens past their prime. Banish them immediately to the rubbish pile*, Ellis had written, but the sentiment had depressed her and she'd left it out.

But Mr Moses, there is no such thing as death, she thought. *There is only trans-for-may-shun!* That's what Miss Stranks would have said, but so much for Miss Stranks and her patchwork of second-hand philosophies. Sitting here was like being sentenced to a kind of death. As of today, Ellis was no one with nothing and nowhere to go. She was no longer a quiet landlady running a neat, plain lodging house for women and girls. All she had to show for the past quarter of a century was a rented house full of shabby furniture and a ridiculous notion she'd save herself by writing a book of anecdotes about tossing tea leaves onto your hydrangeas to ensure they were the bluest in the street.

No wonder people laughed at her. She'd heard them do so often enough. *She may be one of them cabbage-munchers*, Alf Ostler had said to somebody at one of their first street meetings. *But she fires off them fancy letters to the government like there's no shortage of coal in the stokehouse.*

Ellis held out her hand. 'Go on then.'

'That's the way, Els.'

Girl patted out another trail of Sweet Tooth. Ellis coughed as she took a sniff and it tingled in her nose. Her heart began to beat thumpingly fast. She put her hand to her chest and looked at Girl, wondering what she was supposed to feel. She'd hoped it would be like opium, the so-called flower of forgetfulness. She could write about the uses of the poppy in her next column, which would be sure to pique the interest and the ire of the readership in equal part.

Girl began to hum a smoky tune. Ellis leant back against the doorframe, watching the dark sparring with the light. Back when Mrs McCarthy had run the house, the chokos ran thick and wild. The tight tendrils of the passion fruit vine clawed their wiry fingers at the air. River beans had scaled their bamboo stakes in their search for sun. The smell of lavender, rosemary, basil and peppermint had tinged the air.

Some nights when Ellis was lying in bed, a touch too much brandy having passed her lips, she let herself believe she'd have a house of her own one day, one with a real working garden, flowers and vegetables, an orchard, a running creek nearby, just like the one she'd worked in as a child with her mother back on the farm at Candlebark Creek in those fleeting days of plenty before her mother had died.

Her hand went to her throat. Girl's powder was no good. It had not let her forget at all. She could see her mother—*really* see her—as if she was standing a few yards away. She closed her eyes. It was no use. She could hear her mother's voice over the sound of Girl's tuneless hum.

Peppermint, Ellis? Warmth of feeling. Dried and crushed, stops the flow of blood when applied to cuts. Marigolds, Ellis? The old people used to dye their hair with its golden petals … good for pairing with tomatoes.

Ellis must have let out a small cry because Girl went quiet.

'Come on, Els. Like I said, it'll do you good to get things off your chest.'

She looked at Girl, at her puffy eyes and the eyebrows plucked as thin as spiders' legs. Maybe Girl was right. Bottling things up didn't seem to be working anymore. She imagined throwing open the upstairs window and shouting out over the broken rooves and half-demolished streets: *After my mother died, I had nowhere to go. I was taken in by Miss Minerva Stranks, the quasi-theosophist, who fell from grace when Kitty …* No, she could never admit to being part of that.

Ellis could feel the heat of Girl's body leaning into hers. She could almost see the tendrils Girl was sending out towards her through the cooling night air.

Ellis lurched to her feet. 'All right then, Girl.' She tried to laugh to distract herself from the expression on Girl's face. 'You want me to tell you something? Well then, here goes nothing. I've been writing a book.'

'You never!' Girl's teeth shone brownly in the light. 'I bet it's one of them posh ladies and gentleman's saucy romances. I always thought you had something going on, hiding away all quiet like. As my old ma used to say, it's the quiet ones you have to watch out for. They always want the lot with bells and whistles. Never the plain old one-two-three.'

'No, no. It's nothing like that.' Ellis felt herself flush again. Now Girl was dipping a finger in her cup, rubbing the syrupy wine across her cushiony lips, making them shine like ripened fruit.

'Come on, then Els. Like my old ma used to say, you can't keep the punters waiting.'

'But you'll only laugh.'

'As if I would.'

Ellis drained her cup and thrust it towards the bottle for a top up. 'Well, I don't suppose any of it matters now.'

'Course it don't.'

'Have you ever heard of the "Green-eyed Gardener"?' Ellis watched Girl's face carefully. Girl shook her yellow hair. 'I'm writing a book about this garden.' Ellis waved her cup at the yard.

'What? You mean this scrapheap here?' Girl stared up at Ellis, her wet lips held back from her teeth as if she wasn't sure whether to laugh or cry. They both stared at each other until Ellis threw her head back and laughed so hard that Girl did the same. Girl shrieked as she staggered to her feet, clutching at her nether parts, tottering off to the outhouse, her feather boa slithering behind her through the dust.

Ellis kept laughing and talking to Girl through the open door. 'You know if you want to believe, you can see anything. You can transform the whole world, brick by brick. You can turn a dead flower back into a bud. You can see a palace where there's really a ruin. Do you know some people think there is no death? There is only *trans-for-may-shun!*' Ellis stopped and wiped her eyes as she looked up at the smudged out stars. Her laughter sounded hollow now. 'But we haven't transformed, have we, Girl? People like us will always be the vanquished ones.'

'The what?'

Girl emerged from the outhouse, her dress hitched up around the tops of her stockings. The softness of her thighs rumpled out. Ellis could smell her from five paces away, every glorious terrible smell screaming *life! danger! desire!* Perhaps it was the wine or Girl's Sweet Tooth or letting herself think of Kitty again, but she had to force herself from not taking those five paces and burying her face into Girl's clammy neck.

Ellis stepped back and steadied herself against a wall.

'It's strange, but I've been thinking about when I first came here, and why I came. I'd been working as a *secretaire spirituelle*, you see. And before you ask, that's just a fancy way of saying I sat at a desk for weeks on end, devouring thousands of words from hundreds of books, churning them around like butter in my head, spreading them out for somebody else to help themselves to the choicest pickings and make themselves fat. That somebody was the most inspiring and captivating orator of our time. Well, that's what *she* liked to think she was.'

Ellis took another gulp from her cup. Girl's eyes were shining. Once there'd been hundreds of pairs of shining eyes, standing there in front of the surging crowds at the Sunday hall on Castlereagh Street, peddling hope to the desperate, the anxious, the baronesses and fishwives, physicians and quacks. Everyone wanted to believe Miss Stranks' encouraging messages delivered from other worlds where Truth and Everlasting Life once bloomed and would surely bloom again for them, as long as they tossed a coin in first.

'Go on, Els,' Girl said.

'You've seen the way I read out the newspapers every day for Mrs Liddy and Clarrie? I know it sounds like I'm pinning tickets on myself, but people used to say I had this gift. Well, not a gift. I worked hard for it. I only have to read a page once and I can store it away perfectly in my mind. A photographic memory, that's what Miss Stranks called it. She said she was blessed with one too. But it's not always a blessing. It can be a curse. But it's how I kept a roof over my head and a crust in my mouth. That's how I met Kitty Tate.'

Girl was peering at her now, her beaded dress shimmering as she swayed in the falling light.

'You dark old horse, you,' she said, and for the first time in all their years of knowing each other, Girl stood there silently, not laughing or joking but looking at Ellis with the gentlest expression on her face. Girl's lips looked even softer and shinier as she held out her stubby hand towards her.

'Why didn't you say you had the touch before, Els? Girls like me need to know there's more to life than hoisting up your skirts for another spiv. It makes us feel better to think there's folks in this world who know them other things. Who can read all them books and ...'

'Claim to see things other people can't?' Ellis stepped back from the outstretched hand. 'It's true. I did see things. The way a leaf fluttered in the wind, a line of pebbles gathered on a doorstep. Then something would happen. Something big. And I'd realise too late that I should have expected it because the leaf or the pebbles were trying to warn me.'

'Sweet Mother of Jesus, Els. We all need someone to tell us when to watch our backs. Or our cheeks.'

Girl began to rub her finger over the scar on her cheek made by one of her former flashmen, famous for carving his initials into his less co-operative wares.

'Oh Girl, it's hard to explain but for people like me the world is crowded with omens, signs, grave portents. You have to try to shut most of them out. If you don't, they'll drive you mad. Or you'll *not* see the things you should have. Or you'll take them the wrong way and ...' Ellis felt her chest tighten again. She turned away to hide her face. She couldn't bring herself to say it: *and then you'll never forgive yourself. Someone will suffer, because*

13

of you and you'll carry it with you forever like a spot on the eye. She brushed at her eyes which were streaming now, not because she'd been laughing and drinking but because she'd let herself utter the name Kitty again.

She stiffened as she felt Girl's soft arms encircle her.

'So, what do you see for me then, eh?'

Ellis shivered as Girl's squashy breasts pressed into her back.

'I'm sorry. I can't. Once I would've done it for you in a flash. Back then, I wanted to believe I was blessed. Everybody wanted to believe what Miss Stranks said. Except for Kitty. They were heady days, Girl. Rich men and poor men lined up side by side.'

'From what my old ma told me, all them hoity-toities were never famous for being shy. A button jammed between your pearly whites, a quick flip of petticoats and off you went.'

Despite the gallant laugh, Girl's voice fell away and Ellis wished Mr Moses' prizewinning roses were growing right there in her yard. She would have picked one and tucked it behind Girl's ear but there was nothing so fine here anymore, and if she'd done that, Ellis might have let Girl hold her like she'd wanted to be held by someone for years. She might have turned around and pushed her fingers through Girl's yellow springy hair and raised her face up to hers, and then all those feelings which she'd shut out since Kitty might have risen up.

She jerked her head back as she felt Girl's lips brush across her cheek. It took all Ellis' strength to untangle herself from her pungent embrace.

'This garden was a real garden once,' she said, stumbling away across the yard. 'When I came here, Mrs McCarthy had turned this rubbish pit into a miniature garden of Eden, overflowing with cabbages, kale, river beans, chokos and pumpkins. I meant to keep it going, but then there was all the talk of the bridge.'

'You slippery old eel, you.' Girl tugged on Ellis' sleeve, trying to draw her back. 'We thought you were up burning the candle, writing out them invoices for the Clements boys, or more of them letters to the government. Alf's been laying bets you been taking notes and snitching on him to the coppers about that time he rolled those scabs down on the docks.'

'Will you or I tell Alf nobody's sitting up half the night writing about *him*?'

Girl raised her moulting feather boa and tossed it around her like a lasso. Ellis let herself be pulled into the broad spongy bosom of Girl's dress with its broken beads and stiff little tassels hanging off. She buried her face in the smell of her, the smoke and sweat, and the other things far less polite than roses, peppermint or lavender. They both stood there, breathing and saying nothing as the yard turned to shadow and the cold air closed in, until Girl's flashman rattled something along the fence, yelling it was time for her to get back on the nest.

CHAPTER
THREE

It was dark in George Street. The motorcars honked and brayed. Rennie Howarth stood smoking at the gallery window. The reflections on the glass had turned her paintings into glittering shards. Perhaps that's all they were, scraps of shape and colour signifying nothing at all.

'Mrs Howarth?'

Rennie heard the gallery owner clip towards her across the floor. She closed her eyes. *What did he want with her now?* 'Yes,' she said, before grabbing her handbag and running out. 'Whatever it is you are about to ask, yes, yes, yes!'

By the time she'd knocked on the doors of several florist shops and filled her arms with spears of orange and yellow gladioli, George Street had emptied, apart from the occasional shuffling overcoat.

Rennie stopped as she saw the lights of the gallery shining out, burning on as if it were the last building left in the world. It was a far cry from her two exhibitions in London after the war when everyone had been desperate to drown out the horrors of the past with staccato laughter, rat-a-tat jazz and sharp-shooting wit. Her favourite gallery in Chelsea had been overflowing with friends, actors, musicians, and the obligatory array of boisterous hangers-on. As usual, they'd drunk on well past dawn. Sleep still felt too close to death. *We exist!* everybody seemed to need to cry, dancing, drinking, gadding about at breakneck speed in motorcars, aeroplanes, or any terrifying contraption that made you remember you were one of the quick and not the dead.

Even her reclusive brother Irving had surprised her by making an appearance at the gallery, his shoulders twitching beneath his coat. His wife hadn't deigned to come. She'd always sneered at Rennie's art and scoffed at the idea of her holding an exhibition. Apparently parading her 'monstrosities for the world to see' was a 'scandalous shaming of the family's good name.'

Not long after, Rennie had jumped at the chance to set herself free. She'd run away from the increasingly poisonous ennui of her London friends and the cloying disapproval of her family, and taken the broad outstretched arm of an Australian man she hardly knew and had sailed away from everything cold, sad and stale. Now here she was, standing on a street on the other side of the world, looking in at the oranges and reds of her paintings vibrating against the walls.

'Very bold and ... er, very modern,' the gallery owner had said, when she'd rushed them in a few hours late.

Yes, yes, she'd thought. *But are they any good?* Standing here now, she knew they were not. Why had she thought this was the way to beat her husband at his own game? Now it was too late. Someone was calling out her name.

'Irene!'

Oh God, it was him. Nobody but Lloyd ever called her Irene. He despised abbreviated names. *If you were christened Irene, Irene it is.* Before Lloyd, she'd always been Rennie; friendly, funny Rennie; ready with a quip and wicked laugh, especially when accompanied by the jolly music of champagne corks.

Lloyd strode towards her. The whites of his spats glowed and blurred in the dark. It was like watching an entire army closing in on her. She dashed into the gallery. People were already in there milling about. As she darted through the throng, she caught the preliminary stutter of polite conversation. Glasses clinked. Cigarettes were lit. At least the paintings looked less visceral in a room half-filled. She managed an exit to the back room to rifle through the cupboards for vases. As she rummaged about in the musty dark, snippets of conversation wafted her way.

'Highly unusual,' one man said.

'At least the frames are good.'

'I wasn't quite expecting this.'

They hate it, she thought. She counted to three, applied her best opening night smile, picked up the two vases and waltzed out into the fray. At least Fortune had shone down one slender ray, for Lloyd had been ambushed at the door by one of his *dulls* colleagues from the Wool and Wheat. As Rennie deposited the flowers, she cast an eye in his direction, wondering when he'd realise what she'd done. There was still the tiniest flicker of hope he'd applaud her, renounce all previous disdain, and praise her as his ebullient, fun-loving, artistic, bohemian wife.

She grabbed another glass of fizz and gulped it down. Lloyd was still playing the impeccable host. He hadn't realised yet.

My wife ... she thought he heard him say. *I knew my wife's little daubs would be just the thing to capture the optimistic mood of the times.*

She knew she should stand with him at the door greeting guests, but proximity to Lloyd was unbearable. Besides, a woman had taken Rennie's arm and proceeded to bark at her.

'While I'm well aware unorthodoxy may abound abroad,' the woman said, 'the *real* artist should not become seduced by the fickle fad.'

Rennie watched the sagging skin of the woman's neck shake as she talked on, dispensing slight after insult, criticism followed by complaint. It was becoming difficult for Rennie to hold her smile. Her face felt as if it might fall apart, that her cheeks would no longer agree to expend the requisite effort to hold up the corners of the mouth against the unforgiving pull of gravity.

She saw Lloyd's face change. *Oh God,* he'd seen it. The gallery was now oven-like. Laughter rose up in yelps. The electric light pounced on people's faces mercilessly, highlighting every crease, bristle and pock-mark.

Rennie gulped down another glass. The gallery owner moved towards her, mouthing something. Rennie bent down to try to hear. Apparently a 'very important reviewer' had been sighted doing a lap. Rennie spotted a stout bow-tied chap stopping at each painting to frown and jot notes in a book. She hadn't imagined a reviewer would come. Who on earth had arranged for that?

Lloyd had spotted him and wasted no time in homing in. Of course, Lloyd had been behind the reviewer. Now he was forced to bail him up, trying to undo what was not yet done.

Rennie began to laugh. Poor Lloyd. He was the one who'd insisted she hold an exhibition and be introduced to 'the right sort of people' in Sydney society. She hadn't wanted to do it at all.

'These charming little pictures will suit the buoyant mood of the times,' he'd said, as they'd unpacked her polite English watercolours, placing them over her newer Australian works-in-progress blazing across a series of easels in the sunroom. 'I'm not sure these crude messy ones would be quite the thing.'

By 'crude messy ones' Lloyd meant Rennie's recent attempts to capture the slabs of light she saw burning across the croquet lawn or bursting out across the blue dome of the harbour sky at midday. On arriving in Sydney two years before, Rennie had been stunned by the overwhelming presence and force of the sun and sky. This was no place for the cushiony hills of Sussex, lacy wildflowers or cottony clouds. Out here, an artist needed to delve into bolder, earthier, flatter colours.

'Why not paint what you see?' Lloyd had said, when Rennie tried to discuss her difficult forays with the Australian palette.

'But this *is* what I see.'

He'd shaken his head and made that infuriating tut-tut sound in his cheek.

In the end, she'd given in, but not quite. Instead of taking in her timid watercolours, she'd smuggled in her latest works.

Rennie looked up to see Lloyd striding towards her, his face a study of cobalt violet slashed with alizarin crimson. She knew that face. It was often the last thing she saw before he grabbed her. But thankfully he turned around, as everybody always did whenever Bertha Collins swept into a room.

'Bertha!' Rennie called, thrusting her champagne glass at Lloyd's waistcoat as she passed.

Bertha shrieked in response amid a frisson of beads swinging wildly from a dress cut so low at the back Rennie couldn't help but stare down the slender ravine of Bertha's *derrière*. Armed with possibly the longest cigarette holder in history, Bertha spun about shrieking at the paintings.

'I'll take it! I'll take it!'

She aimed her cigarette holder at Rennie's smallest, cheapest offering, the jangling purple and red geometric affair, *Hill on Red*. Even Bertha's flamboyance failed to disperse the polite silence which began to close in over the crowd. Once the reviewer had swept off, people gathered in groups, their backs to the walls as they swilled down rivers of French champagne.

Lloyd didn't falter. He stood over the guests smiling, chatting at length to Bertha and her various acolytes. But to the trained eye, Rennie knew he only managed to remain upright because of the molten anger hardening at his core.

It's a flop, Rennie wanted to cry. *A beastly flop*. Why didn't they all go home at once? She felt like an actress whose lines had been blanched from her mind. She was pinned to the stage in the glare of light. Whatever tiny move she made would be projected threefold.

Then all at once, the crowds moved out, blown like butterflies along the street.

Lloyd said nothing as he towered in the shadows by the door.

'Well?' Rennie said, staggering towards him, trying to pretend she didn't care about the punishment awaiting her.

'You're drunk,' he said, and stalked off towards the motorcar, saying nothing, absolutely nothing, as they sped home through the bruise of night.

CHAPTER
FOUR

After Girl had staggered back to work, Ellis fell down on her bed. She was soaked. She was shickered. She was all the words Girl used for being drunk.

It was unnervingly quiet in the house now with the lodgers gone and the bridge asleep. There was nothing to blot out the sound of Girl's working laugh rumbling out across the street. Ellis tried not to think of what was going on behind the shutters, Girl raising her skirts, unclipping her suspenders, rolling down her stockings, lying back on her bed for whichever Jack-the-lad had arrived with enough coins jangling in his pockets. She willed the reedy voice of Girl's gramophone to start up. At last, there it was. *Ain't she sweet* …

Ellis stared at the ceiling. She supposed some people's desire would be inflamed and not doused by overhearing Girl trading in her sole currency. As a child, she'd whispered tracts of the Bible to herself in bed trying to block out her parent's night time sounds, her mother's weeping placations, her father's stifled shouts. His tempers had flared worse at night but they were always there smouldering during the day, only less visible, like stars whited out by the sun.

She turned onto her side. The shadows of the room unravelled to swim about. *Ain't she sweet.* She felt sick. *She's so sweet* … Was that a poem or a song? She couldn't remember.

21

'Speak, child, speak!'

Ellis sat up. There it was again.

'Speak, child, speak!'

She jumped as a hand pinched her shoulder. Cold fingers scrabbled towards her neck. There was the smell of smoking candles, the flick-flick of impatient fans.

Ellis lit a match. There was nothing, just the tangle of her thoughts and the warping dimensions of a half-dark room. She lay back down, closed her eyes and gave in. *Astral travelling*, Miss Stranks had called it, when another part of you separated from your physical body and travelled across time and place. Was that what it was to remember every smell and sound as if you were reliving every joy and sorrow of the past? Or was it simply dream, fear and regret shot through with memory?

Whatever it was, it was happening now. She was back at the farm of her childhood in Candlebark Creek working with her mother in the kitchen garden. Her arms ached as she hauled pails of water from the neighbour's creek trying to save the last of the wretched plants. She felt the slap of her boots tramp through the powdery soil. *Stop. Listen to me Ellis.* Her mother's voice, but she didn't stop. Her father had told her to keep hauling water to try to salvage the withering plants. She pretended not to hear her mother's rasping breath. She ignored the rattle of a pail as it hit the ground. She didn't even stop when she saw the brown glint of spilt water snake its way towards her boots. It wasn't until later she'd stopped to find her mother wasn't there, and although the day had been as still as glass, a tree beyond the fence had begun to flutter. Ellis had watched the tree and had realised—too late—that it was a sign.

Pray for rain. That's what everyone said. *I am praying mother. There's still no rain.* For months the clouds had refused to drop their cargo rain. People could only watch as their livelihoods blew away. But on that day, it was hard to tell where the sky began and the land ended. The dust billowed up towards the clouds which had amassed in bright white pillars and towers. Thick rays of sun flowed out from behind them in shimmering rays as if God himself had tossed down golden ropes from heaven. Ellis watched the tree and prayed to the clouds. She'd seen and heard nothing else until it was too late.

In the blur of days after she'd found her mother's body lying face down in the dust, whenever Ellis tried to pray, she found the words had shrivelled to husks. Whenever she stared at the pages of the Bible, all she could see were the white spaces around the words, running like white rivers carrying away her faith.

Ellis' father began to drink as if grief was a thirst to be quenched every night. Sometimes he disappeared and she sat in the house alone, always alone, listening to the wind and for the sound of his horse. Twice she ventured into the village, only to find him appear from nowhere to haul her back to the house. Some days he took to the whip, slicing at the dying ground, at the starving horses, at the maddened dogs, and barren sky. It was only a matter of time before the whip would be turned on her.

That time soon came. One evening, she heard his horse. She waited in the shed where she'd worked with her mother drying herbs and storing seeds, listening as he raged about the yard, calling for her. There was a buzz in her head as she reached up to the uppermost shelf and took down the jar marked *Belladonna*. She cupped the berries in the palm of her hand. *Belladonna, Ellis, good for the eyes, in small doses, also for rheumatism, gout. But be careful of the berries. There's a reason they're known as the Devil's Cherries.*

'Where's my mug of tea?' he shouted.

She slipped the berries into her apron pocket, ducked into the kitchen and made the tea. One berry would be enough, she thought, as she crushed it and dropped it into the pot. She added extra sugar and set the steaming teacup by his hand. Everything else was in its usual place. She barricaded herself in her bedroom, listening to his shouts, followed by a brief pummelling on her door. She threw on her mother's coat and Sunday hat with the spray of flannel flowers stitched in linen and held together with silver thread, gathered up her few things and waited for the storm to pass.

As soon as she heard silence, she opened the door and saw her father bending over, staggering about the kitchen, his outstretched hands clutching at the air, his mouth working open and shut, not a sound coming out.

She steered him to a chair and cupped his chin in her hand and managed to pour a glass of vinegar and water down his throat, enough to undo the berry's work. His hands clutched at her, and she almost faltered until she saw his eyes, black with anger. She picked her way through the broken house, filched more food from the pantry and ran away from the barking dogs, through the whispering night, past the wire-ribbed cows and listless trees. She could think no further than every hurried step. Several times she saw the shadow of her father looming and receding across her path, or she heard the whip and stamp of his horse. She wasn't sure how long the power of a single berry would keep him from pursuing her, and her only compass was her mother's words: *If anything ever happens to me, Ellis, you must leave here. Go to the city, to the Benevolent Society for Women and Girls in Castlereagh Street. They taught me my lessons. They know me there.*

Ellis could see herself as a girl of sixteen entering the city for the first time, trying not to cry as she clutched on to the sides of a bullock cart. She flinched at every screech of an omnibus and cringed at the cries of the barrowmen. She stared at all the different kinds of people jostling beneath the canopies of glittering shops brimming with every imaginable ware, and blinked up at the giant letters painted on the side of a two-storey house: *Gilbey's Dry Gin—An Excellent Summer Drink!*

The streets were like creeks in flood. Even the buildings seemed to ride the swell as if trying to crib another inch of space. Chimneys belched black fountains of smoke. Horses' hooves clattered. Ladies clutching parasols slipped through the traffic in flickers of white. Boys darted in front of them as quick as sparrows, sweeping up the horses' muck.

Ellis caught sight of herself in the window of a bakery, her threadbare dress, her mother's Sunday hat, the dusty flannel flowers bobbing up and down on the brown tangle of her hair. Her reflection dissolved into a tray of pies and loaves of bread. Her stomach lurched. She hadn't eaten since the night before. She'd been forced to hand over the food she'd brought to the man who'd given her the ride on the cart.

'How else you pay?' he'd said, eyeing her as she'd emerged from the scrub five miles out from Candlebark Creek.

She'd sat bolt upright all the way, watching, listening, waiting for any move from him, or any sign of her father leaping from the trees and flagging them down, but there'd been none. Now at last he said they were nearing Castlereagh Street. Nobody would know her here.

The buildings grew taller and arched in over them. The air was thick with the stink of drains, smoke and dust. There was no room here for trees or sky. She glimpsed the harbour and her heart lifted as she felt the cool breath of salt, and saw the silky grey water criss-crossed by boats, the forest of masts of the tall ships moored at the docks. The cart slowed to a stop.

There was a girl dressed in white, a blue satin sash tied at her waist. The girl was standing on the steps of a grand-looking hall craning her neck, looking for someone in the clamour of street. A finger of sun caught the dark tresses of the girl's hair, lighting her pale delicate face. She frowned as a man approached her with two large boards. *Come Hear the Truth!* was painted on one side, *Follow the Path!* on the other. As the man tried to put the boards over the girl's head, she slipped away from him and ran down the steps.

'Kitty, come back this instant,' said the man.

'I will not.' The girl tossed her hair. She caught Ellis' eye and smiled slightly as she repeated, 'I will not.'

The cart jolted forwards. Ellis watched as the girl vanished from view.

'Let me off,' she said to the cart-man.

'Can't stop here,' he said. 'We're moving now.'

Ellis waited until he slowed at a corner, jumped down and dived into the crowds. She made it to a wall and leant against it. She'd never imagined one street could be so long and have so many different buildings. She looked up at where the sunset should be, but it was no more than a dirty thumbprint in the sky. She tried to ask for directions to the Benevolent Society. Everyone shook their heads or rushed on past. A man with sores on his mouth sidled up to her and whispered 'Lass, lass.'

She tried an old woman singing a ditty on a step. She stared at her leathery face, the stumps of teeth, the ragged handkerchief spread out across her lap holding one lonely coin. It took Ellis a moment to realise the woman was blind.

'Lay-dees Soc-i-e-ty. Up there by the tree,' the woman sang, her milky eyes staring past.

She picked her way through the throngs to the next corner, but there was no tree. The painted sign said *Häuser's Emporium*. Between the bright advertisements for *Robur Tea* and *Epps Cocoa—Grateful and Comforting*, she could just see the faded lettering *Benevolent Society*.

'Closed nigh on ten years ago,' the shopkeeper said. 'You ain't the first to ask for it, nor the last.'

Ellis felt the world go bright as she stepped back out into streets. She let herself be borne along as gusts of wind whipped along the street, toppling hats and ballooning skirts. She took refuge in a doorway and watched a soldier gallop furiously through the traffic.

A group of bystanders called out and shook their fists. Everybody turned as a lady squealed, battling to control her skirts. Ellis watched as the lady climbed down from a hansom cab, her skirts lifting to reveal dainty white boots and a froth of petticoats. Blue velvet ribbons fluttered from her hat.

The lady clutched at the hat as she turned and shrieked, 'Kitty! Why aren't you wearing the sandwich boards? I told you ...' The woman's voice swung away from Ellis on the wind.

The girl called Kitty appeared at the hall door.

Ellis blinked. *It was Kitty. It was her. The I-will-not-girl wearing the white dress who'd tossed her hair and smiled at her from the steps.*

Kitty frowned as the lady loaded her up with parcels. One tumbled to the gutter. Bits of paper escaped and fluttered up like moths.

'Now look what you've done, Kitty. Pick them up. Then get to the door and mind the donation box.'

'Yes, Miss Stranks.'

Kitty's dark hair flared up in the wind. Ellis heard her blaspheme as the lady swept off towards the hall.

Ellis stamped on one of the chits of paper scuttling towards her and peered at the words in the fading light.

ALL SOULS WELCOME

Come and Witness the Truth.

The Much Fêted

Miss Minerva Stranks

Conduit of the Masters,
Authoress of *The Radiant Past*,
The True Path of the Soul
and *The Golden Path*.

WORLD RENOWNED HEALER
of the World's Ills through the Power
of Pure Thought and Correct Diet.

Kitty was back at the hall doors, struggling to keep them open in the wind. She craned her neck and raised her hand to her eyes as if looking for someone in the crowd. A few passing people took handbills. A knot of people went inside. Kitty hardly seemed to notice them.

Ellis felt someone brush past her.

'Are you collecting or distributing pamphlets for the cause?' a man said. He nodded at the clutch of papers in Ellis' hand.

'No, I found them in the street.'

He laughed. 'Well, that is very charitable. Miss Stranks *will* be impressed. Haughty or humble, young or old, we are all the Lord's helpers, as Miss Stranks so regularly reminds us.'

The man positioned himself in the next doorway, struck a match, cupped it in his hand and lit a pipe. The sleeves of his black jacket were cuffed with velvet. The toes of his boots shone like coal. There was a sprig of white flowers in his lapel. His skin was honeyed brown, contrasting with the white of his shirtsleeves and collar, and the pale blue of his eyes which he turned on Ellis again.

'Aren't you going in?' he said. 'You do know Miss Stranks is one the most inspiring orators of our times.'

The smell of the man's tobacco threaded towards her on the wind.

27

There was another smell, the smell of spring, of working with her mother in the garden before the drought. She knew that smell.

'There you are. You found me at last.'

She turned to find Kitty was waving at her. Ellis stepped out of her doorway and waved back. The pipe-smoking man did the same.

'What happened?' he said as Kitty ran to him. 'I waited for the best part of an hour.'

'I couldn't get away. Stranks was late.' Kitty looked up at him and back towards the hall. 'You're not worried she'll see us here, are you?'

The man frowned down at her. 'Nothing of the sort.' He snapped open his fob watch. 'Besides, she'll be in the Green Room tuning up. Hee-hee-haw. Lo-lo-lo, and all that.'

Kitty laughed and tried to take his hand.

'No, I want to look at you.' He stepped back and motioned for Kitty to spin around. She laughed again as the white lace shawl flew out around her. 'My,' he said, 'You are becoming a plump little pigeon.'

'Am I?' Kitty's smile faltered. She drew in the shawl over her dress. 'Then I'll have to tell Mrs Frith to stop feeding me up. You'll do as you promised and tell her today.'

'You're suggesting I enter the lair of Mrs Frith and dare to advise her on how to wield her carving knife?'

'Don't be perverse. You know I mean Miss Stranks. You'll tell her today, like you promised.'

The man peered at his watch. 'Of course I will, Kitty, but this is neither the time nor the place to speak of it. And you know how she is about being late. Sloth is a sign of the sullied soul.'

They both looked up as the hall's doors were caught by a gust of wind.

'We must be patient,' he said.

'Patient? I will not.'

'Come on Kitty. Run along. I won't be far behind.'

Ellis watched as Kitty ran up the steps. When she'd disappeared, the man turned to Ellis.

'You will join us?' He nodded at the street. 'Young lasses should mind how they go in the dark.'

Ellis shivered as the man strode away through the shadows gathering and dissolving along the street. She peered down at the pamphlet again. Miss Stranks sounded welcoming, almost benevolent. She looked up at the hall, at the golden lamp now burning above the door. Amid the dust and smoke and stink, the sweetest scent whirled about her in the air. Lily of the Valley.

Lily of the Valley, Ellis. Where do we find lilies in the Bible? Luke speaks of them, Mother. And what does Luke say? 'Consider the lilies how they grow: they toil not, they spin not.' What other plants do we find in the Bible? Acacia, Almond, Algum, Aloe. And what of the Aloe's many uses? Apply the juice for soothing burns. Or take it as a syrup for the stomach.

She knew she'd find them. A sprig of white lilies lay at her feet. Ellis picked them up.

'Miss? Mr Bradbury says, are you coming in or not?'

It was Kitty calling out to her, one small hand held out towards her in the dark. Kitty's white shawl had turned golden beneath the lamp and for a moment, the wind lifted it from her shoulders causing it to shrug like a pair of golden wings.

CHAPTER
FIVE

Ellis squinted at the brightening constellation of moth holes in her bedroom curtains, slapped a hand to her forehead and sat up. Now she remembered what she'd done. What had she been thinking, drinking and letting her guard down to Girl like that? *Have you ever heard of the 'Green-eyed Gardener'? I'm writing a book about gardening. I'm blessed and cursed with this photographic memory. I worked as a spiritual secretary for Miss Minerva Stranks. That's where I met Kitty Tate.*

She scrambled out of bed stared at her watery reflection in the mirror, at the lines etched around her mouth, at the streaks of silver growing from her head. Surely Girl wouldn't remember much with a skinful of port wine and a nose stuffed with Sweet Tooth. Ellis touched her cheek and put her fingers to her lips. For the briefest moment, Girl's mouth had brushed against hers and she'd almost let herself kiss her back.

'Forgive me, Kitty. It's been so long.'

She wound her scarf around her nose and mouth, opened the door a crack and looked out. Good, there was no sign of Girl. Even Mrs Liddy and Clarrie weren't yet out on their front step. She hurried down Burton Street towards the curtains of dust and turned the corner where the rows of old terraces had been reduced to mounds of broken bricks. Grit stung her eyes as she navigated her way around the dunes of silt which blew in and settled, blocking pavements, filling drains, heaping across the tram tracks like middens of shell and ash. She nodded to one of the men standing knee-deep in rubble. She didn't recognise the others. They looked like dusted ants as they scuttled over the remains of houses, pickaxes slung over their shoulders, gnawing away at the dank innards of bathrooms and the surprised mouths of fireplaces.

At the cry of 'Watcho!' she stopped to watch a chimney shudder towards the ground. The chimneys were always the last to go. *Like me*, she thought. She squinted at the bones of trees. Once, there'd been wattles here, their winter branches weighted down with drifts of gold. Now they looked as if they'd been through fire. The chimney staggered and slapped the earth. A turret of dust hovered in its wake. She walked on, glancing towards the vast shaft cut deep into the earth where legions of men disappeared with horses and carts, re-emerging with swaying loads. All day the earth shook on its axis. Surely the god of Hades would burst up from his lair to lodge a complaint.

Ellis stared down at the harbour, at the edge of a city perched on the lip of the sea. Even over the clamour she could hear Kitty's voice: *Tell me you don't believe in Atlantis, Ellis. Tell me you don't.* She stood at the top of the escalators leading down to the ferry terminal and turned her head away from the frantic activity of the bridge, from the changing angles of the harbour. It was like catching sight of a dead loved one's likeness in a crowd. For those few seconds, the curve of a cheek or the flash of dark hair brought the stab of recognition followed by the chilling realisation that *what once was, is no more.* Only last week she'd passed a line of abandoned houses, their broken shutters creaking in the wind. She'd known they were marked for demolition but the next day when the houses were gone, their absence opened up strange new vistas. Everything looked larger or smaller, more raw or decrepit. A line of shirts and dungarees might have flapped for sixty years in the slow-moving shadow of a corner hotel and suddenly the hotel with its yeasty smells and hosed-down tiles had disappeared. Now the whole world could see into the mossy backyard of the neighbouring house. She couldn't help but look in too and watch a woman as she stirred at the laundry boiling in her copper, rolled up her sleeves, tucked a strand of hair behind her ears, while the husband blinked at the fierce new light burning in his shaving mirror.

She moved down the escalators and kept her eyes on the vast rooves of the work sheds built where the grand old terminus used to stand, its glass dome gleaming like a giant egg illuminating the clutch of shops beneath and the newsstand where she'd bought her *Herald* every day.

She boarded the ferry and stared across the short stretch of water, at the head and shoulders of the Town Hall suspended in the brownish haze. She didn't look across to The Rocks where the chaos was mirrored in symmetry.

Once she'd escaped the press of people at Circular Quay, she lowered her scarf and walked up Macquarie Street with the morning rush. All around there was the clip-clip of shoes, the swish of omnibuses lurching past. *Kitty, Kitty,* they all seemed to say.

When the city library came into view, she crossed the road and looked in at the park and the Moreton Bay Fig trees. Her mouth went dry as she approached the library steps. She laid her glove across the buttons of her coat, raised her chin and took a deep breath.

At the doors, she caught sight of her frown beneath her hat. She brushed the dust from her sleeves and looked down at her shoes, deciding the hasty darning on the ankle of her stocking might be mistaken for a mole on the skin. *Well here I am, Kitty. I've come at last.*

The library's silence swallowed her. She glanced at the desks dotted like islands across the vast floor. Half a dozen men sat surrounded by moats of boxes, papers and books. Electric lights cast pale pools of gold. She looked up at the square of cloud caught in the skylight. Instead of making her way to the request desk, she tiptoed towards the catalogue drawers, her heart thumping like a marching drum. She eased open the heavy little drawer marked *L*. There it was, *Lighted Way, The, Vol. 1, no. 1, 2nd February 1900*, and its almost unending subtitle: *Journal of Clairvoyance, Spiritual, Intellectual Health, Higher Truth and Virtuous Enlightenment through Purifying Nourishment.* Her hand felt detached as she scribbled down the number alongside her usual requests for the latest editions of *The Garden and the Home, The Australian Garden Lover,* and a random selection of perennial favourites, *The Amateur Gardener* and *Garden and Field.* She felt as if she was gliding as she moved towards the librarian's parapet.

'I'd like to see these please.' She sounded as though she was speaking through a folded cloth.

The librarian scanned the list and narrowed her eyes when she came to *The Lighted Way*. 'Month?'

Ellis' body leant forward. She saw the tips of her fingers whiten as she gripped the counter.

'Precisely which month do you require?' The librarian slid her eyes across the shoulders of Ellis' only coat. 'As you know, Miss Gilbey, these newsletters can run into the hundreds.'

'In the case of *The Lighted Way* there was only ever the one.' She heard her voice ricochet about the room. *There was only the one.*

When the librarian had disappeared, Ellis leant against the wooden counter, glad of its hefty weight. She closed her eyes to the distant sound of pulleys and shunting, summoning her requests from the depths. When they arrived, she scrawled the semblance of her signature across a chit. In the corner of her eye she could see the object of her visit, the thing she'd avoided for over twenty-seven years. She tucked it beneath the other publications and hurried to the desk in the farthest corner.

She half-expected to hear a roll of drums, but everyone was intent on their own task. Even the Argus-eyed librarian had abandoned her post. Ellis fanned out the newsletters and eased out *The Lighted Way*. Her head began to roar like the harbour in a storm. There it was, *2nd February 1900*. She covered it with her hands until only the caption beneath the photograph remained visible: *Protégée of the Charismatic Orator, Miss Minerva Pythia Stranks*. She moved her hands slowly down the page until the whole thing came into view. The print bobbed and dipped. There was the sound of rushing, and the distinct feeling of being reeled upwards by the hair.

For there it was, the delicate face of Miss Kitty Tate.

It was some time before Ellis realised she was still seated at the desk in the library. The skylight was the colour of lead. The gentlemen had folded up newspapers and returned their books. The librarian's spectacles glinted in her direction.

She collected up the stack of newsletters and took her time buttoning up her coat. The soles of her shoes tapped beneath her from a distant place. Her hands trembled as she tossed her items on the librarian's counter and rushed out. She ran down the library steps into the arms of a blustery wind. All sound seemed muffled, as if the grind of omnibuses, the clang of trams, the cries of barrow boys, the whinnying horses and honking motorcars were set behind a giant pane of glass. As she hurried past the park, she felt the rising convulsion of a sob. She raised a glove to her mouth, unsure if the sound had come from her.

In the winds of the Quay she stood very still waiting for someone from the library to tap her on the shoulder. *Miss Gilbey, if you'd come with me.* But all heads were turned towards the plumes of dust rising up over Milsons Point. All gloves were held over ears, trying to block out the worst of the day's final blasts. Nobody would notice a woman's sob.

There, over there, she could just see it through the tears, dust and smoke, whole streets of houses were already gone, the outlines of their foundations marked like graves in the earth. It was time to get back to what was left before it was too late, back to Girl, old Mrs Liddy and Clarrie, to squeeze out the last hours of their small ramshackle lives, where she was just a quietly spoken landlady and nobody knew or cared about the terrible thing she'd set in motion all those years before.

She pushed her way onto the ferry and stood by the rail in the cleansing wind, unbuttoned her coat and stared down at the rainbows of oil slicks and the lumps of rubbish bobbing about. Halfway across the water, she drew *The Lighted Way* from the belt of her dress. She let it flap like a flag in the wind before tearing it into strips and tossing them up, watching as the hundreds of words she'd once typed were blown away with Kitty on the wind.

She buttoned up her coat and brushed her sleeves. At last it was over. The reliable machinery of her heart would soon begin ticking again. She alighted from the ferry and walked up the escalators, breathing in time with her steps. By the time she'd turned the corner of Burton Street she was able to call out, 'Afternoon' to her neighbours in her usual calm and unremarkable landlady's voice.

CHAPTER
SIX

'Afternoon Mrs Liddy, Clarrie,' Ellis said.

'Good day, was it? At the library again, were you?'

'Thank you, yes.'

She plied her key to the lock and gave the door a shove. Once inside, she slumped against it. Shadows flickered across the hallway, and for a moment she could still see her favourite lodgers, she could still hear the fresh-cheeked girls staggering in late smelling of sherry or running out the next morning coughing as they jammed on their shoes, hats and coats, trying to beat the factory bell. She could hear the peals of laughter as the lodgers' children hunted for the Easter eggs she'd dyed and painted with stars and she remembered how that laughter had turned to screams when the black-lipped telegrams had started arriving from the front. Now it was over. All of them were gone.

She took off her coat and hat and went to find the dregs of a bottle of rum. She sat at her desk and took a swig. There was no point in trying to write anything now. Every time she glanced at the paper rolled into the typewriter, she felt Kitty's boot stamp on hers, and heard Kitty telling her to pass a fresh sheet. Every time she imagined laying her hands on the typewriter keys, they were Kitty's dainty hands, the knuckles slightly swollen and red but otherwise translucent.

She lay down very straight and very still on her bed, shut her eyes and waited for the stop-work whistle to blow down on the Point. Boots marched past the window. Someone thumped on Girl's door. A siren wailed. Girl laughed. Her mind flitted from one thing to the next. She could see the librarian's glassy eyes scanning the reading room. *Miss Gilbey, if you would.* By now they'd have discovered she'd stolen the only edition of *The Lighted Way.* She could never go back to the library again. In a single stroke, she'd scuttled her future and stirred up the past. But it was worth it, wasn't it, to let go of Kitty finally?

Night shadows lapped the room. She hadn't eaten any dinner and hardly slept. It was as if she was lying on top of sleep, unable to sink into its numbing depths. Too soon, the start-work whistle screeched down on the Point. She threw her coat over her nightdress, stumbled down to the kitchen, fumbled with a match, lit the stove, set the kettle on the hob, thinking one of the lodgers would catch it if it boiled too long.

The cold morning air hit her face. She squashed down her hat and hurried past the now dormant grocer's shop towards O'Malley's, past Alf Ostler's snores rattling the stone-pocked windows of the abandoned houses either side. At the corner she stopped to run her finger over a tuft of fern growing sideways from the brickwork and turned into a laneway where the morning sun was too wide to fit.

A shadow moved behind the upstairs curtains of O'Malley's. There were the voices of men still lingering from the night before. Others would be in for the hair of the dog. She knocked on a side door beneath the sign *O'Malley's Finest Tobacconist in the World.* She looked down the laneway at a sliver of dawn poaching the clouds from grey to white in a curious array of shapes, predictions of wild weather or mild, and for those who could see them, warnings, omens and grave portents. That's what she'd said to Girl the other night when she was drunk. *I see things, Girl.*

The wind nibbled at the hem of her coat. She slapped it down as the door handle clicked. The face of Paddy Forbes appeared, the *Herald* draped over one arm. Ellis held out a coin, took the paper and hurried off, frowning at the day's headline: *MILSONS PT RESUMPTIONS FULL STE ...*

'Miss Gilbey.'

She stopped. Paddy Forbes never addressed her by name. He stared at her as he pulled the door shut behind him and wiped the palms of his hands along the sides of his hair. There was a splash of red at his gingery neck.

'Yes, Mr Forbes?'

The intensity of his stare kept Ellis standing where she was.

'There's word on the street you been writing a book.' He narrowed his eyes as if the word 'book' was something best spat out between the teeth. His fists pumped like pistons at his sides. 'Mr O'Malley wants you to know you won't be writing nothing about *him*.'

'No, no, no,' Ellis said. In the upper window, a curtain moved. 'Tell Mr O'Malley it's only a light-hearted book about gardening.'

She tried a smile. Paddy's eyes fixed on her ankles and sailed northwards up her knees and thighs, across her hips, until they came to rest on her chest. Ellis folded the newspaper across the buttons of her coat.

'So if you'd kindly tell Mr O'Malley I'm writing a book about ...'

The wind kept frisking at the hem of her coat. Paddy's stare moved south. It was then she realised, the torn scarlet lace of one of Girl's hand-me-down nightdresses would be flapping in full view. At the sound of a ruckus from the other side of the door, Paddy turned and thankfully disappeared. Ellis hurried away knowing Paddy, if not O'Malley himself, was watching her go.

She hurried back to the house which was empty and silent except for the wheezing of the faintly glowing kettle. Her hands were shaking as she bolted the night-lock across the front door. In all her dealings with O'Malley's men, they'd never once singled her out. For twenty-seven years she'd kept her head down, mouth shut, eyes open, and up until the other night drinking with Girl, this had been enough.

She lifted her bedroom curtain and looked out. Of course Paddy Forbes hadn't followed her. Nobody had. She looked up at Girl's. The sun had strengthened, striking the houses along the street, illuminating the boarded up windows, gilding the heads of weeds. Ellis imagined Girl lying on the mess of her bed, her soft, damp, bare skin fingered slowly by the sun. *Terrible, tender, treacherous Girl.* Why did everything become so beautiful when it faced the axe?

She waited to hear the sound of Girl's morning cough, followed by the cranking up of the gramophone. There it was. Ellis frowned. It wasn't the usual frantic pick-me-up shimmy of *Ain't she sweet?* but the mournful falsetto of *All through the night*. She knew it then. Girl hadn't forgotten anything.

Standing in the bathroom, Ellis' hands were still trembling. For a moment she cupped them around her breasts. It was so long since she'd felt another's loving touch. The other night with Girl she'd let herself sail dangerously close. Had Girl told everyone about that too? She shivered as she remembered the look in Paddy Forbes' eyes, how they'd moved across the lines of her coat and settled like a blowfly on the scarlet lace.

38

CHAPTER
SEVEN

Rennie Howarth lay very still beneath the linen and merino wool. Playing dead, that's what people called it. She'd done it for hours as a child, hiding from her brother Irving as he'd stormed through the house, complaining that she'd 'trespassed' into his room. So it had been easy to lie as still as a corpse all these years later while her husband Lloyd left the bed, made his usual noises in the bathroom, dressed and hurried downstairs to consult his precious newspaper.

It hurt to swing her legs down from the bed, but she managed to move crab-like towards the bathroom where she splashed her face, squinted in the mirror and puffed some powder over the worst of it.

She wrapped herself in her Japanese silk pyjama coat and went slowly down the stairs. When she was within smelling-distance of the breakfast room, she counted to three and applied her morning after smile.

As usual, Lloyd was walled behind the day's headline: *MILSONS PT RESUMPTIONS FULL STEAM AHEAD.* Mrs Chisholm the maid turned and watched as Rennie began to rifle for a tin of cigarettes in the drawers of the dresser.

Rennie lit her cigarette and eased herself into her chair. She stared down at the starched napkin jammed inside its silver ring. It looked like a doll clasped in half by the kind of corset she thankfully no longer wore, despite Lloyd's repeated protestations that ladies looked 'more fetching' with some 'good old fashioned firming around the middle.'

She held up the enamel-handled butter knife somebody had given them as a wedding present. She adored it. He did not. She angled the tiny blade so it caught the sunlight and flashed about the room. *What an excellent dart*, she thought. Perhaps she should hurl it at one of her paintings. Lloyd could throw it himself. She could stand in front of *Blue Eucalypts at Sunset* or *Ochre Morning Grass* as he flung knives at her like those carnival men did at the seaside.

She stared at his newspaper, wondering if a review of her exhibition had made it into print. Lloyd's posture revealed nothing. He held the *Herald* like a fence between them every morning, or an albatross with its great wingspan stretched out.

On the ship out from England, she'd watched as members of the crew lured and netted one of these magnificent birds. Rennie had clutched Lloyd's arm and asked if it wasn't bad luck to kill an albatross. He'd said something about superstition being for dimwits. The men weren't going to actually kill it, he'd said, just take a few harmless photographs and set it free. She'd felt sick as they'd paraded the creature about the deck, its staring eye scanning the crowd. Eventually the crew had let it go. For the rest of the voyage Rennie wondered which disaster would befall them: a sinking, a grounding, a gnashing storm? Even after their ship was safely docked in Sydney, she couldn't remove the piercing stare of the bird's eye from her mind. It was as if the albatross had been seeing past them, beyond them into other worlds. For there *were* other worlds, she was sure of it; mysterious, magical planes beyond the material and mundane, the elements of which she sought to capture in her art.

She leant across the table to read the listing of throat slittings, which, according to the *Crimes and Fatalities* section, were up this year, followed closely by general bodily stabbings, poisonings, and a spate of back lane shootings linked, it was alleged, to the increasing reach of the crime syndicates.

Woman blinds robber with flour. How resourceful some people were.

'No drownings today?' she said.

Lloyd cracked the spine of the newspaper. *The beast stirs in his lair*, she thought, studying his paw-like hands.

Initially, she'd mistaken his nightly physicality for passion. He'd kissed her hard as soon as she'd entered the bedroom on their wedding night, grabbing her hair, thrusting his trousers against her dress, calling her his little rag doll, his hands pushing up her thighs, lifting her skirt as he parted her legs with his advance-party fingers and rallied the impatient troops, pushing her down on the bed, turning her over, breathing into her hair as he held her wrists.

At first, she'd quite enjoyed being overrun by him. It made a change from the damp drunken fumblings of English chaps. This was marriage. It was harsh. It was their secret. During the day, it thrummed inside of her like a pulse. But when he adopted even rougher tactics, she'd realised. This was not passion. This was not love. She'd tried to resist his nocturnal advances, but he only ambushed her more ruthlessly than before until— well—how could she put it—marks had been made upon the blank canvas of her skin. Marks she'd tried to hide with fashionably high collars and long drapes of oriental embroidered scarves. Chic backless dresses became impossible, as did anything sleeveless, a hellish sentence in the Sydney heat.

Once, her friend Bertha Collins had cornered her in the bathroom at the Australia Hotel.

'Oh that,' Rennie had said, laughing as Bertha pointed her cigarette holder at a bruise that had escaped its careful covering. 'It's paint.'

'On your neck?'

'We *artistes* are a messy breed.'

And so it went on, the lies and humiliations, the daily patching up of the crumbling façade. She could see it happening all over again, tomorrow morning, and all the tomorrow mornings after that, Lloyd in his starched shirtsleeves and braces, Chisholm's starched napkin protecting her master's silken tie. Only the date and headlines would have changed. The same glaring light barged in through the bay windows. The purple potted orchid crouched prettily on the mantelpiece. Chisholm dispensed the same fiery coffee, and there Rennie sat, waiting for the next grenade to land.

She looked down at her side of the toast rack. As per Lloyd's instructions, Chisholm had allocated her one wafer-thin slice. A tablet of butter perched on the lip of the butterdish. Rennie reached forward and took Lloyd's butter and jam, slathered them on her toast and took a bite.

'I expect all the best breakfast rooms of Sydney are abuzz this morning,' she said. She knew she was moving away from the script, but unless she did, none of this would ever stop.

She laughed, for she could hear it now, a hum of disapproval rising like a cloud around the harbour. *Who does that Mrs Howarth think she is coming out here, painting those wild, crude, formless works and passing it off as the latest thing in Modern Art? Did you see those mad cat scratches on the walls?*

Rennie polished off the toast, lit a cigarette and stood by the bay windows overlooking the harbour. This view had almost been enough when she'd arrived. She'd been quite elated standing in her small corner of the sunroom, paintbrush in hand, trying to trap the glittering angles of the midday sun in the hairs of her brush, searching for ways to capture the brassy play between water and sky, with streaks of ultramarine and cerulean blue.

She turned and looked at Lloyd's shoulders. It was so clear now, blindingly clear. She squinted at the harbour again. The wind was firing a volley of arrows at the water. There was no way out, except for one. In a way, she'd always known it would come to this. She'd given him what he'd wanted in a wife, a pretty, exotic pet to be paraded about, successfully annoying his mother, and, she suspected, avenging an old lover.

One day she'd drown herself in the harbour, give herself up to its silky caress. On the voyage out she couldn't help but think about drowning. Everybody did, whether they admitted to it or not, tossed about on a puny raft sandwiched between the great muscle of ocean and the changeable curve of sky. When she'd put this to Lloyd he'd patted her on the bottom and told her not to be *dulls*, a word he'd previously criticised her for using because, he said, it sounded 'childish and cheap.'

But drowning would not be *dulls*. Apparently it was almost languorous, falling downwards as if flailing through a brightly coloured dream. What was death but a change from one state to another? That's what the theosophists had said. Well, soon it would be her turn to make headlines.

A woman of unknown identity, aged in her early thirties, well dressed, fine Italian shoes, long black hair, of pale English complexion, was found in the Harbour. The police say …

What would the police say? Would they note the 'drownee' was a little too round for the latest straight-lined, slim-hipped fashions, or that she'd dressed rather carelessly for a woman in her position, as if she was in a hurry to leap from a life of privilege into the wash? She'd want people to know she'd been an artist.

An unknown lady with violet paint jammed beneath her nails.

Yes, drowning was the best option left, except there was one tiny complication. Her brother Irving was already en route from England, arriving any day expecting to stay. Could she wait until he arrived, or should she spare him the scandal and do it today?

She heard Lloyd rise from his chair, toss down the newspaper and squash his table napkin into the cloth as if breaking its neck. *Watch out for the albatross*, she almost said. There was the sound of the front door opening.

'Don't eat anything too substantial,' he called from the hallway, apparently unable to resist a parting shot.

He trotted out the word 'substantial' to remind her that despite her unusual height, she would never rival his towering dimensions, physical or otherwise. Lloyd's hands were the size of spades. His blue eyes pierced like searchlights. His spine was erect, telegraphing to the world the newly acquired soundness of his stock. This house on the harbour was imposing. The tennis balls he fired across the net on weekends to his office underlings were executed like missiles, followed by his explosive cry of *'shot!'* Everything about him was impressive, everything except for his pretty, unruly English wife.

Rennie rummaged through the newspaper. Lloyd had succeeded. There was no mention of her exhibition. But then again, she'd not quite failed. Her work had now been aired in both hemispheres. That was a small something to leave behind.

She sat down in his chair as Lloyd barked something about cocktails at the Australia Hotel at six o'clock sharp. In Rennie's coffee cup there was a ripple as the front door slammed. The Australia Hotel at six o'clock? She ran to the hallway and put her eye to the panel of stained glass beside the front door. Lloyd was bathed in navy blue, his satchel tucked under one arm, marching bluely down the path. She turned to the mirror and touched her face. She wasn't sure if the face belonged to a woman about to drown herself. Something irrepressible still burnt in the eyes.

No, it could not be today. Today should be devoted to what she loved. She'd go to the Art Gallery and look at art, remind herself how the Great Masters had persisted in the face of hardship, petty-mindedness and ridicule.

And yes—that was it—she would not come back.

She ran upstairs and threw open the linen cupboard, messing Mrs Chisholm's neat piles. She'd read about robbers breaking into houses and walking away with people's worldly belongings draped over their shoulders. She shook out two pillowcases and dashed into the bedroom. She wondered what she'd need, and how long would she need it— whatever it was—for. She pulled open drawers and filled the pillowcases with a tangle of underthings and scarves, gloves, handkerchiefs, shoes, a sketchbook, a tin of her favourite watercolour paints, pencils, brushes, cigarettes and the lavender flower bag she'd embroidered with geometric patterns.

She heard Chisholm clashing pots and pans in the kitchen sink, found her best hat, kidskin gloves and new season's spring green woollen coat. She dressed quickly but artistically because today was the day. She'd lain awake planning to end it all so many times, next to Lloyd's heaving whisky breath, hoping he couldn't guess that through the membrane of skin and skull, his wife was plotting treachery.

She frowned as she clapped open her purse. *Damnation and blast.* She'd spent all her money on flowers for the exhibition. But the flowers had been beautiful, immaculate sculptures of dignity and finesse, holding their poise in the face of disaster, a view echoed by one unknown guest who'd announced the flowers were *by far the best works of art on display.*

She knew Lloyd kept a stash of banknotes in his davenport desk inside a cigar box. Rennie ran downstairs, found the key. Marvellous. There it was. She dropped the roll of cash into her handbag.

As she shut the drawer an envelope fell out onto the floor. She picked it up. *Mr Lloyd Howarth Esquire.* Rennie recognised the tight curvature of the handwriting and frowned at the return address: *Mr Irving Bartlett Esq. 14 Hill Road, London, N6.* That was odd. Why would her brother write to Lloyd and not to her? She'd been dealing with her brother's travelling arrangements for half a year, fielding Irving's endless questions about what to bring and what to leave behind as if he was about to set off into the remotest jungles of the Amazon.

But she didn't have time to think of her brother now. She slipped the letter into her pocket, grabbed a carpetbag from the cupboard under the stairs, shoved the two pillowcases inside it and ran out of the house to be swallowed by the commotion of the harbour and the windy bright.

Chapter EIGHT

Ellis lifted the bedroom curtain. Girl was out there strewing her wet stockings over the railings like sloughed snake skins.

'Have a lie in, did we, Els?' Girl called out, brazen as you like, as if nothing had happened between them the other night, as if she hadn't ratted to O'Malley about writing the gardening book.

Ellis swung open the door, set her teacup on the step, sat down and spread the newspaper across her knee, the same way she always did.

'Here she is,' said Girl. 'Els looks about as weary as a weir, don't she Mrs Liddy?'

'What, dear?' said Mrs Liddy, cupping a hand to the side of her bonnet.

Ellis kept her breath steady and her eyes down as she filled her pipe.

'Still sucking on the old maidenhair, Els?'

'What did you say, dear?' Mrs Liddy said.

'*May-den hair.*' Girl let out a laugh. 'That's what Els here calls her tabaccy.'

'Well, that's very poetic, isn't it Clarrie?' said Mrs Liddy.

Girl let out another shriek as Clarrie waved his dog-eared copy of *The Works of Shelley* and coughed deeply and silently into a rag.

'That reminds me,' said Mrs Liddy, 'when the maidenhair ferns used to grow down all feathery from the walls in the cuttings at The Rocks. That was before those greedy bigwigs came in and ripped them out.'

'Go on, Els,' said Girl. 'Why don't you tell Mrs Liddy about the Ancient Greeks?'

Ellis kept her face blank. 'Do you want me to read out the papers today, or not?' she said. She stared at the headline: *MILSONS POINT RESUMPTIONS FULL STEAM AHEAD*.

'That's if you don't want to give us one of your clever speeches, Els.'

Oh no, Ellis thought. She stared up at Girl. *Had she told her about that too?* Girl stopped laughing. She was down on her haunches, peering down through the dripping stockings and broken balcony slats.

'No hard feelings, Els. We all need a good laugh this morning, that's all. That's no surprise, is it? Ah. You ain't heard the news yet.'

'What news?'

'Alf reckons none of us are going to see one brass razoo from the government coffers. He says it's all over the papers. They're cutting our street in half in two weeks time.'

Ellis ran her eyes down the page. In all the confusion with Paddy Forbes, she hadn't read the papers yet. She gulped a swig of tea, raised her chin, took a deep breath and began to read it out aloud.

For once, everyone stayed silent. Mrs Liddy didn't cry out 'What, dear?' at every other word. Clarrie refrained from coughing or rummaging through his poetry book to throw in a pithy line or two. Girl didn't laugh, burp or curse. Even the ferries hooting in the harbour seemed to hold their breath until Ellis came to the bit about there being no compensation for tenants in Burton Street.

'The bastards won't get away with it.' It was Alf Ostler, bowling down towards them, his usual gaggle of bandy-legged old timers in tow.

'But what can we do?' Mrs Liddy's apple-doll cheeks began to quake. 'They're all saying the bridge will be the pride of the nation, the working man's saving grace.'

Ellis looked at everyone. They all looked so flimsy, as if they'd be blown away in the next big wind.

Clarrie prodded a finger at his book and said, '*A melancholy tale, to give an awful warning, Soon oblivion will steal silently.*'

'Give it a rest, Clarrie,' Girl said.

Ellis stood up. So, it had happened at last. The standoff was over. In a way it was a relief. It was the *not* knowing that had been the hardest thing to have hanging over them, like the sword of Damocles, everyday.

'Clarrie's right,' said Ellis. 'Oblivion *is* stealing in. We all knew nobody could stop that bridge, not when the bridge is the future and ... and ... we're the past.'

Girl was on her feet, thumping the railing, the balcony swaying beneath her weight.

'Well I ain't going to lie down and be diddled out of my rights when all them other people got paid off like ...'

'Like O'Malley?' Ellis heard herself say.

Alf and his mates shifted in their boots. Nobody wanted to be heard saying *of course a man like O'Malley had been compensated*. O'Malley ran the tobacconist, doubling as a SP betting shop. Since the recent crackdown on returned diggers' growing dependence on pain relievers, he'd been doing a roaring trade in Girl's number one favourite powder, Sweet Tooth, while milling a few quiet quid on sly grog.

'It's the truth and we all know it,' said Ellis. 'Burton Street is finished.'

'Now that reminds me of the "nervous rooves" as they called them, back in the 80s,' said Mrs Liddy. She rose shakily from her milking stool. 'That was the last time they knocked the Rocks about. Slum clearance they called it, a fancy name for ...'

There wasn't much that could stop Mrs Liddy once she'd launched into one of her long quavering tales about the common people being pushed about. Ellis lit her pipe and leant against her doorframe. Everybody turned to look as Tom-the-pickpocket poked his head out of a window.

'You still here, Tom? Shouldn't you be down at the Quay harvesting your morning crop?' Girl said.

'The poor live the life of the fugitive.' Clarrie flapped his poetry book open. '*The Earth is like Ocean, Wreck-strewn and in motion.*'

Mrs Liddy began to sob into the hem of her skirts.

'Oh hush now, Missus. We'll be right.' Clarrie patted the old woman's hand. 'My cousin'll be by any day now. We'll stop with him. You wait and see.'

Ellis looked up. The sun had retreated behind a cloud. It was as if the bridge was already up there, its great form rising over them blocking out the sun.

'I say we all go up there and give 'em what for,' said Alf.

Ellis sighed. 'Go where?'

'The minister's office.'

'Alf's right. Come on, Els. It'll be a fizz.' Girl was smiling one of her ripe fruit smiles. 'If you take Mrs Liddy and Clarrie, I'll do the honours with the flask.'

Girl disappeared from the balcony and emerged downstairs wrapped in her boa, camellia-pink coat and hat with two ostrich feathers poking up. Girl helped Mrs Liddy to her feet and swung the milking stool over her shoulder.

'Oh, all right,' said Ellis. 'Wait a minute. There's something I want to bring for luck.'

'What, dear?'

Girl lifted the side of Mrs Liddy's bonnet and shouted 'Els says she's getting something for us. For luck, she says.'

Ellis ran out to her backyard, picked half a dozen nasturtium flowers and grabbed her hat and coat.

'Some people believe they mean victory.' She tucked a flower into Mrs Liddy's bonnet and pressed another between the pages of Clarrie's poetry book. 'Even the valiant unvanquished need help, don't they Girl? You seem to remember everything else I said the other night.'

'There you go again, getting all frilly with your words again.' Girl thrust her fox fur collar towards her. 'Pin it there, bang between the eyes.'

Ellis stepped back.

Girl roared with laughter. 'Once a cabbage-muncher, always a cabbage-muncher, eh?'

Ellis pinned her nasturtium to her coat and held her arms out for Mrs Liddy and Clarrie to cling on. It was like wading through molasses, trying to steer her two frail charges down the street, past the abandoned schoolyard with its thistles and dandelions sprouting up, around the corner past the bones of the terraces and out into the morning bustle of the main street. They marched through the smell of frying fish and chips, past the boarded-up haberdasher and the barber's shop, their windows pasted over with Notices to Quit. She could hear Alf roaring about rights and duties at the front. Girl swaggered behind, bringing up the rear. Half a dozen people joined in. Some cheered. Others jeered.

'You can't stop progress,' a man called out. 'It's your greatest show on earth, mate, your Harbour Bridge.'

'All we're asking for is our rights,' Alf shouted back.

Clarrie began to cough. Ellis asked if he was all right.

49

'It's just me own eternal flames. Lit by the Hun with mustard gas.'

'What, dear?' Mrs Liddy was beginning to turn purple at the mouth.

'I think we should go back ...' Ellis began to say, but she was drowned out by the honking of claxons at a cross street.

A driver climbed out, strode towards them, hands on hips. 'What's going on here?'

'What does it look like?' said Alf.

'We haven't got all day, mate.'

'Neither do we, *mate*.'

'Then you'd better move along. Stop blocking the street.'

'You're the one blocking the bloody street.'

Alf tried to prod the driver in the chest. The driver stepped back.

'I wouldn't do that if I were you, you stupid old bugger. On your way.'

Ellis looked up as a gob of spittle landed on a gleaming bonnet.

'Who did that?' said the driver. 'I'll rub your nose in it, whoever it was.'

'We should go,' Ellis said.

'Stop where you are, Els,' Girl called out.

A handful of rocks flew over their heads and clattered across a car's windshield.

'Call for a policeman.' A man waved a walking cane from his car.

'Scum, the lot of you,' the driver said, rolling up his shirtsleeves.

'Clarrie, did you hear that?' Alf said. 'We're being called scum for fighting for our rights in our own country. S'pose this lily-livered pipsqueak was one of them conchies.'

'March on.' Girl barged past, with Mrs Liddy's milking stool slung over her shoulder. 'Some fights aren't worth fighting by yourself.'

'Out of the way, lady, if that's what you are,' the driver said. 'Or you'll land one square in the jaw.'

Girl's pink feathers stabbed the air. She took up the milking stool, held it out in front of her, jabbing the driver like a lion tamer.

'Hold on,' she said. 'If it ain't Mr Ferris, Sir, sitting there all nice and cosy in his shiny new Thin Lizzy.' She pushed past the driver and sashayed towards the motorcar. 'It *is* Mr Ferris. How's the wife and three little 'uns? Hope you're not working too hard at that insurance game of yours. I'll never forget that pretty view over the docks from your office.'

A scarlet-faced Mr Ferris sat back into the shadow of his cabin.

'Driver, let them pass,' was all he said.

'And a good day to you too, Mr Ferris, Sir.' Girl blew a kiss to the growing crowd. 'Off we go, Alf. Easy as you like.' Girl raised her brandy flask aloft at the front. 'And if you still want your policeman, you'll find him sinking a few, courtesy of O'Malley's.'

Everyone laughed as they moved around the cars. Ellis heard herself laugh too. The motorcars could wait. The whole world could wait for the people—yes, the *people*—to move on past.

Now Girl was singing out, 'One for all, all for one!' in her crackly voice.

Ellis clutched Mrs Liddy's wiry arm, threw her head back and sang along too. That was why nobody wanted to leave Milsons Point without a fight, not because they didn't want the bridge and the work it brought, or because life had ever been perfect or easy here, but because all kinds of people had been thrown together to live side by side either through the accidents of history or of birth. It was the *people* who'd made the place. Most of the houses crouched slightly lower every year. When they lost roof tiles or sheets of iron to the harbour winds, up went another plank of wood and in went another post to prop up a leaning wall or sagging balcony.

The singing stopped when they came to the offices. Alf motioned towards the steps.

'Storm the barricades,' he said, rather half-heartedly Ellis thought.

'Read out the *Herald* again, Els,' Girl said.

'I can't. It's back at the house.'

'You don't need it, do you?' Girl was standing over her in a cloud of port wine. Beneath the fox fur, her cleavage was heaving from the walk. Ellis tried not to think of that cleavage as she let go of Mrs Liddy and Clarrie. 'You said so yourself, Els. You said you remember every word you've ever clapped eyes on, that they sit there in your brain *like seeds in the ground waiting for the rain.*'

Ellis turned away. 'Oh who knows what rubbish I said the other night. Nothing and nobody was ever going to stop them building the bridge. I'm tired, Girl. I haven't slept. I've got nowhere to go. In short, *I've had enough.*'

'Hooplah!' Girl threw up hands. 'Ladies and gentlemen, bring out the dancing girls. *In short*, Miss-Ellis-bloody-Gilbey has a voice on her after all.'

'Oh shut up, will you?'

'That's the way. Throw a bit of curry in while you're at it. It'll do you the world of good.' Girl tried to take her by the arm but Ellis wrestled herself away.

'Don't tell me what's good for me, Girl. You know nothing about me. Nothing at all.'

'And whose fault's that? Years we been neighbours, and there you sit with your lips clamped tighter than a rabbit's arse while the rest of us have a nice old yarn. Don't think we haven't noticed. But we know *something* about you now.'

'What?'

'Now we know you've got a voice on you when you want.' Girl set down Mrs Liddy's milking stool. 'Up you get.'

Ellis blinked at her. 'You can't be serious.'

'We haven't got long,' Clarrie wheezed. 'I haven't, anyways.'

'But I can't address a crowd. Not anymore.'

Girl offered Ellis the flask. Ellis climbed up onto the stool. She stared at the dozen or so faces. *Go on, Ellis. Chin up chaps.* She half-expected to see Kitty's white handkerchief make the sign of the cross. She raised her chin, took a deep breath and recited the main points from the article.

'You've said your piece,' said one of the minister's men.

'Do we think we've said our piece?' Ellis heard herself cry out.

'No!' everybody shouted back.

Ellis scrambled down. Alf motioned towards the steps.

'You want me to go in, Alf? Oh all right. We've come to speak to the man who—who was it, Alf? Who agreed—who *promised*—we'd be paid our dues. Nobody wants to cause any trouble here. If we could just speak to Mr—what was the man's name Alf?'

Alf nodded furiously at the base of the steps.

'The name, Alf.'

'Eh?'

'The man you said we needed to speak to.'

Alf tilted his head and tapped it as if there was water trapped in his ear.

'The man you said you spoke to. Alf. The one you said read all our letters and put forward our petition in an extraordinary meeting with the mayor and the minister.'

Alf mumbled into his yellowy beard. 'There was no man.'

'What?'

52

'I had to tell 'em something. Somebody had to look like they were fighting the good fight.'

Ellis looked down at the people who'd come at Alf's behest. She looked beyond at the clamour of trams, the carts loaded up with goods, the rushing pedestrians, careering omnibuses and motorcars, spurred on by the winds of progress and change, dashing and racing each other to be first, the most, the biggest, the best, to grab what they could in this brand new cutthroat age.

She turned to one of the minister's men. 'My good sirs, if you would be so kind as to convey our humble request to converse with the party in order to corroborate and testify to the veracity of the announcement of the annulment of the promised payment of our dues as per published today in the morning edition of *Herald*, column two, page three.'

The man looked at her blankly.

'For God's sake let the woman in,' said another man.

A cheer rose up from the crowd. Ellis took her nasturtium out of her lapel and held it up. How quickly it had come back to her, Miss Stranks' tactic of unleashing a volley of incomprehensible words.

She was shown to a room with a high window. She stood on a chair and looked out. To her surprise everyone had already gone. She sat for some time, trying to steady her breath and cool her flushed cheeks. Distant voices rose and fell. She stood up at the sound of footsteps, but they faded off. She rehearsed what to say. She'd add in snippets from the letters she'd typed and the articles she'd read.

The post office clock struck a quarter to ten. She went out to speak to a man on the desk.

'Name?' he sighed, not looking up.

She dropped her wilted nasturtium on his blotter and left.

She found Burton Street empty except for Clarrie sitting on his step, leafing through his poetry book.

He looked up. '*Behold the chariot of our Fairy Queen!*'

'Being without a chariot, this fairy queen feels more like *the world's rejected guest*.'

'No go, then, with the bigwigs?'

Ellis shook her head.

'We thought as much. Alf's taken the rest of the mob up to O'Malley's to commiserate.' Clarrie squinted past her down the street. 'I said I'd wait here and watch out for my cousin. He says he'll be here any day to pick us up.'

'You said he lives out west in the country?' She tried to sound cheerful.

'That's right. A bit of a hill to look at. A slip of a river in which to cast the rod. Could be worse.'

Ellis did her best to smile. 'I'm sure he'll be here soon, Clarrie.' She turned away hoping he hadn't heard the catch in her voice.

Before she shoved open the front door she let herself imagine someone was waiting for her too, to take her coat and hang it on the peg, to ask how she was, to give her a warm kiss, but there was no one. She was alone. This is how it was and would always be.

She sat down on the back step and lit her pipe. A wind had sprung up, raising the dust which had floured the bedraggled plants in the yard. She watched as the dust danced a cancan in the air to the relentless hammering down on the Point.

Come on, someone said. She turned around to look, but there was only the dark tunnel of the hallway and the pale flicker of dust. That's all it took now to see Kitty again standing in her white dress calling out to her from the hall steps.

Kitty's dark hair fanned up behind her head. Her small hand was outstretched in the blustery air. *Miss? Are you coming in to hear Miss Stranks or not? I have to shut the doors, you see, against this blasted wind.*

CHAPTER
NINE

The wind caught the hall doors. Kitty told her to hurry as she gathered up her parcels and ran up a flight of stairs to another door.

Ellis followed. Her eyes took a moment to adjust. The hall was like a church, except for the red velvet curtains shimmering across a stage. Two pianos stood below, their lids closed. Thirty or so people were dotted about the first few rows.

'Darn it,' Kitty said. She set down her parcels, peeled off her gloves and began to tug at the string. When she noticed Ellis was still standing at the door watching her, she gestured towards the stage. 'Aren't you going to sit at the front?'

Ellis held out the half a dozen pamphlets she'd retrieved from the street.

'Oh. You can put them there. Next to this damned parcel.' Kitty frowned. Her skin was so white and fine it was as if it had never seen the sun. Her mouth was neither smiling nor frowning, but slightly skewiff. Her eyes were the colour of cornflowers, bright and blue, and dark-edged. *Cornflowers, Ellis, what do we say they are like? Scraps of heaven, mother.*

Kitty eyed her with an expression of gentle amusement. 'You're not from here, are you?'

Ellis raised a hand to her dusty hat, and felt herself begin to blush. She tried to deflect Kitty's stare by motioning towards the parcel. 'I can help you untie it, if you like.'

'Help?' Kitty laughed. 'That's a dangerous word to trot out around here. But since you have, here. You can open this and put these new pamphlets with the books.'

Ellis set the new handbills next to the stack of books: *The Radiant Past, The Light of Hope, The Ecstasy of the Masters Leading Us Onwards to the Afterlife*. All were authored by Miss M. P. Stranks.

They both turned as a gong shimmered behind the curtains. Kitty sighed and dragged a chair to the desk, nodding for Ellis to do the same.

'I don't blame you for wanting to stay near the door,' she said, fanning herself with a pamphlet. 'You never know what you'll catch if you sit down there.'

The curtains swept open. Kitty closed her eyes and laid her head back against the wall. A ripple ran through the audience: *There she is. Miss Minerva Stranks*. Ellis watched as Miss Stranks glided across the stage. A book was clamped to her bodice. Her hair was swept up beneath her hat in a wide blonde puff. The blue ribbons of her hat danced about. She looked taller than she had in the street. Her cheeks were chiselled, high and fine. Her eyes sparkled as she moved her smile slowly across the audience.

Someone called out 'Amen.'

'Come to me! For we are gathered here to hear the Truth!' cried Miss Stranks.

Ellis glanced at Kitty. Her eyes were still closed, her hands upturned in her lap. Miss Stranks raised her book to the air.

'I beseech you, holy Masters, come to me!' She frowned and tilted her head as if somebody was whispering in her ear. 'So be it,' she said, nodding. 'Amen. It is thus.' She then informed the audience tonight's lecture would open with a brief reading from her latest book, *The Brightening Way: Daily Exercises in the Cultivation of Pure Thought*, copies of which were available at the door. All hats turned briefly in the direction of Ellis and Kitty. Ellis shrank in her chair.

And so Miss Stranks' lecture began. Her voice was as rhythmic and melodic as a lullaby. Tracts from the Old Testament were mixed in with others Ellis had never heard before, 'planting the good seed in the lotus-petalled heart', 'harvesting great spiritual wealth through word, thought and deed' and 'lightening the cosmic soul by banishing impure thought through the divine bodily temple.' She then spoke about the Masters who trod the earth as Wise Ancients, borne out of great wisdom attained over many lifetimes and devoted to progressing man by undertaking the work of God.

'They are here amongst us!' Miss Stranks thrust her book towards the corner of the hall. Everybody turned and looked. 'The age of miracles is not yet past! It is here! It is now!'

A man stood up and shouted 'Hallelujah!'

'You sure it wasn't a bunyip you saw?' somebody laughed.

A few people joined in. Kitty snapped open her eyes. 'Who was that?' she whispered. 'Did you see?'

'Third row,' Ellis said. 'Second hat nearest to the aisle.'

'Interesting.' Kitty smiled and returned to her position, eyes closed, head leant back against the wall.

A flush of colour had come to Miss Stranks' cheeks. Her eyes scanned the audience, the smile frozen on her face.

'I see there are doubters amongst us tonight. Pay them no mind, poor souls. They remain deaf and blind to the Masters' truths. We must never cast them out. They are not yet pure of heart. Impurity is caused by many things, sin, sloth, greed, and by eating meat.'

The two bunyip men by the aisle left their seats noisily, and staggered towards the door, laughing. Miss Stranks watched them go.

'Drink will stupefy the soul. Now, where were we? While all men are equal,' Miss Stranks said, 'animals depend on our help. To feast upon their flesh is not only a betrayal of their trust, but a vile and foolish sullying of the soul. Meat is death. Not life.'

The idea of eating anything made Ellis' stomach leap. She was so thirsty her tongue was a strip of leather in her mouth. She wondered about asking Kitty where there was a water tap, but a few more people had risen from their seats and were making their way to the door.

'We will pray for you,' Miss Stranks called out. She moved to the front of the stage to smile at her remaining listeners. 'Blessed are you, the good people gathered here. You are the true foot soldiers for the cause. You are truly blessed.'

A spatter of applause broke out. Someone called 'More!' A woman ran up and tossed a posy of white roses onto the stage. Miss Stranks scooped them up, flourished them in the sign of the cross and threw them back.

'Come back next Sunday for your fill of the Truth. For there is nothing purer or mightier than the Truth!'

With that, the curtains jerked shut.

'Well.' Kitty flapped her gloves at the desk. 'I may as well pack up. Pack. Unpack. Fetch and carry. That's all I do.'

People had begun to file past. There was the occasional clink of a coin and the odd murmur of, 'Bless you girls.'

The white roses woman made a beeline towards Ellis with a gleaming eye. 'You are truly blessed, child, to be in the service of Miss Minerva Stranks.'

'But I'm not in her service.'

'Hush. Savour your blessings, child. Do not deny.'

'Thank you, Madam,' Kitty said, moving from the desk to usher her out. 'Indeed, we are all truly blessed.' When Kitty returned, she whispered, 'The trick is to smile, agree and get rid of them as quickly as possible.'

Ellis looked around. The hall was now empty. She felt a streak of panic rise inside of her.

'Well,' Kitty said. 'After all the sound of fury—nothing. I hope you weren't expecting something more.'

'I'll help you with those pamphlets if you like.'

Kitty looked at her. 'No, I'll manage, thank you. You can go.'

Ellis felt her head begin to swim. She could not go. There was nowhere to go. She watched as Kitty stopped packing to rub at her hands.

'Oh, don't worry,' Kitty said, flashing a tired smile. 'It's not so bad. I've tried to tell her the work on the new typewriting machine has made them worse, but she's always on at me. *Hands at the ready, while I speak.* Apparently pain in the hands is evidence of the Hell Broths broiling away inside me, a manifestation of my sinful thoughts.'

They both turned as a man appeared at the door. It was the pipe-smoking man Kitty had kissed out in the street.

'What have we here?' He smiled at Kitty as he approached. 'The maid hath procured another maid?'

Kitty laughed. 'She blew in from the street and helped me with the pamphlets, that's all.'

The man's gaze settled on Ellis. 'Quite the little helper, aren't you Miss?' His hand went to his lapel. 'And what a fragrant sprig of lilies you have there. A charming congregation of the lost and found.' He winked at Ellis before turning back to Kitty. 'Miss Stranks is calling for you. I will see this young lady out.'

He moved to take Ellis by the arm. Ellis stepped back and stumbled against the desk. A stack of pamphlets fell to the ground.

'Steady on,' he said. 'I won't ...'

'Thank you, Mr Bradbury,' said Kitty. 'I shall see her out.'

Bradbury moved his smile from Kitty to Ellis before clicking his boots and striding away.

When he'd gone, Kitty said, 'As you can see, Mr Bradbury may be very chivalrous, but he is not for sale, if you know what I mean.'

Before Ellis could answer, a voice rang out in the stairwell. 'Kitty?'

'It's her. Quick. She'll box my ears if she suspects I'm dallying. Help me with these.'

Ellis heard Kitty cough as they rushed to gather up the books and pamphlets and ferry them out to the stairwell. Ellis stood at the top of the stairs, looking down at the stray handbills eddying about the lower steps.

'I'm sorry,' Kitty whispered. 'I can see you need help. But I can't. Not now. Come back next week and ...'

They both turned as Miss Stranks' voice rang out behind them, 'Kitty? There you are.'

'You must go,' whispered Kitty.

'But who is this?' Miss Stranks loomed at the upper door. The honeyed voice was gone now. 'Why have you not *cleared* the hall?'

'Oh, she was only helping me collect the runaway pamphlets in the street.'

'You are here to help *me*, Kitty, not to hire your own. And look what you've done now. You've made me late.'

Ellis saw something flicker across Kitty's face. She knew that look. It was how she'd felt when her father had begun to taunt her, and she'd begun weighing up whether to stay or run.

Ellis stepped forward. 'It's my fault, Miss. I wanted to give you these.' She held out Mr Bradbury's sprig of lilies.

'Lilies of the Valley,' Miss Stranks said. 'Bradbury, didn't I say earlier, "I see a little flower girl with sweet white lilies adorning her hair?"'

'Indeed, Madam. But the cab is waiting to take us back to the house.'

The house, Ellis thought. They all lived in a house. She could see it now, a grand city house with fires in the grate, food on the table, lilies in the garden. She looked at Kitty who'd moved away to cough into her handkerchief.

'Lilies are in the Bible, Miss,' Ellis said. *'Consider the lilies of the field.'*

Miss Stranks raised a hand for her to stop. 'But we know Luke refers to the Easter Lily or the Madonna Lily, not the Lily of the Valley,' Miss Stranks said.

'Mint, mulberry tree, mustard, myrrh.' Ellis' words came out in a rush. 'They're in the Bible too. Marigolds, motherwort, dahlias, daphne, delphiniums.'

'Enough, child. Give me your hand. Let me see it. Aha. 'Tis as I thought. You are from the country. See Kitty? See the callouses on her hands? A sign of *real* work. Are you here alone, child? No. Hold your tongue.' Miss Stranks raised her chin and half-closed her eyes. 'Your mother has recently gone behind the veil.'

Ellis felt a tightness grip her throat.

'You mustn't mind, child. There is no death. There's only transformation. And your father? He too is dead.'

Ellis felt herself begin to sway. Miss Stranks was wrong. Her father wasn't dead. She'd only used one Belladonna berry, not enough to kill a grown man. She could see him raging about the farm, cursing his departed wife, his runaway daughter, blaming them both for his ruined life. The thought flashed through her mind that it was better to let Miss Stranks think he too was gone. Ellis heard herself speak. *'Do no wrong, do no violence to the stranger, the fatherless, nor the widow.'*

'So you know your way around Jeremiah, child,' said Miss Stranks.

'For in thee the fatherless findeth mercy.'

'And Hosea. Where did you learn your Bible so well?'

'My mother was a teacher.'

'As am I.' Miss Stranks turned away to fuss with her hat. 'Keep the lilies, child. You've received my blessing. Off you go.'

Ellis looked over at Kitty who ever so slightly shook her head.

'Please, Miss,' Ellis said. 'As you can see, I'm a very hard worker. And I believe the Masters await the soul's emergence from its barren state to plant the seed and harvest the bounty in the many lotus-petalled heart and will to return to life through the turn of the wheel through the unsullied temple of body and soul. The age of miracles is not yet past! It is here! It is now!'

Miss Stranks glared at her. 'You are either a fool or a fraud. Or am I to believe you are able to read, write *and* recite?'

Ellis nodded.

'The theosophists have sent you here to spy on me.'

'The who, Miss?'

Miss Stranks clapped her hands at Kitty. 'Fetch one of my books. Bradbury? Are you seeing what I am seeing?'

Kitty produced a copy of *The Golden Path*.

Miss Stranks flipped it open. 'Read this page in full and recite it back to me.'

Ellis blinked at the words. Unlike the Bible with its familiar rhythms, some of Miss Stranks' sentences ran to half a page. Too soon, the book snapped shut. Ellis closed her eyes and let the words flow back to her. For years she'd recited the Old Testament for her mother by the fire. There'd been so few books in their house after her mother's small library had been carried away on the quick brown tides of a flood. *But we still have the Good Book,* her mother used to say. *And as long as you can read and remember, you'll have the world.*

Ellis began to speak. 'The heart which finds itself bound with chains of greed shall never be called free nor the heart manu ... manufactured ... a pleth-or-a of tarnished words, thoughts and deeds by the ingestion of impurities from the material realms ...'

'From?' said Miss Stranks. Her cool blue eyes had begun to shine.

'From the sacred and divine source of ...'

'No. From which page and publication?'

'Page fourteen of *The Golden Path of the Soul* by Miss M. P. Stranks, Miss.'

Miss Stranks clasped her hands together in delight.

'Bravo,' said Bradbury.

'Enough! *If* this child is blessed with a photographic memory, the kind which Mr Scott-Elliott so famously possesses, that will make two of us under one roof.'

'What do you mean? Under one roof?' Kitty said.

'Were you asked to speak, Kitty? No, you were not.'

Miss Stranks motioned for Ellis to follow her down the stairs. Ellis looked across at Kitty who was staring up at Bradbury.

'Come, come,' he whispered. 'Look on the bright side, Kitty. This is what you wanted. More hands make light work, and all that.'

Ellis followed Miss Stranks down the stairwell to the shiver of the street. She looked across at the doorway where she'd been huddling an hour or so before. If it hadn't been for Kitty, she'd still be at the mercies of the city. She tried to catch Kitty's eye as Bradbury helped her up into the cab but Kitty had lowered her head as Bradbury heaved himself beside her. Ellis noticed how his leg lolled against Kitty's skirts. Ellis stared out at the blackened streets trying to calm her breath. It was too extraordinary to believe she'd talked her way into finding sanctuary, for tonight at least.

As they clattered through the streets, Miss Stranks talked on about her reputation for Good Works, how she took girls in, girls with no prospects or visible means of support. With hard work, even the most hopeless and corrupted cases could be saved.

The cab came to a halt outside a large house. Dark fir trees quivered either side. A tiny ruffle-hatted maid struggled to hold open the front door against the wind. Ellis stared up at the two enormous gilt-framed portraits of Miss Stranks smiling down from opposite walls.

'But your name.' Miss Stranks turned to inspect her.

'Ellis.'

'Speak up. And your Christian name?'

'Ellis.'

'But that is not a girl's name.'

Ellis' head had begun to spin. Black and white floor tiles throbbed beneath her feet. She knew she mustn't give her real surname, Gifford. Her father might come looking for her, and drag her back to Candlebark Creek. She closed her eyes and tried to think. Huge white letters glimmered: *Gilbey's Dry Gin—An Excellent Summer Drink!*

'Gilbey,' she said.

'Gilbey? Bradbury, where have we seen that name before?'

'Perchance, Madam, upon the label of a bottle of gin.'

Ellis heard Kitty laugh.

Miss Stranks sighed and strode towards Ellis, one gloved hand held out.

'Remove this awful hat.' Ellis flinched as Miss Stranks ripped it off and flung it away, then placed her hand on top of her hair. 'Feel the power of the Lord.'

Miss Stranks' fingers dug in like claws. A series of blinding colours flashed through Ellis' head. When the hand was withdrawn, the flashes stopped. Ellis felt her knees give way as the black and white floor buckled and rose up to hit her face.

She woke in a bed in the dark. The bedclothes were like planks nailed across her chest. Her hair was wet. She was wearing a stiff nightdress, perfumed with what? She lay very still as she heard the shout.

'I will *not*. I will *not*.'

Kitty's voice.

She woke to find slits of light filtering in through a barred window. Her bed was surrounded by a wall of travelling trunks, hat boxes and crates. She squinted at the labels: *Paris, Londres, Bayreuth*.

A slight young girl flitted about the room and set a tray on a crate. There was a glass of milk, a bowl of steaming oatmeal, a quartered apple, pieces of walnut flesh.

'I'm Mabel-the-maid.' The maid smiled an impish smile and made a curtsy. 'You must be Ellis Gilbey. And you must be very hungry.'

Ellis tried to answer, 'Thank you, Mabel-the-maid,' but no words would come.

Miss Stranks strode in, clapping her hands for the maid to leave. In the morning light, Miss Stranks' blonde hair looked grey. Flakes of dry skin speckled her cheeks. Her sharp blue eyes flicked over Ellis.

'As I was saying, you are here for two reasons, child, and two reasons only. Firstly, Kitty has been failing to do her work. Two, if you can recite as well as you claim, you will be of use. The moment you are no longer of use, there will be no reason for you to avail yourself of my hospitality. Understood?'

Ellis nodded.

Miss Stranks gazed down at the tray. 'Ah, the apple.' She picked up a piece. 'Alas we no longer live in a Golden Age. Fruit does not drop from the bough and the Gods do not dine on walnuts.' She popped the apple into her mouth, her jaw moved energetically as she chewed.

Walnuts? Ellis thought. Were they in the Bible? *Walnut, wheat, willow.* Miss Stranks pounced on the walnuts.

'We live in an ugly age. Men gamble with their souls. They lie and cheat. They devour God's creatures, fouling the body, stoking murderous thoughts. Repeat after me: I will eat no meat, nor will I lie or cheat, while I live in the house of Miss Minerva Stranks.'

Ellis repeated it and glanced down at the oats.

'You say you are from the country, child, and know hard work. It seems we are at one on that.'

Ellis looked up at her.

'Not all of us were born with silver ladles in our mouths. We must transform ourselves if we are to rise. I've risen far but I never forget. I now work in the service of God, not by tilling the soil or tending the crops but by weeding the falsehoods from the souls of ...'

'Under falsehood have we hid ourselves.' The words tumbled out of Ellis' mouth before she could stop herself.

Miss Stranks raised her hand. 'Speak only when you are spoken to. A photographic memory means nothing if you do not do as you are told. Work hard, be clean and honest. That's all I ask. As a great sage once said, hard work reaps, what hard work must.'

Was sage in the Bible? Ellis' mother had grown sage leaves for wiping the teeth, for improving the memory.

'Wash, dress and be at the desk at the strike of the very next gong.'

Miss Stranks swept out. Ellis grabbed the bowl of oats and spooned them down. Cries of 'I will *not*. I will *not*,' rang out. Doors batted back and forth. Footsteps tattered up and down the stairs. There must be other girls here, Ellis thought, besides Kitty and herself.

CHAPTER
TEN

How alive Rennie Howarth felt escaping the house, running down the hill towards the ferry, swinging her carpetbag as she went. As she waited at the wharf, she glanced across at the other passengers. *Thank God.* She recognised nobody at all.

She stared at her watch. It was already after ten o'clock. Fridays at ten, she was supposed to take tea at the Ambassadors Cafe in the Strand Arcade and sit in the booth marked *Reserved* with Bertha Collins and her gaggle of giggling friends, as darting little waiters served pots of China tea.

She only went because Bertha had asked for 'moral support', although it was doubtful Hercules himself could support the elastic morals Bertha relished bragging about. It was like sitting in front row of a dreadful play, trying not to laugh as Bertha tilted her head coquettishly, nodding as she pretended to listen to the tedious titter about what frightful thing had taken place at the Easter picnic races or at cocktails on the balcony of the Australia Hotel, despairing over the varying quality of silk, the idiosyncrasies of husbands, maids and children, while prodding tiny forks at lobsters in aspic, ooh-ing and ah-ing at three-tiered plates laden with fresh madeleines, while never actually eating a thing.

Before Bertha rose to leave, she always tossed in a particularly scandalous anecdote about being whisked away for the weekend with an olive-skinned sheik to a grand house somewhere on the river where 'everybody who was anybody' apparently flocked for notorious all night house parties, causing Bertha's friends to scream in horror and delight. Bertha then thrust out her arm and said to Rennie, 'Shall we two loose ladies take our leave?'

'But why do you suffer them?' Rennie had once said to Bertha as they escaped the café in Bertha's gleaming motorcar.

'Why do you?'

'Well, I ...'

'You have no answer, do you Rennie, which makes you as equally guilty of duplicity as me. Let me drive you home and I'll tell you what *really* happened with my hot-blooded sheik when I chaperoned him out to the river and everyone became too tedious so we dashed away to drink champagne and toast the sunrise on a rocky crag.'

But today Rennie would not see Bertha. In fact, given the debacle of the exhibition, it was possible Bertha might not want to be seen with *her* ever again. To lose Bertha's friendship would be a blow. Bertha was the only person she'd met in two years in Sydney who'd borne any resemblance to her contingent of London pals. Something deliciously daring rose up in her whenever Bertha was in the vicinity. She felt brave and rambunctious again; a feeling which had been snuffed out the instant she'd married Lloyd.

Rennie first laid eyes on Bertha in an article in *The Home* titled 'The Automobile and the Woman' profiling the 'new breed of feminine motorists of Sydney.' *Now that's the kind of a woman I need to meet*, she'd thought. She'd torn the article out and made the mistake of showing it to Lloyd who'd muttered something about women in trousers constituting 'the thin end of the wedge.'

'But who is she?' Rennie had said.

'Old Judge Collins' wife? Quite the hyena, so they say.'

Rennie thought Bertha looked marvellous in her mannish Tweed suit, one patent leather boot placed up on the running board, her dark smile curling into a sneer. Rennie promptly ordered her dressmaker to run up the same outfit, but being somewhat stouter in bust and hip, she'd tried it on once and tossed it out. She then set about inviting Mrs Judge Collins to the house for lunch.

On their first meeting, Rennie had been shocked at how flummoxed she'd felt, as Bertha leant in the doorway, frowning at her pinned up hair.

'You don't find it rather passé?' Bertha had said, swiping her long black glove through the vortex of smoke that seemed to accompany her wherever she went. 'I'd say you'd look just the berries with a Louise Brooks bob.'

Rennie had patted the back of her hair as if trying to make it vanish then and there. Of course most of her London chums had lopped their locks off, but Rennie had held back. Her thick, dark hair was one of her most enviable attributes, or so everyone had always said.

Bertha continued to stare at her as she downed a glass of fizz, her mischievous eyes glittering beneath her fringe causing Rennie to blush—not just her face—but her entire body inside and out in hot, distinct, pulsing, disarmingly rhythmic waves.

'How *is* Lloyd?' Bertha had said, on the previous Friday rendezvous outside the Strand.

Bertha had looked particularly eye-catching, marching through the gawping crowds, dressed in her jodhpurs and pith helmet, tossing her driving goggles over her shoulder.

'Lloyd?'

'Your husband, dear. I hear he was promoted to Big Chief at the Wool and Wheat.'

'Was he? I had no idea.'

'Rennie, sweet. Do promise me you aren't wafting off again. I know the world went mad with it for a while but swear to me you haven't slipped under the spell of that slippery Rasputin lookalike, what's-his-name? The theosophist.'

'You mean Mr Leadbetter?'

'Comrade Leadbetter gives me quite the pip, with his preposterous ring and ghastly beard and all those rumblings about his penchant for 'educating' boys. What a load of old guff all that grand temple-building on the harbour turned out to be, waiting for Jesus to tiptoe in his nightshirt through The Heads. I simply had to go down and see it for myself. As for the presence of the female accomplice, *L'Indienne* ... The great and the good pretended to prostrate themselves. What a boring affair it turned out to be, immersing oneself before the Glorious One is no fun, Rennie. No fun at all.'

Mrs Besant, Rennie thought. *She means Annie Besant.*

Thankfully she'd never let slip to Bertha that she'd also been drawn to the theories of the theosophists. Everybody had been after the war. Half of Britain and Europe were lying dead, as were both her parents who'd been felled months apart by the Spanish 'Flu. The theosophists' ideas seemed to offer a modicum of surety and comfort. *You are a link in the golden chain,* one of them had told her at her first meeting, holding out a welcoming hand, and Rennie had laughed too loudly for too long for no reason at all, so that everyone had peered at her until she'd stopped, and she'd wished she could have slinked like a chain down through the cracks in the floor.

Even now when the nights with Lloyd were at their worst, she repeated those words to herself. *I am a link in the golden chain,* for there had to be some reason for her existence, hadn't there, other than being prey for Lloyd?

Still caught in a fug of champagne, she'd dragged herself to weekly theosophy meetings in a dim little room in St Johns Wood, wanting to believe all they said, that one's soul toiled on through the ages, that death was not such a bad thing after all, that there was hope and life on the next plane, that there were godly Masters who walked the earth flinging lifebuoys of wisdom to the floundering.

But doubt had punctured her enthusiasm. Death *was* terrible. It was cruel and unfair. Who cared about the next life when the one you were already living was a wreck?

'Such brouhaha over nothing,' Bertha had said, swatting a waiter with a glove. 'All that rum talk about being strapped to the interminable Wheel of Life, only to bunk in with all those crackpots and wowsers, spinning on until eternity. I think I should become rather ill. And why one would want to come back for another round of *this* when you might be reborn as a horsefly, or worse, a thick-ankled shop girl. Live life now, I say, then down the hatch.'

And everybody had roared with laughter. Except for Rennie.

Well, today was Friday and here she was, the residue of last night's champagne still tingling through her veins, sitting on a ferry burrowing on through the steely wash.

She disembarked, her carpetbag pulling ahead of her like a bolting dog. She laughed as she stumbled ashore and found a post to lean against. She lit a cigarette and observed the city of strangers streaming past. She picked out a few people she felt she *should* know by type. If she were in London, she'd have downed a few cocktails with the tallish woman in the bronze tasselled coat with the Italian shoes. She'd have been acquainted with, and perhaps even dallied with, the pink-eared peeled-looking man with the boater and striped satin tie. But she was in Sydney and despite two years living in the harbour city, she still knew really nobody at all.

She looked at the water. How dark it was. How cold and opaque and … well, final. Barely an hour before she'd contemplated giving herself up to it, but now she was going to the gallery to look at art, to kneel before the Great Masters she worshipped, armed with her sketchbook and pencil, so she could be reminded and inspired by their talent, bravado and tenacity. She'd leave her luggage at the cloakroom, stowing her belongings in exchange for a tag. What bliss it would be to spend one's days doing simple, useful, practical things; checking coats in, checking coats out. *Number 43 Miss. Sir? Number 62.*

She almost dropped her cigarette as a blast of smoke shot up in the air. The entire Quay turned and looked. Barely a yard away, a man fell to his knees and clamped his hands over his head, causing several people to stumble into him. Heated words ensued, until another chap intervened.

'You right there, dig? There's nothing to worry about, mate. They're only blasting for the bridge.'

When the kneeling man realised what he'd done, he scooped up his belongings and scurried off, his eyes flashing from side to side. *Of course*, Rennie thought. The man's harried expression reminded her of her poor brother, Irving. Eight years on from the Great War, some men hadn't yet waded ashore from the hellish swamps of mud and blood.

She opened her handbag and stared down at the roll of banknotes lying inside. Was this what her life had amounted to, stealing from her husband? But it was more than an act of petty larceny. It was her fight to retain the shreds of who she once was and would be again.

She turned away and patted powder to her nose. She was ready to go straight to the gallery and observe real art because, whatever Lloyd did or said, she was still a real artist, at least her hands and a small percentage of her thoughts were those of an artist. If only her hands and thoughts would more easily meet.

Her fragile resolve faltered as she entered the gallery. She'd tried banning herself from making the obvious and heartbreaking comparisons since she'd arrived in the southern hemisphere, but couldn't help notice the ceilings weren't as high as London's National Gallery. Those were either vaulted or daubed with gold. At least the Romanesque floor tiles offered a tinge of authenticity.

She took off her glove and crouched down. The tiles were hard but soft, cool but warm. The eyes of a guard were on her. Rennie flashed a smile. The guard tipped his hat and ambled off.

She stood for some time in front of the early Australian works. She stared down at her sketchbook then up at Thomas Waiting's *A direct north general view of Sydney Cove*, 1794. Autumnal trees flanked the path where two gentlemen in white breeches talked, the hallmarks of industry at their backs. She moved to John Eyre's *View of Sydney from the West Side of the Cove*, 1804. The foreground in purples and browns suggested the formless gloom of the past, while above and beyond, the white-walled houses edged a harbour pulsing with life.

'Some views are false,' she said to herself. A woman standing several feet away turned and looked at her. Rennie smiled and said, 'Hello.'

If the woman hadn't stalked off, Rennie might have struck up a conversation with her, admitting she didn't warm to these early works and the woman might have agreed.

'Is it their measuredness that puts one off?' Rennie might have said, a finger held to her chin. The woman might have smiled and begged her to continue, in which case, she would have.

'This measuredness may have been borne out of the desire to be precise ...'

So as not to cause offence to this woman—who was clearly Australian by the frump of her coat—Rennie would concede that it was rather charming to think these early artists had carried views of Home in their heads across the seas, and that they were painting what they wanted to see rather than what was actually in front of them. But the woman had not smiled. She'd frowned and disappeared.

A gong sounded somewhere. Already? Gallery closed.

She sat smoking on the gallery steps, wondering if it might be better for everybody if she turned to stone like the round-bosomed chimeras huddling on the grass to be climbed on by children and bothered by dogs. She took off her hat and imagined tossing it across the street. It was the kind of thing Bertha Collins would have done to great effect. But she was not Bertha. She'd never have an ounce of Bertha's pluck or aplomb.

She unpinned her hair and shook it out. Lloyd was mad for her hair. When they'd first met in London he'd said it was her 'most pleasing natural feature'—her most pleasing 'unnatural feature' being the ridiculously heavy beaded dress she'd borrowed from one of her more glamorous friends.

Lloyd liked her hair from the back. He liked to breathe urgently on her cheek, turning her over, calling her his little rag doll, raking his fingers through it, as if classing wool. *The way your hair hangs in ribbons of light between ropes of dark.* She wasn't sure Lloyd had actually said that. Interesting words were not a commodity he prized very highly.

She stared at the shadows bounding across the parklands that were almost deserted except for a few men settling under sheets of newspaper amongst the rambling roots of trees. She walked until she found a stall in the roar of the street to buy another tin of cigarettes. As she peeled a note from the roll of cash, the man at the newspaper stand turned to watch a large car honking and swerving along the street. Rennie turned to watch it too. Good heavens! It was Bertha Collins at the wheel, frightening the daylights out of a poor lad selling oranges from a cart. A square-shouldered man seated beside Bertha gesticulated for the lad to get out of the way.

Rennie frowned. No, it couldn't be. *Lloyd?*

She stepped out from the kerb for a better look but no sooner had she done so, she was yanked back. She heard herself cry out as she fell to the ground. A gritty rush of wind from an oncoming motorbus whooshed past her face.

'They almost had you there, Missus,' a man said, panting as he helped her up.

Rennie thanked him and told him she was absolutely fine, holding out the palms of her dirt-grazed gloves as proof—see? Not even a scratch. Shaken, she sat for a moment on a step of a shop.

Lloyd with Bertha? No, it couldn't be. Bertha would never be interested in a man like Lloyd. She'd find him instantly and mind-numbingly *dulls*. She scrabbled in her handbag for a match but instead she fished out the luggage tag from the gallery. *Damnation and blast.* She'd completely forgotten to retrieve her carpetbag.

But Lloyd with Bertha?

She made her way through the blur of the crowds. Her eyes filled with tears as she moved through the teeming streets. She paused at a doorway of a grand looking theatre where a thousand slivers of Mrs Lloyd Howarth (*is that who I've become?*) were reflected back in multiple mirrors and flashing ceilings of arching gold.

Why was Bertha driving Lloyd about?

She walked on, stopping now and then to stare at her reflection in the glossy windows of shops.

When it was dark enough she walked down to the Quay, looking out at the lapping blackness, glittering with the reflection of lights. Ferries were still charging about. Some were strung up with pretty lights, swinging like pearls across a woman's dancing hips. Bertha danced like that. She was hungry for dance. When Bertha drove her home from the tedious Friday meetings, she regaled her with tales of parties she'd attended which were 'just the zip'. Sometimes Bertha stopped the motorcar and demonstrated the latest steps on the side of the road, egging Rennie on to try them out to the whoops of laughter and hooting claxons of passersby, as she recounted the nights spent with all manner of artists, jazz musicians, actors and writers. Rennie didn't say she'd been to much wilder parties in London before she'd made the rash decision to give it all up for a stolid Australian. Sometimes she tried to interrupt Bertha's tales to ask the names of the particular artists she met, but Bertha had invariably moved on to the next racy tale of swimming naked in fountains at midnight, or sliding off into the dawn with various men.

'My passions are my compass,' Bertha had once said.

Rennie had been intrigued, even more so when Bertha added that her 'desires could not be quenched with any one man.' It was not hard to see why Bertha didn't want to sate her passions with her husband, a beefy old judge thirty years her senior but then to hear that Judge Collins had actually *agreed* that one partner was not enough?

But Bertha with Lloyd? Bertha could have any man in Sydney and beyond. Why would she bother with such a bore, and worse, in the same stroke, betray her best friend? No, Bertha must have seen him on the street and offered him a lift. Appalled, if not flattered, Lloyd had accepted, pleased he'd been able to prove his worth by yelling at the orange-selling lad while gathering extra evidence that women drivers really were the thin end of the wedge.

Rennie looked around. The Quay was peopled only by shadows. How stupid to have forgotten to retrieve her bag from the gallery.

It could not be today then. She would have to go back to the house. She waited for what felt like hours for the ferry, crouching by the churn of water, smoking and crying silently beneath her hat.

When she arrived at the house, she stood for a moment outside the gates. Everything was lit up. Blocks of light blazed across the lawn. She let herself in and went straight to Lloyd's desk and squashed the wad of pound notes inside the cigar box. Next thing, Mrs Chisholm was at the door, unsmiling and shelf-bosomed in her starched apron.

Sickening dinner smells roamed the house.

Rennie stood in the bedroom frowning at the glittering evening gown Chisholm had laid across the bed. She'd completely forgotten about cocktails at the Australia Hotel. She went into the bathroom and ran a bath. Wiping her hand over the steam of the mirror, she peered at her body as a portrait painter might, studying the depressions and the hills, the landslips, new creases and pouches of flesh, the creamy shadows invaded by splotches of dark. She touched a finger to a mustard-coloured bruise breaking like an egg yolk down her shoulder blade. She wondered what Bertha would say to that. And as for Mrs Lloyd Howarth, whoever she was, it was almost time to put her out of her misery.

CHAPTER
ELEVEN

Ellis would have sworn she hadn't slept a minute except that she woke with a start at the first cry of 'Watcho!' The industrial harbour symphony was already in full swing. She counted to five, waiting for the blast to shake the window pane. She covered her face with the blankets until the cornices stopped raining dust. She could hear Girl out on her balcony. Mrs Liddy and Clarrie were out there too. She wasn't sure if anybody still expected her to read the newspapers aloud to them on the front step, now that the news they'd been dreading had finally arrived. Nobody had mentioned anything about the debacle at the minister's office, except for Clarrie and his *behold the chariot of the Fairy Queen*. Alf Ostler hadn't dared show his face.

She made a cup of strong black tea and fished out the tea leaf swimming about in it. She squashed it between her fingers. It was soft. A soft tea leaf heralded the unexpected arrival of a female visitor. Ellis flicked it away. The only visitor would be Girl trying to sweet talk her into something else she'd regret.

Her mouth was gluey. She'd drunk too much brandy the night before, trying to chip away at the lump of an idea that refused to take shape for her next 'Green-eyed Gardener' column. She'd ended up lying on her bed trying to block the whoops and grunts coming from the shutters of Girl's house.

She scuffed down the hallway, kicked at an empty tea chest and a pile of newspapers. It was urgent now. She needed to find herself a room.

She dragged herself up Burton Street to buy the morning newspaper from O'Malley's. With every step, the urge to blame someone or something grew inside her. But there was no one else. It was all her fault. Once again, she'd left everything too late. Her eyes flicked north as two crows cawed back and forth in a distant Norfolk Island pine. She tried not to count their cries. An even number predicted rain, an odd number, a sunny day. Six cries. Then seven. Eight. She sighed at the sky. Pillars of clouds had begun to build. *Pillars and towers bring rain and showers*. First she'd seen the tea leaf, then heard the crows and now the looming clouds. Signs were everywhere this morning, jostling for her attention in the raw morning light.

It wasn't a relief to be back at the house, standing in the backyard in the grey and white flicker of morning sun because it meant it was time to face *Apartments, Board and Residence* again. Her eyes wandered to the *Wanted* column. It seemed to run for half a mile. She circled a few possibilities, including those stipulating *working single man only*, or *respectable widower*. The only desirable woman, it seemed, was a *refined lady of certain means*. Normally, she might have laughed. She tore out the column and jammed it into the pocket of her coat.

It was nearly ten o'clock by the time she'd knocked on the sixth door. The façade of number 5 Hobbs Street was porridge grey. A layer of soot adorned the woodwork like a relic of Victorian mourning ware. But, Ellis told herself, perhaps this room (*working man, unfurnished, electric light*) might be the one.

'It's gone,' the woman said, through the crack of the door. 'I thought it was him come back to put the money down.'

'You're still waiting for someone to secure the room?' Ellis peered in past the woman. It looked better than the five cockroach-infested rat-holes she'd just seen. She raised her chin and took a deep breath. 'I don't suppose there's any chance I could have a look. It's for my brother. He's sober. Honest. Single. Works on the Harbour Bridge.'

The woman's eyes brightened. 'The bridge? Well, all right then. But don't go getting any ideas.'

Mustiness engulfed her as soon as she stepped into the gloom. Three red-cheeked children were engaged in a fractious tug of war with a piece of string at the base of the stairs. Ellis caught sight of a downstairs room with a tiled fireplace. It was devoid of any furniture or holes in the floor, and not a bad size. The window opened onto the street the same as her room at Milsons Point.

'Not that one,' the woman said. 'Up.'

Ellis looked up the stairs. Apart from the children shrieking and lolling at her feet, there was no other sign of habitation in the house, not a single chair, hat peg, coal box, or wooden crate. She followed the woman up the creaking stairs, noting the ragged hem and shoes plodding ahead of her. The woman stopped and turned to catch her breath. Ellis saw the enormous stomach sticking out. So that was it. Number four was well on the way.

'I can go up and see for myself,' Ellis said.

The woman shook her head and waved her on. The room wasn't bad. The window offered a stripe of sky. Compared to the mildewed cells she'd already seen, it was cleanish, except for the clumps of pale mushrooms which had taken root in the cornices. But, she told herself, a dab of vinegar and ash would soon see to that. Overall, there was no bad feeling. Well, none that leapt out at her.

Ellis turned to the woman who was leaning against the doorframe, clutching at her skirts. The woman flinched at the sound of the doorknocker.

'That'll be him,' she said.

Ellis' heart fell. The man was back with the deposit. She waited for the woman to go down and answer the door, but she stood where she was, holding her skirts, listening, closing her eyes. There was another thump followed by a child's wail.

'Simmer down,' the woman yelled, rolling her head against the doorframe. The yell reverberated around the room.

Ellis went to the window and tried the sash. A man could be heard retching in the yard below. There was the disquieting smell of burning lard, creating a waxy sheen across the walls. The huge bulk of her landlady's stomach was riding so low, Ellis wondered if there'd be time to ask to see the bathroom and kitchen before a newborn slithered out to gulp its first breath at their feet.

'Who else lives here?' she said. 'My brother would want to know who his neighbours were.'

'Look, if he don't come back in the next five minutes, you're welcome to it. You, or your brother.'

Ellis turned away. She should've realised the woman would see through her lame invention of a brother. She waited for the inevitable spiel about women tenants not taking any gentlemen callers but it didn't come, either because the woman thought her too old and scrawny, or that she was *not that kind of woman*. Well, she wasn't that kind of woman, but not in the way most people thought.

'It's yours for the taking,' the woman sighed. 'As long as there's six weeks board put down in advance.'

Ellis felt the heat rise to her face. *Six weeks in advance?* Downstairs the children's screeching notched up another octave. Ellis stepped away from the door across the spongy floor which dipped so sharply in the corner she had to put out her hand to right herself. She brushed the plaster from her gloves. Despite the damp, there was no evidence of fleas or leaks, only a smear of hair oil from a previous head of hair leaning back in bed. She tried not the think about that head, or why it had carried itself off elsewhere when rooms like this were so hard to find.

She began to pace along the walls, persuading herself the desk would fit sideways by the window, the bed behind the door. The wardrobe could go along the hallway passage and help deaden the sounds of the house. Three screaming children were not ideal but they were probably just unsettled by the coming and going of strangers.

'The advertisement said electric light.' Ellis tried to sound matter of fact.

The woman didn't answer before she stomped out. Ellis flicked the switch. The room stayed dark.

Back out in the street, Ellis stared at her list. It had been the best room so far, but *six weeks down in advance?* The modest funds she'd squirreled away from her writing and typing work would barely cover that. It was no surprise the other man hadn't come back to secure it. She tried to imagine herself going in and out of the broken front gate, putting her key in the lock, climbing the stairs, rolling a sheet of paper in to her typewriter, but ...

But according to her list, the only other possibility (*for those who favour cleanliness and good home cooking, hot bath, every comfort, whole balcony*) lay on the other side of the harbour, beyond the thick brown air of the breweries and therefore, well beyond her means. She stood at the corner and looked back at the street.

'Nice day for it, sweetheart,' a man said, swaggering past.

She watched the way he swung up on the balls of his feet, the smart suit and tie, the smell of hair grease in his wake. Another man appeared from the other end of the street, dressed equally as sharp. *Please*, Ellis thought, hoping he wasn't the man bringing the deposit for the room. Both men met up and moved to stand in a doorway across the street from number 5.

Ellis turned to go. As she did so, she was almost knocked down by another man hurtling around the corner. *Watch it*, she almost said, until she saw the hunted look in his eyes, the missing teeth and unshaven chin. She stepped back and watched him run down Hobbs Street towards the house. The two other men slunk back into the shadows opposite, watching on.

'Open up, will you?' The unshaven man pounded on the door.

Ellis waited to see the landlady appear at the door. The two spivs moved out of the shadows and crossed the street.

'Well, lookee here,' one of them said. His hand moved towards his jacket pocket.

The unshaven man stopped banging on the door. He turned slowly to face the spivs, looking about the street as if trying to figure out his best chances of escape. There was the flick of a wrist, the flash of metal. He lunged at them with a blade. There was the sound of children crying and the woman screaming inside the house.

It took hurrying the length of several blocks for Ellis to calm her breath and comprehend what must have happened. The so-called landlady must have been about to be evicted herself, advertising rooms for rent to wring out a few quid from hapless lodgers like herself. She'd probably already let the rooms half a dozen times, making a tidy bundle before vanishing. But she and her man must have become greedy. They'd asked for larger and larger deposits. They'd hung on too long and now the spivs had caught up with them.

So much for being an experienced landlady who knew the ropes. She should have realised it was a trap, the empty rooms, six weeks in advance.

Ellis threw away the scrap of newspaper and made her way back slowly towards the ferry. It was less than two weeks now before the demolishers arrived to knock down her door. *But my book,* she thought. She had to believe in her gardening book. It was her small raft to cling to on the rising tide.

CHAPTER
TWELVE

She couldn't face trudging back to Milsons Point. She sat on a park bench and surveyed the cheerless trees trapped in their allotted squares of earth. Mr Moses would have been proud of such public acts of horticultural miserliness.

Shoals of pigeons moved across the grass. The smell of urine wafted up. A bed, not a bench, was all most people asked for in this life. And nourishment, safety, the chance of love. Ellis sighed. How her fear had eased the first time she'd seen Kitty Tate's welcoming face.

A pigeon approached her with its oil-slick body and question mark head.

'Sorry. No bread today.' Another approached with a disbelieving eye. 'It's true. I might have been a liar back then, but I've had no heart for such things since.'

A man walking by cast her a disapproving look. The woman on his arm offered Ellis a crooked smile, either out of pity or politeness. Once, she might have fallen for a smile like that. Just a tiny slippage, so small nobody else would have noticed it. It might have happened while she was waiting at the ferry or queuing at the post office. She'd fall in love with the tumble of a woman's hair, or the loose stitches hanging down from the hem of her dress, or the way she brushed a stray crumb from her lip. These temporary slips of the heart had never troubled her much. By the time she'd reached the ferry gate or had set her envelope on the post office counter, she'd fallen out of love with the unknown woman with her unhemmed dress, and was back clasped tight in the memory of Kitty's arms.

Now she'd reached the dry plains of middle age. She was still alone. That was a victory of sorts, or was it? To the eyes of the world, she was drained of colour, purpose and passion. She looked up at the couple walking away, at the sureness of their steps, at the comfortable swing of their arm-linked coats. *If you only knew*, she thought. *What I've done. How hard I loved.*

On that first morning at Miss Stranks' house, she'd raced to get ready— not to be at the desk in time for Miss Stranks—but so she could see Kitty Tate again.

A dress hung from a hook behind the door. She held it to her face. It smelt of Kitty. She fingered the darns and stiff strips of greying lace. Her own clothes were gone, except for her boots sitting battered but polished beneath the bed. She hunted for her mother's hat. *That awful thing*, Miss Stranks had called it. It wasn't the hat itself Ellis wanted, but the clutch of flannel flowers her mother had stitched with silver thread.

She hurried to the bowl of water and patted water onto her face, arms and feet. She touched the place where Miss Stranks' hand had rested on her hair, still unsure if the flashes of golden light had been real or if she'd imagined them.

She crept down the corridor towards the smell of eggs and toast. Peals of laughter rose up the kitchen stairs, interspersed by the clatter of cutlery. She hesitated on the stairs. Mabel-the-maid appeared swaying beneath an enormous tray of crockery.

'We need a dumb waiter,' Mabel said. 'You know, like they have in all the big hotels.'

Ellis tried to hide her ignorance of big hotels and dumb waiters by saying, 'Sorry, have you seen my hat?'

'Miss Stranks told me to throw it out. They'll give you one of Kitty's hand-me-downs.'

Ellis felt tears rush to her eyes.

'I see. You wanted to keep it, did you?'

'It's not the hat. It's the white flowers stitched on it with silver thread.'

A voice called out. 'Mabel? Have you taken that tray up yet?'

Ellis moved to let her pass. 'Thank you,' she said, but Mabel had already hurried off.

'Well if it isn't our newest foundling,' said the cook. 'I'm Mrs Frith, and Lady Godiva over there is Miss Kitty Tate.'

Kitty shook her long dark hair. 'Lady Godiva indeed! Ellis knows perfectly well who I am. You are an inimitable wag, Mrs Frith.'

Mrs Frith shrieked as she toiled between the stove and bench. 'You're the what's-its-name wag, not me. You make me laugh so hard, one of these days I swear my insides'll burst clean out.'

'And where would we be then, Mrs Frith?' said Kitty. 'Will Miss Stranks be forced to plunge her fork into haggis for lunch?'

Ellis slid onto a chair and looked about at the kitchen chock-full with every kind of sack, bottle, packet, jar and tin. The dresser was crowded with pots and pans. Dozens of shining utensils hung on a series of hooks from the rim of a suspended bicycle wheel. Mrs Frith spun the wheel around and plucked down a ladle.

'That marvellous contraption,' said Kitty, pointing her fork at the wheel, 'is Mabel's latest invention. I keep telling her she mustn't hide her light under a maid's hat. She wouldn't tell me where she found it. I suspect some poor lad is riding about with one less wheel.'

Mrs Frith shrieked again and patted the damp expanse of her apron. 'Oh Kitty how you make me laugh. My insides are all churned up.'

'My apologies, Mrs Frith. I shall try to be more funereal from now on.'

A gong beat frantically in the hallway.

'Oh blast their eyes.' Kitty pushed her plate across the table.

'Not eating your eggs again?' said Mrs Frith. 'Mark my words. You'll fade away.'

Kitty stood up. 'Come, Ellis. You mustn't be late on your very first day. Or they'll eat you up.'

Kitty ran up the stairs ahead of her. Ellis followed, and found her standing at the mirror in the hallway, pulling back her hair and pinching her cheeks.

'Oh, do please tell me I look half alive,' Kitty said. 'Lie if you have to. I won't mind.' She turned to Ellis and smiled. 'I see she's put you in one of my old dresses. You look quite sweet in it, even if you are as thin as a nail.' Kitty plucked a white lace shawl from the hallstand and draped it around her shoulders. 'Do I look sweet too, or like a plump little pigeon?' She swung around. Her dark hair fanned out above the whiteness of the shawl. She stopped to peer at herself in the mirror.

Ellis didn't know what to say. 'You look ... lovely.'

'Oh, you are sweet, peering at me with those pretty green eyes.' Kitty leant in and kissed her on the cheek. Ellis blinked at the feel of soft cold lips on her skin.

A man's voice called out from behind the door. 'Come.'

Kitty squeezed her hand. 'Whatever happens we must stick together, you and I. But first, I'll let you in on a trade secret. Whatever she does or says, the trick is not to let her see you care.' Kitty tossed her hair. 'Like this, see? Chin up, chaps. Shoulders back.'

Kitty stepped away from her across the room and seated herself at a desk behind a large machine. Two walls were wallpapered in light blue diamond patterns. The others were taken up by bookshelves. The sun streamed in from the windows at Kitty's back making a dark halo of her hair. Beneath it, her white lace shawl glowed.

Bradbury motioned for Ellis to follow Kitty and sit on a stool beside her. Miss Stranks strode in, sniffing the air.

'Bradbury, you've been smoking that stinking pipe again.'

'Not guilty.' He thrust up his hands in mock protest. 'Perhaps the culprit was Mrs Frith. I have it on good authority her nostrils have been known to combust.'

Ellis heard Kitty stifle a laugh.

'We are here to work,' said Miss Stranks. 'Not to joke. Or smoke.'

A posy of violets was tucked into Miss Stranks' bodice. Their little faces seemed to pucker as she marched about the room, straightening picture frames and shuffling papers into perfect piles. The violets' sharp scent wafted through the air. They reminded Ellis of times on the farm before the drought, working in the kitchen garden, her mother beside her, weeding the beds, moving their frostbitten fingers between the plants. Sometimes her mother had talked of her life before she was married when she'd been taken in by the Benevolent Society and been trained to work as a governess in some of the best houses in Sydney. *Don't you miss it mother?* Ellis had once asked. *My garden is now my library,* her mother said. *Every flower and tree is like a book. What do we use violets for, Ellis?* And Ellis would run through the list of plants and their uses. *Violets pounded down as a syrup keep the digestion regular, mother, and help to cure sleeplessness and inflammation of the eyes.*

Ellis felt a stamp on her foot. She looked down to see Kitty's boot inching away. She jumped as Miss Stranks clapped her hands above their heads.

'Sit up straight, child. Eyes to the front. Pass Miss Kitty a piece of paper *before* she needs it. Understood? We'll start on my speech for Sunday next. All at the ready?' Miss Stranks cleared her throat, and began to speak in the same honeyed tones she'd used at the hall. 'And so 'tis our task as Higher Beings while navigating the untamed currents of this life ...'

Kitty's fingers began to work the keys. Ellis tried not to jump with every strike. She wanted to cry out that the machine was magic, punching letters into the page. She looked around. Nobody else seemed to think it was. She looked at the hundreds of books on the shelves. Thousands of girls like Kitty must have written them out on machines like this. She flinched again as a bell rang on the typewriter. Kitty swatted at a lever, before plunging on. Ellis felt another stamp on her boot. Once again the keys had stopped.

'What is it now?' said Miss Stranks.

'Paper,' said Kitty. She frowned as she rubbed at her hands.

Ellis rushed to offer her another sheet. Kitty fumbled as she tried to roll it in.

'Get on with it,' said Miss Stranks. 'You've already derailed my train of thought.'

'May I?' Bradbury leant in and rolled the fresh paper smoothly into place.

Kitty mouthed 'thank you.' Bradbury winked in response.

Miss Stranks resumed her lecture voice. 'For it has been ordained that man is not on this earth to undertake great burdens without ... without ...' She moved to stand in front of the desk and stared down at Ellis. The waiting sheet of paper trembled. 'Without forgetting that the simplest humblest peasant is nearer to God in the garden.'

At the sound of the gong beating in the hallway, Kitty stood up and rubbed at her hands.

'Kitty, did I say you may leave your post?'

'I'm sorry, but I cannot go on. It's as if there are knife-blades stabbing at my hands.'

Miss Stranks marched towards Kitty, placed her hand on her head and forced her to sit back down. 'Your pains are the result of your *karma*, Kitty. Hell Broths percolate within the minds of the sinner. Do as I've told you. Think pure thoughts and all pain will away. Back straight. Chin up. All at the ready?'

Ellis saw Kitty try to swallow a sob. Tears splashed onto the typewriter keys.

'May I suggest a brief adjournment?' Bradbury said. He drew out a handkerchief and offered it to Kitty.

'Oh, very well then,' said Miss Stranks. 'But we'll have to work through the lunchtime gong. *Vite!* Kitty. Off with you. *Tout de suite!*'

Kitty ran from the room so quickly her lace shawl slipped from her shoulders and fell to the floor.

'Come back here and pick it up at once,' called Miss Stranks.

Bradbury stepped in to retrieve the shawl and draped it across the back of a chair. Ellis sat glued to her seat as Miss Stranks and Bradbury eyed each other.

'You take such an interest in our girls,' said Miss Stranks.

'I'm glad you think me attentive, as one who humbly aspires to your lofty positioning as a Higher Being. But if you'll excuse me, I'll see if Miss Kitty is ready to return.' Before Miss Stranks could answer, Bradbury made a little bow and left the room.

Ellis remained at the desk. Miss Stranks stood at the window behind her.

'I know what you're thinking, child. You think your new employer is perhaps too harsh. But this is the real world. Like it or not. Girls like Kitty are careless. They turn their noses up at opportunity. And why do you think that might be?'

Ellis tried to think of what to say. 'I don't know, Miss.'

'Of course you don't. Unlike you or I, girls like Kitty fritter away their opportunities—simply because they can.'

Bradbury reappeared. His face was flushed, his hair tousled at the back. He brushed down his sleeves and smiled at Miss Stranks. 'Miss Kitty will need more rest. The morning at least. Perhaps we should remove to the other room and see how this one fares with the books?'

Miss Stranks sighed and gestured for Ellis to leave the desk.

Ellis' heart was thumping as she was shown into the adjoining room. The bookshelves rose so high there were ladders to reach the upper shelves. Slivers of dark red wallpaper peeked out between paintings of sweeping hills, sailing ships, bowls of fruit, ruffle-collared ladies and gentlemen. A pair of yellowing potted palms flanked the long windows overlooking the street where Miss Stranks began to pace back and forth. Dark red curtains hung either side, their edges and tassels faded to pink.

'The dress fits you well enough.' Miss Stranks motioned for Ellis to spin around. 'I suppose the hair cannot be helped. God giveth and taketh as He sees fit. Sit. At the desk. Back straight. Chin up. Eyes to the front. Hands folded *neatly* in the lap.'

Ellis sat down.

'Write.' Miss Stranks nodded at the inkwell, silver pen and blotting pad. Ellis took up the pen and felt its weight. She put the nib to her lips.

'It's a writing stick,' Bradbury laughed. He looped his hand through the air. 'One writes with it.'

Miss Stranks advanced on her. 'You cannot write if you slouch like a ...?'

'Slouch?' offered Bradbury.

'Sir, have you not heard the old saying: the joker is no longer the joker if he repeats himself?'

'Excuse me, Miss.' Mabel-the-maid entered with a message on a tray.

'Now, what is it?' Miss Stranks snatched up the letter. Her eyebrows arched as she read. 'The dirty beggars!'

Bradbury extended a hand for the letter but Miss Stranks had already scrunched it in her fist and tossed it at the fire grate.

'They think they can tell me what to do. That I, Miss Minerva Pythia Stranks, should be *advised* on the content for my speech for Sunday next.'

'Hmm,' said Bradbury. He raised himself slowly from his chair. 'I thought such a thing was on the cards. Forgive me if I speak too plainly, but this might be the chance we've been waiting for. We have talked before many times about the ways we might *enliven* our lectures and ...'

'... And I also speak *plainly* when I say I refuse to lower myself to acts of cheap pettifoggery.'

'But you do agree we must increase our share, that we mustn't be trumped by the theosophists. Your small but loyal flock still speaks of you in high regard.'

'It seems everywhere I go they speak only of Mrs Besant,' said Miss Stranks. 'She has lit a fuse. The whole nation holds its breath for her illuminating return.'

'And that is where I spy a chink of light.' Bradbury stepped forward. 'While the nation waits, *we* shall keep them occupied.'

Ellis sat pinned to her seat as Miss Stranks and Bradbury talked on. She couldn't follow everything they said. There was mention of 'adding colour' to the Sunday halls through including 'more mystical dimensions' via enlisting some of the 'theosophists' more tantalising tropes.'

'One thing remains constant throughout the millennia. The lost seek belonging. The sad seek hope,' Bradbury said. 'Give them what they ask and they'll scurry back hungrier and in greater herds every week.'

'You're not suggesting we try out the elements which got us into hot water last time?' said Miss Stranks.

Bradbury waved a hand. 'We will not be trying anything if we cannot build, let alone hold, our ebbing crowd.'

Bradbury moved to stand behind Ellis' chair. He smelt of tobacco, of the city, of men.

'If this one is as we think she is, we'll make hay fast,' he said.

'Meaning?' Miss Stranks glared at Ellis.

'Why re-invent the wheel when it ain't yet broke? This lass claims she can read, write *and* recite. She's already shown she knows her Bible. Why not send her back to another fertile source? Set her to trawling the works of Mrs Besant and Madame Blavatsky. Use what *they* use to draw people in. Everybody knows you are blessed with a fine memory and an enchanting voice, Miss Stranks, so why not harness the expertise of the Masters and use it for our own good?'

'You mean we steal the good bits and pass them off as our own.'

'Inspiration, flattery, call it what you want. Whatever fair words spring from your lips in the course of spreading God's message shall be yours and His words alone. But I must away. My doctor is preparing an unguent for Miss Kitty's hands. I suggest you allow her to rest while you busy yourself with our new recruit.' Bradbury clicked the heels of his boots and strode out.

'You heard him.' Miss Stranks dragged the ladder along the bookshelves. 'To work.'

Miss Stranks marched up and down the shelves, directing Ellis where to set the ladder, which pamphlets and books to retrieve. Strands of Miss Stranks' hair sprang from her puffed out hair. Her cheeks were in high colour as she flung books at the desk in a series of thumps: *The Harbinger of Light; The Austral Theosophist; Free Thought; Nineteenth Century Miracles, Or, Spirits and Their Work In Every Country of the Earth; The Story of Atlantis.* She motioned for Ellis to sit at the desk. Two enormous tomes crouched before her: *The Secret Doctrine* by Mme H. P. Blavatsky and *Isis Unveiled: A Master Key to the Mystery of Ancient and Modern Science and Theology.*

'I've read both of them, of course. Go through them and find the most interesting bits.' Ellis tried to listen as Miss Stranks stood at her shoulder reeling off a list of instructions. The smell of violets tinged the air, but their sweet smell was tainted by the bitterness of Miss Stranks' impatient breath.

When Miss Stranks swept out at last, Ellis glanced around at the gleaming furnishings and ornaments. She went to the window and looked down at the street. Boys were out wheeling barrows of fruit. Men dipped their hats and swung their walking canes. The new tips of leaves were like a mass of small green flames burning on the branches of the street trees. Everything looked in its rightful place, while here she was, trying to save herself by gaining a toehold in a strange house. If she failed, she'd have to try elsewhere. But where was 'elsewhere'? Huddling in doorways, navigating the treacherous currents of the streets, forever on the look out for her father while she scoured the city for another kind of Benevolent Society who'd take her in?

She turned to the awaiting books. All she had for now was her facility to read, write and recite. *We must stick together, you and I.* That's what Kitty Tate had said. Ellis touched the place on her cheek where Kitty had kissed her. Miss Stranks was wrong. Poor Kitty was lovely, gentle, and beautiful and not careless at all.

Madame Blavatsky's *Isis Unveiled* loomed like a rock. Ellis lifted the front cover and ran her fingers over the frontispiece. Miss Stranks had said she'd already read the book in full but as she tried to turn the pages, she found none of their edges had been cut. With no knife at hand to open them, Ellis flicked through the newsletter, *Theosophy Australis* but was stopped by the photograph of Mrs Annie Besant. The eyes were striking, soft, dark and very kind. Her pale hair was swept back on one side. A high white collar framed her face. Her chin rested on her hand. A large pale stone ring glittered on her finger. There was another photograph, Madame Blavatsky. Ellis stared at the eyes. They were huge, entrancing, unnervingly steady and probably blue. Madame Blavatsky seemed to smile without smiling. The more you looked at her eyes, the more you were drawn into them until you were plunging at great speed through the dark tunnel of time and space, up into the sky, down into the sea, to everywhere and nowhere all at once.

Next was the booklet *Theosophy for the Novice Querent*. Ellis consulted a battered Oxford English dictionary. 'Novice' she knew but 'querent' and 'theosophy' were not to be found.

After flicking through the *Novice Querent*, Ellis learnt 'theosophy' was a mixture of two Greek words 'Theos' for God and 'sophos' for wisdom, thereby meaning Divine Wisdom. Fortunately, the author used the idea of a garden to suggest planting seeds of hope in the hearts of all men, a garden where all men were equal, whatever creed, colour or race. Watering the soul with pure intent, thought and deed allowed all men to flourish and move on to a higher plane. Ellis was struck by the notion of respecting every rock, stone, plant and tree. She thought about the farm, about the whining dogs, the starving cows, the horses rearing beneath the whip.

There was a knock. It was Mabel. Ellis was wanted immediately in the blue parlour next door.

Her mind went blank. All the words she'd memorised had fled. She tried to summon up Mrs Besant's calming eyes and Madame Blavatsky's soothing stare. Would Miss Stranks turn her out as soon as she discovered she'd not even opened *Isis Unveiled*?

PART TWO

PART TWO

CHAPTER
THIRTEEN

Apart from the rather muscular clouds crowding in from The Heads, it was a typical blue Friday morning. Seven days had passed since the debacle of Rennie Howarth's exhibition, and seven nights since Lloyd had deigned to speak more than two words to her. This new tactic of descending into silence had added an enervating dimension to his usual ploys.

Rennie lay in bed staring up at the shadows huddling around the ceiling rose. Sometimes, as she'd lain beneath Lloyd's weight, she'd imagined the hands of the artisan who'd fashioned the plaster flourishes overhead. There it was, clinging like a useless lifebuoy upside down above the bed of a married couple who no longer spoke. She lifted her own hands into the hair. The engagement ring felt a little tight. Despite what Lloyd said about her increasing weight, her hands remained pale and elegant, except for the flecks of paint she'd put there herself to cover up the latest round of bruises.

'I shall paint what I like,' she'd said, when he'd stormed into the bathroom the night before, showering her with chits of paper. 'I sold one painting, didn't I? I sold it to Bertha Collins.'

Rennie had watched him as she'd said Bertha's name. Through the veil of steam, she saw the way Lloyd had straightened his shoulders and hitched his trouser leg, the skin across his neck reddening as he bit back the urge to speak. There she'd sat in all her nakedness, the once warm embrace of water turning cold.

She felt around for the cigarettes. *Damnation and blast.* Chisholm had been hiding them again. There was nothing else for it but to descend to the battlefield of the breakfast room.

Lloyd was there, holed up behind his newspaper. Rennie's few breakfast things huddled on her side of the table. She rang the bell.

'Tea,' she said brightly when Chisholm finally arrived. 'China tea. With honey and milk.' As Chisholm meandered off, Rennie added, 'And a large bowl of oats with cream and honey, followed by toast with butter and two eggs Benedict.'

Her request failed to cause even a ruffle of Lloyd's newspaper. She stared at the pages. His great paws had already robbed them of their pristine crispness dutifully provided by Chisholm every dawn, plying her trusty iron, sparing her 'Lloyd-and-Master' the inconvenience of encountering a wrinkled sentence, a folded word or an errant blob of ink. Rennie wondered what Chisholm thought as she slid her iron over columns of stocks and shares, the personal announcements, weddings, funerals, the call for *Honest Reliable Quality Staff—Absolutely NO LOAFERS need apply!*

She peered at the page. *Man falls down escalators, Milsons Point.* What a very modern mishap. She read on. Apparently the man, aged in his late sixties, had bounced 'all the long way down' but was not killed.

Now something else had caught her eye.

HISTORY UNDER THE HAMMER

It was dust to dust yesterday for some of the oldest buildings in the Rocks ... a sad and solemn occasion for those forced to bid farewell to their homes for the building of the Sydney Harbour Bridge. A shiver ran through the assembled crowd and handkerchiefs were raised to women's eyes as the auctioneer slammed his hammer on history ... all gone in a matter of moments for a few pounds each ... the grim faces said it all ... the final nail in history's coffin.

'Jolly sad.' She stirred her tea loudly. 'Isn't it Lloyd? To think of all those poor people uprooted for a beastly bridge.'

Lloyd didn't answer. She felt like she'd been left to soliloquise on stage for as long as she could go on before her voice turned hoarse or she was roundly booed off. Chisholm wandered in with a tray. Rennie pointed her cigarette at HISTORY UNDER THE HAMMER.

'What do you think, Mrs Chisholm?' Chisholm lowered the tray, glanced at the page and said she didn't know ma'am. 'This Harbour Bridge building business,' Rennie persisted. 'What do people think?'

Chisholm repeated that ma'am, she didn't know and then, if that would be all, might she return to corning the beef?

'Corning the beef? Is that all the woman can think about?' said Rennie, when Chisholm had finally scuttled off. 'Really Lloyd. All this has to stop.'

The newspaper shivered in his hands. She waited. Her heart began to flip. Her knees trembled beneath the table but her upper half was holding steady. She'd be ready with a perfect wifely smile when he lowered his newspaper.

'All this has to stop.' He lowered the paper and scowled at her. She could hear he was trying to keep the reins tight on his voice. Spittle had gathered at the corners of his mouth, the whiteness of it contrasting with his face, neck, and the scarlet shine of his pate. 'I see. Mrs Howarth thinks the biggest building project this nation has ever seen must grind to a halt. Throw down your pick-shovels at once lads, give up your paying jobs, because a lady—an artist no less—holed up in the lap of luxury on the harbour at her husband's considerable expense, has had her conscience pricked by a few wily slum dwellers playing the bleeding heart. Shall I dash off a letter to the editor now?'

At least she'd goaded him to speak.

'There's no need to bother,' she said. Her voice sounded light, ambivalent even. She added a silly laugh. 'I'll write one myself.'

'You, Irene? You do speak such utter rot.'

'It was dust to dust ... It's horrible to think of it.'

'Then I suggest you don't. It's called life, Irene. Progress. But what would you know of that, sitting up there in your bower daubing away, filling your head with all manner of romantic nonsense? That may have suited you and your London fops, swanning about with your high-born noses stuck in the air. Shall I be the one to break it to you? Welcome to real life in the modern age. The bridge is already bringing substantial benefits to all of us, and for that people must pay the price.'

'What people, Lloyd? Not us.'

'Would it make you feel more noble if you suffered too?' Rennie jerked back in her chair as Lloyd tossed his napkin at her. 'Shall I spread a rag beneath the privet bush for your bed? Or furnish you with a lamp so you can visit the caves along the sea walls and lie down with the dossers and the fly-by-nighters, lending your ear to their tales of woe?'

'What would you know of woe? You have no heart, bleeding or not. You've only ever cared about success, about what happens at the blasted Wool and Wheat. That's why you snared me, as an upper class trophy to show off to your boorish family. But I failed you, didn't I? I failed you in the worst way possible. I have failed to bear you a son and heir. Now you seek to wound me by stepping out with my only friend, with Bertha Collins.'

With that, Lloyd stood up, threw down the newspaper and moved towards her. Rennie could see the pulse beating in the side of his neck. He moved in over her. She stared down at the steaming oats. He expected her to cower, to beg forgiveness, to fall to her knees, but she would not do it. Not this time.

She raised her eyes to meet his. 'If you are going to strike me, then strike me now.' Her voice wasn't loud, but it was loud enough.

She waited for what seemed an age. His eyes flinched. He cursed and finally moved away. She heard him punch the hallstand before the front door slammed. Rennie sat rigid in her chair. Her words clanged about her in the air. She'd never called Lloyd's bluff before and now that she had finally done it, what was she supposed to do next?

She leapt up and paced about. She stopped to stare out of the bay windows and smoked countless cigarettes before remembering the bowl of oats. Despite being a little on the stodgy side, she spooned the whole lot down, followed by two clammy eggs and four damp squares of chewy toast.

She returned to the bay windows to make sure he'd gone. The bare twigs of the jacaranda scratched at the glass. Once, she'd never tired of looking at that tree, the fern-like leaves, the purple flowers making a carpet across Lloyd's blessed lawn, the flat little pods spinning and clapping like tiny castanets. Now it was bare, as if it had shed all of its grandeur and had entered a period of austerity. All the while, beneath the bark, unseen, beneath the ground, the tree continued on making preparations to bloom and flourish again, quietly remaking itself.

It was clear now what she needed to do. This time it was easy. She'd rehearsed the whole charade a week before. She didn't hurry as she moved about the bedroom. She remembered where she'd put the luggage tag from the art gallery. There it was. She ran her fingers over it. *Number 10.* She'd tucked it away with a handful of gold jewellery and the letter she'd completely forgotten about, mysteriously addressed to Lloyd from her brother Irving.

She stared at Irving's handwriting. What could he want now? All of his travel arrangements for coming to Sydney were in place. She'd corresponded with him tirelessly, covering every last detail about his proposed sojourn south. You'd think he was preparing to set sail to the furthest planet, prevaricating about this, vacillating over that. *Yes,* she'd said over again, he could stay with them for the entire six months. *No,* he didn't need to bring fishing rods, saddles, pianos, spades, quinine, light bulbs, castor oil or any other thing he invented to worry about. She always had to steel herself before opening any of his letters. She'd tired of writing back every week, so she'd begun to send a series of quick sketches instead. *We have everything here,* she'd scrawled across the bottom of one. *Except the Sussex sleet—and please do not dream of bringing that!!* which she supposed had either mortally offended him or succeeded in allaying his many fears because his barrage of anxious missives had finally ceased.

Rennie wondered if Irving was ill again. It was to be expected following his wife's recent death. But if his nerves had returned at full pelt, he'd have been incapable of affixing a postage stamp let alone manoeuvring a nib. It wasn't helpful to think of Irving and his nerves today, or to relive the smell of hospital, the cloying silence, the heartrending noise as stony-faced nurses led her along echoing corridors, unlocking and relocking a series of doors as if entering the underworld, never quite knowing if she, the visitor, might find herself entombed in purgatory with him, like those slaves who'd been forced to lie down with the Pharaohs, their tongues cut out.

Downstairs in Lloyd's study, she unlocked the drawer in his davenport. The wad of money had grown inside the cigar box. Underneath it, she found a scrap of newspaper folded into a tight square. She smoothed it out. *Chisholm,* she almost called. *Bring forth your trusty iron.* But she stopped herself when she saw what it was. It was the article she'd torn out months before about Bertha Collins gadding about Sydney in her motorcar.

Her eyes filled with tears. So, it was true then. Bertha had betrayed her for Lloyd. Why else would he keep her photograph, except as a trinket to gloat over when he supposedly came down to work late at his desk? Before this morning's clash, it would have made her feel sick. But now it made her more determined than ever before.

'I don't know when I'll be back,' she called to Chisholm, as she strode out into the blustery air. She imagined Chisholm recalling those words when Lloyd came home and discovered his wife had upped and left. The traitors and gossipers would dine out on it for months. *Fancy that English flibbertigibbet leaving Mr Wool and Wheat!*

Rennie walked down the path with a new earnestness in her step. Nothing was going to stop her now. She'd go straight to The Rocks to bear witness to 'the sad and solemn occasion' herself, armed with her sketchbook. Lloyd was wrong. She'd never been afraid of exposing herself to the harsh realities of life. She knew more—because she *felt* more— about the brutality of living and dying than he ever could.

But she was stopped in her tracks by Bertha's motorcar thrumming across the front gate. *Bertha?*

'At your service,' Bertha said, swinging down from the driver's side.

Rennie's breath went from her. Her husband's mistress had been directed to ambush her in broad daylight. What a stroke of genius. Lloyd must have telephoned Bertha to cover himself. *Strike me if you are going to, Lloyd. Strike me now.*

'You do look a little peaky,' said Bertha. 'Beastly day to be going out.'

But Rennie would not be fooled. She smiled and said, 'Dastardly, yes.'

Bertha held open the door with a charming grin. How clever Bertha was. How intrepid. That is why Rennie had wanted to meet her and know her, but now she realised, she'd mistaken her friend's derring-do for ruthlessness.

'Such a ghastly day to be tossed about out on the ferry,' Bertha said, adjusting the cravat ruffling at her neck.

Rennie looked back at the house. She thought she saw Chisholm watching from the bay window. They were all in on it together, an unassailable triumvirate. But things were different now. She would outwit them all at their own game. She gave Chisholm a salute and climbed in.

'Our Lloyd thinks of everything,' Rennie said, before Bertha rocketed forward.

Our Lloyd. That would hit the bullseye. She was becoming rather good at this.

She looked across at Bertha and caught the slightest flicker of panic gnawing at the edges of Bertha's usually splendid mouth.

At the Ambassadors Cafe, Rennie sat very still as Bertha laughed and talked with her fatuous friends. Their wedding-ringed hands fluttered through the smoky air. Rennie felt strong and tranquil, beyond their reach. When somebody finally directed a question to her—it was Bertha inquiring about Rennie's—meaning Lloyd's—plans for the forthcoming picnic regatta on the Hawkesbury—Rennie threw her head back and blew out a spout of smoke, leant forward and stuffed two madeleines into her mouth.

It was one o'clock by the time she'd escaped them, refusing Bertha's insistent invitation to drive her home.

'You are too kind,' she said. 'I prefer to walk. I have an appointment.'

'Not with a strange man, I hope?' Bertha said, with a racy laugh.

'No. With destiny.'

Despite the grand words, tears smarted in Rennie's eyes as she walked away. Finding and keeping true friends, she knew, was rare indeed. But now she knew Bertha had never really been her friend. She had worked against her, like everyone else.

As Rennie stopped to dab a handkerchief to her eyes, she noticed a woman on the corner selling flowers from an old suitcase.

'Roses, sweet peas, boronia,' she called.

How ingenious. Rennie stopped to peer at the flowers, and inhale their scent. To think such things of beauty had been locked up and transported inside this battered case. She took off a glove and swept her hand over the flowers' soft heads. Like her, all of them had been severed from their roots, waiting to be bought and carried away to who knew where, for pleasure and for sorrow, for marking the big things in life like births, deaths, and marriages.

Births, deaths and marriages? she suddenly thought. *But why in that order?*

She considered several varieties before being drawn to a single yellow rose. The woman's face was kind as she attached it to a clutch of ivy leaves and pinned it to Rennie's lapel.

She walked on until two uniformed men swung open the doors of a department store and looked at her expectantly. The glittering interior called to her. She relented and was greeted by all manner of shiny things. Moving from one counter to the next, she pressed her gloves against the glass, peering at baubles and trinkets, observing an elderly woman clasping a diamond-studded wristwatch on the ruddy mottled folds of her forearm. Two shop girls hovered around the woman's chair, advancing with mirrors, murmurs and encouraging looks. *It won't help*, she wanted to say.

Catching sight of herself in a mirror, Rennie whisked the last of the tears from her eyes. In her youth, people had likened her to a Grecian goddess with her thick dark hair and the proud line of her nose. After she'd married, and failed to produce a child, she'd gained a little weight, perhaps to console herself. Then she'd gained more weight and the compliments stopped. *But you have such lovely hair and eyes*, people sometimes said, as if the rest of her was best ignored.

She was hungry. Fortunately, there was a tearoom on the upper floor. She ordered a pot of tea *without* Chisholm's so-called slimming lemon slices and *with* milk and sugar—accompanied by a sturdy slab of orange cake setting sail on a stout wave of whipped cream. She smoked several cigarettes before demolishing the cake, however it was impossible not to notice the women at the next table staring. Perhaps they knew her or perhaps they were just rude. Of course. They knew about Lloyd and his new *belle amie*, Bertha. Rennie recognised the woman in the brown hat with the nose like a greyhound's bolting around a track. Perhaps the woman had been at her exhibition, tittering pointedly into a champagne flute.

'Hell-oo!' Rennie cried, waving her cigarette.

The women responded with tight hellos before turning to whisper behind their hands. Rennie opened her sketchbook with a flourish. There could be nothing better than drawing the women at the table as they really were, the conspiratorial tilt of their hats, the bitter lines of their mouths. After a few moments, she stilled her pencil and let out a cry. She'd not drawn the women at all—but Bertha. She stood up and bumped the table, clattering the crockery. Everyone turned to watch as her chair slammed to the floor. Rennie shelled out some coins, grabbed her things and ran sobbing down four flights of stairs.

When she'd composed herself sufficiently to hail a taxi, she told the driver to hurry to the Art Gallery.

The cloakroom man took forever to retrieve her things. There were no questions or comments, no sign that this transaction signified Mrs Lloyd Howarth was on the cusp of exchanging one life for the next, not even 'We thought you was never coming back for this lot missus', or 'We nearly tossed it into the rubbish bin', only a disinterested nod. That done, she hailed down another taxi to Circular Quay. She felt perfectly all right as she looked out of the window and up at the sky which was crowded with tall clouds like grand architectural follies, colonnades suspended in the darkening air. *And look at the light.* She drank in the colours, sipping at it like nectar, edging the clouds with gaudy reds, oranges and pinks, colours any serious artist would make sure to avoid because they were too beautiful to be believed. *Like heaven*, she thought.

She took out her sketchbook, looked across at The Rocks and attempted a rough sketch, but the bulk of daylight had already gone. She stood by a ferry gate trying to think. There was enough money for a nice room at the Australia Hotel, but that would be foolish. Everybody knew Lloyd there. There had to be somewhere else.

Lights had begun to twinkle across the stretch of water. She reached into her pocket for a cigarette but instead drew out the envelope from her brother Irving. How odd. There seemed to be two letters inside of it. She pulled out the first. It was addressed to Lloyd.

My dear Lloyd,
Several complications best not discussed here prevent me from travelling, as per our original arrangements.
In the light of your concerns about my sister's erratic displays of behaviour, I think it best to quarantine her from any news of my delayed arrival. I reiterate my support for exploring all courses of action, including the procuring of professional nerve treatment, however I

believe this is a matter best further discussed during the course of our ongoing correspondence.

Your Brother-in-law, in gratitude and in haste,

Irving Bartlett, Esq.

People queuing turned and looked as Rennie cried out, 'I support all courses of action for procuring professional nerve treatment ...?'

So *that* is what all this had been about. Lloyd wanted to lock her away so he could trade her in for Bertha Collins. *But nerve treatment?* Well, Irving certainly knew all about that. She supposed Irving had never mentioned to Lloyd he'd spent four years locked in a hospital after returning home from the Somme. It was not the sort of thing one talked about. She never had. It hadn't seemed proper to tell her new strappingly healthy husband the harrowing truth. What did Lloyd Howarth know of war when he'd spent its entirety insulated from the stinking hell of the trenches by his conveniently 'essential role' thousands of miles away in the antipodes at the Wool and Wheat? She'd had more exposure to military atrocities herself during her volunteer visits to help out at the local hospital than he ever would, sitting all night with the moaning, the sorry, the half-melted, the wishing-they-were-already-dead. Nobody wanted to hear about grown men's minds being blown to bits when it should have been enough for them to have escaped with most of their body parts still intact, and a handful of medals to try to pin back together the shreds of their lives.

'All aboard,' a man shouted.

Rennie turned to see the ferry that would take her back to Lloyd and the house.

'Where's that one going?' She pointed towards another ferry preparing to depart.

'Milsons Point.'

She stuffed Irving's letter back into its envelope and ran to the gangway. Before she set foot on it, she stopped to stare at the water churning between the wharf and the ferry. *So easily,* she thought, *I could slip in and down and ... it would all be over.*

'You getting on or not, lady?'

The man had begun to draw in the ropes. She stepped onto the gangway. A girl with a frightful pink-feathered hat held out a chubby hand towards her.

'That's the way. We were all laying bets you was planning on walking across.'

A few people laughed. Rennie laughed too and had to stop herself from crying out, *Now I cross the River Lethe*. She stood very still at the front of the ferry. Perhaps it was the extraordinary light or the lurch of the water, or the timely interception of Irving's letter—if not Bertha's mocking smile—*not meeting a strange man, I hope?*—but leaving one life for the next was not so hard. It was like feeling her way along a tunnel of silk, soft, like a dream, or like drowning, she thought.

When the ferry reached the wharf Rennie stood for a moment to do a quick sketch of the escalators cut into the cliff. So much for the march of progress. The escalators weren't working. She plodded up them, her bags as heavy as sacks of coal. When she reached the top she looked along the darkening street as people scuttled after trams, hurrying back to their ordinary lives.

Well, this would be *her* life now, cast adrift on a sea of dust. She had no idea where to go but it felt completely right to walk past the haphazard little houses built in on each other, no bigger than dog-boxes. Others looked as if they'd been shelled. Many stood roofless. The tattered remains of balconies scraped and banged in the wind. Strips of wallpaper flapped like mouldering streamers. It was all quite fitting for purgatory.

She stood for a moment trying to sketch it in the dying light and continued up the hill, through the olive green shadows, the smell of stale cooking and fetid drains. She turned her head as a woman shouted, 'Of *all* the things, Arthur, you went and …'

She smiled and walked on, realising she would never hear what poor Arthur had 'went and' done. She came to a corner. She could see the pink feather-hatted woman from the ferry lumbering up the slant of a narrow street. The woman had smiled so guilelessly at her as she'd offered a complete stranger a friendly hand.

Rennie stopped by a schoolyard to look through the bars of the fence, wondering if the full light of day would render the buildings less dispiriting. It was hard to imagine children learning and playing in such an uninspiring place, munching apples, scraping knees, running home to report the injustices and the triumphs of their days.

She crossed the street and drew back into a doorway as a group of men sauntered past. Thankfully, they walked on. She began to trudge up the hill, following the path of the pink feathers which disappeared inside a door. Rennie walked on but stopped as she heard a chesty laugh ringing out from behind the shutters of a precarious balcony. She turned and looked about the street. She would return to draw it in the light, the boarded-up houses, the buildings sagging into dust.

Her eye caught the faded sign in a window opposite.

WOMEN'S AND CHILDREN'S
LODGING HOUSE
Small, neat rooms

INQUIRE WITHIN

Rennie smiled when she saw the house number. Perhaps the theosophists had been right. Everything *was* linked in a golden chain, for the house number was the same as her luggage tag from the gallery: number 10.

She pressed her face to the dusty pane. A rag of a curtain blocked the view. She turned her ear to the window. Over the evening hum of the harbour, there was the distinct sound of a woman's voice speaking rather earnestly over the tap-tap-tap of a typewriter.

CHAPTER
FOURTEEN

Ellis was pounding through the 'Green-eyed Gardener' when she heard the knock. She continued on, trying to keep the rhythm up. All day she'd been attempting to pack up the house. After dinner, she'd stood on the back step smoking her pipe, staring out at the expanding sea of nettles taking over her yard, worrying about what to write for her next column. That's when she'd realised. The subject for her next column had been staring her in the face.

'Nettles,' she said, plunging down the keys. She'd taken to speaking as she typed. With no lodgers anymore to overhear, it helped to keep her awake.

'One bright morning, when Mr Moses peered through the much-used spyhole in his fence, he was both delighted and appalled by the sight of a great dark tide of nettles surging towards his perimeter, heaving onwards like the Spanish Armada ...'

The knock sounded again. She raised her voice.

'... Like an army overrunning his enemy's lands. According to Mr Moses, nettles were the height of slovenliness and neglect. Why else did they flourish in abandoned grounds? Fearing they would rampage through his own defenceless plot, their stinging leaves plying their invading arrows in a sustained attack at his prizewinning chrysanthemums ...'

Another knock. Ellis closed her eyes, trying to hold the thread of her thoughts. There was an old saying of her mother's about soothing the sting of nettles by applying dock leaves. *Nettle in, dock out /Dock rub nettle out.* At last, Mr Moses' imperious tone was coming back to her. He was in his element, at war with the nettles, preparing to do battle with the symptoms of lassitude and decay.

Ellis took a sip of brandy and sat back to admire her work. The nettle was turning out to be excellent fodder for the gardener, writer and cook alike. There was nettle soup, nettle tea, and nettle pudding. Perhaps she'd include a recipe for nettle porridge.

There it was again, the knocking sound.

She stood up, switched off the light, went to the window and looked across the street. Girl's shutters were closed, and Girl would never announce herself so daintily.

A shadow fell across the corner of the glass. Ellis drew back. What if it was one of O'Malley's men, or those two spivs she'd seen scuffling outside the bogus room for rent on Hobbs Street?

She crept down the hallway. The house felt as if it was expanding in the dark, its walls stretching, becoming thinner and weaker against the advances of the night. She felt about for the sharpened stick she'd taken to keeping behind the kitchen door and she switched it about like a sword as she crept back up the hallway, unsure if a lunging or beating motion was the most effective for fending off attackers.

She waited behind the front door. The knocking stopped. When she thought she heard the sound of footsteps moving off, she returned to the bedroom window and lifted the curtain half an inch. There were only the usual oily shadows flickering across the street.

Back at the typewriter, she lit a match and held it aloft. She looked up Mrs McCarthy's picture and sighed. So much for finding a nice quiet place to write her book. Tomorrow she'd have to go out again at first light and see about securing herself a room. Tonight she'd write until dawn if necessary, finishing off the nettles and perhaps starting another column on the multitude of uses for the poppy.

She switched the light back on. 'Nettle beer.' And took another sip of brandy. 'An excellent remedy for rheumatic joints.' She touched a hand to her chest. Her heart was racing beneath the buttons of her writing jacket. 'The nettle's fibre is not unlike that of flax and hemp ...' She'd read that in one of the older herbal books, an anecdote about an English gentleman visitor greatly admiring a Scottish housewife's nettle napery after he'd slept between her 'soft nettle sheets' and dined from her 'fine nettle tablecloth.'

She sighed and glanced over at her bed. The nettle was beginning to roam too far and wide.

The knocking started again. This time it was louder. Ellis felt about for the stick.

'Hell-oo?' A woman's voice, high, sad and long like the evening cry of the currawongs.

Ellis switched off the light and went to the window but the woman must have pushed herself up against the door. She crept across the room and into the hallway, blundering into the dismantled bedsteads.

'Hell-oo? Hell-oo in there?'

Ellis heart was belting now. Either she opened the door—or put up with being interrupted for the rest of the night. She clutched the sharpened stick and eased the front door open, her boot chocked against it just in case.

She almost laughed when she saw a milk-skinned woman with dark black eyes and reddened nose. The woman's bare knuckles were raised as if about to knock again. Her hat was made of fine pale straw, fashionably moulded to the head. Against the falling darkness of the street, smoke swirled around her in a diaphanous cape. Her silk white stockings glimmered against the cobblestones as if her torso had been set on two pillars of light. Ellis' eyes went to the woman's lapel where a yellow rose rested its delicate head against a spray of ivy leaves.

'Yes?'

As the woman put out a hand to steady herself against the wall, her handbag slid along her other arm and fell down across the front step, wedging itself in the gap of the door. Two orange leather gloves slithered after it.

'Oh thank heavens, you've heard me,' she said, trying to peer past Ellis into the house. 'I've come about the room.'

Ellis closed the door behind her a little more. The woman stepped back into the street, scrabbled about in her coat pocket and drew out a tin of Polo cigarettes. Ellis waited as she lit one and pointed it at the window.

'It says here, should I require a room, I should *inquire within.*'

Ellis was still trying to absorb the combination of the rose, the ivy, the expensive hat, the fine green coat, the soft leather gloves, the gleaming stockings, the red-rimmed eyes and the blue swathe of smoke.

'So that's what I'm doing,' the woman said. 'Inquiring *within.*' She flashed a brilliant smile, the warmth of which was almost visible, zapping across the air between them like an electric ray.

'I ...' Ellis began to say.

'I'm so glad you heard me. I've been on one extraordinarily long journey and I'm completely exhausted.' The woman drew hard on the cigarette, raising her head and blowing it out in a line above her head, revealing a section of her silky neck. 'My apologies. Let me explain. It all began last week, you see, when I went to the gallery to look at art and the chap in the cloakroom handed me a tag and the number on it said number ten—but I forgot my bags so I returned there this morning after I'd read about the frightful—but thankfully not fatal—accident on the escalators down there.' She turned and waved down towards the Point. 'So I went back to the gallery and lucky for me, my bags were still there, intact.' She paused to draw again on the cigarette. The coal flared in the falling light. 'And now I'm here, undertaking a very serious mission, to bear witness to the desperately sad destruction of The Rocks and Milsons Point. What a state it's in. I think it's all jolly sad. I really do. Well. Here I am.' She blinked at Ellis, as if expecting her to say something. 'You see, my luggage tag said number ...'

'Ten, yes.' Ellis heard Girl's shutters scrape open. 'I'm sorry. There aren't any rooms here. Not anymore. Not in this street.'

The woman stepped back and frowned at the upper windows.

'Oh I see. You're full.'

'We're not full, we're ...' Ellis raised her hand to her chest. Her heart had begun to flutter, as precise and fast as a hummingbird.

'Marvellous, then. It seems we're both in luck. The woman turned and waved a hand at the darkening sky. 'I should very much like to find myself a bolt-hole before the heavens open. You know what they say about pillars and towers.'

Ellis stared at her. *Pillars and towers?* Ellis blinked up at the sky. The previously rosy evening light had been overpowered by a purple-black billow of clouds. She opened the door a little more and held out her hand to test for rain. As she did so, the woman swung around and sat down on the front step, put her head into her hands and began to sob.

'You right over there, Els?' Girl called down.

'No. Yes. It's only a lodger come to see about a room.'

'A lodger? That's leaving it a bit late. Tell 'em we're all about to sling our hooks.'

Ellis looked along the blackened street. There was the sound of boots coming down the hill. It was beginning to rain in heavy determined drops. The woman's shoulders were heaving up and down.

'Look, you'd better come in,' Ellis said, and almost added, *But don't go getting any ideas.*

She bent down to help the woman to her feet and inhaled the smell of expensive perfume and cigarettes. She steered her inside past the bedsteads, navigating between the piles of newspapers and half-packed tea chests. She felt the woman's soft hip brushing against her own as they moved towards the stairs where the woman sat down with a thud.

'You're very kind,' she said, as she began to wriggle out of her overcoat.

The coat was merino, if Ellis was not mistaken, with watermarked emerald satin for its insides. When Ellis took it, she felt its weight before draping it over the banister.

'I can pay a good price for the night if you ...' The woman's words were interrupted by a cough.

Ellis went to the kitchen and poured a glass of water. She rubbed the glass over with a cloth and fished out a strand of something in it. The woman clamped a fist around it, her dark eyes clenching as she gulped. It was then Ellis saw the cuts and bruises spread across her hands. So that was it. The woman was in *that kind* of trouble.

'Look,' Ellis heard herself say quietly. 'I was about to put the kettle on.'

She went back to the kitchen, unable to believe what she'd said. She was meant to be emptying the house, not filling it. But then again, it was only for the night and she needed the money more than ever now, and a woman with that kind of trouble could hardly be turned out this late.

Standing at the stove, Ellis held her hand to her chest. There it was again, the distinct sensation of fluttering in her chest. She went to the pantry and shook the cake tin. Mrs Liddy's rock cakes were always a bit on the nuggety side, but nothing a sprinkle of water and quick warming up wouldn't fix. As she set out the tea things on a tray, she remembered the tea leaf she'd found in her morning cup. She'd ignored the tea leaf in the same way she'd ignored the warning signs for the vacant room at Hobbs Street. Now a woman had appeared unannounced on her step—a rich lady lodger who was offering to 'pay a good price' to stay one night.

Ellis looked at the tannin stains on the tray and the chipped cups rocking back and forth on mismatching saucers. She began to wipe a teaspoon down the front of her jacket but stopped herself. What was she doing polishing a teaspoon for an unknown lady who'd wandered over onto the wrong side of the tracks?

'Here,' she said, setting the tray on the floor. The floorboards were dotted with drifts of hair, plaster and dust. She kicked at a moth wing caught in a web.

The woman sipped at the edges of her tea. Her cheeks began to colour up. She flashed Ellis another electric smile.

'Wouldn't you like to see the room?' Ellis said, turning away. She raised her cup towards the ceiling. 'It's plain but clean. Small but neat.' The woman stared at her as if she'd spoken in a foreign tongue. 'The room? Wouldn't you like to see it first?'

'Oh yes.' The woman came to her feet, wobbling as she picked her way up the stairs, the white gleam of her stockings disappearing into the darkness.

Ellis stayed at the bottom of the stairs and closed her eyes, tracing the steps moving above, the way the woman paused at the window, tried to lift the window sash. She heard her say something about 'links in a golden chain' over the increasingly heavy beat of rain.

'I'll take it,' the woman called down, balancing herself at the top of the stairs.

Careful, Ellis almost said. *Careful Kitty.*

'Only if it doesn't cause a fuss.' The woman's face crumpled as if she was about to cry. 'I promise to be no bother at all.'

She *was* like Kitty, even though her eyes were brown, not cornflower blue. Not scraps of heaven, but scraps of rich dark earth. 'I'm sorry, what did you say?' Ellis said.

'What do we do about a bed?'

'I'll have to bring it up.'

'We. There's the two of us now, isn't there? *We* can carry up the bed. Together. I can help.'

Ellis was about to turn her attention to the bedstead when she caught the smell of burning cakes. She hurried off to rescue them.

'Here,' the woman said, when Ellis came up the stairs. She smiled at the rock cakes. Ellis had chiselled off the worst of the blackened bits. The woman took a large bite, chewing eagerly as she produced a roll of notes out of her handbag. Ellis blinked at the money. It was more than she'd make taking in a woman and two children for over two months.

'I'll go down and fetch some change,' she said.

'No. Don't. I'm so grateful you let me in.'

Ellis crossed the room and tugged at the blind. She couldn't possibly take such a large amount for a room like this for a single night, could she?

'Would you mind if we left the blind up?' the woman said. 'I like to see the stars from my bed. I'm an artist you see, or I thought I was.'

Ellis felt her body jolt. *I like to look out at the heavens from my bed.* Wasn't that something Kitty used to say?

She turned to see the woman pacing about, the look of joy on her face. She was saying the room felt so perfectly right, that she'd dreamed of this room, of its stillness and calmness, that being here was equal parts heaven and destiny. Her voice was very upper class and—what? *Familiar.* But Ellis had never seen this woman before. She'd remember seeing a face like that—the smooth white cheeks, the large dark eyes, the sweep of black hair, strands of it looping down now from beneath the hat, wisping across the creamy softness of her neck.

She turned around to apologise about the blind, but the woman had left the room. The roll of money was on the floor. Ellis picked it up and tucked it up her sleeve. The woman had said to keep the lot. She obviously wasn't thinking straight. Tomorrow morning, Ellis would do the right thing and give a part of it back. She looked across at Girl's. *Sweet Mother of Jesus, Els,* she'd say if she'd been listening in. *Never look a gift horse in the mouth. It'll only kick you in the pearly whites.*

'I'm Rennie, by the way.' The woman had run up the stairs again, tossed down her bags and held out her hand. 'So let's have none of this Mrs so-and-so or Miss this-and-that *guff* which is far too *dulls* when Rennie shall do perfectly well.'

Ellis looked at the cuts and bruises on the outstretched hand, and the glinting huddle of diamond rings.

'Oh that,' Rennie said with a laugh. She wiped her hand across her dress. 'A little too much fervour while jousting with the Prussian blue. One of the many hazards of being an artist, I'm afraid.'

Yes, you are afraid, Ellis thought. She held out her hand, taking care to place her fingers away from the so-called paint.

It was almost nine o'clock by the time Ellis had extended the potato and fennel soup with a cup of water, stirred in a dash of caraway seeds for taste followed by a slosh of brandy, washed the dishes, made a pot of tea and sat down again at her desk to do battle with 'The Green Eyed Gardener'.

Her new lodger had hoed into dinner. They'd sat in an enforced but comfortable silence as the rain thumped down. There'd only been one awkward moment when Rennie had looked about the kitchen, holding up her empty plate as if expecting a second helping. When she'd realised there was none, she'd laughed and said very loudly over the rain, 'How silly of me. I'd forgotten you weren't expecting a guest,' and put the plate back down.

Ellis rubbed at her eyes and sighed at the typewriter. In *Mr Moses' blissful ignorance, he decried the many uses of the nettle* ... no, cross out ~~blissful~~ ... *however patiently his neighbour explained the benefits, he refused to be convinced by the many useful properties of the nettle such as digging them back into the tired soil in order to rejuvenate* ... Ellis stopped typing. Above the steady beat of rain, she could hear Rennie pacing back and forth overhead.

She looked over at her wardrobe. If she hadn't locked the roll of money away herself, she wouldn't have believed it had happened at all. What a windfall. It was enough for her to put down for a decent room—without mushroom-sprouting cornices, devious landlords, spivs or bailiffs—and perhaps, if she stretched it even more—a room boasting *all conveniences, hot bath, good table, every comfort* and a *whole verandah* to herself.

She jumped as a gust of rain slapped against the windowpane. She left the desk to make sure the window was shut. The glass vibrated beneath her fingertips. Rivulets of water had begun to make their way inside. She repositioned the scraps of paper in the sills, wondering if Rennie had closed the window upstairs. The thought of going up to check flashed through her mind, but then an image came to her of Rennie lying back on her bed in an emerald green nightdress, with edgings of fine mantilla black lace—

her smile shining out—her hair spun out like black silk across the pillows and sheets, her pale, soft, breasts heaving slightly as she raised her eyes as a brutal map of bruises came into view, welts and marks etched all over her front and back.

She lifted her curtain and looked out at the rain. She stood in the hallway, absorbing the changed timbre of the house. The echo of empty rooms was muffled by the rain, and softened by the presence of another body in the house. She found herself hesitating at the foot of the stairs. Rennie's light was still on. Over the beat of the rain she could hear her cough. The smell of cigarettes wafted down.

She stood in the kitchen and tried to turn her thoughts to the usual mundane tasks of a landlady such as finding the bucket to catch the drips in her room. But she was no longer a landlady. She was no longer sure who she was.

She opened the back door and stared out at the windy night. The rain swept in and cooled her face but it did little to calm the wild beating of her heart.

CHAPTER FIFTEEN

Her heart was beating so loudly Ellis thought Miss Stranks would hear it all the way across the parlour.

'A day's rest,' Bradbury was saying. 'That's all the doctor asks, plus regular application of the unguent to soothe the pains in Miss Kitty's hands.'

Miss Stranks raised her pointed chin and stared at him. 'You fuss too much. The girl won't thank you for it, you know. And however impressive her lineage, she must do like the rest of us and earn her keep. Her parents expect nothing less. They wouldn't have placed her in my care if they thought she was getting off scot-free. She'll learn to adapt whether she likes it or not.'

'One day's rest won't hurt though, will it?' He turned to smile at Ellis. 'Besides, the other girl is here now.'

Miss Stranks glared at Ellis. 'What are you doing there loafing about?'

'Come,' said Bradbury. 'Let's turn our minds to the Sunday speeches. I believe Miss Ellis has been busy diving for pearls of theosophical wisdom.'

Miss Stranks gestured to the typewriter. 'Sit. Where Kitty sits.'

Ellis slid onto Kitty's chair, placed her fingers on the keys and peered at the gleaming *Remington* sign, at the army of letters waiting to be ordered into legions of words. She prodded at the letter 'K' and waited to hear the satisfying *plunk* as it struck the page.

'Hands at the ready,' said Miss Stranks. 'Back straight. Write!'

Ellis withdrew her hands. 'I thought I was going to recite, Miss, not write. Not on this.'

'What's the difference? Read, write. Read, recite.'

Ellis lowered her head to hide her face. Her lip had started trembling.

'Perhaps,' said Bradbury. 'We should leave Ellis to try the machine by herself and type out what she remembers. I'm sure a trove of pearls will spring from her fingertips.'

When the hallway was clear, Ellis crept into the other parlour and tucked *Theosophy for the Novice Querent* into her dress. Once back at the desk, she opened a drawer, set the booklet in there and began to type, slowly at first, until she managed to reproduce a whole paragraph.

> The world is the Lord's classroom. All must begin as students, on the lowest rung of the lowess class before we learn, and only then may we move up class after class, rung after rung, till we have known the Lord's lessons; then we shakl leave that school for evermore.

Ellis looked up. Bradbury was watching her from the door. She eased the drawer shut to hide the booklet as he strode across the room and positioned himself at her back. He leaned in over her shoulder, his smoky breath going in and out as he read. After some minutes he took up a pencil and corrected the words 'shakl' and 'lowess'.

'There,' he said.

His face was so close she could see each glossy hair of his eyebrows, the dark curve of thick lashes, the fine lines around his eyes. He looked at her expectantly, organising his lips into a charming smile. His eyes searched her face as if he was waiting for her to say something, or to laugh and toss her hair like Kitty did. Ellis kept her expression blank.

He frowned. 'You're an odd one, aren't you Miss Ellis?' He straightened up. 'It seems you do not need my assistance to sally forth and conquer the unknown. Impressive work. Carry on.'

The gong beat in the hall. Bradbury checked his watch and strode away.

Ellis went to the window and looked down at the street. A ragged-looking man had stopped to watch Bradbury leave the house. A filthy sack hung from the man's back. His bare feet were as grey and gnarled as lumps of wood. His trousers barely clung to his bony frame. Bradbury made a great show of tossing him a coin. The ragged man caught it and frowned up at where Ellis was standing. She wondered how she must look to him, a young woman in a freshly laundered dress, staring down from the windows of a grand house. She had to stop herself from banging on the glass and crying out, *I don't belong here either* ... but the man had returned to scrounging on the street.

'He hasn't gone, has he?'

Ellis turned to find Kitty at the door. Ellis motioned towards the window. Kitty ran to it.

'Oh blast him. Why didn't he wait for me to come down? Was he talking about me to Miss Stranks?'

'I don't know, Kitty. But I wanted to ask you something about you and Mr ...'

They both turned at the sound of Miss Stranks chastising Mabel-the-maid in the hallway.

'Quick. She'll skin me alive if she sees me down here,' Kitty said. She dashed from the room to hide behind a door. 'Bring my tray up later. Ask Mrs Frith.'

Ellis returned to the desk and forced herself to plod through another paragraph from *The Novice Querent.*

We have four bodies: The Physical, the Astral, the Mental and the Causal. The Physical body is the fleshly temple. The Astral body is more refined and influenced by the ebb and flow of strong reactions and desires. If Man could control these emotions, peace would reign and there'd be no violence or malice in the world.

Ellis stopped. The vision of her father in a drunken rage flashed through her mind. She plunged on, determined to head off the perilous direction of her thoughts.

As a new century dawns we shall prosper if we plant the fertile seeds of love and respect in hearts of all men. Divine Wisdom is being amassed at every corner of the earth by those with the power to leave their Physical bodies and travel Astrally through time and space, to gather the Truth of the ancients who once inhabited the glittering city of Atlantis, sunk beneath the waves.

Ellis stopped again. Atlantis. This was something she could see, a once grand city buried beneath the sea. She read on. Apparently in Atlantis, True Religion had brought enormous material and spiritual advancements benefiting its blessed inhabitants until they lost their true direction and fell to sin, causing God to send forth Noah's obliterating flood. Now, scattered fragments of the Great Wisdom remained, lying like hidden jewels at the base of all the world's major religions. Gradually, these fragments were being retrieved for the building of the Divine Wisdom, otherwise known as theosophy.

Ellis sat back and rubbed her eyes. A gong sounded. In another hour she'd be summoned to prove her worth to Miss Stranks.

She hurried through the rest of the chapter but to her disappointment, Atlantis was not mentioned again. She walked along the bookshelves and plucked out the slim booklet *The Story of Atlantis: A Geographical, Historical and Ethnological Sketch* by W. Elliot-Scott. The sentences were long but the idea of a city sunk beneath the sea lay glittering like a prize beneath the dense paragraphs. Apparently the author had a remarkable capacity for memory and was able to see things almost magically. This allowed him to travel back in time to retrieve the Wisdom of the Ancients of Atlantis.

She scanned down the page. Disappointingly, there was little discussion of the lost city itself. The author seemed more concerned with the kinds of 'root races' he claimed had once inhabited it. Some races were hairier, smaller and darker skinned. They had no ability to think, plan or remember much. In contrast, the wiser, paler-skinned races were more refined, boasted fierce intellects and vast spiritual, mental and physical attributes. In short, they were higher beings.

Ellis frowned and glanced back at the *Novice Querent*. One of the things she'd liked about theosophy was its belief in equality between all men. There it was on page four. *We must begin by loving every one, no matter what may be the colour of their skin … and whether he be rich or poor.*

She returned to the shelves and found another booklet, *Atlantis: the Antediluvian World* by Ignatius Donnelly. Happily, it opened with a dreamlike fable passed down by the great ancient philosopher Plato, *The Dialogue of Critias.* There were descriptions of the city, the Temple of Poseidon housing the 'golden pinnacles', a pole carved with the country's laws and embossed with a mysterious metal called orichalcum. On the other side of the pole, horrible curses described the fate of those who disobeyed. Lush gardens surrounded the temple, fountains, and refreshing baths which ran cold and hot all year thanks to the advanced engineering skills of the Atlanteans. The land beyond was fertile, drenched by sun and ingeniously watered by a complex system of irrigation canals: *The air was redolent with fragrant herbs, blooming flowers, ripened fruit, crystal waters, arable earth … and every kind of root, herbage and verdant tree flourished there.*

Ellis sat back. If only there'd been some kind of irrigation system on the farm at Candlebark Creek. Instead, the rivers had run with dust.

Once again she was summoned to the blue parlour. Her mouth went dry when she saw Miss Stranks standing at attention by the window. Her face was flushed. Bradbury was in his shirtsleeves fanning himself with a newspaper. Mabel arrived with a pitcher of iced water, lemon and mint.

'Would you like me to open the windows, Miss?' said Mabel.

'What?' said Miss Stranks. 'Heavens no. I can barely hear myself think without having to contend with the hullaballoo of the street.'

Mabel offered Ellis a glass.

'*Vite!* Over by the mantelpiece.' Miss Stranks clapped her hands.

Ellis' knees were shaking. She tried to appear calm but it was as if during the short walk from one room to another her mind had drained of all she'd read and her vocal chords had seized up. She turned away to face the mantelpiece. It was imperative she do well or Miss Stranks would toss her back to the streets to scrounge like that ragged man she'd seen from the window.

She did as Kitty had advised, took a deep breath, put her shoulders back and chin up, but it didn't help. One sentence became tangled with the next. Whole paragraphs slipped away.

'The astral and the mental and the ... there are planes of nature, and sub-planes too and ... the etheric double is the colour of gray ... it comes in the form of an egg—I mean—an aura ... because man has many emotions which he must control ...'

She could see the top of her hair bobbing up and down in the mirror over the mantelpiece. She heard Bradbury cough. Or was it a laugh?

'Which books are you attempting to enlist as your source?' This was Miss Stranks. Ellis managed to rasp out the title, *The Novice Querent.* 'And?' said Miss Stranks.

Ellis gripped onto the mantelpiece and shook her head.

'You mean to tell me this is all you've read? One flimsy beginners booklet?'

Ellis stared at the blue wallpaper. The diamond-pattern design shimmered blue, green then grey. She closed her eyes. The diamond-pattern pulsed in orange and red behind her eyelids. 'Atlantis,' she said.

'What?'

'*At-lan-tis.*' She almost shouted it.

'Atlantis?' That was Bradbury. His boots clipped back and forth. 'By Jove, we just might have it. Atlantis. Of course.'

'Turn around at once. Look at me when I speak to you,' said Miss Stranks.

'No, wait,' said Bradbury. 'Let's hear what the young lady has to offer on Atlantis.'

The heat had risen in the room. Ellis felt her throat relax. She closed her eyes and imagined she was far away where there was no pain, sorrow or humiliation, only the cool embrace of the soft, warm sea. It wasn't so hard to do. Her Mental Body had unmoored itself from her Physical Body before. In the week before she'd run away, her father had swayed over her and the thinking-feeling part of herself had risen up from her body until she was looking down on the grey-yellow farm from high above, sailing with the crows and bypassing clouds.

When she finished reciting, there was silence in the room.

'You may turn around now, Ellis,' Bradbury said.

'I knew she had it in her.' Miss Stranks' eyes were glistening. Her hands were clasped as if in prayer. 'I knew it when I singled her out from the crowd on that night at the hall.'

'Agreed. She is skilled in recital but does not have the delivery. Even a small, friendly audience seems to unsettle her.'

'With practise she will overcome it. Everything can be overcome with hard work, pure thoughts and ...'

'But we need her to be ready for next Sunday.' Bradbury began to pace across the room.

'When her back is to us,' said Miss Stranks, 'there is a natural rhythm and, dare I say it—*authenticity*.'

'Agreed.'

'But people expect to see her face. They crave the eyes. Look at me, child. Do not sulk.' Miss Stranks' smile vanished. 'But your eyes are burning red. You've been rubbing at them, haven't you? You look like a lizard. What a fright.'

'In heaven's name, do be quiet!' Bradbury's hand shook as he flung it out towards Miss Stranks. Miss Stranks stepped back, her face frozen in shock.

Bradbury bowed his head. 'I beg you, Madame. Forgive me. I have raised my voice most indecently. Please, let me explain the reasons for such an uncouth display. My exuberance was fuelled by the fact that you have just put your finger on the heart of the matter, so brilliantly, I didn't want to lose the thought.' He offered Miss Stranks a charming smile. 'The audience *craves*, you said?' Miss Stranks managed a stiff nod in reply. 'We *crave* what we desire but cannot always have. We chase after it and try to grasp it, like a child running after a rainbow. That is the nub of it. See? Bear with me, if you will.'

He clipped across the room, plucked up Kitty's lace shawl and swirled it before him in the air.

'We may just have the answer under our noses. But we'll need a hat. One of the broader-brimmed varieties.'

Miss Stranks' expression moved from horror to amazement to admiration. She rushed from the room and returned with a straw boater.

'Set her by the window with the light behind her.' Bradbury moved a chair into the sun. Ellis was told to sit. Bradbury placed the hat on her head and draped Kitty's shawl over it.

'Come now, Miss Ellis. Once more, with feeling, as they say. Plato's description of Atlantis.'

Ellis blinked out through the lace. Her knees were no longer shaking now that she was sitting down. The veil did help a little, not because it obscured the steely eyes of Miss Stranks and the encouraging smile of Bradbury, but because it smelled of Kitty. She closed her eyes knowing that Kitty was with her, urging her to secure a place in this house. *We must stick together, you and I.*

When she'd finished, Miss Stranks said, 'I predicted this. You remember I said at the hall: *I see a girl with sweet white lilies adorning her hair?*'

'Indeed.' Bradbury took out his watch. 'I must make haste if we are to place an advertisement in the newspapers for Sunday next.'

Miss Stranks followed him from the room.

Ellis removed the hat and veil and wiped her brow. That was twice Miss Stranks had mentioned seeing a girl with white lilies in her hair. But Ellis hadn't been wearing the flowers in her hair when Kitty had invited her into the hall. She'd offered Mr Bradbury's lilies to Miss Stranks as a wilting, battered posy.

CHAPTER
SIXTEEN

Rennie raised her hand as she perched on the lumpy lodger's bed. The ceiling was so close, she could feel it shaking from the pounding rain. She shivered as the smell of wet wool enveloped her. Waving her cigarette improved things a little and, if she closed her eyes, it was almost like the smell of autumn, of rambling through flame-coloured woods as a child, tramping through the mud and leaves and sodden grass, past the little thatched cottages crouching in the valley. Yes, it was the smell of oldness and newness; hope, youth and possibility, and it made her want to take out her sketchbook and draw it all.

She smoothed out a page and licked the tip of her favourite pencil, but stopped as the words *my husband is being unfaithful with my best friend* insinuated themselves into her mind.

'My husband,' she said to the room. 'My husband has run off with my best friend.'

Nobody could hear her. The rain was so loud, she could've taken up playing the bagpipes without anybody turning a hair. She stabbed the pencil at the page, moving her hand quickly, trying to capture the sullied glory of her new surroundings before they shed their strangeness. It wasn't the usual subject for a work of art, which made her all the more determined to pin down the murk and grime and make her own 'crude messy little' masterpiece here and now.

In the yellowy electric light, she peered at the mould-coloured wallpaper which didn't quite reach all the way up to the cornices, the swollen window with its lopsided blind, the heavy bedstead wired together. The bedroom floor dived away at a dizzying slant. The electrical wires were exposed around the light switch, which was missing its brass covering. The handleless door gaped ajar, opening to the odd-shaped corner where it seemed the builder had forgotten to leave enough space for a proper landing.

Her attempt wasn't bad for a preliminary sketch. One day she'd transfer it to canvas, adding a jumble of watery greys, browns and greens to capture the room's idiosyncrasies dissolving into chaos. There'd be no need to include a figure in the final picture. If she worked on it, the room would *feel* inhabited as if the breath, nightmares and dreams of past tenants clung to the walls.

It was then Rennie felt afraid. It was far easier to reduce an overwhelming sight to a dab of scenery on a page, than it was to face the fact she was destined to spend the night in it. She frowned at the tatty blanket and threadbare pillowcase, and tried to think cheerful thoughts as she lay back on the bed, but it was like curling up on a sack of cotton reels. She leapt back up, took out Irving's envelope and began to pace about. It was almost too extraordinary to have found such incriminating evidence in Lloyd's desk. Perhaps he'd wanted her to discover it. Yes, that was it. The whole thing had been premeditated. Her running away had saved him the trouble and cost of carting her off to an asylum himself.

She lit a cigarette and read down the page: *I wholeheartedly support your suggestion of seeking a professional cure for my sister's nerve treatment from your 'top-notch' physician ...* If it hadn't been written in Irving's hand, she'd never have believed her brother was capable of taking part in such a devious conspiracy. Although he had been puffed up with his own self-importance since birth, Rennie had never considered him a man given to deliberately devious acts. She'd always tried her best to overlook his many failings, knowing he'd suffered enough for what he'd done and seen in the mud- and blood-soaked fields of France. The wracking nervous twitch and his tedious descent into pedantry simply had to be tolerated, although only in small doses, for the urge to escape him gripped her within minutes of their every meeting.

It was clear he was being influenced by Lloyd. Men like Lloyd made it their business to sniff out the weaklings in the pack.

Rennie folded the letter away. But what was this? A second letter in the same envelope? *Good Lord.* She'd forgotten she'd found it at the ferry wharf.

She smoothed it out. This one was not addressed to Lloyd—but to her.

Dear Rennie,

I have been greatly troubled to hear that your husband has been behaving in a less than decent manner. This unpleasant development has left me no other option than to arrange your immediate passage back to England. A berth has been booked on the 20th of September on the *Seastar.* It is fully paid. All you need do is appear. Make sure to mention this to no one. I trust you will keep safe until we meet.

Awaiting your swift and sensible response,

Your brother,

Irving.

Rennie threw the letter on the bed and rummaged for the other one. She stared at the two letters. They were both written in the same hand.

'Dear God, Irving! What have you been playing at?'

Was this why his series of anxious missives had suddenly stopped? Had Lloyd been intercepting them? She scouted about for the envelope. There was none, and therefore no proof he'd addressed the letter directly to her. It could all be part of an elaborate trick. Irving had sent the letter to Lloyd who'd conveniently left it lying about in his davenport—so she'd find it. Then, when she tried to board the ship on the suggested date, Lloyd would be lying in wait, ready with his henchmen to bundle her off for nerve treatment.

She strode across the room but after two and a half paces she'd reached the door and could only pace back another two. What a devil of a development. She'd never sleep now. How could she even hope to in such a grimly Spartan arrangement? Besides, she was still ravenous. And she could never sleep when hungry. Why hadn't she packed a little picnic for herself? It was all too awful to contemplate.

Dinner had consisted only of an entrée-sized bowl of watery soup and a dry crust of bread. Although she had to admit, the soup was surprisingly tasty despite its lack of body. All through dinner the rain had flung itself down in fractious bursts, confusing the smattering of communication with her taciturn but not entirely unfriendly landlady, Ellis Gilbey. Rennie had tried to ask a few questions about the house, about the Harbour Bridge, about the resumptions bearing down, but Ellis seemed not to want to hear.

'Funny soup,' Ellis had said when Rennie had finally ventured down into of the kitchen. Her new landlady had been standing at the stove wielding a wooden spoon at a blackened pot. 'Funny soup?' Rennie had said. 'No,' Ellis had said. 'Fennel—*fen-nel* soup.' And both of them had laughed, their mouths agape as the rain rumbled on around them like distant guns.

Her stomach was complaining now, rumbling as loudly as the rain. Damn more dinner. She could use a drink. She moved her hands across her belly until she found the place where her hips always ached. Lloyd liked to grab her there until her skin turned red, burning and pinching beneath his grasp. She could feel him now, his fingerprints embedded beneath her skin. She wondered how long it would take to shed all evidence of him.

Safe, Irving had said. *You must keep safe.*

She felt suddenly calm. For whatever the failings of her current surroundings, she was safe—she'd foiled Lloyd at his own game. He'd be dealing with the policeman now. She could see it so clearly, as if she was sitting in the front row for a play: the doorbell ringing in the wings, the dishevelled detective stumbling in to wipe his muddy boots across Mrs Chisholm's spotless carpets, sneering as he assessed the house, the capacious drawing room, the looming oak cabinets, the shimmering paintings, the gleaming family silver, all of it shouting *establishment*. The detective flicked open his notebook and levelled his first question at Lloyd, 'Any chance your wife has been abducted, Sir?'

Lloyd hesitated, moving his cigar-thick fingers across his roughened chin, draining a glass of whisky, leaning against the mantelpiece like a sportsman nursing a broken rib, stalling for time as he weighed up the potential benefits of the police pursuing that line of thinking instead of the truth.

Turning slowly, he met the detective's eye.

'I do not disagree,' he said. 'Unpleasant as it is, I concede abduction cannot be ruled out.'

Pleased with his command of the double negative, Lloyd repeated that his wife had not appeared particularly unhappy at the breakfast table. She was never unforthcoming in gadding about, idling in the department stores, taking tea with her gaggle of lady friends.

'Nobody could say I've not provided her with every comfort, for God's sake,' he said, waving his whisky at the room.

On cue, Chisholm bustled in, supporting whatever fiction her master had confected before asking if she might return to the kitchen to wrap the *boeuf en croute*, Sir, or stuff the goose.

Lloyd strode about the room until he stopped rather suddenly at one of Rennie's timid Sussex watercolours.

'But,' he said, ruffling his hair. The policeman raised his eyes from his pen and notebook. 'This may not be significant, but ...' He went on to say his wife had been pestering him to let her hold an art exhibition. He'd advised against it, of course, being a pragmatist. Perhaps the publicity had caught the opportunistic eye of the underworld? Thieves were drawn to art like bees to honey, were they not? Before he could expand, Bertha Collins' motorcar was heard skidding to a muddy stop.

There she was. Rennie could see her now, striding up the path, fighting her way through the bucketing rain. Lloyd made sure to affect a chaste, gentlemanly welcome as he thanked Bertha for braving the elements in his hour of need.

'Judge Collins' wife,' he said, introducing her to the detective, making sure everybody knew exactly who they were dealing with.

The detective watched on as Bertha ridded herself of one dripping cape, and two sodden gloves, revealing a breathtaking and barely skin-covering creation of beads, tassels and Chinese silk. Standing sentinel by the roaring fire, Lloyd poured another round of double whiskies, thumping a fist on the mantelpiece as he decried the scourge of a city crawling with thugs carrying guns.

'A man can no longer read the daily papers without being assailed by tales of toughs marauding about in gangs,' he said. 'I'll be blowed if I don't dash off a letter myself to my old friend, the Minister of Police, demanding more officers patrol the streets.'

At this, the detective put away his notebook and exited.

And so things would proceed without anybody having uttered one word of the truth. The truth was that Lloyd had both ravaged and lavished his wife with equal fervour. After a night of particularly brutish marital passion, he returned home bearing luxurious gifts, instructing Chisholm, his admiring witness, to help him unwrap them while Rennie waited to be draped in a series of glamorous things. *Everyone must pay the price*, he often said.

'Well, this is what happens when you can no longer pay the price,' Rennie said.

Since the debacle of the exhibition, his gifts had stopped. An eerie silence had stalked the house. How tiring it was. Every night she was on the lookout for Lloyd's next attack, waiting, listening, never knowing how and when it would arrive. Now she was here, in safe but gloomy territory, far from Lloyd and out of reach of Irving's probable conspiracy.

She prodded the unforgiving mattress one more time. It was as hard as the sandstone at Mrs Macquarie's chair where she'd gone to sit full of hope when she'd first arrived, pink and fresh with wifely eagerness, hauling her easel and box of paints, trying to make friends with picnicking strangers sunning themselves in the harbour light. But she had not made friends with anyone except for Bertha.

Rennie leapt up again and began to pace. It was all her fault. She'd allowed herself to be swept away on a whim by a man she didn't know and hadn't loved, wanting to believe in the span of his shoulders, the depth of his pockets, wooed by the wide, flat accent and the surety of his stride. He'd offered her something no other man could: the possibility of leaving behind everything she'd known and lost, to live far away in a warm, golden land, thousands of miles from the weeping wounds of Europe, where the unbearable grief of losing both her parents, and the changed personality of her brother, had almost sent her hurtling towards the precipice. She'd tried to escape everything by drinking and dancing until dawn every night, but the thrill of hunting fun had waned, leaving her with an empty purse and a sour taste in her mouth.

Rennie stopped pacing. She wondered if her landlady could hear her marching up and down. She smiled, for it was actually quite funny to be tramping across a shoebox of a room wearing her favourite London dress and Florentine dancing shoes. It was also a tiny bit thrilling to think nobody in the world knew where she was. She wondered if that was how explorers felt as they squelched on through the unchartered wilds, danger converging all around, not knowing which fate awaited: unparalleled glory; grisly disease or humiliating defeat.

But the smell was becoming sickening now. Rennie went to the window and wrestled it open half an inch. The rain rushed in like a waterfall. She managed to force it shut again, but not before a large puddle had formed on the floor. She looked across at the light switch, hoping the water wouldn't lap its way towards the electric wires and cause some kind of cataclysmic combustion. She'd read of such things, spontaneous ignitions of a deadly domestic kind, especially in buildings tacked together on the cheap. It was a relief to see much of the puddle drain down through the cracks in the floor.

There was nothing else for it. She'd have to try to carve out a place to sleep on the rock of her bed. At least it *was* a bed, an island of refuge upon which to cling for one long, spine-wracking night.

She pulled the linen back from the mattress and tried not to shriek at the sight of two dried brown lakes of stains. The flat leather buttons reminded her of flaps of wizened flesh, as if a series of belly buttons had been sewn into the ancient lump of horse's hair. She felt her eyes fill with tears. She'd mistaken the smell of this room. It wasn't the scent of hope and possibility, it was the reek of desperation and poverty. But she couldn't leave now. It was late and dark and beating with rain.

CHAPTER
SEVENTEEN

Ellis looked up. At last, her lodger had stopped pacing up and down. She left the desk and wedged fresh scraps of paper in the sill. In the corner of the ceiling, several brown buds of water had formed, ready to drop. She moved the bucket and steeled herself for a night of writing bedevilled by the percussion of drips, if not the movements of a particularly restless lodger.

She took another sip of brandy and frowned at Mr Moses and his bellicose crusade against the invading nettle hoards. She'd barely written two words when the tap-tap-tap began again overhead. Over the base drum of the rain, Rennie's shoes added a staccato beat. A sound like that could drive a person mad. Thumping a broom on the ceiling crossed her mind, or a rake. That's what Mr Moses would have done. Actually, Ellis thought, it was exactly the kind of sound to prompt Mr Moses to return to his spyhole in the fence in an effort to discover its irritating source.

She sat back and closed her eyes. Tap-tap-tap. If she let the ideas flow, the whole scene would come to her, fully formed. She sat forward and plunged her fingers on the keys. The tapping sound was coming from the usual culprit, Mr Moses' *avant-garde* neighbour. Through the spyhole, Mr Moses could see him out in his shirtsleeves beneath the persimmon tree, chipping down through layers of his well-draining, friable humus which had been formed from years of digging in untidy weeds, nettles, lupins, seaweed, manure, compost and the like. His neighbour laboured on cheerfully, whistling as he chipped away. Tap-tap-tap. Mr Moses stood transfixed. What in heaven was the blighter playing at now? A fish pond. Good heavens. The man was adding a fish pond into his already wildly unruly plot.

The fish pond was a coup, Ellis realised as she committed the idea of it to the page. People liked ponds. They featured in the new, large modern gardens which accompanied the new large modern houses, all of which seemed to grow bigger, colder and less cosy and increasingly needed to be called 'homes'. Ponds were tranquil. They were grand, cool. And dangerous. They invoked halcyon days of a privileged childhood, feeding the ducks with scraps of bread, glimpsing the golden flash of fish, or tossing in a coin to make a wish, or peering down to run your fingers through the tadpoles and slime.

Mr Moses would never normally dream of sacrificing a section of his immaculate garden to something as pleasurable as a pond, not until he'd seen his neighbour chipping away at the bedrock. Now he would have to build one too, but on a more fitting scale. A fountain would furnish his, he decided, as he surveyed his garden for the most promising site. While his neighbour made do with a ramshackle home-made affair, Mr Moses would order a statue of Neptune or a pert bare-breasted nymph to adorn his fountain. He'd set it in the front garden towering over his award-winning rose bushes contained by clipped box, burbling as a centrepiece to his impeccably raked paths.

Good, Ellis thought. She was pleased to have thought of the nymph. Nearly every good story led you back to the Greeks. She left Mr Moses to planning the mechanics and aesthetics of his fountain—an idea so brimming with potential advances and failures it would stretch for several future columns. There'd be no end to him arguing with sculptors and the people who made fountains.

Tonight she'd devote the rest of her column to nymphs, specifically the blue water lily, *Nymphaea caerulea*. It was said to be linked to the water nymph Lotis who'd died from a broken heart after being forsaken by Heracles. Hebe, the goddess of youth and spring had turned Lotis into a purple lily. Two nymphs, Dryope and Iole, found the lily while gathering flowers, but when Dryope tried to pick it, the stem spurted blood. Dryope was then turned into a lotus tree, instantly forgetting all ties with her past and family, hence the term, 'the lotus-eaters', souls who'd sampled the seeds of the lotus tree and roamed the world, amusing themselves with earthly pleasures, immune to their own histories.

Ellis sat back in her chair and cradled her brandy against her chest. So much for Girl's port wine and Sweet Tooth. Lotus-eating was what she needed at a time like this.

She left the desk and sat on her bed. At least there was silence now overhead. The rain drummed all around. She glanced over at the wardrobe. Rennie's money was safely locked away. Tomorrow, she'd go out early and secure herself a decent room. For the first time in her life, her purse would be full. She'd see what she wanted and be able to snare it for herself. She pictured herself bowling up to a grand front door, being shown through a large, light-filled room with its own well-appointed bathroom and kitchen, and a shining harbour view. As she was about to make her offer, she caught the landlady staring down at the darning in her stockings and the thinning weave of her coat. *It's gone*, the landlady said, hurrying to see her out.

But I have the money, Ellis thought.

Did she really have the money? There was still the conundrum of whether to hand back some of Rennie's rent. She'd prided herself on being scrupulously honest ever since the deceptive days of Miss Stranks. Just because her landlady days were almost over, it didn't mean her standards should lapse. But then again, Rennie had flatly refused to take the money back and she'd drawn the notes from her purse so nonchalantly. Money meant so little to people like that, while for those in Ellis' position, they'd never seen such a stack of 'Fisher's flimsies' in their lives.

What she could do with that amount!

Ellis took off her writing jacket and laid it over her typewriter. Together with her meagre savings scraped together from typing the Clements Brothers' invoices and her monthly column, she almost had enough to secure a good, clean, dry room for at least a few months, a room with a sparkling blue view of the sea, her desk by the window, finishing her book with the harbour winds blowing in, ruffling her papers as she typed, inhaling the scent of roses, sun, honeysuckle, mint, parsley and salt. There might even be enough to buy a new winter coat, stockings, and a pair of shoes.

She turned off the lamp. It was hard to believe any of this had happened at all. But it had. Proof was up there hammering across the floor again, tap-tap-tap. She could see Rennie's face, her luminous white cheeks streaked with tears as she darted back and forth. *I could go up there*, she thought. *Take her up a drink.*

She raised her glass in the dark. 'To my windfall, and to Mr Moses and his blessed fountains.'

There, she could sleep now. But she couldn't sleep. Snippets from the 'Lady of the Lake' poem flared in her mind, something about the water lily raising its white chalice to the light. If she closed her eyes, she could be back there lying in the dark surrounded by Miss Stranks' suitcases and travel trunks, staring up at the ceiling in the huge echoing house, listening for any sign of Kitty Tate crying out, imagining she could see through the ceiling plaster, the floorboards and the Persian carpets which separated them, her white skin glowing in the dark.

CHAPTER
EIGHTEEN

As Ellis recited the tracts on Atlantis for Miss Stranks beneath the veil, Bradbury's words rang through her mind. *We crave. We hanker after what we desire but cannot have. We are like children trying to grasp the rainbow.* At night she wept for the past and feared for the future but the thing she *craved* was seeing Kitty again, for Kitty had stopped coming down to the kitchen to pick at her meals and joke with Mrs Frith. There was just an empty chair at the table and being regaled by Mrs Frith's ever-expanding list of bodily complaints.

The five o'clock gong marked the beginning of a long day. Ellis washed and nibbled a little bread while Mrs Frith complained about her clicky knees and puffy ankles. Ellis sometimes asked about Kitty, but Mrs Frith would only roll her eyes and say, 'Never you mind. Girls like Kitty always make it their business to get what they want.'

She then entered the red parlour to read more about theosophy and its connections to Atlantis. At noon she supped on a watery soup and a heel of dry bread on a tray at the desk. She read while she ate, or she stood at the window watching the people pass in the street. It was back to the books until the two o'clock gong when she was called into the blue parlour, was told to sit and put on the hat and veil, and recited all she'd read. She was then quizzed at length by Miss Stranks.

'And what did you eat in Atlantis, child?'

'They ate no flesh, Miss. Although Plato does mention meat.'

'Yes, yes. What else?'

'Nuts, fruits and berries plucked from the bough. Chestnuts specifically, and something thought to resemble the cocoa-nut with a hard skin and clear milk inside.'

'And how did you attire yourselves?'

'The ladies wore flowing white robes and fragrant flowers in their hair. Some wore blue ribbons at their waists, and bodices with pearl buttons and white lace shawls. The men wore robes with golden belts. All wore golden sandals.'

Ellis had not actually read anything about Atlantean clothing, but she'd recently discovered the illustrated plates of a very beautiful book in Miss Stranks' library, *The Myths of Greece and Rome* full of dreamy-eyed goddesses posing in filmy white dresses and flowers in their hair. Miss Stranks seemed delighted with every new detail she provided and so Ellis began to add a few more.

Sometimes Bradbury appeared, reeling slightly as he plumped down into a chair, his legs splayed out as he fidgeted with his watch. 'Pretend I'm not here,' he mouthed, giving Ellis a wink.

One evening, Ellis was sent to the kitchen for supper. Mrs Frith told her it was 'off' until after 'the event'.

'What's off? What event?'

Mrs Frith rolled her eyes and whacked her wooden spoon inside a pot.

Ellis ran up to the red parlour and was surprised to find Mabel and Bradbury shunting furniture. An octagonal table had been set with a vase of dark red roses, a globe of the world, a halved oval of violet-coloured crystal, and a feathered mask. A single carver chair had been painted gold and was positioned in front of the fireplace. Two lamps swaddled in dark red lace were set on the mantelpiece.

'Sit, child,' said Miss Stranks. She was dressed entirely in white. A heavy gold pendant hung from her neck threaded on a thick gold chain. Ellis recognised the pendant's complicated pattern from an image on the cover of one of the theosophy journals. The three concentric circles cut with a crucifix shimmered as Miss Stranks moved about. There was a large ring on one of her fingers. The pale puff of hair had been replaced by a firmly pulled back arrangement brushed tightly to one side and held by a series of pins.

'Well?' Miss Stranks spun around to show herself.

Bradbury clapped. 'The addition of the Atlantean Cross is a masterstroke. You are indeed the incarnation of Mrs Besant.'

Miss Stranks clasped her hands together and laughed. It was curious to see her laugh. Her lips seemed too thin and pale to allow for bursts of jollity. She was still laughing when she produced another smaller cross pendant on a length of blue ribbon and swung it back and forth before Ellis' eyes.

'Tie this at your neck.'

Bradbury added the hat and veil.

'Pretend none of us are here,' he said.

'Remember, child,' said Miss Stranks. 'You are truly blessed. You have the gift. Do not disappoint. Simply do as you have learned. Take us back to Atlantis.'

It seemed a fuss for one of her usual recitals. Everyone fell still at the ringing of the doorbell. All the lights were extinguished, except for the two lamps on the mantelpiece. Through the veil Ellis saw Mabel usher in several figures. She looked up at Miss Stranks who was standing beside her, her white dress glowing in the half-light. Three women and two gentlemen sat down and peered at her. Miss Stranks took a breath and raised a hand.

'Welcome. Be still. Listen and watch. For it is time. It is here. Come to me! Oh Wisdom of the Ancients, of Masters of Truth and Light. For we have been visited by one who has travelled so far and she has entrusted us to hear her tales of that fair and grand city—Atlantis.'

One of the ladies raised her opera glasses to peer at Ellis. 'Atlantis?'

'Mais oui, Madame.' Miss Stranks' voice grew louder. 'A city we all claim to know but what, in fact, do we know of this lost city sunk beneath the murky depths? I am here to tell you that Atlantis is not gone. It is here right now in this room, in the form of this child who has travelled thence via the astral plane. Speak, child, speak.'

Miss Stranks' hand tightened on her shoulder. Ellis was breathing so hard the veil sucked in and out. Sweat had begun to trickle underneath her arms. The pendant felt cold and heavy at her neck. Bradbury stepped forward and addressed the guests.

'Ladies and gentlemen. You have been selected for this evening's private viewing on the proviso that you shall not pass one word of what you shall witness tonight, for as you can see, our conduit is shy. This is to be expected. Timidity is a sign of sensitivity. Reticence is an indication of authenticity.'

'Be assured Sir, we are both honoured *and* discreet,' one of the gentlemen said.

The woman beside him tapped her fan on the arm of her chair in agreement.

'Speak child, speak!' Miss Stranks moved to stand behind her chair. Her hands went to Ellis' shoulders. 'You are amongst friends here, child. You may speak now.'

Ellis stiffened as Miss Stranks' fingers moved in underneath the back of the veil.

'We are all at the ready.'

Ellis felt the fingers move towards her neck. She jolted forward. Miss Stranks pulled her back and pinned her down to the chair.

'Do you want to remain of use in this house, or would you prefer to return from whence you came?' she whispered.

Oh God. Now Ellis understood it all.

What do you wear? Miss Stranks had asked during the long hours drilling Ellis on details of Atlantean life. She'd never dared correct her. She'd always answered, *They wore white robes, Miss.* Never once had she replied using the words 'we' or 'I'. She'd never pretended she'd been in Atlantis herself.

'There was no poverty, hunger or begging in that great land, was there child?' Miss Stranks was saying. 'Do not be shy. You're amongst friends here. True believers of the cause.'

'Hear, hear,' said one of the guests.

Miss Stranks' fingers caught hold of the blue ribbon at her neck. She tugged at it so hard, Ellis coughed. She saw a sliver of light appear at the door. A white figure sidled in. It was Kitty. Ellis' heart lifted. Kitty crossed herself with her white hanky, raised her chin and put her shoulders back. *Chin up chaps. We must stick together, you and I.* She knew that's what Kitty's signal meant. She had to go through with it, or else.

'Atlantis is a fair city …' Ellis heard the familiar words stumble out. The ribbon relaxed at her neck. 'We walk the grand streets drenched in golden sun ... We worship the God Poseidon, founder of our land, father of Atlas. We are peaceful. We are all free.'

After the guests had been bundled out, up went the lights. Ellis blinked at the room. Kitty was gone. So too Mr Bradbury.

Miss Stranks' cold fingers tore off the pendant. *'Ordinaire.* Your recital was *ordinaire.* What were you thinking? And Mabel, stop loafing about. Go and instruct Mrs Frith to *halve* all Ellis' meals from now on. Now get out. All of you.'

Ellis ran from the parlour but stopped when she saw Kitty on the stairs. Bradbury was with her.

'But you promised,' Kitty was saying.

'How could I have said anything to her tonight? We had the guests.'

'But you promised you would.'

Bradbury stepped up towards Kitty and kissed her on the mouth. Kitty clung onto him, kissing him back, her hands running through his hair.

'Bradbury?' Miss Stranks shouted from the parlour.

He tried to pull away, but Kitty kept kissing him.

'Stop it,' he said, unpeeling her hands. 'Do you want to risk everything?'

'Don't you? Let her see us. Let her see what she *must* already know.'

'Bradbury? Where are you?' called Miss Stranks.

'Be patient Kitty. That's all I ask.'

Kitty stepped back, blinked at Ellis, turned on her heel and ran upstairs.

Ellis did not return to her bedroom as ordered, but crept back up to listen in the shadows as Kitty argued with Miss Stranks somewhere above.

'Ellis? I thought I saw you there.' It was Mabel flitting along the hallway.

'Is that where Kitty sleeps? Up there in the attic room?'

Mabel nodded.

'But Miss Stranks' room isn't up there, is it? She's down the hall in the one with the double doors.'

Ellis returned to her room and lay on her bed. She stared out through the barred window at the diluted city stars. *You and I must stick together, Ellis.* It didn't sound as if Kitty meant to at all.

When the house was quiet Ellis felt her way in the dark. Three flights up, she found the door. She could hear Kitty sobbing.

'Kitty?'

Kitty sat bolt upright in her bed. 'Oh. It's you.' She lay back down and pulled the bedclothes up around her.

Ellis waited.

'Well, what do you want? You know she'll roast you alive if she sees you up here.'

'I wanted to see you. I wanted to talk.'

'I don't know how you can show your face. I didn't think you'd go through with it. I thought you'd lock yourself in your room or refuse, like I do when she tries to get me to perform for her cronies like a circus seal.'

'But I didn't know what she wanted me to do. Not until I was in there with all those people.' Ellis rubbed at her neck where Miss Stranks had pulled the ribbon tighter and tighter. If she hadn't played along, how hard would Miss Stranks have pulled, until she'd choked?

'Don't take me for a fool, Ellis. You may play the sweet country innocent, but you knew exactly what you were doing, trying to ingratiate yourself with her. And with *him*.'

Ellis felt her throat tighten. She began to cry in loud, rolling sobs.

'Shh,' said Kitty. 'They'll hear us.'

Ellis knelt down and covered her face with her hands. She'd grown so thin, she could feel the bones sticking out beneath her skin. That's all she was now, pain, bones, humiliation and skin. She flinched as she felt a hand touch her shoulder.

'Get up.' Kitty took her by the hand. 'Shh now. Come here. Lie with me.'

Kitty led her to the bed, raised the counterpane and laid it over her. Ellis had never felt anything as soft, the mattress, the pillows, the gentle hands of Kitty as she stroked her hair. Ellis stopped crying and looked up at Kitty's cornflower eyes.

'Shh,' said Kitty.

She felt Kitty lie down behind her, her hands clasp about her waist. She felt Kitty stroke her hair, and kissed her lightly on the cheek.

'I know,' she said. 'We're both trapped on the same damned sinking ship.'

And at that moment Ellis knew she had never felt so wretched, or so loved.

She woke to the sound of Kitty's shouts. The bed was empty. It was still dark.

'I will *not!*'

She went to listen at the door. She could hear footsteps. Voices. There was a moment of silence broken by an unknown man's thundering voice.

'You will do as Miss Stranks tells you Kitty, today, tomorrow, and for the entire duration of ... until the *accouchement.*'

Accouchement? Ellis knelt at the keyhole but there was only black. There were no more voices. She waited for Kitty but she didn't come. She huddled under the blankets as the grey dawn light filled the room. Church bells pealed in the distance. There was the sound of Mabel's first gong. Ellis waited for it to finish and made her way back down carefully to her room.

After a meagre breakfast, she found Kitty back at the desk in the blue parlour pounding away on the typewriting machine. Her hair wasn't done. Her face looked silvery, her eyes were puffy. Before Ellis could speak, Miss Stranks arrived clapping her hands.

'Sunday is a day of work.' She glared at Ellis. 'You, go to the other parlour.'

Ellis paced about the room next door. *Ordinaire*, Miss Stranks had called her performance. She wondered if this was the moment Miss Stranks would toss her out. *Don't let her know you're scared of her*, Kitty had said. Several gongs came and went. Finally, Miss Stranks swept in. She didn't look at Ellis, but went straight to the octagonal table and pounced on the violet crystal. She moved to her usual station at the windows, the sun streaming in behind her, and held the crystal up so that it cast diamonds across her face.

'Such a plain little object when you see only its outer skin. But from where I stand, it contains a glittering prize.' Miss Stranks peered down at the street. 'Why, there he is again, that God-forsaken tramp.' She rapped on the windowpane. 'You down there. Get away. Go and bother someone else.'

She turned back to Ellis. 'Man reaps what he sows, does he not? Which brings me swiftly to the matter at hand. What will you sow, Ellis? Seeds of hope and prosperity, or doom and austerity?'

Ellis felt the heat rise to her face. 'I don't know.'

'Oh don't play the *ingénue* with me. You've already sewn your bitter crop, as per your appalling performance last night. I've said before you are truly blessed and I've said that like me, you appear to have the gift. It was a mistake to tell you these things. I see that now.'

Ellis stared down at the carpet. The silhouette of Miss Stranks was overlaid with the carpet's dark patterns flowing like rivers, knotted and parting and knotting again.

'Life is series of choices. Frittering away your God-given talents is one choice. It means very little to me what you do, of course, unless you intend to cause me trouble. Are you a troublemaker, Ellis? Is that why you came? I know your type.'

Ellis looked up. Miss Stranks was stroking the crystal as if it were a pet.

'You think you are made of stronger stuff because you come from the country. But you forget, I also know the hardships of country life. My father was a shearer, as tough as a tree. Not one of those trees with wispy branches and feathery leaves. A tree with branches so strong you could string up two men and it wouldn't break. My mother ran an hotel in the country. The bar was her stage. Every joy and horror of the world unfolded there. I can't tell you how many drunken admirers and detractors we turned out every night. It wasn't a pretty life, Ellis. But for all my misfortunes, I chose to develop my own gifts. I suppose everybody has told you how I saw the Virgin Mary walk out from the scrub behind the cattle yards when I was eight years old. There she was in her blue mantle. Of all people on God's earth, Our Lady chose me. She had these bits of wattle seed and sticks in her hair and she brushed them off. Just like that. She smiled at me. At me alone, nobody else, and in that moment, I knew I was truly blessed for evermore. People laughed when I told them. I didn't care. I've been ridiculed and underestimated all my life. But they won't dare to after Sunday next. Why? Because I am not careless, Ellis. Like you, I know what it is to go to bed hungry, to wake in the morning so thirsty you have to lick the dew from the grass to have a drink.'

She raised her head.

'Go on. Take a good hard look at this room and everything in it.'

Ellis glanced at the gilt-framed paintings, the cut glass ornaments glittering on the mantelpiece, the walls of leather-bound books.

'Every item proves I've made a life for myself. I will not risk losing so much as a button for anything or anyone. Understood? So, your choice is quite simple. It is time to nail your colours to the mast. Either you pull your weight as part of our crew and venture on with us to Atlantis, or you disembark.'

Chapter
NINETEEN

Rennie flailed about on the bed. How anybody was expected to carve a decent night's sleep from this lump of rock was beyond her wildest imaginings. She'd tried lying on top of the musty bedclothes to escape the blankets that twirled around her like strangling vines, but it only caused her to become cold and shiver in the clammy damp. Her bones ached. Her mind leapt between one startling image and the next. Two letters? Both from Irving? Which damned one was the truth? Every so often she sat up, lit a cigarette and swung the match about, trying in vain to discover the source and proximity of an alarming cascading waterfall sound.

She woke exhausted and fearing the first day of her new life had already rotted on the bough. There was the taste of earth in her mouth. She whipped out her pocket mirror, half-expecting to find her tongue had been colonised by a brownish moss.

She sighed at the room which was washed with a gelatinous light. The window had steamed up like a milky eye. She wiped the hem of her nightdress across the glass. It had stopped raining at last, but the view was obscured by the sporadic tumble of water overflowing from the gutters above. In between bursts, she could make out the grey huddle of buildings. She watched as a bent-up stick of a man stumbled along the muck-plaited street, coughing and spitting as he went. If he turned left at the corner, she would go back to Irving on his blasted steam ship. If he turned right, she would ... well, she'd do something. She peered at the man. Good Lord. He kept stumbling on, charging at the rubble, straight ahead.

She shoved up the window and considered the lopsided balcony opposite. The threat of more rain hung like a wave waiting to break. At least the sun was doing its best to prise the clouds apart. She squinted down at the gleam of the street, fished about for her sketchbook and began to draw the missing slats of the shutters opposite, the mouldering bricks and sopping wood. That would take her mind off things. At the sound of a rough laugh coming through the shutters, Rennie stepped back from the window. She watched in horrified delight as a chubby fist appeared, followed by the now partially naked pink feather-hatted woman she'd spoken to on the ferry the night before. The woman coughed as she emptied a bucket from the balcony. It was as if Rennie had stepped inside one of the Dutch masters' paintings where moody damsels with pouting lips did ordinary things, filling milk jugs or pouring tea.

Tea, she thought. *That would jolly things along.*

She threw on her dressing gown and ventured down the stairs.

It was dim on the stairs, but she didn't dare try the light switch.

'Hell-oo?'

She hoped Ellis was already up, boiling a kettle or stirring a hearty pot of oats. The kitchen, however, was empty. She pondered lighting the stove herself, but everything looked too antiquated and perilous.

The back door needed to be tugged at. Reluctantly it opened to a sodden world. The only signs of life were the three fat bronze flies waiting on the wall. Rennie shooed them away and frowned at the rain-battered yard, with its falling down fence, wet logs of firewood and turgid jungle of knee-high weeds. The path to the outhouse was partially flooded. There was nothing else for it. She eased off her shoes, hitched her dressing gown up into her belt and dashed out.

The bathroom was an equally sorry affair. She breathed only through her mouth as she stood in the humid dankness to scrub her hands with a surprisingly fine rose-scented soap. *Good heavens*, she thought, eyeing herself in a blotchy sliver of mirror. *Imagine if they could see me now.*

When she returned to the kitchen, there was still no sign of her landlady.

'Hell-oo?'

She decided to try the room at the front of the house where she'd heard the typewriter pounding away. A faded sign saying *Private!* was nailed to the door. Rennie knocked, and waited. There was no response. She knocked again and put her ear to the door.

'Ellis? I was rather hoping for a cup of tea.'

Her voice echoed around the empty house. She felt like an actor who'd arrived too late, calling out her lines from the wings of a theatre already emptied of its audience. She knocked again and turned the handle, pushing ever so slightly on the door.

'I do hope I haven't disturbed you.'

There was nobody in there. Rennie gasped as her eyes adjusted to the veritable Aladdin's cave. Everything seemed to glitter and hum in the soupy dark. A red and black striped gentleman's smoking jacket hung on the back of a chair set at a narrow desk, groaning beneath scraps of paper engulfing an ancient-looking typewriter. An exotic red and gold counterpane had been thrown back against the bedposts of a heavy brass bed, accompanied by two purple silk cushions embroidered with Oriental dragons in silver and scarlet thread. A statuesque amber-coloured wardrobe was jammed in behind the door. Lloyd's gloomy heirloom wardrobes had always reminded her of upended coffins. In contrast, this one was enlivened by an intricately carved frieze of leaves and voluptuous fruit—not the kind of thing Rennie had expected to find in a down-at-heel place like this.

Her heart thudded in time with the sound of water pinging into buckets. She approached the wardrobe to brush her fingers over the warm, silky wood, reading its carvings as if they were Braille. What a contrast to the lodgers' room upstairs. There was no nauseating odour for a start. This room smelt of Christmas, a mix of orange peel, rum, cinnamon, cloves and pipe tobacco. The whole effect screamed *authentic bohemian*.

A dark thrill rose inside of her, for even though she was caught in the most despicable of conundrums herself, she'd stumbled upon something deliciously curious. She looked over at the desk where a stack of paper teetered on the edge. She couldn't help but take a peek. Several papers drifted towards her feet. She looked down at the words *Clements Bros. Wares of Distinction*, and the listing of items and costs in neat columns. But the desk held the real treasure: *Water lilies?? linked to the story of Lotis who was … Proper name for fountain-makers? Fish pond. Fountain. Why stop there? Moses will surely aspire to a moat.*

Rennie flicked back further.

Mr Moses grimaced at the advancing army of nettles preparing to breach his perimeter … And back further still. *On planting parsnips by the light of a waning moon, it has been claimed farmers of yesteryear worked without their trousers when planting out their parsnips crops, allegedly as a way of testing the coolness of the ground …*

Rennie let out a laugh and thumbed through a large scrapbook, stuffed with clippings. All of them were the same, years of columns titled 'The Green-eyed Gardener'. The most recent one began with *On planting parsnips by the waning moon.*

Her eyes ran down to the name of the author, *Scribbly Gum.* She'd heard of Scribbly Gum. Bertha's tedious friends at the Ambassadors Café had argued endlessly over it. Apparently they found Scribbly Gum objectionable. They thought it was 'rum' to poke fun at some poor, earnest chap, making him the butt of jokes as he went about improving his garden. What was wrong with wanting your garden to outshine all the others in the street?

But this was simply too funny to believe. Was her landlady—Ellis Gilbey—really Scribbly Gum, or was it some sinister and rather sad obsession? But Rennie knew it was in fact true, for it was too deliciously incongruous to be otherwise. While the well-heeled argued over a wronged Mr Moses, or sided with the author's irreverent jibes, Scribbly Gum sat dreaming up mischievous things in her dank little room surrounded by an eclectic array of oddments, tucked away in a falling down slum terrace where the only garden was a fetid yard choked with dust, mud and weeds.

Rennie jumped as she heard a gramophone begin to crank up across the street, followed by a woman's raucous laugh. She stood listening and waiting, her heart leaping like a hare. It was the same feeling she'd felt as a child when she'd stolen into her father's study and drawn pictures in his precious books, or had waited for her mother to reprimand her for tossing her kippers to the dog.

'Morning Alf,' she heard the woman call out.

Only a ragged curtain separated Rennie from being seen. If a gust of wind lifted it, she'd be caught red-handed in Ellis' *Private!* room. She turned to go, but was stopped in her tracks by the watercolour glinting above the desk. Tears came to her eyes. It reminded her of Sussex, of walking through the summer hills, sketch book in hand, her father striding ahead of her in the gloriously gentle afternoon light telling her to look at the butterflies hovering, to listen to the wrens chattering, to watch the orange crepuscular rays of sun as they streamed out from behind the clouds, to study the dark green lines of the hedgerows in the valley hurrying off into infinity.

She stared at her own face reflected in the glass, wishing it were as easy to be transported to another place by simply remembering it. She turned as the sound of boots splashed in the street. A shadow flickered across the windowpane. She hurried from the room and almost forgot to close the door. As she bounded back up the stairs, she could hear the *Private!* sign scraping back and forth.

Panting slightly, she watched on from her upper window. Ellis Gilbey was down there in the street, one hand held up shielding her eyes as the woman on the balcony called to her.

'Any news we should know about, Els?'

'I thought you'd heard enough.'

'What do you reckon, Clarrie? Are we up to here with news, or not?'

The bent-up little man called Clarrie picked his way through the puddles towards them.

'So you survived the hurly burly, then Clarrie?' Ellis said.

'The tempest must unleash its fury now and then.' He waved an old book above his head. '*Stair above stair the eddying waters rose.*'

Good heavens, Rennie thought, the poor misshapen little fellow was quoting one of the Lake poets, though exactly whom she couldn't quite recall.

An old woman in a bonnet appeared and began to whisk a broom at the sea of brown puddles lapping at her step.

'Morning Mrs Liddy,' Ellis said. 'Do you want me to read out the papers this morning?'

'What, dear?'

'I reckon we'll be right now,' Clarrie said. 'It's grand of you to ask, but my cousin'll be by any moment now to pick us up.'

'Good for you. I'm sure he will.'

'Pardon me,' Clarrie said attempting a stiff little bow. *'But now my heart is heavy, and would take lone counsel from a night of sleepless care. Pardon me, that I say farewell—farewell!'*

'Oh it cuts me up Els. After all this time. Well it don't feel right. To think we have to head off to all these different places, places we don't know.'

The pink-feather woman fluffed up her hair as she spoke. Her ample breasts bobbed about in grubby sockets of satin and lace. Rennie noticed how Ellis didn't answer but turned away. The woman didn't seem perturbed by Ellis' snub, in fact she seemed encouraged and crouched down to speak through a flurry of stockings hanging from the balcony rails.

'Els, how's that late night lady lodger of yours? Me and Alf was just saying, now there's a pretty windfall to land in your lap.'

Rennie pulled back from the window. *Late night lady lodger?* They were talking about *her.* The woman's voice had dropped to one of those huffy whispers actors produced, supposedly inaudible to the other players on stage but capable of reaching the back row of an audience.

'I thought it was the Queen of Sheba herself, when I had a look. Slumming it down here, is she, with the riff-raff?' Rennie couldn't hear what Ellis replied, but it was clear by the brusqueness of her manner she didn't want to be drawn into the conversation. 'What do you say, Els? I'll bring another bottle over later, eh? Take a look at her myself.'

Rennie heard Ellis say something about being too busy packing up house.

'And compiling my gardening book,' she added. 'Now that the whole world knows about it.'

The woman let out a cackle as Ellis shoved open the front door, and made her way briskly down the hallway.

Rennie lit a cigarette. Of course the neighbours had noticed her. The whole street—or what was left of it—seemed to have its ears and eyes on stems. What a fool she'd been. Any one of them might have caught her poking about in Ellis' private things. She'd read of lodging house tenants being hauled before the courts for 'barbering', accused of rummaging in other people's belongings, pleading the lame excuse of being drunk or disorientated, even under the spell of sleepwalking.

She could hear Ellis charging about the house. There was the sound of water stuttering through the pipes, and at last, the happy clatter of breakfast things. Rennie stubbed out her cigarette, applied a grateful, innocent lodger's smile, and went downstairs.

She hesitated at the door of the kitchen. The kettle fretted on the hob but there was no sign of any food. Ellis was bent over the kitchen table, still wearing her squashy hat and threadbare coat, frowning as she circled something in the newspaper.

'Hell-oo?'

'Morning,' Ellis said, not looking up before turning away.

Rennie drew out a chair which scraped rather loudly across the floor. 'Gosh,' she said, trying to collect herself. 'But how marvellous. I see you get the *Herald* in.' She craned her neck to try and see what Ellis had been reading. Several items in the *accommodation wanted* column had been marked heavily in pencil.

'Tea?' Ellis said.

'Oh yes, please.' Rennie almost added *China tea with sugar and milk*; that was the line she trotted out to provoke Lloyd and fluster Mrs Chisholm. She managed to stop herself in time. 'Tea would be—marvellous.'

She watched the way Ellis' compact frame cut through the gloom of the kitchen. The economy of her movements seemed to match her carefully meted out speech, as if nothing should be wasted, material or otherwise. Judging by the state of the furniture cobbled together from kerosene tins, apple crates and tea chests, nothing here had ever been replaced or tossed away.

'Sleep all right, despite the tempest?' Ellis said.

'Yes, thank you. It was—everything was—absolutely marvellous.'

Rennie thought she saw Ellis smile to herself as she took off her hat and coat and hang them on the back of a chair. She waited as Ellis ran her hand through her hair, which was thick and curly, with the odd silver streak running through the dark, and cut very strikingly into a bob.

She watched as Ellis rolled up the sleeves of her cardigan and swept the crumbs from the tablecloth into her hand. She heard her whistle lightly through her teeth. Several sparrows appeared as if by arrangement, hopping in over the back step. Ellis whistled again as she tossed the crumbs into the yard. The birds flitted off.

'I'll cook some oats.'

'Oh, yes please, I could eat a horse.' Rennie's voice bounced around the room. She thought she saw Ellis stop in her tracks for a moment and blink, as if Rennie had said something terribly wrong. 'But only if that's what you usually eat for breakfast,' Rennie added quickly. 'The oats, I mean. Not the horse.'

Rennie laughed, waiting for Ellis to join in, but instead she sighed.

'As you can see, there's not much that's *usual* here anymore. So we may as well go ahead and do whatever is usual or unusual. What do you say?'

Ellis' eyes were on her now. They were a disconcertingly pale, solid, opal green. As Rennie was handed a cup of tea, she realised this had been the longest utterance her landlady had made so far.

Rennie returned the stare, raised her cup and smiled her brightest smile.

'When in doubt, Ellis, I say chin-chin.'

While Ellis washed the dishes, Rennie scanned every column of the newspaper. Her disappearance hadn't yet made it to the missing persons column. It would, she supposed, on the following day. Perhaps the police had advised Lloyd to wait. This would fit their plan of pretending she had been abducted by a bunch of toughs, rather than fleeing of her own volition in order to save herself.

She turned to the page where Ellis had circled rooms for rent. She'd never bothered reading this section before. The rooms looked surprisingly reasonable with *every comfort, clean kitchen, lovely view*. Perhaps she and Ellis could go out together to scout for a place. Ellis would know where to go, what to ask, and the right amount to pay without being fleeced. There'd be safety in numbers, if nothing else.

She watched as Ellis bustled about the kitchen and disappeared up the hallway towards her room. Rennie waited as she heard her opening the bedroom door, wondering if she might sense the air had been disturbed. Thankfully, nothing happened. Rennie breathed out in relief, but despite a belly full of food and a fresh cigarette, the feeling of alarm that had dogged her all night, returned to besiege her.

She frowned at the *rooms to rent* column, raised her head and looked about. Was this the joyless landscape awaiting her now, the brown stuffy air of a rented house? Either she gave in and returned to her 'comfortable life' or she stumbled on alone, sentencing herself to a world of poverty, sleeping in rooms as gloomy as tombs, sighing in kitchens riddled with buckets of rain, forced to frequent fetid outhouses furnished with squares of newspaper hanging on a rusted hook, and slimy bathrooms with sputtering taps. It had been all very well to sit in a hot bath in a house on the harbour, entertaining ideas of striking out on her own, giving birth to a brave new artist self as a recorder of life's significant and harsh realities, but could she really survive trading the 'security' Lloyd offered for a life of this?

She touched her hand to the bruises on her arm. *She's a danger to herself. She runs off without explanation.* That's all Lloyd had to say. And when her brother Irving finally arrived from England and displayed his vast array of fiddly behaviours, not least the incessant shoulder-twitch, Lloyd would muster even more ammunition for his cause. *It runs in the family, these nervous complaints.*

My family, she thought. What did those two words mean to her now? They'd been robbed of their true meaning since her parents had died, and her brother had teamed up with Lloyd to betray her. *All you need do is appear at the dock*, Irving's letter had said. She was not that stupid. Surely even Irving knew that. She tossed aside the newspapers and rummaged for her cigarettes. As she did so, an advertisement caught her eye.

Lane Cove
J. T. Bickley Real Estate
*
***
!!Famous Easy Terms!!
One Pound Down, 10 Shillings a Month
Splendid Roomy Blocks, Market Gardener's Paradise
MAKING GENEROUS PROFITS NOW
For Poultry, Orchards
Flower Farmlets
***
*

She stared at it. *Flower Farmlets at Lane Cove.* The diamond shape shimmered as she read the advertisement again. Lane Cove. Wasn't that where Bertha vanished to with her swarthy sheik for glamorous all night parties? Or was it somewhere on the Hawkesbury? She couldn't quite recall. But even if it was the same place, which she doubted, Australia was so big, and besides, she had no interest in being swept up in Bertha's party-going nonsense anymore. The image of a pretty little farm growing flowers swept through her mind. How noble, simple, humble and *real* a life that would be. And how desperately now she wanted it.

She leapt up from the table and bit at her knuckles as she tried to think. She frowned at the yard. It was bleak and damp except for one bright diamond of water trapped on a nasturtium leaf. It was then she made the link: the diamonds of her engagement ring and the diamond-shaped advertisement for the little flower farm at Lane Cove.

She stared at the ring. It would fetch a good price, along with the other few pieces she'd salvaged from the house. After all these months of fretting, one night spent lying awake in a dingy lodging house had crystallised her thoughts. It all seemed so clear now. She would not—and could not—ever go back to Lloyd. Tomorrow she'd pack a picnic and venture out to Lane Cove to sit in the winter sun amid the wildflowers and gentle ferns, listening to the swish of the eucalypts, the bounding of kangaroos and the laughter of kookaburras, far away from the city with its backstabbers, cuckolds and gossipers. She'd bunk down in a cosy country inn and explore the environs, assessing the possibility of buying a flower farmlet of her own. She didn't know if she *could* buy a farmlet of her own, legally, but *damnation and blast it all*—she'd certainly try.

She looked up at the squeak of birds darting overhead. Two green parrots pushed their narrow shoulders through the air, the iridescent oranges, greens and yellows of their under-feathers flaming in the sun.

She turned to look at the back of Ellis' house, the faltering eaves, lopsided windows, and the crooked little rooms. If she stayed here while she exacted her plan, it would be the perfect foil. Despite its obvious privations, Ellis seemed genuinely kind, honest and intriguingly odd. Not only that, it appeared she was the real Scribbly Gum. Rennie imagined Bertha shrieking with delight on hearing this, except that Rennie was never going to speak to Bertha ever again. Yes, this was the place. There were no other tenants rattling about who might be tempted to report her whereabouts to the police, or undertake a little 'barbering' themselves.

Rennie strode back into the house. 'Hell-oo? Ellis? I was wondering ...?'

But her question was interrupted by a cry of 'Watcho!' followed by a tremendous blast so strong it actually moved her hair. She coughed as a flurry of damp plaster hurried down the walls.

'Gosh,' Rennie said, as Ellis entered the room, seemingly oblivious. 'Is that coming from the bridge? I thought they might have downed tools given all the rain.'

'Rain or shine, foul or fair.'

'But how ghastly,' Rennie said, frowning up at the ceiling. 'Will it hold? Or shall we all be killed?'

Ellis shrugged. 'It only has to stand for another week or so.'

'I see, another week.' That was sooner than she'd thought, but it would have to do. 'And then, Ellis, if you don't mind me asking, where will you go?'

'Well that's the burning question.' Ellis eyed Rennie sharply as she said this. Her eyes really were very arresting. There was an unusual depth and yet a definite guardedness to them, as if their owner knew they might betray her inner thoughts too readily if she allowed other people to study them for long.

Ellis flicked her eyes away and stepped back, as if unsettled by Rennie's proximity.

Rennie smiled and persisted. 'The burning question to which, I take it, there's still no burning answer?'

Ellis moved past her and began to bolt the back door. Rennie tried again.

'I realise you must wonder why I'm here, why I've come. As I said last night, like everybody else I've been transfixed by the building of the bridge. But when I read about those heart-rending auctions at The Rocks, I had to up sticks and see for myself, not only to record history in the making—or the unmaking, should I say—but to *live* it, to *breathe* it, to soak it in.' Rennie stopped to watch another flurry of dust race down from a cornice. 'You must all be beside yourselves. I don't know how you live with it.'

'Most don't. They've already left.'

'But not you, Ellis.'

'So it seems.'

'But why?'

Ellis scooped up a section of the newspaper, folded it in half and stuffed it into her coat pocket. 'Why is not always the most useful question we think it is.'

'Indeed,' Rennie said. 'But I was wondering if I might ask you something.'

Rennie squeezed the diamond-shaped advertisement in her pocket. If she was going to save herself, she had to blunder on *rain or shine, foul or fair.*

'Yes?' Ellis placed her hat over the tousle of her hair and began to wind a long fraying silk scarf around her neck. The rim of her hat hid the upper part of her face. The scarf was pulled up to obscure her mouth.

'My armour,' Ellis said, causing the scarf to suck in and out as she spoke. 'Against the dust.'

'Doubling ingeniously as a disguise,' Rennie said. She felt her eyes fill with tears again, for the whole answer had just materialised in front of her as if by a miracle. She gathered her hair over one shoulder in one single tress and scissored her fingers across it.

'I hope you don't mind me saying so, Ellis, but before you put on your hat, I was admiring the dashing style of your hair. I wondered if you'd be kind enough to recommend me your hairdresser.'

CHAPTER
TWENTY

Hell, Ellis thought. What had she agreed to now? She sighed at the sparrows as she carried a chair out into the yard and set it in a triangle of sun. Once, she'd been talked into cutting Girl's hair in exchange for a bottle of grog and it had been about as easy as trying to wash a cat.

Rennie smiled one of her brilliant smiles as she raised her hands in a yawn and sat on the waiting chair, her hair glowing like polished rosewood in the sun.

'Did you grow your own flowers here once?' she said as she flipped open a notebook. 'I've spied a few remnants doing battle with the weeds.'

Ellis glanced down at the book. The silhouettes of ruined buildings filled one page. On the other, petals of a nasturtium flower appeared before her eyes in a few deft strokes.

'There was a bit of a garden here once,' Ellis began to say. 'Before ...'

'Before all this beastly bridge building business? *The final nail in history's coffin*, one of the newspapers called it, and seeing it here, being right here perched on the edge of the abyss, I can only agree. Most people prefer to remain blind to the extent of the disruption of others, don't you think? They don't understand we're all a link in the golden chain. So long as their bacon arrives piping hot for breakfast and the rain holds off for their tennis parties, and their lawns are clipped.'

The words *link in a golden chain* hung in the air. Ellis tried not to let her old bias rise up. Hundreds of thousands of people like Rennie dabbled in theosophy, as was their right. It still was very fashionable, its appeal perfectly understandable. And whatever her lodgers believed or not, it had absolutely nothing to do with her.

Ellis set the scissors on a crate next to a bowl of water, took a breath and considered Rennie's skull. The scalp was as white as wax and she wondered if the hair might bleed when she cut it, like Dryope and the purple Lotis flower. She dipped her hand into the warm water and sprinkled some on the hair.

'How short?'

That fluttering sensation had started again in her chest. She stepped back as Rennie produced an ivory-coloured Bakelite comb, its spine stuck with white and red roses. She tapped it on the base of her skull.

'There-ish, don't you think?'

The cuts and bruises on Rennie's hands were raw in the light. Whoever or whatever this woman was escaping was merciless.

'All right.' Ellis took up a tress and snipped it off. She watched as it slithered like a live thing down Rennie's back and landed beside her shoe. Rennie moved her head to look down at it.

'Gosh.'

'You want me to go on?'

'Rather. This is all so—so incongruous.' A spurt of cigarette smoke shot up as Rennie began to laugh. 'Oh dear, I shall have to remain very still and quiet or we'll both end up dealing with a rats' nest.'

Ellis waited until the laughter stopped, eased the scissors under another ribbon of Rennie's hair and cut. This time the blades sounded clean and decisive. She supposed she might get into a rhythm the same as she did on the typewriter, but Rennie had begun to wave her arms about.

'I've been sitting here, Ellis, wracking my brains trying to remember the most eye-popping article I saw in the newspaper the other day. Now I've remembered. It was to do with some dreadful backward little village in the Austrian Tyrol. They'd introduced a bob tax on every woman who dared to pursue the "decadent mode" of bobbing her hair. A bob tax? Can you believe it? I had to read it over twice.'

Ellis took another snip. 'Yes.'

'You can? Really?' Ellis stopped snipping as Rennie waved her cigarette. 'Everybody I told wouldn't hear a bar of it. *Oh you do speak such utter rot*, they said. Do you think I could find the blasted article to prove them wrong? I damn well turned the house upside down. If only I could remember what those venal officials said in defence of inventing this travesty. A bob tax, I ask you. Whatever next?'

Ellis waited for Rennie to be still again. There was the sound of dripping all around them in the yard, as if a wall of vapour had risen between them and the outside world. In the distance, the hum of the harbour wore on, interspersed by a series of earth-shattering blasts. She placed the scissors near Rennie's left ear. It too looked waxen, a delicate sculpture not made of flesh. Ellis reached out her hand to touch it, to brush away a stray hair. She brushed a few more from Rennie's shoulders, flicking her fingers down her back, over the shoulder blades, down the soft curve of her back. She was glad Rennie couldn't see her face. There was another loop of hair on Rennie's neck. Then she realised. It wasn't hair. It was the edge of a bruise, blooming like a dark flower towards the lower reaches of the skull.

'I already feel half naked and gloriously free,' Rennie laughed. 'Is that how you felt when you had yours lopped?'

Ellis tried to think how best to deflect yet another pointed question. *'But if a woman have long hair, it is a glory to her, for her hair is given to her for her covering.'*

'Good Lord, again.'

Rennie jolted back and clapped her hands. Ellis withdrew the scissors just in time.

'St Paul, verse fifteen, chapter eleven, the first book of the Corinthians, actually,' she said, before she could stop herself.

Rennie swivelled around and tried to look up at her. Ellis could see down into the rose and ivory cavern of her mouth.

'But that's exactly what those fiendish bob taxers trotted out in support of their case against the hairdressers wanting to follow the—oh, I've forgotten exactly what else they said.'

'To follow the fads of Paris fashion?'

Rennie threw her head back and laughed so hard, the few remaining tresses danced a jig.

'I cannot believe it. You've remembered the entire dastardly thing word for word. Good heavens, you *are* full of tricks.' Ellis turned away, pretending to do something with the bowl of water while Rennie continued. 'Well, that is the most remarkable thing I've heard in an absolute age. You're the first articulate, erudite, worldly person I've met since wading ashore this wild brown land who not only *reads* the same absurd things as me, but tucks them away in the memory. Who'd have thought? Really, it is the most extraordinary stroke of luck that I came here, don't you think?'

Rennie tossed her spent cigarette at the weeds. Ellis heard it fizzle out. She waited for Rennie to settle again.

'Would you grow them again, if you could? Flowers, I mean,' Rennie said.

'If I could.'

'But you can't?'

Ellis tried to get back into the rhythm of the scissors. The bob was taking shape now. A pile of hair lay at her feet.

'I suppose it depends on the burning answer to the burning question, as I said.'

'Indeed it must.'

Ellis could almost see Rennie's thoughts darting about like bright fish. 'Is it easy, do you think, to grow lots of flowers?' she asked.

'From memory, it takes a bit of work.'

'From memory? I think you've already proved your remarkable capacities on that score. So you've grown flowers before, Ellis? You've plunged your hands into the soil? Watched the buds rise and blossom in the scented air?'

'Yes and no. Years ago.'

'In the country?'

Ellis stopped. That was one too many questions in a row. Ellis waited before she spoke. 'The country and the city.'

'I see. And will you stay in the city, do you think?'

'So it seems.'

'But you wouldn't be averse to the country life.' This was said as a statement, not a question.

'There's no point in feeling averse or not.'

'Oh I see. I expect not.'

Ellis snipped on, trying to make progress before Rennie began firing more questions.

'Me, I love the countryside. I was brought up in the south of England, you see, with sweeping hills and wildflowers and, well, never mind.' Rennie held up a hand. Several diamond rings glinted in the sun. 'I suppose you'll be taking all of your furniture with you wherever you go. The beds, kitchen table and what-not?'

'I'll just need to see how it looks at the front,' Ellis said.

'Of course. Shall I close my eyes?'

Ellis hesitated. It had been easier to work unseen behind. Now she felt exposed. She glanced down at the front of her dress. A lump of porridge had streaked her skirt. She splashed a little water at it.

Rennie's eyelids trembled as she clenched them shut. Ellis directed the blades at Rennie's delicately plucked eyebrow, sliding it slowly across the translucent skin of her temple. She could see the fine lines around the eyes, but even close up, it was hard to tell her age. Early thirties perhaps? That would mean she'd been born just before the turn of the century, around the same time Ellis had last seen Kitty Tate.

'I want the fringe to come down to rest on my eyelashes.' Rennie flashed open her eyes and peered at her. 'Like this.'

It was becoming hard to concentrate. The bird wing sensation was beating so loudly in her chest it was a wonder Rennie couldn't hear it. She slid the blades under the fringe and snipped a dozen or so smallish cuts.

'There,' she said, stepping back. 'All done.'

Rennie looked up and gasped as she patted the back of her neck. 'Hello neck! There you are!' She leapt up and began to dance about as she ran her hand over the new topography of her skull. 'Bertha Collins said I'd look like Louise Brooks if I lopped it off and now that I have, she'll never get to see it. Tell me, Ellis. What do you think? Do I look like a movie star?'

You look like you, she wanted to say. 'See for yourself.' She gestured towards the bathroom and Rennie rushed off. There was a peal of laughter and much splashing of water before she emerged.

'Well this doubles as *my* new disguise, Ellis. Oh but wait. Here.'

Rennie took a note from her pocket and switched on one of her radiant smiles. 'Will that do?'

Ellis waved the money away. 'It's on the house. Speaking of which …' This was her chance to mention giving back some of the rent, but something stopped her. It was Rennie's persistent line of questioning.

What had she been after, asking about tables, beds and chairs? 'It's late. I should be going out.'

Ellis began to sweep the hair into a pile. Rennie came over and touched it with the toe of her shoe.

'I almost feel we should bury it.'

'The birds will make good use of it,' Ellis said. 'Or ...'

A stab of shame stopped her from suggesting Rennie would fetch a good price for the hair. Ellis knew exactly who to sell it to. Rennie touched her arm and smiled at her. Ellis looked down at the hand resting on her arm. She moved away, and continued to sweep.

'I have to go out. I'll wait while you gather up your things.'

'Oh.' Rennie's smile evaporated. 'Well actually, I was going to ask you about my room.'

'The room?'

Rennie's eyes looked even bigger without the heavy frame of her hair, like wide dark glittery lakes.

'Would you mind terribly if I stayed a few more nights?'

Ellis stopped sweeping. *Yes*, she wanted to say. *Yes. Please stay.* 'I'll have to see.'

She looked down as Rennie's touched her arm again. She could feel the heat of her hand move down through the sleeve of her cardigan and all the way down onto her skin.

'There was one more thing I wanted to ask.'

Ellis pulled away to toss the bowl of water at the yard. Rennie opened her cigarette tin, took out a scrunch of newspaper and held it out. Ellis blinked at the words. *Flower Farmlets!! ... one pound down now ... splendid roomy blocks!!!*

'I was wondering if you might allow me to stay, so that I might keep a little *pied-à-terre* here while I find out about securing one of these plots in Lane Cove. Tell me, Ellis, what do you think?'

Pied-à-terre? Ellis wanted to laugh out loud. It sounded like something Miss Stranks would have said, throwing in French words to make herself sound more sophisticated than she was. *Don't blink at me Ellis, with those bloodshot lizardy eyes of yours. If you took the trouble to consult the Larousse dictionary, you'd find it means 'a foot to the ground', a room to call one's own in the middle of the town.*

CHAPTER
TWENTY-ONE

'Q uelle surprise. Look at these crowds.' Miss Stranks' eyes widened above the frantic beating of her fan.

'I'm astonished to hear you are surprised, Miss Stranks,' Kitty said. 'As Mr Bradbury says, rumours are like rabbits. They spread and breed with impunity.'

Miss Stranks shot Kitty a sharp look. 'Alight this instance! *Vite!*'

Ellis felt sick as she stared out at the people flocking at the base of the hall steps.

'No, wait,' said Miss Stranks. Her cheeks were in high colour. 'Bradbury, you shall shepherd me to safety from the mob. Kitty will give out the handbills and mind the door. Ellis, you walk up and down wearing the sandwich boards until Bradbury escorts you backstage to change into your stage attire.'

As Miss Stranks prepared to be helped down, Kitty whispered to Ellis, 'Congratulations. Stranks thinks you'll make a tastier sandwich filling than I ever could.'

The sandwich boards squashed her breasts, bruised her shins and dragged on her neck. It was almost impossible to dodge through the crowds. People laughed and pointed, or bumped into her deliberately.

A boy ran up and tugged a strand of hair which had escaped from the large bonnet Miss Stranks had insisted Ellis wear to hide her face.

'Follow the path!' one man said, as he did a rude little dance behind her. 'I wouldn't mind following that all the way up a dark alleyway.'

Bradbury waved for Ellis to leave the pavement and meet him in the side lane. Her shoulders lifted as he unstrapped the boards.

'That wasn't so bad. Cheer up. Does that feel better?' he said.

'Like I could fly.'

He rearranged the bonnet on top of her hair. 'Don't worry. You'll scrub up all right once you're dressed.'

Ellis looked across to see Kitty frowning at them from the hall steps. *It's all right*, she wanted to say. *I will be all right. And so will you.* She raised her chin and put her shoulders back in solidarity, but Kitty had already turned away.

She followed Bradbury's black boots down the lane, in through a gate and a door at the back of the hall, into the smell of powder, dust and wax. At the top of a flight of stairs, he stopped and motioned towards a door. *Green Room* was painted across it. He motioned for her to look through the keyhole.

The sound of a voice came from the room. It was Miss Stranks. 'Hee-hee-hee, lo, lo, lo, ai-ee-ai-ee-ai-eeee.'

She could just see her, tapping the base of her chin, turning her head, gazing at herself in the mirror as she wriggled her narrow lips out while making squealing sounds. Bradbury bent down beside her and chuckled silently as he looked through the keyhole. He was standing so close to her, she could feel his breath on her cheek.

'Our little secret,' he said, as he motioned for her to follow.

The corridor grew darker as it burrowed further underneath the hall. The walls seemed to fold in overhead. Ellis noticed a red feather caught in a cobweb hanging above, pointing like an arrow. *Stop. Go back.*

'Your quarters, Madam.' Bradbury clicked his heels and made a mock salute.

Her 'stage attire' was hanging on a peg. The simple blue silk dress didn't have buttons and the usual clasps, but was to be wound around and allowed to fall freely except for the golden cord tied at the waist. A pair of Miss Stranks' gold sandals, several sizes too big, made a slapping sound whenever she walked, and would serve as Ellis' Atlantean footwear.

In the dimness, she caught the moving glint of Bradbury's eyes. His hands went to her bonnet and removed it.

'Let me take it off for you. There. That's better. You have such lively hair, Ellis. But they have bruised you, the straps of the sandwich boards.' He moved his hands to her shoulders and down her arms. 'Relax,' he said. 'That is the key. To relax.' He rubbed her shoulders. His hands dropped, moving across the bodice of her dress.

'Sorry,' she heard herself say as she stepped back.

He pulled her to him. 'Shh, now shh.'

His chin jutted into her forehead. Her cheek was squashed against the rise and fall of his shirt. His leg jutted into her skirt. He was panting and saying 'shh, shh' over again, pushing his hands into the front of her dress, lifting up his knee to force hers apart. She was up against the wall now, the back of her head jammed against the cold stone. Her feet were lifted off the ground. She struggled to push him away, but he seemed to be everywhere, on her mouth, on her hips, jabbing up between her legs, thrusting her against the cold stone of the wall.

'Bradbury? Where are you?'

He pulled back so quickly she hit her head against the wall. Once again, the voice of Miss Stranks rang out. One of his hands was at her throat. His eyes challenged her not to make a sound. His breath was all over her, the stink of rum and the stale scent of perfume she recognised—it was the scent of Kitty Tate.

'Bradbury? Are you there?'

He let go and pushed her at the wall, straightened his collar, wiped his face with his sleeve and strode towards the white figure of Miss Stranks.

The back of her head was pounding. The place between her legs ached. She slid to the floor.

'What are you doing lounging about?' Miss Stranks loomed over her. 'Get up this instance. You are not dressed.'

Ellis blinked up at her. Another face appeared. Bradbury's.

'I'm afraid Miss Ellis has been less than cooperative. I have been trying to convince her, 'tis nothing more than a case of nerves.'

'Nerves?' Miss Stranks helped pull her to her feet. 'Bradbury, go and see to Kitty at the front of house.'

She felt like a marionette being jerked about by a puppeteer. Miss Stranks turned her roughly as she wound her into the blue dress, and marched her towards the stage. Then it was Bradbury on her again, his fingers on her neck as he pushed her across the stage towards Miss Stranks. The curtains were still shut. She could hear the shuffle of feet and rising hubbub of voices on the other side.

She blinked at the two blue lace-clad lamps placed on plinths behind a gold-painted chair. Bradbury told her to sit. The Atlantean Cross was a dead weight around her neck. The only thing that kept her seated was knowing Kitty was there, that Kitty alone would believe her and understand.

She closed her eyes and tried to calm her breath. *I am here, but not here*, she told herself. The gong sounded in the wings. Silence fell. The curtains swept back.

Miss Stranks cried out, 'Speak, child, speak!'

She blinked at the sea of faces, the flapping handbills, the restless hats, the clumsy movement of latecomers pushing past each other to find seats, followed by laughter or hisses of *shh!* Her heart was pounding as Miss Stranks raised her hand and called for the Masters to come and send down their holy light. She shivered as she felt Bradbury's fingers go to her shoulders. She could see Kitty's face shining like a sliver of moon by the door. She kept her eyes on Kitty, waiting for the white kerchief to make the sign of the cross. North, south, east and west. *I'm with you, Ellis. We must stick together, you and I.*

And so it began. The now familiar words gathered in small herds in her throat, stumbling and galloping out through her mouth—was it her mouth? She felt like a machine, a typewriting machine spitting out lies. In her mind, she took Kitty's astral hand in hers. Together they plunged down into the warm embrace of silence, coolness, peace and serenity, swimming away to a lost world where the lands were green and there was no malice or violence or drought or death, and chestnuts rained down from the boughs, and every kind of flower and tree nodded in the sunny air.

There was applause. She heard it, but didn't hear it. A posy of purple lilacs fell at her feet. Miss Stranks pretended to smile at her. There was the release of Bradbury's fingers from the ribbon at her neck, followed by the push on the back of her dress as he huddled her away, the lace shawl and hat still in place.

'Don't let anyone see her,' whispered Miss Stranks. 'Put her in one of the dressing rooms.'

Bradbury said nothing as he locked her in a dressing room. The threat of his intentions said enough. Ellis shivered again as she heard the crowd's applause rise and crash like a wave landing at the slippered feet of Miss Minerva Stranks.

'Come back next Sunday for your fill of The Truth. Our new newsletter will be for sale at the door, the very first edition of *The Lighted Way*.'

Ellis removed the shawl and hat and stared at herself in the row of mirrors. There were four in total. *We have four bodies*, she thought, as she touched the places where Bradbury's fingers had been. *Which one is mine?*

Kitty wouldn't look at her on the trip back to the house. What did she know? What had he said? Bradbury's repartee with Miss Stranks continued as usual. She saw how his hand disappeared in the froth of Kitty's skirts, how Kitty did not move to push it away.

All night Ellis listened out for Bradbury. She set a chair against the door and with every passing footfall, every rattle and creak and cough of the plumbing, she sat up in her bed, but he did not come.

At first light, she crept down to the kitchen. The back door was open. She stared at the golden green rectangle of the yard. In all the weeks she'd been here, she'd never been allowed to go outside 'to loaf about', as Miss Stranks would have said. It was the first time she'd been offered the chance to escape. But escape to what?

The garden was small, with much of it swamped by weeds. She inhaled the smell of damp crushed grass. The cool water soothed the bruises on her shins as she waded steadily towards the fence to where the laden branch of a fig tree hung down from the neighbouring garden. She climbed the rails of the fence and reached up for a fig and felt like a child; a tired, thin, battered child. She almost cried out as the freshness and sweetness stung her mouth. She stowed more figs in her pockets, climbed down to stand in the sun. The sun was on her head, sending its gentle heat onto the bruises of her skull. The gate was just there. She could easily climb it. She could easily run.

'Thief!'

She jumped at the closeness of a man's voice. The head of a rake appeared on the other side of the fence and waved about. She ducked down in the grass.

'I'll get you, you little thief. I saw how many of my figs you took.'

In her hurry to crouch down, she'd squashed the figs in the pockets of her dress. The spreading red juice looked like blood.

'Thou shalt not steal!' The rake continued to swing back and forth.

She ran, head down, back towards the house. Halfway across, she tripped on something in the weeds and looked up at the sound of laughter. Kitty was watching from an upper window. Ellis raised a hand to wave up.

'Ellis? There you are. Miss Stranks has been looking for you.'

It was Mabel-the-maid, calling her back into the chill of the house.

The man's voice rang out behind her. 'Thou shalt not steal!'

Mabel smiled at Ellis' stained dress. 'I can see you've had better luck than me. I've thought of building a ladder there against the fence, with a bucket and pulley system leading back to the kitchen door.'

Ellis couldn't look at her. Surely the whole world could tell what had happened with Bradbury. Her hands trembled as she handed Mabel the squashed figs.

'That's not a bad haul,' Mabel said. 'You were lucky he didn't smite you with his rake.'

Ellis followed her along the hallway towards Miss Stranks' private door. Mabel was called in. Ellis was not. When she emerged, Mabel told her Miss Stranks was 'deeply alarmed' by Ellis' 'provocative and recalcitrant behaviour.'

'She wants me to leave the house immediately?' Ellis asked.

Mabel looked at her oddly. 'No. Mr Bradbury put in a good word for you. He said your hesitation before the lecture was down to nerves, that with his guiding hand you'd bring in even bigger audiences.'

Ellis tried to listen as Mabel told her she would have to rise at four o'clock instead of five to repent for her mistakes, that her meals would be halved until she'd reflected fully upon her ungratefulness and petulance. Something had collapsed in side of her.

She sat on the stairs. How stupid she'd been. Of course Bradbury knew how to protect himself. If she stayed here, his behaviour, his 'guiding hand' would only grow more insistent.

'Psst!' She looked up to see Kitty on the upper stairs. 'I see you've encountered old Mr Moses.'

'Who?'

'The man next door. That's what I call him. *Thou shalt not*, and all that.' Kitty's skin seemed to glow in the morning light. 'You said you wanted to speak to me.'

'It doesn't matter now.'

'It sounded urgent.'

'Not anymore.'

'Well if it doesn't matter, then come up.'

Ellis glanced at Miss Stranks' door. What did anything matter now? She'd wanted to see Kitty for so long, to talk to her away from everyone else, and now here was her chance.

Kitty's room was transformed by daylight. A rich blue and red Persian carpet was spread across the floor. Rosy curtains breathed at the window. Clothing, ribbons and shawls were draped over fine pieces of furniture. Dainty shoes were lined up beneath the bed. Unlike her own dark cell, Kitty's room was all air and light. The larger window looked down over the street and offered shimmering glimpses of the city beyond. The other window overlooked the back of the house. Ellis could see Mr Moses down there balanced on his ladder, tussling with the fig tree trying to saw off the overhanging branch. The rest of his garden consisted of straight white gravel paths and clipped rows of hedges fencing off bright beds of rosebushes, each one pruned to equal size.

She sat down carefully on a velvet chair.

'One day when I am dust this will all be yours,' Kitty said. She was watching her intently, propped up against a wall of pillows on the bed.

Ellis didn't answer.

'Well, what did Strankenstein want with you this time?'

'Strankenstein? You mean Miss Stranks? Is that her real name?'

'Oh dear. I forget sometimes you really are a simple country girl. What is it you wanted to talk about?'

Bradbury is no good, Kitty. He's a bully and a brute. That's all she had to say. But now she knew Kitty wouldn't believe her. Nobody would.

'To leave here,' was all she said.

'That's hardly news. Although you've lasted longer than some. Me, I've been here a millennium.' Kitty laughed again rather loudly, Ellis thought. 'Is that all?'

'If you hate it here so much, why don't you leave too?'

'Oh, I hate it here all right, but I'm not like you. You wouldn't understand.'

'I might.'

'Even if I could leave, I can't. My parents put me here. I am bound to stay. Not forever. Just long enough.'

'For what?'

Kitty frowned and smoothed her hands over her stomach. When she realised Ellis was watching her, she pulled up the bedclothes and let out a bitter laugh. 'Until somebody dies and leaves me pots of gold to do with as I like. That's how it works in my world.'

'Isn't there somewhere else to go and wait while …?' Ellis said.

'Oh, you mean somewhere fun?' Kitty flung off the bedclothes and scrambled out of bed. She picked up a dress, held it against her body and moved around in a dance, flapping the sleeves and fanning out the skirt. 'Shall we go to Paris and waltz in the gardens beneath the Eiffel Tower? Or shall it be Egypt, to burn the soles of our slippers as we dance across the molten sands at midnight in the shadow of the pyramids?'

Kitty held out her hand.

'Up you get. Or can't you country bumpkins dance?'

Ellis rose gingerly to her feet. Kitty flung away the dress and pulled Ellis towards her. She was wheezing slightly.

'Like this,' she said, looking down and moving her feet. 'Da-dah. Da-dum. Wait. Do you want me to show you how real actresses fall down on stage?'

Before Ellis could answer, Kitty had thrown herself to the floor in a tumble of petticoats. Kitty lay motionless, staring up.

'Kitty?' Ellis leant in over her. Neither the bodice of her dress, nor her swollen stomach rose or fell. Her open eyes were as still as glass.

'Kitty. Stop it.'

Kitty's face collapsed into a smile. 'I really had you there for a moment, didn't I?' Kitty sat up and tossed her hair. 'I learnt it from an actress at Covent Garden. I've been there, you see. I've seen all the wonders of the world. My parents took me everywhere. I was so lucky. Everybody told me so. I saw the Great Sphinx with its huge blank eyes gazing at eternity. I've tripped up the crumbling stairs of the Colosseum in Rome and tossed my crusts to the starving cats before the beggars scampered in and took them off. There is a whole world out there, Ellis. A real world, not one to invent and pretend you travel to *astrally*.'

Kitty began to cough. Ellis moved to help her up. Kitty's sleeve felt damp. Her hands were hot. Her face had begun to bead with sweat.

'You look feverish,' Ellis said.

There was a jug of water on the side table. Ellis poured out a glass.

Kitty fell back against the pillows. 'My bed is on fire and you bring me a glass? I ask for freedom and they imprison me beside a cliff. I am like poor Iphigenia, waiting for the sacrifice.'

'Who?'

'Oh, I keep forgetting. You know nothing, do you Ellis. Nothing of any worth or truth.'

'Don't say that Kitty. I do know things.'

'It is not *knowledge* to regurgitate other people's lies.'

'I've already told you. I had no choice.'

'That's another lie.'

'I know about your *ac-couch-e-ment*.' The word reverberated in the air. Kitty began to rub at her hands. 'No,' she said.

'I know about it. And I can help.'

'No you can't.'

'We can find somewhere else together. Somewhere better.'

'You mean like Atlantis? Oh yes, let's go there now, to that magical land. Shall we swim like mermaids holding our breaths, our hair waving beneath the waves?' Kitty's chest was heaving. She grabbed Ellis by the hand. 'You don't believe in any of it, do you? Tell me you don't.'

Ellis looked down at the oily stain of ointment Bradbury had smeared across Kitty's hand.

How could she tell anyone what she believed when she no longer knew herself? What was the truth? Besides, she had begun to see things since reading all those books. Thinking back, she always had. She'd seen the tree the day her mother died, fluttering wildly in a non-existent wind. She'd seen the halo of light falling about Kitty's hair at the first night at the hall. She saw golden flashes whenever Miss Stranks laid her hands upon her head. She'd noticed the red feather trying to warn her to go back before Bradbury had forced himself onto her. And what about her knowledge of Atlantis? Some mornings when she woke, her mind was still whirling with strange, loud, beautiful visions, so intricate and detailed she *felt* she must have walked those streets with those Atlantean people, and worked in their fields tilling crops, or stood in grand caves staring out at a shining sea, the strange rich notes of music echoing. Was speaking about your dreams any less truthful than reading somebody else's words aloud from a book, especially if it meant putting food in your mouth and keeping a roof over your head?

Kitty withdrew her hand and shut her eyes. 'Stranks really *has* you now. But she doesn't have me and never will.'

Ellis studied Kitty's face slowly, in the same way the sighted stare at the blind. She drank in every inch of her, the grey half moons beneath her eyes, the silvered frown, the dark ruffled river of her hair, the fine bones of her face, the crumpled petals of her mouth, the mound of her stomach rising and falling with every laboured breath.

She couldn't bring herself to say it aloud: *But Bradbury has both of us now, doesn't he?*

CHAPTER
TWENTY-TWO

R ennie felt a thrill of excitement as she trotted behind Ellis down Burton Street. What a relief to be out of the dingy confines of the house, to leave behind the two tormenting letters from her brother. She held up the scarf across her face and tried to copy how Ellis skirted around the puddles and picked her way through the rain-soaked sludge. When people in the street stopped to stare, Rennie realised her mistake. She'd set off for her maiden voyage from Milsons Point wearing her new spring green merino coat. Lloyd would spot her a mile away.

She and Lloyd had argued so spectacularly about the coat, it had rivalled the most melodramatic of operas. *But I want that one! No you do not! Oh yes I do! No you do not!* He'd insisted on the drab dark brown but she'd fixed her mind on the vivid green and, for once, she'd succeeded. Eventually, he'd relented but not before delivering the parting shot that the particular shade of green made her look sallow around the gills.

Now she regretted the whole damned thing.

'Where might one hail a taxi?' Rennie said.

'Not round here.'

'But I need one now. Don't worry, Ellis. I'll pay for it.'

'There won't be any until we reach the terminal.'

'Oh. How silly of me.' Rennie tried to sound unperturbed as she followed Ellis through the rubble. Perhaps the films of rising dust would deaden the brightness of her coat.

Once at the vehicular ferry terminal, Rennie found a taxi to take her fare. She waved at Ellis to climb aboard.

'I know we should have waited until we reached Circular Quay, but I can't, you see. There's a view from an office over there I need to avoid.' She pointed at the Wool and Wheat.

Ellis said nothing and sat bolt upright all the way, staring out of the taxi window at the water, then at the crowds of the Quay, one hand held against her chest, the other splayed against the glass to steady herself with every gear change, swerve and toot. When they passed a churchyard, Rennie saw Ellis flinch, turn her head and mumble something under her breath.

Rennie lowered her scarf as they waited at a corner. A man peered into the window. Her hat had been the second mistake. Having brought only two with her, she'd worn her favourite, the Parisian cream-coloured felt, with the Bakelite buckle and lemon ribbon. Unfortunately, it was the one she'd worn when she'd left the house under Mrs Chisholm's beady eye. She glanced over at Ellis' soft grey hat, wondering if she might instigate a swap. Now she was without the usual thick upholstering of her hair, her hat spun around on her head every time the driver took a corner. But what joy it was to be without that heavy blanket of hair, to have entered the company of all the other modern women of her age, feeling the frisson of freedom, sloughing off the weight of ages, even if it did leave one's neck rather open to the elements.

'A bob tax,' she said, trying to catch Ellis' eye. 'I ask you!'

Ellis looked over and offered the modest makings of a smile.

After half an hour staring at the traffic, Ellis sat back and said, 'Here we are. The Haymarket.'

Rennie stifled the urge to cry out no, *no we are not here at all*. This was not the real Haymarket. Whenever she heard the nasally enunciated names of Hyde Park, Croydon, Canterbury or Camden, it brought a wave of disappointment, reminding her she was *here*, not *there*, thousands of miles away from the Real Thing.

She looked out at the market men scuttling about, manoeuvring overloaded barrows, balancing boxes and baskets, darting beneath verandahs, shouting out to each other in rough tongues. It could have been anywhere in England except it was newer, harsher and smaller. Rennie frowned at two peculiar narrow towers rising up over the buildings. Behind them, the sun waved its arms in the sky.

'After a night of pelting rain, now this,' she said. 'Everything is so extreme here, so full steam ahead.'

'Banana ripening towers,' Ellis said, following her gaze.

'We don't have those at the real Haymarket.'

Ellis didn't answer. It was possible her ration of words had already been used up for the day. *I know somebody who'll know about plots of land at Lane Cove*, she'd said, after Rennie had shown her the advertisement for the flower farmlets. *My friend Ned McCarthy. He works at Paddy's Market*. Apparently Ned McCarthy was a minor oracle on all things to do with market gardening. Rennie had jumped at the suggestion. What else could she do? Besides, the lodging house pantry certainly needed fattening up.

The driver leant a grubby sleeve along the front seat and leered at her. Rennie tried not to look at him as she handed over a note. That done, she repositioned her hat, opened the door, aimed her shoe away from the mound of sodden cabbage leaves, counted to three, and clambered out. She waited for Ellis to follow. When she didn't, Rennie tapped on the glass.

'Oh, let him keep the change, for heaven's sake. I've got a flower farmlet to purchase.'

She knew her attempt at jollying Ellis along sounded hollow, but it was the only way she could think of tamping down the fear that was rising in her like the remnants of an overly rich meal. It was possible Lloyd and his cronies lay in wait, even here. She felt the cold whip of his shadow everywhere. *Oh go away, will you Lloyd*, Rennie thought as she closed her eyes to the thought of him and turned her mind to coping instead with the decidedly fruity market smell engulfing her.

'I am completely at your mercy,' she said, when Ellis finally emerged from the taxi, looking flushed. 'Shall we go and meet your friend?'

'Here.' Ellis emptied a handful of coins into Rennie's glove. 'And watch your purse.'

Rennie dutifully emptied the coins into the pocket of her coat. Despite the bustle, some people seemed to have nothing better to do than to stare at her as she negotiated her way through ankle-deep layers of rhubarb leaves. As Ellis led her deeper into the market, she felt the fever of activity infect her, the bawling chorus of the barrow boys, the girls haggling over price-war bread. Everything seemed to brim with life. Her only regret was forgetting to bring her sketchbook.

'I've been trying to think of his name,' she called to Ellis, who was beetling ahead through the throng. 'There was a Frenchman, famous for a series of portraits of blind bean sellers and toothless cheese merchants at Les Halles.'

As Ellis burrowed on, Rennie stopped to watch an old woman tying together clumps of asparagus with wisps of string. She bought three bunches and asked the woman where she might find some bread, tea and cheese. The woman replied something gummy and unintelligible. Rennie looked up to see Ellis zigzagging away from her. She strode after her, careful to keep sight of the squashy mushroom of a hat toiling on through the masses until the hat stopped at a stall at the end of the aisle where—good heavens—a tall, slender man beamed behind wicker baskets overflowing with vegetables. The man's hair was flaxen beneath his hat. His face was tanned and lean, as if he'd spent his whole life working beneath a caressing sun. *My, my*, Rennie thought.

'Els?' Rennie heard him say. A soft red and white cotton kerchief was knotted at his neck. His forearms shone out in smooth nut brown against the pale blue linen of his shirt.

Rennie watched as Ned McCarthy gave Ellis a hug and a kiss on the cheek. Ellis' entire demeanour changed. Her wiry body uncoiled. She swung her hands about as she talked. She threw her head back and laughed a deep, rich, generous laugh. When Ellis looked over towards Rennie, her eyes were a shining jade green.

'The advertisement?' she was saying as she waved Rennie over.

Rennie fumbled in her handbag. 'Oh heavens,' she said, touching her hat. She felt like a child who'd seen a forbidden object in a window and was now so possessed by longings and dreams of its reward, she couldn't think of anything else. 'I seem to have left it behind at the house.' She heard herself laugh too loudly as she held out her hand to Ned, glad she was still wearing the gloves. The wedding rings were no more than a bump. *See, Lloyd? Two can play at this game.*

'Hello, I'm Rennie. Ellis has told me so much about you. What a wonderful place it is here. It's so alive.'

'Rennie wants to know about those flower farmlets they're advertising at Lane Cove.'

'J. T. Bickley Realtors.' Rennie leant forward, and flashed another smile. 'One pound down no more to pay. Splendid roomy blocks, etcetera.'

'Hmm.' Ned rasped a broad, honey-coloured hand across his chin.

He looked at the both of them, back and forth. His eyes were a clear watery blue, like the sun striking the white shallows of a beach. When he turned his oceanic eyes on Rennie, she felt her shoulders drop. *This* was the kind of sun-drenched colonial chap her friends in London had dreamed about: honest, taciturn fellows made of muscle, warm air, hard work and light; men untrammelled by the burden of class or history—not the stuffy mercantile aspirants like Lloyd Howarth and his ilk. Despite the clarity of Ned's gaze, a distinct wall seemed to go up when Rennie returned fire with another smile.

'Do you know anything about them?' Rennie said. 'They sound absolutely perfect.'

'They *sound* perfect,' Ellis said. 'On paper.'

'If you two hold the fort,' said Ned, 'I reckon I know somebody who might.' He gave Ellis' arm a squeeze.

'That's exactly what Ellis said.' Rennie laughed, as she turned to watch him saunter off, his slender arms swinging at his sides.

She waited for Ned to turn and respond with a smile but he disappeared into the crowd. Rennie watched as Ellis installed herself behind the cabbages and served several customers. How simple and pleasurable Ellis made it look, handing over fresh produce for a coin.

'Your friend Ned seems very charming,' Rennie said as she raked through a box of river beans. Ellis was busy noting down sales in a book. 'Does he live at Lane Cove with his cabbages?'

Ellis didn't look up.

'Or nearby, in the city?'

'No and yes.'

Rennie waited. Ellis didn't seem inclined to elaborate, so she tried again. 'Ned lives on a farm, and in the city, with or without his family *and* his cabbages?'

'You could say that.'

'I see,' said Rennie, although she didn't quite. 'How marvellous.' She laughed, trying to cover up the sting of Ellis' reaction. She looked about for Ned's dark hat and sun-coloured hair, but there was no sign of him so she dug a fingernail into the fennel and inhaled its aniseed smell. As she did so, her hat slipped off her head and fell into the potatoes. 'Oh damn this beastly old thing.' She set it on top of a cabbage. 'I don't suppose there's any chance of my finding another hat anywhere here.'

Ellis was now head first in a pile of sacks. 'Try over there.'

'Where?'

'Past the fur and feather.'

'Stupendous,' Rennie said, as she marched off, relieved to leave Ellis to her sudden descent into prickliness.

Rennie smelt the fur and feather before she saw it. She couldn't bear to look at the long clawed toes of the chickens and ducks huddling together in cages. Others contained rabbits. She knew their eyes were following her, a glistening mixture of pleading, accusation and fear. She let out a small cry as she caught sight of a stoat tied to a length of twine, running up and down a man's shoulder. The air was thick with feathers, cackles, grunts and farmy smells as Rennie hurried past, coughing into her glove. The floor was carpeted by hay and a repulsive mosaic of bird droppings. Sparrows and pigeons flapped at her like flame-crazed moths.

At last she came to a section selling tufts of claret-red amaranth, bundles of hemp, tables spread with yellowing sheets of piano music, and candlesticks fashioned from sawn-off pipes. Finally, there was a row of stalls with oddments of clothing hanging from a dizzying arrangement of poles and wires. As Rennie approached, she realised the wares were second-hand. *How silly of me*, she thought. *Of course they are.* It was too late to back out now. One of the stall owners had spied her over a pile of bedraggled scarves. Rennie smiled at the items, catching the inevitable whiff of sweat, lavender water and mustiness. She fingered an evening gown with a bodice adorned with *fin-de-siècle* lace.

'May I see that one?' She pointed to an old black velvet mourning hat sitting atop a hatbox.

It looked like something her mother might have worn in a stiff-lipped photograph at an old-fashioned garden party, a mother who was not in mourning officially, but who'd spent her life swimming about in a well of bitterness, carping at her husband, punishing her daughter while lavishing praise on her undeserving son.

The woman poked a pole at the hat. It felt like being at the fair as a child, winning her first prize at the coconut shy. She remembered how her brother Irving had complained to their mother that she must have cheated. How else could his little sister have triumphed over him? Her mother had made Rennie surrender the prize to him, beneath the distracted eyes of their father.

Rennie remembered all this as she peered inside the hat. It was the smell of it, she thought, the oldness and staleness of the stifling life she'd fled. There were no small creatures or stray hairs immediately apparent to the naked eye and it was reassuring to find *Monsieur Étienne, Paris* stamped on the brown curl of the label.

Rennie put it on. The black lace tumbled down over her face. The woman waved her towards a mirror belonging to a neighbouring stall.

'I'll take it!' Rennie said, for that's exactly what Bertha Collins had shrieked at her paintings a week ago—or was it a hundred years ago—when she'd arrived at her exhibition in a whirlpool of smoke and glittering beads, pretending she was still Rennie's friend and not the mistress of her husband.

A small crowd had gathered around her to watch. Rennie glanced about at the coats. They weren't hugely encouraging, but she'd need a different coat to avoid being seen by Lloyd and his spies. A purple one with a fox-fur collar slouched on a peg. It was not the style she'd usually wear, but that was the point, to confuse and confound her cunning foe. The woman swung it down in one deft swoop. There was a hole on the left cuff and small teardrop-shaped stain on the back, but apart from that, it looked and smelt possible.

A crinkly-eyed old woman stepped forward and offered to hold Rennie's coat and hat while she tried it on. People murmured. Somebody made a joke she couldn't quite catch. As the shape and smell of someone else wrapped about her, Rennie realised once it would have horrified her to wear a dead woman's clothes, but this old coat was her armour now, as was the hat. The crowd approved. Rennie did a little curtsy and paid the hat-coat woman whatever sum she asked.

She walked back slowly, adjusting to the feel of her new-old clothes beginning to find their own fall and rhythm on her form. Her spring green coat was tucked beneath her arm. She quickened her step when she sighted Ned stationed at his stall. Ellis was sitting on a crate smoking her pipe, laughing with Ned recounting an apparently hilarious tale requiring a series of whimsical hand movements. Ellis slapped her knee and laughed as Ned leapt up to serve a customer. When he'd finished, he tossed several bulbs of fennel in the air in the manner of a juggler. Ellis laughed on through a puff of smoke.

'Yes and no,' Rennie heard Ned laugh as she waited.

'Oh?' said Rennie, leaning in over the table.

'What will it be today then?' he said.

She felt his blue eyes wash over her. 'One flower farmlet at Lane Cove, please, flourishing on a particularly splendid roomy block.'

'Rennie? I didn't recognise you behind all that.'

'*Touché.*' Rennie rolled up the black lace and smiled. 'One disguise, it seems, begets another.'

'I was just saying to Ellis, the word is mixed on those plots for sale at Lane Cove.'

'Oh?'

'Some are fair. But you'll have to be careful when you go out there and see them for yourself. I'd think of camping out there for a while before you buy, see how you like it first.'

Camping? Rennie thought. *Good heavens.* She twisted her engagement ring beneath her glove. 'But some of the plots have potential?'

'You'll need to make sure you have what you need, good drainage, reasonable soil, a functioning water tank, proximity to the river and passable roads and tracks. And watch the houses. Some they're calling cottages.'

'But they're little more than slab huts,' Ellis said.

'While others are more …'

'Substantial?' Rennie said. She felt her smile falter. That was Lloyd's word, trotted out as an emblem of his infallibility. It took all Rennie's strength to flap her glove at the air and laugh as if she didn't care a fig. 'I see. Thank you, Ned. You've been very helpful. Shall we gather our provisions, Ellis, and press on?'

She saw the way Ellis looked at Ned. Ned's eyes flickered as if registering a secret that had been transmitted earlier between the two of them. A streak of disquiet rose in Rennie. What had they been saying about her while she was gone? Had they spoken of her sneeringly like that Girl had done back at the lodging house? *Thinks she's the Queen of Sheba, does she? Hope you made a pretty penny out of her, Els.* She'd plunged into trusting Ellis on sight—and on what grounds? She hardly knew the woman. She'd only spent one bone-splintering night in a dank cavern of a room. It was true Ellis did *seem* kind enough, and her bedroom was cluttered with an astonishing array of interesting things, and she was writing all manner of intriguing things under the pseudonym of Scribbly Gum, but that didn't mean she should be taken on her word, that she wasn't one of those gold diggers or swindlers, an opportunist seeking to entrap a vulnerable, wealthy woman like herself.

'Actually, Ellis,' Rennie said. She patted the pocket of her green coat. 'Would you mind terribly buying everything for the house? There's something I must see to.'

Her hands scrabbled deeper in the pockets, but the considerable cache of coins was gone.

'Damn.'

'What is it?' Ellis said.

'I've been robbed.'

She felt everything drain from her, as if she was made of nothing more than cloth. She heard Ned speak as Ellis took her by the arm and steered her through the shouting, sneering, jeering crowds. When they came to the clothing stall, there was no sign of the thief.

'It must have been that old woman with the crinkly eyes,' Rennie said. 'She was standing right here. She offered to hold my coat and hat. You must have seen her. You must know who she is.'

The stallholder woman shook her head, pursed her lips and crossed her arms. If there'd been a drawbridge on the stall, its clanking chains would have already hoisted it up.

'They'll be miles away by now,' she heard Ellis say, as she led her back to the sunny but distant, charming but elusive, Mr Ned.

CHAPTER
TWENTY-THREE

Ellis rested the hessian sacks of produce on the step of the escalator. She looked back to make sure Rennie was following. There she was, stumbling forward in that ridiculous mourning hat, holding out one hand as if lurching across the deck of a ship. Ellis tried not to look at the fox-fur collar of Rennie's new coat with its flaccid paws and yellow staring eye, or the way it rose and fluffed itself in the breeze, as if preparing to burst back to life. She thought instead of Rennie's creamy face, the dark hair, the way her dazzling smile could cut through the dust and grit. Ellis laid a hand against the buttons of her coat. It was still unnervingly unsettled, her fluttering heart, despite the debacle of the robbery and what that now meant.

Before they'd left the markets, Ned had plied them with cabbage, kohlrabi, river beans, onions, parsnips, carrots, Josephine apples and Emperor pears, a pound of spuds, a block of cheese and a loaf of bread. *Dear Ned*. It was more than Ellis would usually buy to feed the whole house for two full weeks.

She squinted back at the diamond-speckled harbour. Today the bridge men moved in determined swarms through the noise and dust. And like the dust, her moment of hope had risen up only to dissipate. There was only one thing left to do now—hand back all the money Rennie had paid her for the room. The dream of having enough to secure a good room with views, new shoes, silk stockings, hat and coat—was just that—a dream. Tomorrow, she'd have to go out early and look again.

As she walked up towards Burton Street, Ellis felt the hum of a thousand regrets descending on her. In the taxi to the markets, she'd allowed herself a moment of careful exhilaration. It had been decades since she'd set foot inside a paying taxi. *At last*, she'd thought. *It will be all right*. But the moment of exhilaration had soon evaporated. She'd spotted two small yew trees huddling in the yard of a church, shivering like dark feathers in the sun and known it was a sign. Try as she might to pretend it meant nothing, the image stayed with her. And so it had happened, the warning and Rennie's robbery by a 'sweet old lady' pulling off the kind of ruse Tom-the-pickpocket would've mastered by the age of six.

Ellis stopped to readjust her sacks. She looked back to see Rennie walking distractedly, glancing up at a parrot screeching overhead. Rennie then stopped to study something in the dust and gestured for one of the resuming men to retrieve a souvenir from the rubble.

Ellis almost raised her hand to wave, but turned when she heard Clarrie crying, 'The tyrants! The tyrants!'

He was standing with Mrs Liddy beneath Girl's balcony, waving his poetry book about. Alf Ostler and his acolytes were there too. Ellis picked up her sacks and began to walk. At the sight of a policeman emerging from Girl's door, a ridiculous thought flashed through her mind. The city library had tracked her down to arrest her for stealing *The Lighted Way*.

'A policeman?' She heard Rennie panting behind her. 'This will be my husband's doing. He's had me followed. I knew he would. And just when I've bought my new disguise.'

Ellis hurried up the street, ignoring Rennie's cries of 'Wait, Ellis. Tell me if you still recognise me in this hat.'

She couldn't wait. Mrs Liddy wailed. Clarrie's arm was slung around the old woman's shoulders, trying to hold her upright. Alf had sat down on Ellis' front step to mop his face. There was a man she didn't recognise, well dressed, but not a spiv, standing on Girl's balcony, jotting in a notebook.

Ellis dropped her sacks. 'What's going on?'

'You can't go in.' That was Alf.

'Where's Girl?' she said.

She waited to hear Girl's bolshie laugh telling the policeman to watch where he put his greasy mitts. But there was no laugh. There was no

Girl. It was then she saw the blood smeared in a red wave across the wall. Splotches of blood bloomed like poppies in the dust. One pink feather was glued—by blood—to Girl's front step.

'She's been a bit cut up,' said Alf.

A bit cut up?

A group of O'Malley's men were standing further up the hill, looking on from the shadows, scuffing their boots at the cobblestones.

'It wasn't them,' Alf said. 'They're sniffing about, seeing who's trespassed on their turf.'

'*The tyrant whose delight is in his woe*,' Clarrie said.

Ellis couldn't speak. She couldn't think.

'Oh Ellis dear, we heard it all, the terrible screams.' Mrs Liddy was sobbing. 'We couldn't do anything. Nobody could.'

'Where is she? We have to go there.' Ellis looked around. She didn't like the way nobody would meet her eye. 'I have to see her.'

Alf rose slowly to his feet. 'No, you don't, Els.'

Alf had never called her 'Els' before. He'd never called her anything except a cabbage-muncher. She blinked at his singlet. It was covered with blood. The sky sagged and quivered as her knees buckled and she hit the ground.

She woke on her bed. Her shoes were off. Rennie's purple coat was laid over her. The fox-fur collar at her chin smelt of mothballs, lavender and cigarettes. Rennie was seated at the desk, smoking as she leafed through Ellis' notes for 'The Green-eyed Gardener'. Rennie leapt up, trying to shove the papers back into a pile as if she hadn't been pouring over them.

'Splendid, Ellis. You're back with us. Why don't I make us both a nice hot cup of tea?'

Ellis tried to sit up but a small pointed hammer had begun to pound at her temples. She lay back down. She could hear Rennie open the front door and call out.

'She's back with us. Clarrie, can you tell Mrs Liddy? Ellis is all right.'

Ellis felt about for her pipe. Despite her tremble of her hands, she filled and lit it and managed to sit part way up. She lifted the curtain and looked out. The policeman was gone. Girl's shutters were pulled across. How strange to see the balcony railing without its bawdy festoon of stockings—and without Girl—who was lying alone in a hospital *a bit cut up.*

Rennie appeared, smiling over the tea tray. Ellis watched as she set it down on the floor, poured the tea, and handed her a thick hunk of bread topped by half an inch of Mrs Liddy's famous lemon curd.

'I was talking to your neighbours,' Rennie said. 'They're very, well, salt-of-the-earth types. They told me all about you two, you and Girl. I gather she was quite a character.'

Was? Panic tightened in Ellis' throat. She moved to get up. She had to see Girl before it was too late.

Rennie handed Ellis a cup. 'Or would you prefer brandy? I wasn't sure.'

The fox's glass yellow eye glinted up from Rennie's coat. Ellis pushed it away. Despite the hammers multiplying in her head, she managed to rise to her feet.

'Can't I get you something? Here, let me help,' Rennie said.

It was hard to walk but Ellis made the few steps to the wardrobe, unaided. She felt Rennie watching as she unlocked it, lifted the secret compartment in the floor and drew out an old biscuit tin containing her stash of rent money.

'Here. This is yours.' Her voice sounded hoarse, as if she'd been wailing and keening for days on end.

'Oh?' Rennie said.

'I took too much for the room last night.'

'Say, that's quite a sum you have there, with all the shrapnel.'

In the fug, Ellis had taken out all of her savings and shaken them all over the bed, the entire sum of the bibs and bobs she'd scrounged over the years working for the Clements Brothers and as Scribbly Gum. She removed Rennie's share, laid it apart on the satin coverlet and scooped the rest of it away.

A quail's egg-sized swelling had sprung up at her right temple. Nobody had thought to apply brown paper and vinegar, not even a cool cloth. But there was no time now to think of that.

'Have you seen my shoes?' She tried to bend down to look under the bed, but the hammers were threatening to turn into horses' hooves.

'But you haven't had your tea. Sit for a moment. Rest. One sorrow need not turn into two. And two sorrows need not become three.'

Ellis steadied herself, wondering if Rennie had invented that saying. She couldn't recall hearing it before. It was both wise and irritating at the same time. She resumed the hunt for her only pair of shoes.

'I didn't know your friend, Ellis, but she was very kind to me on the ferry when I came here last night. She held out her hand and smiled at me. And do you know, that one simple act saved me, Ellis? It saved my life. I wish I'd told her that at the time. But one doesn't, does one? I heard her calling out to you this morning from her balcony. I watched you both talking from my window. Nobody could have known that within hours she'd be assailed so brutally. It's utterly chilling to think of it. How thin the line between life and ...' Rennie's voice trailed off.

Between life and—death?

'My shoes, have you seen them?' Ellis said.

'I'd like to see to that bump on your head.'

'No need to. It's nothing.'

Rennie moved towards her. 'But it looks simply frightful. And anyway, Alf said to wait.'

'Alf says a lot of things.'

Rennie followed her into the hallway. Ellis felt a fresh wave of dizziness trying to wrestle her to the floor.

'You can't go, Ellis. Not in that state. There's nothing you can do. Alf said ...'

Ellis had to concentrate as she struggled to find the arms in her coat.

'The money's on the bed,' Ellis said. 'It's still early in the day. You'll find another room easily enough. Try Elizabeth Bay.'

Rennie watched on as Ellis eased her hat over the quail's egg on her head.

'But you can't go now. Girl would have wanted you to stay here and make plans for your future. She would have wanted you to think about where you're going to go next. Obviously you can't stay here. Neither of us can. We're both in the same pickle, you and I.'

Ellis raised her head. *Would have wanted* ...? That was the second time Rennie had used the past tense when speaking about Girl. Rennie's diamond ring glinted at her through the whorl of cigarette smoke.

'I thought you'd notice my jewellery soon enough.' Rennie thrust the ring at Ellis as she tried to pass. 'Wait. Feel it Ellis, and tell me it won't fetch a bit.'

'I have to go.'

'But you can't. Your shoes.'

They both looked down at Ellis' stockinged feet. Ellis tramped down the hallway out to the kitchen and out the back. Her shoes weren't there.

'You can't go out like this, Ellis. It isn't safe.'

'Look.'

'No, *you* look.' Ellis flinched at the sudden escalation in Rennie's voice. 'You cannot go and see her because … because it's too late.' Rennie's hand was held over her mouth as if she was trying to catch the words she'd just let tumble out.

Don't say it, Ellis thought. *No. Do not say another word.*

'I'm so terribly sorry. I really am.' Rennie's eyes were racing over her. 'Oh God, how dreadful. How perfectly awful. There's no way to say this to you other than the truth.'

Rennie tried to take her by the hand. Ellis stepped back against the wall. She needed it to keep her standing upright.

'They didn't want to tell you yet. They asked me to sit with you, to see how you were. Clarrie said to hide your shoes.'

Ellis felt her mind go blank. There was a buzzing sound in her ears.

'Don't,' was all she said as she turned away, took off her hat and coat, and hung them slowly back on the peg.

Her bedroom was bathed in harsh white light as if the demolition men had already knocked down the walls and jemmied up the roof. She saw Rennie's shoes arrive on the carpet by the bed. They looked strange, as if they'd landed from a far off place, the expensive leather, the stout silver buckle, the clump of dried mud clinging in a circle with tufts of dead grass at the base of the left heel. Ellis looked at her own feet. Her stockings looked like two old paper bags.

She didn't raise her head as a glass of brandy was lowered into her hand. She saw the russet amber colours dance in the light and the cut of a hundred tiny stars twinkling up from Rennie's diamond ring.

'I'm so sorry,' she heard Rennie say.

It made no difference what Rennie said. Ellis felt her sit down on the bed and take her hand. Ellis could smell her perfume and smoky breath. She could feel her warmth. But it meant nothing. Rennie meant nothing. The hummingbird sensation in her chest, which had begun to beat steadily since Rennie had arrived, was gone. It was the second feathered creature to have died that day.

CHAPTER
TWENTY-FOUR

The *Lighted Way*, somebody cried. *Let there be The Lighted Way.* It was Miss Stranks. Here, now, in Burton Street, looming in white over Ellis' bed.

'Do you hear me, child? To the desk.'

Ellis was at the desk.

'Hands at the ready.'

She put her fingers on the keys. Were they her fingers? She plunged them down. Miss Stranks' voice warped like a passing fire engine's bell.

'Our new monthly journal of illuminating ideas, an enlightened publication of spiritual pure thought, and clairvoyance. Child? Are you listening? Find twenty colourful ideas for *The Lighted Way* before the eleven o'clock gong.'

Words darted past her eyes. *Vegetarian League's Journal Special Ladies' Edition ... The Vexed Diet Question when Exposed to Fresh Air ... The Proper Care of Certain Organs, as per the Female ... Indisputable Evidence of Everlasting Life of the Pharaohs.*

'I am like poor Iphigenia.' That was Kitty's voice.

The pages of a book flicked open in front of her, *The Myths of Greece and Rome. IPH-I-GE-NI-A: Daughter of Agamemnon; sacrificed to Diana. Orestes finds.* There was a picture of Iphigenia, pale-faced, dark-haired, sad-eyed, draped in white, waiting alone on a cliff.

'Time!' called Miss Stranks. 'Hurry up, child. Where is your hat?'

She was in the foyer. Miss Stranks stared down at her.

'You've been rubbing at those eyes again.'

Ellis stared at the blur in the mirror where her face should have been. Her eyes were hot. She'd woken to find them glued shut. She turned as the front door opened. An oblong of light shimmered. Fragrant warm wind swept in.

'Run!' Someone cried. 'Run!'

Night fell in Burton Street but brought no relief. It was only another tunnel back to the phantom world of Miss Stranks.

She was there again, feeling her way through the familiar dark, listening to the breathing of the house. She crept upstairs and let herself into Kitty's room. Kitty wasn't there. The counterpane was flung back. She laid her head on Kitty's pillow, inhaled her smell. She squinted out at the stars fizzing at the window. Her eyes oozed hot thick tears.

'The doctor is here,' she heard someone say.

The doctor?

There was the sound of a man's voice in the hallway, the stamp of footsteps on the stairs. The door flung open. *Rennie?* No. She was still back there, imprisoned in the past with Miss Stranks.

'Sit.' Miss Stranks paced back and forth. Ellis blinked at her moving form.

'Carry on.'

Ellis said nothing. She was at the desk.

'Get on with it. *The Lighted Way* needs to be ready for Sunday next.'

Miss Stranks stalked off. Ellis heard Mabel's voice. Apparently, a girl was waiting to see Miss Stranks.

'What is it, this time?' Miss Stranks said.

'She says she's from the shop girls' coalition,' Mabel said. 'She waited all afternoon yesterday. They're holding a march in the Domain on Sunday. She gave me this handbill.'

'Last week it was the Bird Preservation Society who pecked my ear for over an hour, and while I loathe the practise of using birds for hats, I can't save the *entirety* of the earth's living souls single-handedly. Birds' beaks? Shop girls? Whatever next? Tell her I'll pray for her. Tell her to come to the hall Sunday next. We don't want every Tom, Dick and Mary making a beeline to the house.'

Miss Stranks tossed the handbill away. Ellis asked Mabel to retrieve it. *One for all! All for one! Justice for shop workers. Fair conditions for all! Gather at the Domain, Sunday.*

The Garden and Field. She found it when she'd blundered along the shelves trying to find something to fill the final pages of *The Lighted Way*. She squinted at an article on the 'Clean Culture' movement. It wasn't about Cultivating Pure Thoughts or Unsullying the Temples of Flesh, but about animal waste or fertilisers like blood and bone. They were unnecessary when lupins, nettles and seaweed could be used to enrich poor soils. She'd read as many articles in *Garden and Field* until her eyes were burning coals and there was a pain in her face as if a small hot stone had been placed beneath the skin of her cheek. She damped a kerchief and held it across her eyes.

She must have fallen asleep. She was woken with a jolt. The room was dark. She felt her way across to the windows and squinted at the night-grey streets. Her foot tripped on something. *The Myths of Greece and Rome* was lying behind the curtain in the red parlour. The image of Iphigenia pulsed up at her in the moonlight. But wait, there was something else. A posy of violets had been pressed inside a typewritten note: *For your eyes, Ellis. I would have brought you Ambrosia, but do we have it growing here?*

Ambrosia? The flower of love.

She was at the desk, a clean piece of paper in the typewriter, her hands trembling on the keys: *Your ambrosian words of love are steady points of light in a sea of dark. Forget not mine.* At the sound of the midnight gong, Ellis folded the note away beside Iphigenia's sweet face, and took it downstairs to hide with a pile of *Garden and Fields* beneath her bed.

When all was quiet, she felt her way up the stairs again, holding her breath, swimming her way through the blurry dark towards the white, soft silken arms of ambrosian Kitty. She swayed at the door in the watery dark.

'Ellis?' Kitty sat up. 'Open the curtains, will you? I like to see the stars from my bed.'

Moonlight streamed into the room. Ellis lay down and felt Kitty's hands clasp around her waist. She could hear her wheeze as she brushed Ellis' hair back from her face. She could feel the mound of Kitty's stomach press into her back. *Oh Kitty*, she thought. *We must leave this place. Together.*

'I know,' said Kitty, as if she'd heard her thoughts.

Lying so close, Ellis blinked at the stars, trying to temper her breath and calm the tempest of her thoughts.

'You're not asleep,' Kitty said. 'It's your eyes, isn't it? Do they hurt?'

Ellis felt the hands unclasp. Kitty sat up on her elbow. Ellis turned her head away. She could feel Kitty's breath on her face and the silky stroke of her hair as it brushed down against her cheek. Kitty lay back down and they gazed out at the stars, Ellis the half moon, Kitty the growing full.

The moon had retreated behind clouds. Kitty sat up again and stared down at her, eyes glittering. The crumpled rose of her mouth was so close, it took all Ellis' strength not to lift her hand to touch it. She could hardly breathe as Kitty leant down and kissed her slowly on the lips.

She didn't care when the first gong sounded. She was still drunk on the scent and touch of Kitty. She moved a hand across the bed, searching for the tender warmth of Kitty—who was not there.

Ellis sat up and rubbed at her eyes. Morning sun had invaded the room. Kitty was on the floor, her dress unbuttoned at the back, bathed in misty swirl of gold.

'You must take this,' Kitty said.

'What are you doing?'

'Don't ask me to explain. I can't. Not now.'

Ellis peered at the letter in Kitty's hand.

'If you refuse to take it, I'll—I'll perish. You know I will.'

Ellis left the warmth of the bed. 'Who's it for?'

'Just take it, will you? Do as I ask.'

Ellis took the letter. Her eyes were so bad she couldn't make out the lettering on the front. 'It's for him, isn't it?'

Kitty frowned up at her. 'Of course it is.'

Ellis fled back to her room, washed her eyes and sat on her bed, Kitty's letter to Bradbury in one hand, and the note she'd written to Kitty and had forgotten to give to her the night before: *I forget not your ambrosian words of love. They are steady points of light in a sea of dark. Forget not mine.* She flung the note across the room.

As for the other one, *Ellis, you must deliver this urgently to Mr B* was written across the front.

'What *is* going on?' Miss Stranks swooped in over the bed. 'But what are these? My book of Greek myths? Nobody said you could bring them down here. But wait. What is this?'

Miss Stranks snatched up something up from the floor and laughed. '*I forget not your ambrosian words of love. They are steady points of light in a sea of dark.*' She moved over to Ellis. Her face was crimson.

'Filthy child.'

Ellis closed her eyes and waited to be struck, but Miss Stranks only stood there glowering down. She hadn't found Kitty's letter to Bradbury. She'd found Ellis' love note to Kitty Tate.

'The Hell Broths have been at work again. Your eyes are in a disgusting state. Come here.'

Ellis flinched as Miss Stranks' hand went to her skull. She waited for the fingernails to dig in and for the flashes of golden light. This time they didn't appear. There was just the awful growling of Miss Stranks' voice, and the pinching pressure on her head.

When Miss Stranks had gone, Ellis tossed back her bedclothes, upturned the wooden crates, buckets and trunks, but the letter meant for Bradbury wasn't there.

I'll perish, Ellis, you know I will.

She asked Mabel if she'd seen any of Kitty's letters. She ran down to the kitchen to quiz Mrs Frith. She hovered outside Miss Stranks' private quarters, listening at the door. It was unlocked.

Everything inside was gold, blue and white. A golden four-posted bed was hung with blue tassels and lace. She opened a golden wardrobe jammed with perfumed dresses, adorned with cuffs of fur and feathers. She opened drawers and rifled through the pearls, carved ivory crucifixes, blue leather gloves, indigo shawls and golden rings.

A shadow lapped below the door. Ellis held her breath until it went away and hurried from Miss Stranks' room.

'Ellis?' Kitty was at the top of the stairs. 'Did you deliver my note to Bradbury?'

Ellis climbed a few steps up. 'No,' she whispered. 'Not yet. You must wait, Kitty. Promise me you'll wait.' Ellis turned to see Mabel moving towards the gong. 'I'll deliver it this evening at the hall. It's Sunday, Kitty. I'll see him there. Promise me you'll wait.'

There was the sound of the front door opening. Miss Stranks called for Mabel to hurry up. Ellis ran to the parlour and sat at the desk, staring at the muddle of papers, the mountains of books, the blur of words.

She knew it would come. The cry of 'I will not!' rang through the house followed by silence stretched so taut as if it was willing something to shatter it.

'You're keeping him from me. I know you are. Let him see me.' It was Kitty shouting at Miss Stranks again.

Ellis ran to the door. It was locked. Kitty's voice rose to a scream.

'If you don't let him take me away, I'll tell my parents what's happened here. And then where will you be? Once again, in disgrace, where you belong.'

Another silence. Ellis strained to hear, but whoever was speaking to Kitty was doing so quietly.

'I will not! If you don't let him take me away, I'll throw myself down the stairs. Like real actresses do.'

There were several cajoling voices followed by a scream.

'Like this! Like this!'

There was the sound of running; slamming doors.

'Not under any circumstances is Ellis to be let out of the parlour.' That was Miss Stranks. 'Get back to your posts. All of you.'

More voices. A man's. Not Bradbury's.

The house was in darkness when the parlour door was finally unlocked. A man Ellis had never seen before grabbed her arm, marched her down to her room and locked the door. She paced the flagstones, listening.

She was locked in the parlour again under strict instructions to finish *The Lighted Way*. She sat at the desk. She stood at the window. Sometimes she typed. Whenever there were voices, she ran to put her ear to the door.

'The photograph is ready,' somebody said.

She returned to the desk and rolled out the final sheet of paper. At last she had finished *The Lighted Way*.

The parlour door was unlocked by a triumphant Miss Stranks. Her hair was piled up higher than usual. The rash on her cheeks was still visible despite the dusting of white powder. But her eyes sparkled as she glanced around the room.

'You are finished here,' she said.

Time flickered past the bars of her bedroom window. Silence and stillness smothered the house.

Ellis woke to find her eyes jammed up with yellow muck. Shadows converged. The lines and angles of her room wobbled. She called out to Mrs Frith whenever she heard her puffing past.

'Can you bring me some cucumber or chamomile for my eyes?'

'You mind yourself or they'll *have* me for speaking to you down here.'

Later, Mrs Frith must have relented. A knife blade appeared beneath the gap in the door bearing a half a dozen wafer thin slices of cucumber. Two thinly sliced cheese sandwiches followed.

She wasn't sent for by Miss Stranks until the Sunday afternoon. Mabel-the-maid was in the foyer beside the gong. Miss Stranks was there with another man Ellis didn't recognise. There was no sign of Bradbury.

Ellis blinked at the pile of newspapers on the hallstand. She touched her hand to the print, trying to decipher what it said. *The Lighted Way*. She leant in closer. On the front page, there was a photograph.

Everyone turned as the front door opened. Bradbury's boots clumped across the floor. Ellis could smell rum on his breath. He staggered across the foyer, one hand flung out.

'You drunken fool,' said Miss Stranks. 'To the kitchen, now. Mrs Frith? Make Mr Bradbury a pot of strong black tea.'

'Tea?' said Bradbury. 'That's what you say when you're warming up the old vocal pipes so the Holy Ones can hear you all the way far up in the golden temples in the sky? Tee-hee-hee. Lo-lo-lo.' He tried to lurch towards Ellis, but the other man blocked him. He kept laughing as he was bundled away down the stairs.

'Well now,' said Miss Stranks. 'I planned to surprise everyone with my inaugural newsletter when we arrived at the hall this evening, but there's no time like the present. Bring it here, Ellis.'

Ellis stared at *The Lighted Way*.

'Come on. Or have you grown potatoes in those peasant-girl ears of yours?'

Ellis couldn't understand what she saw. The photograph of Kitty dipped and shimmered. She squinted at the words written beneath: *A Beautiful Death, Miss Kitty Tate was Shepherded Gloriously by Miss Minerva Stranks Across the Threshold of the Afterlife.* She put a finger to the photograph and traced the outline of a delicate stone-white face. White lilies shone like stars against the dark night of Kitty's hair.

'No,' Ellis said.

'What?'

'No!' She was bent in half with the force of the scream.

'Take her back to her room, Mabel,' said Miss Stranks.

Mabel didn't move.

'What's wrong with you all today?'

The other man returned from dispatching Bradbury downstairs. At Miss Stranks' instruction, he advanced on Ellis. She backed away, from Miss Stranks, from the sound of Bradbury's drunken laugh, from the photograph of Kitty lying there.

The front door opened. A gust of warm wind swept in. *The Lighted Way* flew in the air. There it was again. The distinct cry of 'Run!'

CHAPTER
TWENTY-FIVE

There were ten *Heralds* piled up on the end of Ellis' bed, which meant it was ten days since the policeman had arrived to ho-hum at his notebook and fossick through Girl's pitiful belongings. Ellis pretended to be asleep every time Clarrie brought in the newspaper. How could she say she couldn't bear to look at them, that there was no room inside of her to take in one more report on the manner and the time of people's deaths?

She watched the dust motes rise and fall in columns in the light, and ripple and reform with every blast for the bridge. She heard the cries of the resuming men, advancing like drummer boys across no man's land. She stared up at the ceiling as Rennie clipped across the floor. She feigned sleep whenever Rennie crept into her room to poke about at her desk or help herself to a newspaper.

'At last. I've made it to the missing persons column,' Rennie announced.

Ellis said nothing. She was incapable of anything except breathing in time with the heavy tides of her heart.

She woke to hear Rennie bounding downstairs. The front door was flung open.

'Ahoy!' Rennie cried.

Mrs Liddy's broom fell silent in the street. Clarrie coughed. Alf Ostler began blustering on about how he'd taken to keeping a pitchfork beneath his bed in case any more toughs set foot in Burton Street.

'You'd better arm yourselves,' he said. 'It could be any one of us next.'

Ellis sat up and lit a pipe. She waited to hear Girl's cackling reply: *Who's got a pitchfork living here, Alf? Give it here and I'll show you where to put it.* But there was no reply, just the echoing cries of 'Watcho!' followed by another pane-rattling blast.

When the blast had subsided, Ellis heard Rennie call out, 'Ned McCarthy? Ahoy there.'

Ned was here? Ellis waited for him to appear, but no one came.

She made her way down the hallway to the outhouse, past the flies buzzing over unwashed plates, the scalded pots, empty port wine bottles and saucers with teetering pyramids of cigarette ash. Ellis blinked at the dusty brightness of the yard. She sat in the outhouse, looked up at the stars of light shining through the holes in the iron roof. She considered washing and dressing, but no. Not yet.

She returned to bed. After few hours of dozing, she heard the key in the front door.

'Shh,' somebody said. A series of boots entered the house. She thought of Alf's warning about keeping on hand a pitchfork, or its equivalent, the pointed stick she'd kept behind the kitchen door. *If they come, let them*, she thought.

Someone was moving furniture about. She caught Alf's voice, 'Take it easy, will you? We don't want you smashing all the little lady's crockery.'

She almost laughed, but she couldn't laugh. That would be treachery.

She listened to hammering in determined rhythmic taps. A tea chest was heaved. The bedstead was shunted down. Rennie marched about dispensing instructions in a cheery voice, stopped only by the blasts.

'*The earthquakes of the human race/ Like them, forgotten when the ruin/ That marks their shock is past.*' That was Clarrie.

Mrs Liddy stopped sweeping her broom at the front step. 'Morning Tom,' she said.

Not Tom-the-pickpocket come to try his luck. But Mrs Liddy had headed him off with one of her I-remember-when lamentations about the little folk being done over by the bigwigs.

At last, there was Ned McCarthy's voice. He arrived like a beam of colour in her room. He set two sacks of fruit and vegetables on the floor and asked if he might sit with Ellis for a moment.

'The old place, eh?' He perched on the side of the bed, and took off his hat and looked about. The morning light caught the golden shimmer of his hair. 'This old place has lasted until it's lasted, I suppose.' He smiled at the picture hanging over the desk. 'Mum was a good one, wasn't she?'

Ellis wanted to nod, of course she did, but she couldn't seem to make herself.

Ned took her hand and held it tight. Ellis saw how his chin began to tremble, how a tide of emotion rose in his sea-coloured eyes. She wanted to reach out and stroke his cheek, but he turned away and wiped the back of his hand across his nose.

'Hang on, I've brought you something,' he said.

He went out into the hallway and reappeared with a large basket. He set it on the floor beside the bed. Ellis looked down at the parcels of damp newspaper and sphagnum moss. The smell of pollen, earth and damp rose up.

'Righto. These are cuttings from my garden to start you off,' he said. The trembling chin was gone now. He smiled as he touched his hands to each plump parcel of dissolving ink. 'Seedlings too. From what I've heard, the cottage itself should be all right.'

The cottage, Ellis thought. *He was talking about Rennie's flower farmlet at Lane Cove.* During those first fractured days following Girl's death, Rennie had persuaded her to pitch in her meagre savings and buy into the cottage with her. *You could grow the flowers, Ellis, and I could paint them. You said you'd love the country life. We can't stay here. Don't you see? It would be just the two of us. Wouldn't it be heavenly?*

'For what it's worth, I think you've done the right thing, Els,' he said.

Ellis looked at his eyes, those bright pools of light. So, it was true then. Today was the day. She was going to leave Burton Street. She raised a hand to her chest. All this had to be packed? She frowned at her desk and the piles of paper fallen to the floor. Then she remembered the nettle column she'd been working on. She'd missed her deadline for 'The Green-eyed Gardener'. Worse still, she hadn't told the editors of *The Gardeners' Almanac* she was moving away.

She gestured for Ned to bring her a paper and pen. He stood by the bed and watched as she wrote: *My dear Editors, Scribbly Gum is going bush to start a garden of her own. Shall I continue with the Green-eyed Gardener, or would you prefer me to retire?* She folded it in half and scrawled *URGENT* across the back of it.

'I'll see it gets there.' Ned placed his hat on his head. His expression changed at the sound of Rennie approaching. 'But you will watch it now, with ...?' He slid his eyes towards the sound of Rennie's voice.

Yes, Ellis said back with her eyes. Ned kissed her on the cheek and left.

There was the sound of a truck idling in the street. Ellis lifted the curtain. The Clements Brothers' fine polished shoes emerged from the cabin. She heard them greet Mrs Liddy and step through the activity. They installed themselves at her bedroom door and politely enquired about her health. When Ellis couldn't manage to find an answer, they admired 'the workhorse' of her old typewriter and bemoaned the fact they'd be losing their 'trusty invoicing secretary' after all these years of 'impeccable service'. They slid a departing envelope into Ellis' hand and offered to repair the damaged leg of her old wardrobe. They told her they'd already arranged for two of their men to drive Ellis and her 'furnishings' out to Lane Cove for 'the removalling'.

Ellis managed a nod. They departed, leaving a waft of hair tonic in their wake. She opened the envelope. Another minor windfall. She tucked it away in her cardigan pocket. She heard Rennie intercept the Clements Brothers in the street. Ellis couldn't catch all that was said. The word 'marvellous' came up over again in between gushes of Rennie's laughter.

'Ned? You're back,' Rennie said. 'What fun.'

Ned joined in the discussion, something about Rennie's splendid new chairs and mattresses being delivered straight away. *Dear Ned.* There he was at the beginning and the end.

Ellis looked up to find Rennie ushering a workman into her room.

'Here it is,' Rennie said, meaning the wardrobe. 'Such a handsome fellow. It's wonderful to know he'll leave here with the requisite number of legs.'

Ellis wanted to say, *it's a she, not a he.* She rose from her bed waving the man away. She closed the door and dressed herself, slid the Clements Brothers' windfall inside the biscuit tin and took it out the back with Ned's garden-in-a-basket. She washed herself in the bathroom and sat on the back step. She smoked two pipes of maidenhair and stared out at the yard, waiting until she could feel the softness of Girl next to her. There she was. She could smell her musky smell. She could hear her humming a saucy tune. One of Girl's chubby fists was held out. *Have a snifter or two, Els. It'll perk you up.*

'Ellis?' Rennie called.

Girl nudged her again and faded away. Ellis tried to concentrate on what Rennie was saying.

'Ellis? Did you hear what I said?'

Apparently a boy had arrived with an urgent reply from the editors of the *Almanac*. Rennie handed her the note. Ellis read the words and brushed away the twitch of a smile on her lips. *As you know, Miss Gilbey, gardeners never retire. We await your next instalment in due course. I trust you (and Mr Moses) will travel well.*

She sat on the stairs, Ned's seedlings and her biscuit tin at her side, watching as they dismantled her life and carried it into the light. Every crack, stain, scratch and scrape, every frill of dust was illuminated before it disappeared into the back of the Clements Brothers' truck. When it was all done, she didn't allow herself to linger in each shell of a room. She tried not to notice the empty sound of her steps or where the plaster had cracked and floured the floor, or the swathes of damp advancing and retreating across the walls. She simply went to each window and opened it. It seemed fitting to let the harbour winds blow away the last traces of all the souls who'd ever passed through here.

For the last time, she took her hat from the peg and wound her scarf around her neck. She thought she heard the house sigh as she stepped out into the pale shadows of the street. Everyone was gathered there. Mrs Liddy had brought a tray of jars and cups. Paddy Forbes—O'Malley's right-hand man, no less—produced a bottle of sherry. Nobody spoke as he filled Ellis' glass.

'To Girl,' she finally said.

Everybody looked down at their sherries. Ellis took a deep breath, raised her chin and put her shoulders back.

'To Girl,' she said again. This time her voice was calm and even. She held her glass up towards the empty slant of Girl's balcony.

That done, the driver leapt into the truck and cranked it into gear. The other man heaved himself after him. Rennie was wearing the veiled hat and fox-fur coat. She dashed after them and cried out, 'All aboard. Come on, Ellis!' She held out an impatient glove.

Ellis blinked up at the cabin as Rennie squeezed in beside two men, laughing as she wriggled into her seat.

Ellis turned to Ned. 'I'll sit in the back.'

'What? With all the furniture?' said Rennie. 'One of these chaps won't mind riding shotgun, surely?' Rennie motioned for the ruddier, balder, fatter, older one to climb down.

'No. I'd prefer it.' *I'd prefer not to see.*

'But you can't.'

'Yes, she can,' said Ned.

He cleared her a space in the back between the kitchen table and the wardrobe. Once she was ensconced, he passed her the biscuit tin and basket of plants. Ellis clutched them to her coat and closed her eyes. The driver ground the gears and the truck began to shudder down the street. *Stop*, she thought. She opened her eyes.

'Stop! Wait!' somebody called out.

'Stop,' Ellis said.

'Why? What is it now?' Rennie called out from the window.

The driver shunted to a halt.

'Wait.' It was Clarrie limping towards her, flapping his poetry book. 'At last, the fairy queen rides in her chariot. My cousin'll be by any minute now so I reckon he'll have me so busy fishing, I won't need this old thing anymore.' He pressed the poetry book into her glove.

Ellis looked down at it and tried to speak, but Clarrie had already turned away to limp and cough back up the street.

She was glad to be alone as they inched through the chaos of Milsons Point. On they went through the endless suburbs until, at last. They were in the trees.

PART THREE

PART THREE

CHAPTER
TWENTY-SIX

The sky was bird's-egg blue. *See Lloyd? I've done it.* Rennie smiled out at the trees. The further the lorry thumped along the track, the more her mind buzzed with daring images and new ideas. As soon as they were settled, she'd experiment with her paints; she'd pile her palette with Payne's grey, French ultramarine and one of the yellows and finally capture the grey-green hues.

On they went. Once or twice, she urged the driver to go faster, but being one of those chip-on-the-shoulder types, he either obliged and thudded them straight into a muddy pothole, or pushed his hat back and began to whistle as if he hadn't heard. Rennie wound down the window. The cabin was beginning to smell decidedly fruity. She lit another cigarette and kept on smiling, despite the driver's petulance.

Finally they passed the village of Lane Cove. Strangely, there was no one about. But there was a haberdashers, butcher, wide-verandahed hotel and a general store.

She had to hang on as the driver swung left onto another wheel-rutted track. The other man fell against her with a thump. Every now and then she craned her neck to try to see if anyone had been following them. As yet there was no sign, but she knew Lloyd had both time and resources on his side.

Rennie let out a cry as the glittery glimpse of the river caught her eye. And yes. Two chimneys. Hurrah! And a roof. But oh. It looked rather ramshackle as they skittered through the gate past the faded sign flapping in the wind: *Arcadia*. They ground to a stop next to a rusted iron drum and a wheel of barbed wire. Rennie stared at the cottage. It was large and low. Various porches and rooms dived off this way and that, as if somebody had thrown it down from a great height. She looked up as a wind fizzed through the trees. Large white birds with yellow crests stood like stout candles in the branches staring down. One let out a hideous screech, causing the others to add to the cacophony before taking flight.

'I suppose that's the Australian way of saying welcome.' Rennie tried to sound jolly as she flipped open her cigarette tin.

'Whatever you say, Missus.'

Oh God, she thought as the men leapt out of the driver's side and disappeared behind a tree.

Ellis had already climbed down from the back. She walked straight past them as if in a daze, not saying a word, the biscuit tin clutched to her chest, and Ned's battered basket in hand. She seemed intent on reading the sign on the gate where she stood for some time, her face a blank. That done, Ellis walked to the cottage and tested each step of the porch with her boot before setting her things by the door. She wrenched the door open and disappeared. It seemed like forever before she emerged.

'Brooms, buckets, mops,' was all she said. Her demeanour gave no hint of what level of horror or beauty awaited them inside.

Suddenly Rennie felt unbearably hot. She flung off her hat and tore off her gloves. She stared down at her fingers, at the pale indent where the wedding rings had so recently branded her as Lloyd's damaged goods. Oh God. What had she done?

It had all seemed so much fun back at Ellis' house, the mad decision to sell off her jewellery and buy her own small square of earth. It had felt like a honeyed dream, waltzing off with Ned McCarthy up the street, the sun shining on his angelic hair, the dust and rubble at their backs, envious eyes watching as she'd laughed and chatted on to Mr Taciturn Ned. For those few moments, she hadn't cared if Lloyd or Bertha, or the whole damned lot of them had seen him chaperoning her through the ruinous streets. They'd stood together outside the Clements Brothers' Emporium, their twin reflections etched across the displays of fine furniture and pristine settings of home. Ned had said 'Come on,' and they'd entered the shop together and walked down the aisle towards the counter, not quite arm in arm, but very much with the air of being old friends—if not man and wife.

When she'd shown the Clements Brothers the items of jewellery she wanted to sell, they'd discreetly suggested applying soap to ease off the rings. All the while, Ned had stood there, silently watching this intimate and irrevocable act. The Clements Brothers had kept their word. They'd asked no questions and paid a fair price. Then it was time for Rennie and Ned to trip off to the dubious real estate offices of J. T. Bickley Esquire. Once inside, he'd considered a sheaf of papers, trying to slow things, she thought, before informing her at length of the pros of cons.

'Who needs more cons?' she'd laughed. 'The city is already bristling with cons.'

Now that she'd done it, it was both blissful and terrifying. The men were beginning to thump and scrape things in the back of the lorry. Rennie knew she should climb out, but she couldn't yet. Her eye was caught by a drop of water shimmering in a clump of grass. It sparkled at her, blinking and twitching like a diamond. *Yes*, it seemed to say. *You have done the right thing. You are the link in the golden chain.*

She looked along the track. There was no sign of Lloyd, not yet. At any moment he might converge in a wail of sirens with a battalion of policemen. And until he did, she'd keep to her plan of eking out a simple, humble, bucolic life here in the bush, with only the joys of nature to admire, absorb, sketch and paint—simply for art's sake. She tried to hold her smile as she blinked at the empty track, at the walls of trees crowding in, the thick, heavy silence penetrated only by the cackles of birds and the disquieting fidget of leaves whispering in foreign tongues.

CHAPTER
TWENTY-SEVEN

Ellis peered up at the slouching ceilings. She trod carefully across the creaking boards. At any moment they might open up and swallow her. She felt no emotion as she inspected each room, nor as she took up the broom. It wasn't until she tried not to think of Mrs Liddy ploughing her broom through the house for the very last time at Burton Street, that the realisation hit her. She had finally left. She carved narrow paths with her broom through layers of leaves, paper and dust, and chased several cockroaches the size of rats. She apologised to a colony of redbacks before sweeping them out. She knelt down in front of the fireplace and tussled with a vine which had ventured down the chimney to twine itself around the grate. She stamped her feet to ward off snakes as she braved the long grasses at the back of the house. She put her ear to the cold belly of the water tank and managed to wrench on the tap to fill a bucket. She mopped the floors, wiped the windows with wet newspaper, emptied the kitchen cupboards of old tins of bully beef, removed the skeletons and droppings of mice, and peered at the possible treasures stuffed under the house.

She stood in the garden and looked at the lines of the roof. Ned had been right. The bones of the cottage were good—*and it was theirs*.

She heard Rennie claim the largest room at the front of the house as her bedroom. *Good*, Ellis thought. She'd liked the sleep-out immediately, the long and narrow afterthought of a room with its missing louvres, lurching floors, and the vine leaning its elbows along the sills.

She could hear Rennie directing the removalists, as they grappled with a heavy wooden couch she'd bought from the Clements Brothers. There were grunts and curses as they tried to upend it and coax it in. The room seemed to contract around its bulk. Three more chairs needed to be hefted in, apparently. How many chairs had Rennie bought?

'No. More to the left,' Rennie said, waving her cigarette. 'Oh no, not there. It'll catch fire if you jam it like that against the hearth.'

The rigmarole continued until all the beds, cupboards, chairs and boxes were heaved inside. Ellis made sure the kitchen was set out with enough pots, pans, crockery and cutlery to see them through for the first night.

'You sure you'll be all right here, ladies, on your own?' said one of the men.

'But we're not on our own,' Rennie laughed. 'There's two of us.'

'Thank you, yes.' Ellis said quickly. 'Ned McCarthy will be out here soon with the horse. Please give my regards to the Clements Brothers.'

Ellis and Rennie stood on the porch as the truck swept off, the roar of the engine diminishing like a wave breaking in the distance. Neither of them spoke as they watched the dust rise and fall along the track.

'I've really gone and done it now,' Rennie let out a silly laugh.

'We'd better collect some wood for the fire before it gets dark.'

'What fun this all is,' said Rennie, but in her voice there was a quavering of doubt.

The cool of night engulfed the house. A wind swept in. Ellis lit the kerosene lamps and set a small fire in the sitting room grate. They perched on Rennie's enormous chairs surrounded by a sea of boxes and swathes of newspaper. Neither of them spoke as they chewed through the dry egg and potato pie Mrs Liddy had baked. *Mrs Liddy*, Ellis thought. She took a swig of sherry to help it go down, and wondered if Clarrie's cousin had come to collect them yet. As the sherry wended its way down the byways of her throat, she closed her eyes and willed herself to picture her old neighbours being driven away on a cart by a kindly man to somewhere pretty and comfortable, over the hills way out west to where the soil turned red and trees rose up as pale as bone, but the vision wouldn't hold.

Rennie remained silent, smoking and sipping her sherry, staring at the fire. Ellis saw her flinch as the wind whipped up beneath the iron roof.

'What was that?'

'The wind, I expect.'

'No, the other sound. It sounded like scraping, or … a car. Could there be a car coming out here at this hour?'

'I'm sure it's just the wind.' Ellis went to the window and peered out. 'I can't see anything.'

'Of course you can't. It's pitch black.'

They both looked up as the wind rumbled through the roof.

'See? It's only the …'

'No. It wasn't that sound. It was more of a … oh I don't know. A grinding sound. Like someone dragging something metallic, sharp, heavy.'

She means an axe, Ellis thought. This kind of unsettling talk could go on all night if she didn't put a stop to it. Ellis went to the kitchen. As she passed Rennie in the sitting room, she hid the frying pan behind her back.

'You're not going out there, are you?' Rennie said.

'I'm sure it's just something come loose in this wind.' Ellis tried to keep her voice calm.

'But shouldn't you at least take the lamp?'

'Wait here.'

'No, I'll come with you. I can't stay in here alone. What will I do if you don't come back?'

'I'm not going anywhere.'

Ellis forced herself to smile over her own growing sense of unease. It couldn't have been a car, could it, or a truck? She hadn't liked one of the removing men, the way he'd gawped at the tight cut of Rennie's dress and sworn under his breath as she'd ordered them about.

Ellis let herself outside and stood on the porch. She shivered as her eyes adjusted to the windy dark. She raised the frying pan in front of her, half as a shield, half as a weapon, and followed the path of the scraping sound which finally brought her to a piece of metal flapping back and forth outside Rennie's bedroom window. She managed to wrestle the metal to the ground and set two rocks on it to hold it down. She looked in at the window, at the flickering light emanating from the fire and lamps, at Rennie's wide new bed, her clothes and sketchbooks flung about the floor.

The moon stayed shy. The occasional star flickered behind the moving lace of high cloud. She stood on the porch and looked out across the trees to where the distant glow of the city lit night's dark hem. Over there across the tops of the trees lay the other world, her old world with its familiar labyrinth of falling down streets, their shattered edges soothed by the silken salve of the harbour where the white footsteps of the wind left their mark. It wasn't hard to imagine she was back there now, disembarking from the last ferry, moving around the corner and up the hill, her boots tapping across the dusty cobblestones. There it was, the yawning door of number 10. She peered in at its hollowed-out skin and turned to make sure Mrs Liddy's and Clarrie's house was empty too. She couldn't bring herself to look across to Girl's balcony. She wished she'd thought to leave a flower on her step, something bright pink and visible in the dark. Now only Alf Ostler remained. Ellis imagined him snoring away at number 17, fingers of moonlight stroking the tines of the pitchfork stowed beneath his bed.

She peered into the sitting room window. Rennie wasn't there. Ellis let herself back inside. Rennie leapt out at her like a jack in a box.

Rennie gasped when she saw the frying pan. 'So, you *were* on edge as well as me. Tell me, who or what was the culprit?'

'An old sheet of roofing had come loose. That's all.'

'That's all? It sounds rather serious.'

'Nothing a touch of ingenuity wouldn't fix.'

Rennie smiled at her, as if about to continue quizzing her.

'It's late,' Ellis said. 'I'm turning in.'

She covered over the fire and made her way to her room. She was half undressed when she heard Rennie call out.

'We are safe now, aren't we? Tell me we are.'

Ellis was thinking of Girl, the bruises and burn marks on her arms, the scar on her cheek, now lying blue and cold in a pauper's grave. *So much for safety, Rennie*, Ellis wanted to say. *Look at Girl. Look at her life, the bravado instilled from birth. She's more qualified than anyone to tell you that safety can only ever stretch so far.*

After about an hour of lying awake listening to the sounds of the house, Ellis heard her bedroom door open. She lay very still and kept her eyes half shut. She could see Rennie standing there, her white face, her dark shock of hair, the glint of her eyes casting about the room. Ellis continued feigning the breath of a sleeper, but her mind raced. What did Rennie want? She saw her toss her hair over her shoulder as if it were still long. Rennie coughed and waited, then was gone.

Morning barged through the bare windows. Cockatoos shouted in the trees. A flock of magpies took turns tossing up and swallowing their golden notes. Ellis lay very still. If she moved, it might all collapse. She closed her eyes to the gold-drenched light. She already knew every inch of this place, the brown shadows lurking in corners, the silvery webs spinning down from the beams. She knew the ship-like creaking of the roof above and the slow click-click of the floors below. She recognised them all, not because she'd already had time to explore but because they belonged to her childhood at Candlebark Creek.

She should have sat up and leapt out of bed when she heard Rennie cough and clatter pots and pans about, but she couldn't seem to move. So, it was true then. They'd done it. *One pound down now, no more to pay, splendid roomy blocks, sight unseen.* After all these years, she was back living amongst the trees in the air, light, clouds and sky. She had a room of her own, with a desk and typewriter by the window, a view of the trees. Outside, there was the garden waiting to be made beside a craggy cliff which cast its great shadow towards the cottage. For the moment at least, she had a place. Why then had she woken in the night, weeping quietly, wanting to die? Because as soon as she'd seen this place, old memories she'd tried to lock away had been exposed, rising up as sharp as the outcrops of sandstone she'd tripped over in the backyard when she'd scrounged for firewood. Even though she knew the wryly named *Arcadia* wasn't the farm of her childhood, she knew it was the ghost of it.

She forced herself to sit on the edge of the bed and dress. She stood at the window and looked out at water tank. *Home. Would she ever dare to call it that?* She'd forgotten the presence of natural silence, the constant undertone to the buzz of a blowfly, the flutter of moths, the rising shrill of cicadas, the busy march of ants. She raised her head. In the distance, there was the mirage-like rush of water. She knew it then. It had been the proximity of a river which had made her weep.

They'd not had a river at Candlebark Creek. Their small creek had been no match for the years of drought. They'd been forced to carry water from a fetid waterhole miles away with the pitiful aim of keeping everything alive. She had failed and everything had died.

She should have known. She should have seen. She'd heard her mother struggling with the pails. *Listen*, her mother had gasped. *Listen to me, Ellis*, but Ellis had worked on, trying to save the last of the plants. And even though she'd heard the rattle of the pail as it hit the ground, and although she'd seen the precious water escaping across the ground glinting towards her in the sun, she'd still turned to watch the leaves of the gum tree flicker and dance. She'd gazed up at the clouds sailing overhead, a raft of golden ships, and let herself become entranced by the rays of sun flowing down like celestial ropes.

By the time she'd found her mother, she was lying face down by the garden fence and even though the day was as still as glass, a wind had swept up and ruffled the back of her mother's dress. Her hair had been lifted and fallen back down. And for those few seconds, Ellis had prayed that it was not the wind, but her mother's breath.

CHAPTER
TWENTY-EIGHT

F our weeks. Could it really be only four weeks since they'd landed at the cottage? Rennie crouched down beside the sandstone cliff and cupped her cigarette in her hands. Whatever Ellis said about the cliff, she'd been pleased to find a natural turret rising at the back of the cottage. *Sight unseen.* So what if the cliff blocked the sun to the garden beds? It was still only early spring and already the sun threatened to burn every living thing to a crisp.

She peered at the different colours and lines in the rock. Every inch of it cried out to have its likeness splashed onto a canvas in a blocky mosaic style, in yellow ochre, madder rose and burnt umber. One day, when Ellis was being less monosyllabic and a bright choir of flowers sang brightly from their beds, Rennie would hold a small soirée here. She'd hang all of her artworks on the cliff, draping the other sections with a sheet painted with ivy-clad ruins, sun-baked hills, satyrs cavorting with buxom red-lipped maidens, strumming lyres. Or, she thought, as she chivvied her trowel at the rock, why not blast a section out and fashion her very own grotto? She could paint all kinds of frescoes on the walls. She'd escape in there in the summer heat to laze about drinking gin and lime. She could hold small gatherings for all her friends, except of course, she had no friends living out here. Even if she'd dared take a tiny detour from pursuing the country life to dip her toe back into the social whirl, there'd been no time for anything so far but work, work, work.

So much for living the green and pleasant Arcadian dream. For four back-breaking, fingernail-splitting weeks which already felt like four months, they'd spent every hour sieving, trenching, flinging rocks from dawn until dusk only to wake and find more rocks had infested the beds overnight.

'Growing stones,' Ellis had called them. 'People once believed stones grew back over night.'

Rennie had stopped her tedious stone-breaking task to respond to the longest and most interesting sentence Ellis had uttered since they'd arrived.

'Once believed?' Rennie's laughter had echoed a little too shrilly against the cliff. 'I'd say they still damn well do, Ellis, don't you think? With unabashed impunity.'

But Ellis had not laughed back. She'd simply continued throwing her hoe at the earth as if trying to behead some kind of mythical multi-headed creature that promptly sprouted another.

Should I stay, or should I go? The question rattled so loudly and so often through Rennie's head, she wondered if Ellis could hear it too.

On that first morning here, Ellis had appeared like a somnambulist on the front porch. Tears had poured from eyes. She'd looked frail and wild-eyed, not the wiry, taciturn, dry-witted landlady she'd been before Girl's murder. How could Rennie think of leaving when it was clear how much Ellis depended on her now?

Ellis hadn't displayed such an outpouring of emotions again. In fact, she'd revealed not one thing. Every day she leapt out of bed to work like an automaton in the sun. She didn't seem to feel the blisters spreading across her hands. Her thin body never seemed to tire, or if it did, she drove it on relentlessly. She stopped only to wipe sweat from her brow, to eat, drink and ponder aloud where to plant Ned McCarthy's seemingly endless array of seedlings, or to stand and puff on her pipe, squinting at the beds, working from a plan in her head about where to mark out boundaries, away from the encroaching shadows of the cliff. While Rennie was still feeling about for her first morning cigarette, Ellis was already thumping about the kitchen, spooning down great bowls of oats and molasses in silence, gulping sweet black tea, dressing the same way every day in dusty breeches, straw hat and baggy shirts. Whenever she talked, which was an increasingly rare event, the subject was always gardening.

Yesterday, Rennie had discovered Ellis bent down over another batch of seedlings provided by Mr Elusive Ned. Rennie had crept to the door and heard her whispering to them. When Ellis realised she was being watched, she was unperturbed.

'Some people believe all plants have souls,' she'd said. 'The Greeks certainly thought trees had souls.'

'Well,' Rennie had laughed. 'I'm not about to argue with the Greeks.'

She threw down her trowel and frowned up at the porch. Her sketchbook perched on a makeshift easel besieged by seedlings sprouting in rusted tins, broken chamber pots and apple boxes which Ellis had discovered in 'the treasure trove' beneath the house and set on rocks or in moats of water to avoid the onslaught of snails and slugs. An ancient pram squeaked down dusty paths, reborn as a wheelbarrow. Lupins were to be grown and stamped upon to drive away the lines of invading ants. String would be dipped in creosote to lie around the cabbages. Eggshells had been smashed and scattered around to protect any tender shoots. Tea leaves were flung. Peelings and scraps were tossed into Ellis' mysteriously named 'clean culture' compost pile. Apparently she'd read about it 'years ago, in another life.' The compost was 'clean', she said, because you didn't sully it with 'the remains of dead animals.' Affable marigolds were planted beside friendly tomatoes because apparently they were 'companions'. Bean and pea seeds were rolled in paraffin to fend off mice. Onions were planted around the edges of beds to repel the rabbits. Horses' hair was to be collected and wound around the trunks of all future fruit trees to thwart the upward climb of insects—and heavens knew what else was going to be done in Pan's name. And with every hour, Rennie found it more difficult to ignore the persistent refrain of her thoughts: *But dear God, is this what I came here for?*

The night before she'd closed the door to her bedroom and reread Irving's letters. *Your passage has been booked on the 20th September. All you need do is appear.* She'd held both letters up to the light as if trying to divine their veracity. Was Irving on her side or not? Or was he merely trying to lure her out so that Lloyd could lock her away for eternity in the Australian equivalent of Bedlam so he could gad about with Bertha Collins? The sailing date was now only two weeks away.

Rennie turned her head. What on earth was Ellis doing now? She could hear her muttering as she tossed fistfuls of seeds at the earth.

'One for the crop, one for the crow, one to die, one to grow.'

'What a ghastly saying,' Rennie said but Ellis didn't seem to hear.

Well, it would be both of them who perished from discomfort and overwork if Mr Kelp-and-Kale Ned didn't arrive soon with their much-needed horse and cart. She'd paid for the horse herself in full before they'd left, her funds having fallen maddeningly short for the outright purchase of a motorcar. A full month on and the horse was yet to canter up the track. Until Flicker, Firefly or Flossie arrived, she and Ellis were forced to take it in turns to trudge through the Never-Never into the so-called village to gather a new batch of supplies.

While the hike to civilisation did release Rennie from the back-breaking tedium of raking at the dust, the track was long and wracked with stones and there was always the distinct feeling of being watched. Even though it was easy to believe there was nobody else living within shouting distance, or 'within coo-ee' as Ellis insisted on saying, other people were tucked away behind the trees. More than once she'd heard the tinkle of music, the shouts of laughter, the roar of passing motorcars. Whenever this happened, she'd had to force herself not to throw down her trowel or abandon the axe and dash to the gate and cry out 'ahoy there.'

Rennie looked up. At last, softness had come to the evening sky as it cast its rosy colours over the cliff. She watched the birds diving into clouds of gnats. *In their tiny beaks*, she thought, *they usher in the silken threads of night*. Not that Ellis seemed to notice. There she was, still toiling away.

Rennie went up to the porch and held out her hands in the bronzing light. Cuts, scars and an intricate web of dirt had become ingrained like filigree across her skin. The white gash of her wedding ring had been long buried beneath the grime. There was satisfaction in knowing that the muscles in her arms curdled with every stroke of the rake, rather than as a result of a bullying husband's fists. But with every hour of toil, she worried about the damage to her beautiful, willowy, artist's hands—if not to her sensitive creative mind.

She hadn't realised there'd be no time for art out here. There wasn't any time for *life*. Of course, she'd longed to escape to the country, but this was not the kind of country she'd quite meant. Yes, she'd been desperate to run from Lloyd's stifling world, but sometimes one did miss things.

Sometimes one longed to see and hear and smell and—well—*be amongst* the madding crowd—especially on a Friday night.

How far she felt from everything at that very moment, rubbing at her aching hands, standing on the porch in her ghastly clothes, watching Ellis slaving on. She'd known she'd have to pay a high price to free herself from her husband's yoke and it had not been so hard to dissolve in the hazy film of the eucalypts, but the longer she was here, it was becoming more difficult not to let her mind wander beyond the garden and the cottage. It was harder not to stray from the rock-strewn track which led to the village where the woman in the grocer shop frowned whenever Rennie asked perfectly clearly and politely if she might trouble her for a pound of tea or a day-old newspaper as the woman gawped at her, saying 'Beg par?' over again.

Ellis advised Rennie to carry a stick whenever she ventured from the house, 'to ward off the snakes.' But she couldn't be bothered with that now. She grabbed her cigarettes, sketchbook and pencil and walked quickly down the side of the cottage, across the track, down through the bushes and the scritch-scratch trees, breaking into a run as fast as her boots would allow, feeling the prickle of freedom as she skittered over roots and stones, not caring if she tripped, her arms whipped by thorns and twigs until she could hear, smell, and see the multiplicity of beguiling elements that made up the long cool flow of the Lane Cove River. She loved the river. It was both a comfort and a temptation.

It was almost too dark to sketch but she wanted to try to capture *something* of the day, the dark parentheses of currents besieging the rushes, the wallpaper bark peeling from the trees, revealing the enigmatic scribbles made by unseen insects.

There was not a soul here but her. A woman and a river, both moving towards unknown ends. It struck her that, at that very moment, nobody in the world knew where she was. She stared at the water, its surface moving deceptively slowly, driven on by the churning turmoil beneath. So easily, she thought, she could give herself up to the currents there. She finished her cigarette and watched as it fizzled out in the water and was ferried away downstream. She rose to her feet and held one boot over the bank. She could smell the muddy water and hear the cool, silent invitation of the river. She closed her eyes. How simple it would be to take one more step.

But what was that? She turned her head. There it was again, the distinct sound of laughter coming from further up the river, followed by the hooting of a claxon which meant it could not be Lloyd. Perhaps it was a band of happy holidaymakers scudding about on a jaunt. She lunged back up the bank, a mixture of elation and fear rising inside of her. But the car was gone.

When she reached the cottage, the ubiquitous Brunnings gardening book was lying open on the step. Ever since Ned had sent it along with packets of seed, Ellis had treated the thing like a bible, reading it every night and repeating swathes of it at the most unexpected moments. *It says we must sow these in the warmer months. According to the book, we must …* There was no doubt that Ellis' photographic memory was an impressive trait—but perhaps it was one best appreciated in small doses.

'Champagne anyone?' Rennie said as she ran up the steps. She clawed at her hair to remove the sticks as she strode through the living room with its handsome new chairs. She stepped down into the kitchen which was deserted. Still? At this hour? Why hadn't Ellis begun to cook? Through the tiny window, she could see Ellis working like a navvy in the dusk.

'Champagne or cocktails?' Rennie sighed to the makeshift pantry, which boasted little more than the tight bricks of cornbread Ellis insisted on baking every other day, several earnest carrots, a bunch of bendy turnips and a bag of onions on the sprout.

The vegetarian diet had been fun, at first. Coupled with hard work, the extra pounds had fallen off, but now she was becoming somewhat browned off with it. Unable to boil an egg herself, Rennie could only appear grateful and chomp away on her woody walnut cutlet or whatever noble delicacy Ellis had rustled up that evening to grace their plates.

But tonight, if Rennie had her own way, she'd be off to the Australia Hotel to order the oysters in aspic, followed by the rack of lamb. She'd wire her brother Irving and tell him she was on her way back 'under her own steam', travelling under a false name back to England. *Oh poor old England.* Could she really bear to go back there? Once repatriated, why should she stay in that mouldering tomb? As soon as she'd returned she'd pack herself off to one of those fashionable artists' colonies on the Mediterranean to mingle with other authentic artistic sorts.

She felt lighter as she stared at the gloomy shadows, but the lightness was snuffed out as she remembered the unsettling dream she'd suffered the night before, prompted no doubt by the persistent noises in the night, the shrieks and cackles and mysterious barks and cries particular to the Australian bush. In the dream, all the animals she'd ever plunged her knife and fork into reappeared in a caterwauling throng, gathering about her bed, staring at her as they staggered about with missing limbs, chunks taken from their bleeding flanks, wingless chickens, tongueless oxen, all beseeching her with accusing eyes as they stampeded throughout the house, and lumbered down to leap into the river.

If that's what a vegetarian diet did to you, why on earth would you persist? Tomorrow, when it was her turn to tramp into the village again, she'd stop by the family butcher with the sign in the window saying *freshly killed*, and bring home a decent lump of meat and announce to Ellis she had temporarily abandoned her newly adopted herbivorous life while the delicious scent of *real* cooking filled the house.

Rennie opened the window, impatient for tonight to be over so tomorrow would arrive.

'Ellis, can't you come in now? It's far too late. What are you up to out there in the dark?' She was aware she was beginning to sound like a boarding school mistress or a nun chastising her sinful charges. *Oh God*, she thought. *Is this who I've become?*

'It's Friday. I thought we'd agree to stop early on Fridays. Really, Ellis, what is going on?'

In the fading light, she saw Ellis stop. She couldn't quite hear what Ellis said, but she stood there for some time, as unmoving and inscrutable as a sentinel.

Next day, Rennie was up early, eager to trek into the village. She'd not slept well. She'd lain in bed scanning the night for the hum and buzz of human activity, laughter, music, passing cars, anything to stave off the return of her ghastly animal dream, and to distract her from fretting over what to do about Irving's free ticket back to England.

How far away that all felt now. She lit a cigarette and marched away from the cottage, pleased with the wad of damp newspaper she'd stowed in her basket to wrap around the meat and keep it cool during the walk back. After about half an hour she saw a frill of rising dust ahead. *Excellent.* Finally Mr Azure-eyed Ned would gallop in on the winged back of Pegasus. But then she heard it, the grinding of a motor car. She scurried off the track, prodded her snake stick at the ferns and positioned herself behind a tree. If it was Lloyd he'd thunder up to the cottage only to discover she wasn't there. She wondered what Ellis would do. Welcome him with a frying pan?

There was the sound of women's laughter over the approaching sound of the car.

She held her breath. There it was now. The car roared past. She caught sight of two women and two men. Both women were blonde and neither man was as solidly built as Lloyd. She stepped out from her hiding place as the car made a *whumphing* sound and screeched to halt. She ran back to her tree. There were shrieks of laughter.

'You've driven straight past the turn off, you fool,' somebody laughed.

The car ground backwards, jerked forwards and skidded off down a side track. Rennie waited until the dust dispersed. She stood at the turn off. She glanced back along the track to the village and gazed up at the sun. The car couldn't have gone very far. It wouldn't take a moment to have a look. She walked quickly until she saw the tyre marks swinging off the track and down through a wooden gate, half-hidden by ferns. She thrashed her snake-stick about and looked up. Through the trees she caught a glimpse of a high gabled roof with chimneys painted handsome red, dotted with fancy ornaments in celandine green.

She brushed back the ferns and stared at the sparkling brass sign, *Riverslea*. She tossed away her stick and quickened her pace along the tree-shadowed driveway. The width of her smile increased with every step. The architect of this truly modern house had been playing tricks. The actual size of the creation was concealed until you came close enough to its stylish, bold presence. There was a series of large garages to the left, suggesting a fleet of cars. Only two were visible, neither of which she recognised. A long, cool dark-tiled verandah surrounded the house. Lush potted palms waved softly in the breeze, contrasting with the warm sandstone brickwork. A towering fountain in the form of a squarely chiselled kangaroo bubbled in the middle of the sweep of a circular drive way.

She stopped. One more step and it would be too late to turn back. *Everybody who's anybody goes to the parties at the river house*, that's what Bertha Collins had said. Could this be the same house? She had to know.

She had to look. Either that or she'd end up withering away, a perfect nobody, in the Australian bush.

She counted to three, took off her hat, patted her hair and before her nerve deserted her, marched out from the trees and ran up the front steps. She lifted the heavy brass knocker and let it drop. As she waited, she peered inside the wide front windows at the large room dotted with cushions in magenta and gold satins and silks. The walls were covered in large abstract paintings and offset by floor mats in the Cubist design which had been so fashionable in London before she'd left.

'Hell-oo?'

Nobody answered. She made her way around the side of the house, through a pretty English walled garden with fronds of honeysuckle and pink and red roses perfuming the breeze, and into a tunnel of wispy trees. She hadn't felt so excited since—oh what did it matter now? She'd discovered something wild and exotic all by herself. She raked her fingers across the surface of a small pond where the mouths of goldfish could be seen nibbling clouds, and peered into another window. She gasped at the sight of a grand piano.

Excellent, she thought, as she ran down the path and through a gate. She stopped when she saw large sloping lawns sweeping down to an avenue of weeping willows trailing their branches into the river, the very same river she had sat beside so many times with her sketchbook, smoking, worrying, wondering how long she'd last this kind of life. Everything here looked so different, silky, lazy, placid. Chunky stone sculptures adorned the grass or rose up from the dizzying array of flowerbeds. A bronze shield hung on a wall.

The sound of singing appeared to be coming from a hatch beneath the house. Rennie marched towards it.

'Hell-oo? Anybody home?'

'Mademoiselle Jeanne?' A pink-eared man appeared, to the sound of women's laughter.

'Bonjour, monsieur. I'm terribly sorry, but you are mistaken. My name is not Jeanne.'

'*Santé*.' He offered her a half-drunk bottle of champagne.

Rennie turned as the sound of claxons hooted at the front of the house. A woman in an orange turban and flowing gown walked towards her across the grass, flapping an enormous oriental fan.

'Welcome ashore, Miss Jeanne.' The woman's face creased in delight as she looked Rennie up and down. 'What fun we'll have painting you.'

'I'm terribly sorry, but I think you're mistaken. I'm not Miss Jeanne.'

The fan-woman bent down to fend off an orange puff of a dog which had begun to dance about at the hem of her filmy skirts. A curiously sylphlike fellow in a sailor's jersey and black beret arrived and called the dog back.

'This is Miss Jeanne,' the fan-woman said to him. 'Our model. Whisk her off to the studio. Show her the gowns. We'll begin with the Roman, I think and then the Greek.'

There was an enigmatic smile from beneath the beret, before he picked the dog up and stowed it gently on his hip.

'I'm so terribly sorry,' Rennie laughed. 'But I'm not Miss ...'

All eyes now turned towards the monsieur who'd arisen from the hatch beneath the house and screamed as he dropped the bottle of champagne.

'Oh dear, it seems we shall have to do without Monsieur's latest exposition of Stravinsky until later. I'm sure you are familiar with the challenges of the artistic life, Miss Jeanne.'

'I do hate to disappoint you, but I'm not Miss Jeanne. I'm your neighbour. I'm in the rustic stone cottage down the track. I'm an artist, you see. My name is Rennie Howar ...' Stupidly she'd almost blurted out her married name. She let out a laugh to cover herself.

More people began to appear, chatting and ambling across the lawn. Her breath left her as she caught sight of Bertha Collins flouncing through the gate in a galaxy of glittering beads. But no, it wasn't Bertha. This one was too broad of shoulder and thick of limb.

She turned to find the fan-woman smiling at her. 'Do stay and join us now that you've materialised.' She put out her hand. 'My name is Olga De Witt. You'll have heard of my husband. All frightfully controversial. But I make it a rule never to listen to guff. How very fortuitous to have found us tucked away down here, even if you are not Miss Jeanne. We're holding a painting class any moment *sans* the model, as it now turns out but I'm sure we'll find something else on which to focus our artistic passions. Stay, won't you? We could use your expertise.'

'Well ...'

'That's a yes, I take it? Bravo.' Olga touched Rennie's arm. 'I don't suppose I could interest you in an early glass of French fizz?'

'What bliss.' Rennie laughed and patted at her hair. 'But would you mind terribly if I powdered my nose before we begin?'

'Powder away.' Olga waved her fan towards the house.

Rennie stood in the large bathroom, touching her hands to the pretty soaps, perfume bottles, the bevy of lipsticks, combs and powders. She stared at herself in the mirror. She was almost unrecognisable now with her bobbed hair, and leaner sun-browned face, both of which seemed to have bestowed her with a new air. It wasn't the emblem of freedom exactly, not yet. She applied a pencil to her eyebrows and stopped for a moment to peer at her eyes. Despite her emboldened exterior, caution and fear still lurked not far beneath the surface.

There were voices outside. She slapped on some powder and lipstick and opened the door to find a group of women crowding around the lookalike Bertha Collins girl.

'Is your sister coming, Claudette?' somebody was saying to her.

'Oh no,' Claudette replied, with a dismissive wave. 'It's all too rum to think about. Bertha's still caught up with that ghastly social-climbing jumped-up fellow from the Wool and Wheat. We've tried to beat some sense into her. But you know Bertha and her one tracked mind.'

That beastly wool and wheat fellow. It was Lloyd. Bertha really had run off with Lloyd! Rennie stifled a yelp and pushed her way past Claudette or Bertha whoever she was. All along, she'd known it was true. She wanted to laugh. She wanted to scream. *I was right all along!*

As she strode out of the house and across the grass, Olga called out to her. 'There you are. We thought you were lost.'

Over the symphony of popping champagne corks, Rennie laughed, 'As a matter of fact, I've never felt quite so found in all my life.'

CHAPTER
TWENTY-NINE

Late afternoon shadows lapped across the garden beds. Rennie was still not back. Ellis put down her hoe. She sat on the porch and looked across at the seedlings Ned had given her. How long ago that now felt, as if it might have happened to someone else.

She smoked a slow pipe but could not relax. She went into the kitchen. Dirty plates and cups were piled in the sink. A pair of knives lay across each other in an X. She uncrossed the knives and frowned. No, that was foolish. Nothing bad had happened to Rennie and nothing would.

She stood on the front porch and looked along the track. A frill of dust hung in the distance. She set off towards it through the gate, following the line made by Rennie dragging her snake-stick behind her. After some minutes, the line stopped. She stood at the turn off to a narrow side-track, and crouched down to inspect the skidded marks of tyres.

Now and then, Rennie's footprints were visible in the dust. She followed them until they swerved off the track and down through a gate where the stick lay abandoned amongst the ferns. A swatch of ferns had been freshly clipped back to reveal the gleaming brass sign: *Riverslea*. Ellis rubbed a finger over the lettering. So this was the source of those late night sounds. A grand house by the river. Ned had made passing mention of such places, not that it had interested her. And now Rennie had found one. Of course she had.

She could see a slender figure striding away from her, a fluffy orange dog stowed on one hip.

She kept her distance, but walked on until she saw the house. Half a dozen motorcars were parked haphazardly around the modern style of fountain Mr Moses would despise. Spears of pampas grass nodded pale feathery heads. Curious-looking trees were dotted about the grounds. Some had large odd-shaped leaves, lateral branches, trumpets of red flowers.

She'd seen enough. She turned to go.

'Hello, there.'

Someone had seen her. She quickened her pace back along the track.

'Hello there!'

It was too late now. She had to stop. Ellis turned and raised her hand to the sun. The slightly built figure was now a silhouette, the dog's orange fur a glowing ball of light.

'Are you from the artist cottage too?' The voice was high and soft. There was something odd about it. 'Won't you come and join us?'

'I'm afraid I ...' Ellis' voice trailed off.

'They're almost finished painting your friend.'

'My friend?'

'Rennie. She's making the most fascinating model and instructor. She keeps leaping up to see if they've captured her likeness or made her into a so-called crude messy monstrosity.'

'There's nothing the matter, then?'

'You'd better come and see for yourself. Olga will never forgive me if I don't introduce you.'

Ellis looked down at her own dirty trousers and boots and began to brush at her sleeves.

'Oh, don't worry about that. You should see how I usually get about.'

As the figure turned and walked towards the sun, Ellis realised it was a woman.

There was the strangest feeling of coming out of a dream as Ellis walked behind the striped sailor's shirt and black beret. Every detail seemed to leap out as she walked past the fountains and down the side through a very English garden with roses, honeysuckle and hollyhocks. Next she was in an Australian section where clumps of grey spiked bushes dripped in a waterfall of bright red flowers, a kind of grevillea she'd never seen. Tufts of nodding russet-coloured grasses were alive with the whirr of insects. Drifts of white flannel flowers brightened an untamed bed of greenery. Beside them waratahs raised their waxy flaming heads. Wattle trees draped across the path. Green and red kangaroo paws raised their slender hands to the sky. She'd never seen these plants arranged in this way. Mr Moses would have run at them with a machete in one hand, Brunnings gardening book in the other.

Ellis stopped when she saw the people lying about on the grassy banks beneath the trees. A small rotunda stood in the centre of the lawn. The columns were twined with ivy and hung with diaphanous curtains. A woman dressed in white cloth reclined on a wall of purple satin pillows set between potted palms. Yellow roses adorned the woman's short dark hair. A bowl of red grapes and figs lay in a brass bowl on her lap. A group of painters sat pasting away at the canvases, seemingly entranced by their subject's dark red mouth, jet black eyes and luminous skin.

'Another artist? We *are* in luck.' A woman in an orange turban flapped an oriental fan in Ellis' direction.

'Ahoy there!' The model in the rotunda sat up. 'Marvellous. There you are. I'm sorry to disappoint you Olga, but our newest interloper is not a painter. She's a writer. And not just any old writer. You'll all know her but you won't know her, if you know what I mean. It's supposed to be a closely guarded secret, but I cannot bear secrets. As you say Olga, we *are* in luck, for we have amongst us the most mysterious and clandestine gardening columnist of our times. Everyone, meet the one and only Scribbly Gum.'

'*Rennie*? Is that you?' Ellis said.

'Oh, that is too funny. Did you hear? Apparently I am unrecognisable even to my closest friends. I'm supposed to be a Greek goddess. Or am I Roman? One too many glasses of fizz and I can never remember who I am.'

Everyone laughed. Ellis felt herself wither inside. She turned to go, but somebody had come up behind her with a tray of drinks.

'Are you really the infamous Scribbly Gum?' called out the woman with a fan. 'My husband would buttonhole you all night, but alas for him, and hurrah for us, he's not here. Do you plan to write scandalous things about my garden here?'

'You'll have to try harder than that if you want to find out what she's working on now,' Rennie laughed. 'Not that she has been working on anything literary since we arrived. She'll refuse to tell you, so I will. Not that she's told me officially, but I've guessed what she's up to. She's gathering all her 'Green-eyed Gardener' columns in the one place, peppering them with myths and stories and old wives' tales woven in with the odd floral moral.'

'Floral moral!' somebody laughed.

Ellis felt sick now, standing there in her old clothes in this spectacular garden with its crowd of glamorous strangers, all staring at Rennie's creamy white breasts barely contained by her silken sheet as she summoned someone to find a cigarette. A lad leapt up and furnished Rennie with a fresh one.

Ellis felt a light tap on her arm. It was the woman who'd intercepted her at the gate, smiling at her, elfin-faced, dark eyes sparkling.

'Would you prefer something else to drink?'

Ellis tried not to stare. There was something unsettling about her, and it wasn't just the pleated trousers, sailor's top, the beret, or the paisley cravat casually tied at the neck. 'Thank you, no.'

'Oh Ellis, don't be such a dry old stick. Let your hair down for once and stop being so *dulls*,' Rennie laughed. 'It never killed anybody to loosen up and have a spot of fun, fun, fun.'

'Ellis?' The woman almost dropped the tray of drinks at their feet. She was staring at Ellis. 'It *is* you, isn't it? I thought it was when I saw you back there at the gate, but I couldn't quite believe it. I thought it must have been a trick of the light. It was the pale green of your eyes. Nobody else has eyes like that. She held out her hand and smiled an impish smile. 'I always knew we'd meet again.'

'I'm sorry I'm ...'

'I'm not sorry one bit. I'm Mab. But you might remember me as Mabel.'

'Mabel?'

'Mabel-the-maid.' She set down the tray, took off the beret and dropped into a curtsy. 'Otherwise known as the long-suffering underling to the indomitable Mrs Frith with her puffy ankles, bilious stomach and clicky knee. And that over there in the orange turban flapping her Japanese fan at all and sundry is my great friend Olga De Witt, who employs me, but in rather different circumstances than our notorious Minerva Stranks. You may have heard of Olga's husband, the free-thinking ethnographer, hailed in Europe as the next great thing? I do some sculpting and keep Olga company during his long absences. He's off wading through the Big Wet up north as we speak, collecting a myriad of ancient languages on his gramophone.'

Ellis blinked at Mab—at *Mabel*? With her hair cut short, her pointed face and minus the housemaid's apron and white ruffled hat, Ellis could just see that yes, it *was* her. Mab curtsied again, casting her eyes down as she pretended to strike an imaginary gong. Ellis slapped a hand to her forehead and began to laugh. Mabel-the-maid was *here*? She grabbed a glass of champagne and took a gulp.

'But whatever is it, Ellis? Am I so very amusing lying here?' Rennie motioned for Ellis to come over to her. 'I'm sorry I absconded, but they needed me here in the name of Art. I meant to come back to the cottage as soon as I could, I really did.'

'Mabel?' Ellis said, shaking her head. 'Mab? No, I can't believe it.'

'You look well, Ellis. A bit tired around the edges, perhaps, but aren't we all?'

'So do you,' Ellis said, and it was true. Mab looked like a different person from the harried young girl who'd rushed about at Miss Stranks' bidding all hours of the day and night. Now her cheeks were sun-touched. Her eyes were clear. Her clipped hair was glossy in the falling light. The impish smile remained.

'It must have been all that cabbage munching in our youth,' said Mab.

Ellis laughed again. 'That's the one thing I stayed with, cabbage munching.'

'Meat is death, girls, not life!' Mab's voice sounded so similar to Miss Stranks, Ellis felt a shiver run through her. 'Me too Ellis,' Mab added. 'I can't harm anything with a memory.'

They stood saying nothing for a moment, as if the significance of what Mab had just said had struck them with equal force.

'I never thought I'd say this,' Ellis said at last. 'But to find you here, like this, means Strankenstein was at least right on one count. The age of miracles is not yet past.'

'It is here!' Mab said, flourishing her hand. 'It is now!'

'Indeed it is.'

'You made the spinning bicycle wheel for Mrs Frith's armoury of egg beaters and wooden spoons. I remember being impressed by that.'

'One of my earliest attempts to turn one thing into something else. Not that Mrs Frith ever stopped complaining about her ladles whizzing around too fast and making her giddy.' Mab's smile faded. She lowered her voice. 'You remember that last day at the house?'

Ellis stared down into her glass.

'Come on,' said Mab. 'Let's go inside.'

Ellis heard Rennie call out from the rotunda. But it was too late. Mab had taken her by the arm and was leading her up the steps to walk back together into their pasts.

CHAPTER
THIRTY

Mab led her into a library of sorts, but it was nothing like the oppressive libraries of Miss Stranks. There was one large wall devoted to books. The other walls displayed an eclectic array of arts and crafts. African bronzes bedecked the mantelpiece. Aboriginal paintings on sheaves of bark stood beside small figurines carved from stone, studded with amethyst and turquoise. Large windows looked out onto the river. Mab positioned herself by the fireplace.

'You remember?' Mab said again.

Ellis moved to the window and looked out.

'Run!' someone had cried, and Ellis had run from the house, from Miss Stranks, from the drunken advances of Bradbury—and the shock of seeing the photograph of Kitty splashed across the front cover of *The Lighted Way*. She'd blundered through the streets, with no idea where she was going. She only knew she had to get away. The streets were teeming. Everyone seemed to be walking in the same direction.

At some point she'd stumbled into a group of girls.

'Hold up,' said one of them. 'You'll wreck my sign. I stayed up all night painting that.'

Ellis squinted down at the sign. *All Work, Low Pay*. Another sign said *We Say No!*

'Come on,' said one of the girls. 'Or we'll miss the march and nobody will see your ruddy sign.'

Ellis walked along behind them until they entered a park. She ran to a tree and hauled herself up. Below her the crowds converged and moved like one great creature towards a building on the edge of the grass.

'All for one! One for all!'

A woman had taken to the steps of the building and began to speak. 'Welcome everyone.'

So much for speeches, Ellis thought. The words 'equality', 'hours', 'wages', 'fair conditions for shop girls' came towards her on the breeze, and she remembered the girl who'd come to the house to see Miss Stranks, her pamphlets calling for justice for all shop workers. She remembered how Mabel had said, *I'm sorry Miss Stranks can't see you but she says she'll pray for you*.

The crowd cheered. Another woman came onto the steps and cried out, 'Your applause for Mrs McCarthy, our tireless campaigner. We'll meet here again Sunday next.'

Mrs McCarthy waved the woman away. 'Don't thank me. It is every one of *you* I should thank for coming here today,' she said. 'It's *you* who have stood up for all the others who have no voice.'

'One for all, all for one!' the crowd yelled back.

Eventually the cheering died away. People began to drift off in small knots leaving streamers and scraps of paper on the grass. Ellis was about to climb down to hunt for dropped coins when she saw a boy clambering up the tree towards her. She shrank back and clung to her branch.

'Hello,' the boy said. He was holding out something in the palm of his hand. 'Look, I found this drying out on the grass. See?' Ellis squinted down. 'It's moss,' he said, touching his finger to it. 'If I plant it again quickly it should be all right. Do you live in this tree by yourself?'

When Ellis didn't answer, the boy turned to wave to a shape walking towards them across the grass. 'Mum, this shop girl says she lives in this Moreton Bay Fig all by herself.'

'Righto,' the woman said. 'And how's the eating up there with all those figs? The Garden of Eden, I don't think.'

Ellis recognised the voice. It was the woman who'd given the 'fair and square' speech on the steps.

'Figs are found elsewhere in the Bible,' Ellis said. 'It's not their fault they've been equated with the downfall of Adam and Eve.'

'*Equated*, eh? Well I don't mind saying I don't know the Good Book too well myself, but for those that do, comfort's found where comfort's due.' The woman raised her hand to the sun and smiled up. 'You'd have a good view from up there. How many do you think we drew here today?'

'I don't know,' Ellis said, rubbing at her burning eyes.

'Go on, love. Give us a guess. One hundred? Five hundred?'

'At least four hundred, counting hats.'

'Very wise too, to be counting hats. We'll use that figure to rattle the cages of the establishment. But first we'll need to sort out some recompense for all that counting. No working for nothing, that's how it goes. Me and young Ned are going back home for a pot of soup.'

'Soup?'

'Potato and pumpkin, zest of orange, sprinkle of nutmeg and a suspicion of cream. Ned, my lad here, grows the best pumpkin this side of paradise, not to mention parsley, kale, cucumbers, river beans, fennel and potatoes. Early Iona potatoes, aren't they Ned? How's about you come down from your tree-house perch and join us for a bowl so we can compare our crowd numbers properly? Then you can run straight back here and mind your figs.'

'All right,' Ellis said, as the woman took her hand, helping her to climb down. She could just make out the form of thistle-haired Ned running on ahead.

'Mrs McCarthy's the name,' the woman said. 'You might have heard me mouthing off.'

They walked in silence through the evening light. Ellis could feel Mrs McCarthy next to her, her slow solid walk and the steady movement of her coat. Mrs McCarthy kept hold of her hand as they waited for the ferry at the wharf. Ellis wondered if someone might see them from a passing boat and mistake them for a proper family. She could hear Ned whistling as he skimmed stones across the water. The harbour was one huge glittering moving shape, blue and velvety beneath an even huger night.

'We're in one of the palaces on the right,' Mrs McCarthy said as they turned into Burton Street.

Lights blurred out across the cobblestones. There was the sound of laughter, and calls of 'I hear you pulled in a fair crowd today' and 'Put the wind up the bigwigs, did you?'

'Ned?' Ellis heard Mrs McCarthy say, as she steered Ellis up into the house. 'Run along and see if Mrs Liddy can spare us a dash of rose water and sulphate zinc. And we'll need some vinegar to fix this poor girl's eyes.'

'Would you like another drink?' Mab said.

Ellis nodded. She watched Mab pop open the door of a cabinet secreted in one of the bookshelves and pour two brandies into large crystal balloons. Mab settled herself back by the fireplace and offered Ellis a cigarette. Ellis shook her head and took out her pipe.

'So you imbibe the foul tobacco leaf as well?' Mab said.

'My maidenhair,' Ellis said without thinking.

Mab let out a laugh. Ellis felt the heat rise to her face. She tried to turn away to hide her embarrassment, and began to step across the room, but was tripped up midway by a leopard skin rug, complete with head, its jaw locked into a permanent roar.

'Sorry about that,' Mab said. 'Olga doesn't quite share the "all creatures great and small" precept. So, you were saying, you were found by Mrs McCarthy's son, Ned.'

Ellis sat down and tapped the bowl of her pipe. The old pull of opposite emotions—between keeping quiet and speaking her mind—was in full swing, but sitting here with Mab, the urge to speak was winning out.

'There's no rush, Ellis. We don't have to say anything we don't want to.'

'No. That's the strange thing. Sitting here with you here, I *do* want to. I feel as though I *have* to speak. I suppose that sounds dramatic.'

'It sounds the least dramatic thing I've heard all day.'

They both laughed.

'All right, then. I can't tell you how long I lay in bed with cabbage poultices over my eyes, listening to the comings and goings of other lodgers in the house. Mrs McCarthy came in regularly, "Righto, Ellis, here's some fresh cornbread with a dollop of Mrs Liddy's famous lemon curd." I was lulled to sleep by the winds coming in off the harbour, lifting the edges of the day's humidity. I heard young Ned chatting to his plants in the backyard. When I was fit enough to stand at the window, I saw the blur of green tumbling over fences, outhouses and woodpiles, threatening to smother the night-cart lanes.'

Ellis stopped. There were some things she could not say, not even to Mab who looked so kind and gentle sitting there by the fireplace, and who already understood a good part of it. She couldn't say how it was to lie in bed week after week in Mrs McCarthy's house, waking to find night pressed over her face, wondering if the dark was night or the seep of blindness she'd feared so much—or death—death that Kitty now knew for herself, spinning like a white star in the endless black of whatever matter or reality constituted her after-death, far beyond Miss Stranks and her claims of knowing the surest route to the afterlife, far away from the glittering lost city of Atlantis.

She gulped at her brandy.

'When I was strong enough, I helped Mrs McCarthy with the basic chores, cooking, shopping at Paddy's Market where Ned had begun selling his vegetables to a barrowman.'

'Was it all right?' said Mab. 'Living there?'

'It was nothing like working for Miss Stranks. There was food on the table, laughter on the stairs, sun in the yard. Mrs McCarthy held meetings in the kitchen but they weren't like Stranks' so-called parlour events. In winter, they roasted potatoes and cooked damper in the stove. In summer, the windows were shoved open and somebody slugged some firewater into Ned's passionfruit punch. I was free to join in but I stayed in my room. Sometimes a man arrived with a typewriter and I'd lie in bed listening to the bitter-sweet rhythm of fingers tapping away at the keys.'

'Bitter-sweet because it reminded you of Kitty?'

Ellis blinked at Mab. 'Because it reminded me of everything.'

'Go on.'

'One day Mrs McCarthy discovered I could find my way around a typewriter. She passed around the hat and bought me a second-hand machine from her friends the Clements Brothers. She said "A girl who can type has nothing to stop her getting on in the modern world." Later, she arranged for them to give me a bit of work typing out their invoices. I was lucky. Work like that was hard to find.'

'Good for her.'

'Life went on like this for four years or so until Mrs McCarthy was offered a job on a progressive north shore council. "Why not take over from me?" she said. "You almost run the place anyway." She'd already schooled me in what she called her "fair and square rules of the house." Her first rule was never to let a lodger run thin with the rent for more than a month. "Although it breaks my heart to say it, Els. This is a business, not a charity—which doesn't mean you can't be charitable at heart— charitable but smart. Number two. Never fall in love with a lodger, but seeing this is a women's and children's lodging house, you won't need to worry there." *No I won't*, I thought, but not for the reasons Mrs McCarthy imagined. Well, maybe she did. As I said, she was progressive in all things. Even love.'

Ellis stopped. Had she said too much? She looked up at Mab, but her expression had grown even more tender. Mab's eyes were brimming with tears. They were gentle eyes, softened by having seen and felt too much. How had she never noticed those kind eyes beneath the ruffled housemaid's hat?

Ellis took a deep breath. 'You see, by the ripe age of twenty, I'd decided to never make the mistake of loving anyone ever again.'

Mab looked down at her glass and swirled the brandy. 'And have you kept to that, Ellis?'

'Almost. Yes.' There, she'd spoken the thing she'd kept clamped inside of her for all these years. She felt her head go suddenly light, as if a great weight had been cut from her neck. 'And you?' She couldn't help but smile at Mab's soft frown.

'Me?'

'Where did you go? What have you been doing for the past twenty odd years? That is, if you don't mind speaking about it.'

'Oh well, there's nothing much to say. I worked in a few other big houses and hated it. Like many others, I managed to escape when the war came. That's when I met Olga. We were helping to glue soldiers' minds back together, teaching basket weaving, cobbling, woodwork, stone carving, that sort of thing. I revelled in making something out of nothing. After so long cleaning up after other people, it was bliss to be able to create something with my own hands.' Mab stubbed out her cigarette. Compared to the slightness of her frame, Mab's hands looked remarkably strong. 'But look Ellis, now that I've found you after all these years, there's one thing I need to tell you.'

'Oh?'

'But I think we should have another drink first.'

Mab flitted across the room. Every now and then Ellis could picture Mab's younger self rushing up and down the stairs carrying her beater for the gong, or swaying beneath piles of newspapers, or ferrying sumptuously laden trays for Miss Stranks.

'I have to warn you. It's about Kitty.' Mab's back was turned as she said this.

'Kitty?' Ellis felt the old tightening of her throat.

'Are you sure you want to hear it?'

Ellis managed to rasp out a small, 'Yes.'

Mab sat down on the low table in front of her and fixed her eyes on her. 'There's no easy way to say this, so I'll dive in. Is that all right?'

Ellis nodded.

'I was there, you see. I was there with her when they took those photographs after she died. When I realised what they were doing, I tried to stop them. And when I realised I couldn't, I stood by Kitty. I washed her. I laid her out. I put those white lilies in her hair. I tried to give her some dignity. I made sure she looked beautiful, even in death.'

'She was beautiful, wasn't she?'

Mab looked away. 'But that's not all. During that time I found out something else.'

Ellis was thinking about that morning at the city library, how it was to see the white lilies studded like stars in Kitty's hair, her picture plastered across the front page of *The Lighted Way*, how she was real but not real, there but not there.

Ellis drained her glass and stood up. She felt the urge to run, to leap over the table and run out of the room. It took all her strength to stay where she was. She'd grown used to her memories for all these years and now her grief—her guilt—had grown around them in the same way a tree's trunk grew around a rock until both the rock and the tree risked mutual destruction if prised apart.

She moved towards the bookshelves and ran her fingers along the books. 'Do you know what happened to her? Miss Stranks, I mean?'

Mab left the table and stood on the other side of the room. 'Chicago was the last I heard. She made sure to get out before the full scandal hit the papers. I gather she almost died on the voyage out. I suppose her own "Hell Broths" finally had their way.'

'If she is still alive,' Ellis said, 'I expect she's treading the boards spouting the same old hokum, taking perfectly wise, ancient arguments from anywhere she likes and spitting them out as self-aggrandising nest-feathering nonsense.'

They both turned as voices rose in the garden.

'Stay for dinner, all of you,' Olga De Witt called. 'Mab, where are you? We'll have such a feast.'

'I'm sorry. Once a maid, always a maid.' Mab bobbed into another curtsy, but this time neither of them laughed. 'You'll stay, won't you?' she said, as she turned to go.

The dinner was a luxuriant blur, a heady stream of good food, laughter, music, wit and wine. Mab sat beside her, chatting about her plans to make more sculptures and fountains.

'I want them to be beautiful *and* useful,' she said. 'I'm working on an amphitheatre for one family. Italian fountains for another, with grottoes, follies, and dry stone walls. An irrigation system and a water theatre.'

'A water theatre?' Ellis said. 'You mean setting fountains around a stage?'

Their conversation was regularly interrupted by Olga's requests for more champagne. Then the pink-eared Monsieur leapt up to play a thunderous piece on the piano and conversation was brought to a halt.

Ellis left the table to stand against a wall as Monsieur whipped up a jazzy tune which the young ones in the room recognised and sang along with, 'Chilly, chilly night'.

'I haven't heard that in an age,' Rennie laughed, raising a glass.

People jigged about as Monsieur tinkled up and down the keys. The music went on until everyone fell down—everyone except for Ellis who stayed leaning against the wall. Every now and then Mab caught her eye and held her gaze across through the noise and smoke and Ellis had to shake herself. *Mabel—Mab—was really here?*

Someone produced a piano accordion. Monsieur stood up on the piano stool and began to pump out a French folk song. Everybody joined arms and danced. Rennie was still dressed as a Greek goddess. She swirled at the centre, swinging her costume about until she stopped dancing and draped herself across a chaise lounge. An admiring chorus surrounded her. She peered over their expectant heads at Ellis, and shot a look across at Mab.

'Ellis darling.' Rennie flung out her arm and twisted an empty glass. 'I'm absolutely parched. Fetch me another round of bubbles, you old grump.'

'Allow me,' said a lad, leaping up.

'No, I want Ellis to do it,' Rennie said, and everybody laughed, except for Ellis.

Ellis said nothing as she left the room and slipped away from the house.

She heard Rennie stagger after her.

'Ellis? Come back. How can you be so unbearably dour? It's a party. And parties are meant to be fun. You've been full of woe ever since we came out here.'

Ellis waited in the shadow of a tree watching as Rennie stumbled down the front steps and lurched towards the motorcars. She slapped her hands at the bonnets calling out. 'I know you're hiding in there, Ellis. Oh do come out and talk to me. I can't bear this silence one moment more. Why does everyone try to punish me with silence?'

Two of Rennie's young painting charges appeared. Rennie turned and screamed with laughter as one of the lads tripped and fell headfirst into the fountain.

'Why, ain't that the cat's pyjamas? Ellis, come and look.'

Ellis turned to find Mab was behind her, watching her.

'Are you all right, Ellis?'

'It's nothing.'

They watched as Rennie leapt into the fountain to flail about. Her white robes were now translucent and clinging to every valley and hill of her body.

'And Rennie is your ...?'

'She was my lodger. Now we share the cottage down the track. Well. We did.'

They were face to face now. Mab stepped forward and hugged Ellis, but it was more of a clutch, the grab of two bodies clamped together awkwardly. Mab's small breasts pressed against hers. She inhaled the warm curl of her neck. It fitted so neatly and Mab was so light in her arms, so clear in her manner, and warm—and *hell*. Ellis threw back her head and began to laugh.

'What is it?' said Mab.

'That's what it is. You're so damned familiar.'

Mab raised a finger and rested it on Ellis' lips. 'Of course I am. You already know me. You know who I am, and *what* I am. We recognise something in each other. We always did.'

'Ellis?' It was Rennie zigzagging towards them across the grass. Ellis pulled Mab back into the shadows.

'For God's sake Ellis Gilbey. You can't walk back to that dirt-floored hut by yourself in the dark. I have something to tell you. It's important. I cannot bear all this secrecy one moment more. I want to speak to you about the cottage, about my damned ticket home.'

Mab trembled slightly in Ellis' arms. They both watched as Rennie stumbled past.

'I see. She's leaving you and going home,' said Mab.

Ellis blinked. 'So it seems.'

'By "home" I take it she means England.'

Ellis didn't answer.

'Ellis?' Mab said. 'I've been wanting to ask you something all night. It's about Miss Stranks. Do you remember the henchmen at the house on that terrible day?'

Ellis extracted herself from Mab's embrace and turned away. Mab. Rennie. Kitty. Miss Stranks. Their faces and voices were whirling around in a jumble inside her head.

More people had emerged from the house to run down the steps and leap into the fountain. Somebody had brought out a series of lamps. Beams of light swung across the garden in golden slants. Rennie ran towards the light and began to dance. Olga rushed towards her and tried to wrap her up with a fur stole.

'Do you mind them swimming in your fountain?' Ellis said.

'It doesn't matter what I mind,' said Mab. 'Olga commissioned them. They're mine but not mine. I'm sorry. You'd rather not talk about Stranks again?'

'Of course I remember the men at Stranks' house. How could I forget?'

'I remember how one of them tried to grab you before I opened the front door and told you to run.'

'What?' Ellis said. She looked at Mab. Her face was half-covered by shadow. 'What did you say?'

'Perhaps you don't remember when I told you to run.'

'*You* told me to run?'

Mab was staring at her, her eyes sweeping over her in the dark. 'Just like I slid those slices of cucumber under the door and those sandwiches when Stranks tried to starve you half to death. And I left you that note about the ambrosia.'

'You sent me the note? But you couldn't have. The note was typed. Nobody else could type in that house except for me and Kitty.'

Mab stepped back. 'Now it's my turn to be shocked. *Now* I understand. All along, you've thought it was *her*. You thought that was all thanks to Kitty Tate.'

A thousand visions flashed before Ellis in the dark. She was drunk. She was tired.

'I tried to speak to you so many times,' said Mab. 'But that thug was prowling everywhere and it was already enough of a job keeping out of Bradbury's way. But now I see what's happened. Oh Ellis. All this time you've blamed yourself for Kitty's death.'

Ellis closed her eyes.

'But you mustn't,' said Mab. 'It didn't happen because of you.'

'Stop. You don't know what you're talking about. Kitty gave me a letter to deliver to Bradbury. But I lost it. She thought he wasn't coming back. I told her to promise me to wait, but she didn't wait.'

'Listen to me, Ellis. It wasn't you.'

'I lost the letter—and—Kitty ...'

'Threw herself down the stairs? Is that what you think?'

Ellis could hardly speak. *Yes*, she wanted to scream. *Yes, Kitty was meant to wait for me to come back. Why didn't she wait? I'll show you how real actresses fall down the stairs. Like this!* she'd cried. *Like this!*

'But that's not what happened.'

Ellis peered at Mab. What was she saying? *Hell*, she was drunk. She stared past her, raising her eyes up to the stars which were hanging down so low she could almost feel the burn of their icy heat.

'No, look at me Ellis. Listen when I say: Kitty did not throw herself down the stairs. It was them. I heard them talking while I was laying out her body. Stranks, Bradbury, and that so-called doctor. Do you understand? She didn't jump. And she didn't fall.'

'But I heard her scream. Bradbury hadn't come and she wouldn't wait.'

'Bradbury *was* there with Miss Stranks,' said Mab. 'I'm not sure exactly who pushed her. One of them, both of them, all of them. I didn't stay around long enough to find out. But I do know this. *They* killed her Ellis. They wanted her gone. Kitty was too dangerous. Her family were old money. They'd left her with Stranks while they went to India to "follow the path." Kitty couldn't go, not just because of her delicate health. Apparently she'd become attached to one of the leading theosophists and it had caused a huge scandal. Her parents had connections with all the big names. Stranks wanted them to be in her debt so she could rack up more favours for herself. But she didn't want Kitty *there* in the house, if you understand what I mean. She knew what made Bradbury tick. Kitty's liaison with him came as no surprise.'

'No, you're wrong. This is all wrong. Kitty died because of me.'

Ellis staggered back. Mab reached out for her. She pushed her away. She could hear Rennie laughing about drowning herself in a fountain of fizz. But she didn't care about Rennie or anyone else. Ellis sat down hard on the grass. No, it couldn't be. All these years the pain of Kitty's death had hung where it belonged—around her neck. And now Mab was telling her she was wrong? She looked up to see Mab standing over her.

'Ellis, listen.'

Ellis staggered to her feet. 'No. You listen to me. This was a mistake. All of this was a huge mistake.'

Mab tried to take her by the arm, but Ellis had found the driveway and stumbled on.

She woke in an unrepentant morning sun, her cheek jammed against the splintery boards of the cottage porch. Flies buzzed around her mouth. A line of ants ran over her wrist. The silence was sliced by the screech of cockatoos. She managed to sit up and haul herself to her feet.

She lurched through the house and washed her face, staring at herself in the watery mirror of her wardrobe door. Then she remembered. *Mab.* She'd pushed Mab away from her.

She hunted for her pipe amongst the mess of papers on her desk and found only an empty tobacco tin. She boiled a pot of water and made a cup of strong black tea. She went out to the garden and crouched down against the cliff. The tea turned cold as she wept. She pulled herself together enough to heat more water to steep a pinch of dried yarrow, nettles and rosemary for her hair. She washed, dressed, brushed her teeth, and sat on the front porch, watching, waiting. Nobody came.

It wasn't until after she'd woken, propped up against the verandah post, Clarrie's poetry book lying open on her knee, that she saw the figure on the track, no darker than a pen-stroke striding through the rising haze of dust.

Mab raised her arm to wave. Ellis hurried inside and shut the door of her sleep-out. She lay down on the bed, hoping Mab would go away. She heard Mab let herself in and step across the floor.

'I've brought you something,' she said. She felt Mab climb onto the bed behind her. She could feel Mab's fingers lightly touch her hair. 'You smell like a herb garden. Give me your hand.'

There was the taking of her hand, the unfolding of her fingers, the feel of a small cold weight placed in her palm. She frowned at the white tile carved with a spray of star-shaped flowers.

'Flannel flowers,' Mab said. 'I remember you had some pinned to your hat when you came to Stranks' house. You asked me to find them for you. I never did. So here's my approximation, carved in soapstone, no less. I've been up all night finishing it. I must say, it looks like you could use a paperweight while you finish writing your infamous gardening book.'

Ellis blinked at the flowers, at the delicate precision of Mab's handiwork.

'And I've brought something else.' She felt Mab stroke her arm. 'Not from the past, or for the future, but for now. First, your pipe, which you left behind last night. And secondly, a very late but very special delivery of maidenhair.'

They both laughed. Mab leant in over her and brushed her lips across Ellis' ear and then her cheek. *And I am alive*, Ellis thought as she pulled Mab towards her and kissed her mouth.

Ellis composed the letter as the early morning shadows strode across their naked limbs.

Dear Editors of the Australian Gardeners' Almanac,
I regret to inform you that Mr Moses died suddenly while attempting to tame a wild rose. Would you consider a new monthly column about

239

a woman establishing her own country garden where she eventually holds gardening classes, music and poetry recitals, stone carving lessons and various other artistic and horticultural pursuits? If so, I should like to publish it under my own name.

Lying here with Mab, drifting back and forth through the silvery membrane between lucidity and sleep, she could see it all, the fruit sweetening on the bough, the thriving herbs, the bountiful harvest of vegetables, the swathes of flowers glowing in the sun.

Beyond the fence, choirs of birds sang hymns in the trees. Chairs carved from sandstone were dotted between tables brimming with food and wine. The sharp sweet scent of mandarin blossom filled the air. Blue water lilies clustered on sun-dappled ponds.

She could hear a truck pull up at the gate. She saw how the expressions changed on the grey faces of the poorer city folk she'd invited to spend the day far away from the relentless grind, grit and smog.

As evening fell, a new tide swept in. Rennie arrived from who knows where to a fanfare of claxons, a gaggle of equally glittering characters in tow. Mab darted about putting the final touches to the stage they'd dug out into the side of the cliff, flanked by a quartet of burbling fountains.

Ellis waited in the shadows of the grotto as the first notes of a piano accordion silenced the crowd. She saw herself prepare to step out on to the stage to recite the poetry she'd written herself. She took a deep breath and glanced down at the garden which seemed to float in the flicker of lamps, then up at the white stars blossoming on the inky arch of night.

Sources

p. 29 and p. 60: 'Consider the lilies how they grow: they toil not, they spin not ...' Luke 12:27.

p. 47: 'A melancholy tale, to give an awful warning,/ Soon oblivion will steal silently.' Percy Bysshe Shelley, 'Queen Mab', *The Complete Poetical Works of Percy Bysshe Shelley*, ed. Thomas Hutchinson, Oxford University Press, London, 1965.

p. 48: 'The Earth is like Ocean, Wreck-strewn and in motion ...' Shelley, 'Queen Mab'.

p. 53 and p. 74: 'Behold the chariot of our Fairy Queen!' Shelley, 'Queen Mab'; and 'The world's rejected guest ...' Shelley, 'The World's Wanderers'.

p. 60: 'Do no wrong, do no violence to the stranger, the fatherless, nor the widow.' Jeremiah 22:3; 'For in thee the fatherless findeth mercy.' Hosea 14:3.

p. 146: 'Stair above stair the eddying waters rose.' Shelley, 'Spirit of Solitude'.

p. 147: 'But now my heart is heavy ...' Shelley, 'The Cenci'.

p. 156: 'But if a woman have long hair, it is a glory to her, for her hair is given to her for her covering.' St Paul, 15:11 Corinthians.

p. 181: 'The tyrant whose delight is in his woe ...' Shelley, 'Queen Mab'.

p. 194: 'The earthquakes of the human race ...' Shelley, 'Queen Mab'.

Acknowledgements

To everyone who helped turn this work of fiction into a reality—thank you—especially:

~ Sue Martin, Alison Ravenscroft of the La Trobe University for sharing ideas, books, wisdom and opportunities;

~ Carrie Tiffany, Alex Craig for giving precious time, clarity, and for opening doors; Rebecca Starford for all the valuable comments; thanks also to Martin Hughes of Affirm Press;

~ Helen Burns, Jane Camens, Jane Meredith, Lisa Walker for writerly encouragement;

~ past and present staff of the Northern Rivers Writers Centre and Marele Day for the watershed Residential Emerging Writers Mentorship; thanks also to the staff of my local RTRL library;

~ my writing group Sarah Armstrong, Jesse Blackadder, Hayley Katzen, Amanda Skelton for shining so many lights;

~ long-distance friends Jen Castles, Jo Harrison, Karen Adams;

~ Charlotte, Daphne my eternal thanks and respect;

~ my dear departed parents for adventuring, remembering and then forgetting; and my brothers and sisters and their families for helping me get back on my feet, with special thanks to Annie, Stella, Madeline for the music and the books;

~ the Art Gallery of South Australia and the estate and relatives of the remarkable Dorrit Black for allowing her painting 'The Bridge' to illuminate the cover;

~ my agent Fran Moore for the perennial enthusiasm and faith;

~ Pauline Hopkins, Renate Klein, Susan Hawthorne, Deb Snibson, Maree Hawken, Helen Lobato at Spinifex Press: my gratitude for welcoming me so warmly in, and for the artful editing suggestions and inspired design;

~ and lastly and firstly to my wellspring, Delma Corazon. *Thank you*. For everything.

MORE FROM SPINIFEX PRESS

Haifa Fragments: A Novel
khulud khamis

As a designer of jewellery Maisoon wants an ordinary extraordinary life, which isn't easy for a tradition-defying, activist, Palestinian citizen of Israel, who refuses to be crushed by the feeling that she is an unwelcome guest in the land of her ancestors. She volunteers for the Machsom Watch, an organisation that helps children in the Occupied Territories cross the border to receive medical care. Frustrated by her boyfriend Ziyad and her father who both want her to get on with life and forget those in the Occupied Territories, she lashes out only to discover her father isn't the man she thought he was.

Raised a Christian, in a relationship with a Muslim man and enamoured with a Palestinian woman from the Occupied Territories, Maisoon must decide her own path.

A beautiful story of intertwined cultures and relationships with the rhythm of hope, mixed with the creative drive for life, justice, meaning and love.

—ALEX NISSEN, feminist peace activist

Pb: $26.95
ISBN: 9781742199009
Fiction
Rights: World X UK English language Europe, X Italy

My Sister Chaos
Lara Fergus

2012 WINNER, Edmund White Award for Debut Fiction, USA
2012 FINALIST, Lambda Literary Award for
Lesbian Debut Fiction, USA

An obsessive-compulsive cartographer trapped in the mapping of her own house. A painter turned code-breaker trying to find the lover she lost in the war. Two sisters on a collision course.

In *My Sister Chaos* two sisters escape an unnamed war-torn country into separate lives of exile. The cartographer is obsessed with keeping the world in order, but finds it unravelling under her own demands. Her sister, an artist, arrives unexpectedly. Her very presence is a sign of chaos for the cartographer. But in spite of this, the sister has a firm grip on the real world, and a greater connection to the past.

Chaos and order in tension provide the scaffolding for this compelling work of fiction. Presented within a world of obsession and trauma it asks whether any of us is immune to the forces of destruction.

Told in overlapping first-person narration, it is schematically ingenious and meticulously constructed ... [A]t its core this novel shows a deep compassion for the human predicament of when to control and when to surrender and what, finally, might be a rational response to an irrational situation.

—*New Internationalist*

Pb: $24.95
ISBN: 9781876756840
Fiction
Rights: World X Macedonian, Tamil

Juno and Hannah

Beryl Fletcher

1920, deep in the New Zealand bush, a settlement of Christian fundamentalists live a life of austerity and isolation. It is a place where there is little space for compassion, particularly for the women who can never rid themselves of Eve's original sin. The elders rule over the women, children and young men, meting out punishments for transgressions as ordinary as self-reflection.

Sisters Juno and Hannah have grown up in the community, but when a stranger washes up on the river bank and Hannah goes to his aid, she finds herself accused of necromancy. The girls flee but are quickly forced to accept help. Hannah, unsure who is friend or foe, finds herself dependent upon and attracted to the man into whose lips she breathed life.

Juno and Hannah is a remarkable novella. The vivid New Zealand landscape reflects the journey of the sisters with its bounty of beauty and resources but also with its scars, wrought during the early days of colonisation.

High gothic bush yarn, Juno and Hannah has all the ingredients of love, quest, humour and endurance played out against a background of rural 1920s life, eugenics and cult religion. Simply told, fast paced, Beryl Fletcher's new novella abounds with vivid evocations of the natural world and some unforgettable female characters.

—STEPHANIE JOHNSON, author of *The Open World* and *The Writing Class*

Pb: $24.95
ISBN: 9781742198750
Fiction
Rights: World

*If you would like to know more about Spinifex Press
write for a free catalogue or visit our website.*

SPINIFEX PRESS
PO Box 212 North Melbourne
Victoria 3051 Australia
www.spinifexpress.com.au